PRAISE FOR HOLLY CRAIG

'An exhilarating and accomplished action-packed thriller, *The Shallows* will have you gripped right from the start.'
—B. A. Paris, author of *Behind Closed Doors*

'*The Shallows* is a gripping thriller about survival and the murky depths we can go to for wealth and prestige. Relentlessly fast-paced and packed full of tension, it's the definition of a page-turner.'
—John Marrs, author of *Keep It in the Family*

'A stunning thriller . . . Glamorous, tense, gripping and twisty . . . What a ride!'
—Shalini Boland, author of *The Silent Bride*

'This one is fast, fun and twisty – A great read!'
—Sarah Bailey, author of the Detective Woodstock series

'Immersive, compulsive storytelling . . . *The Shallows* will hook you and keep you reading long into the night.'
—G. R. Halliday, author of the Monica Kennedy series

'Packed with twists and turns, this is a rollercoaster of a thriller that will leave you guessing – and your adrenaline spiked! I read it in a weekend.'
—Ali Lowe, author of *The Trivia Night*

'The author we've all been waiting on . . . Her talent does NOT disappoint!'
—Paula Johnston, author of *The Lies She Told*

'A dark and murky read that is ultimately filled with epic, strong women. *Desperate Housewives* meets *Dead Calm*.'
—Susi Holliday, author of *The Hike*

'*The Shallows* is a brilliantly written observation into how well we know those closest to us, both physically and emotionally. Superbly rich in setting, fantastically tense in atmosphere. I flew through it.'
—L. V. Matthews, author of *The Twins*

'A relentlessly gripping thriller with unguessable twists.'
—K. L. Slater, author of *The Girlfriend*

THE
RIP

ALSO BY HOLLY CRAIG

The Shallows

THE RIP

HOLLY CRAIG

Text copyright © 2024 by Holly Craig
All rights reserved.

Published by Thomas & Mercer, Seattle

www.apub.com

Amazon, the Amazon logo, and Thomas & Mercer are trademarks of Amazon.com, Inc., or its affiliates.

ISBN-13: 9781662508189
eISBN: 9781662508196

Cover design by Will Speed
Cover image: © Trevor Payne / Arcangel; © bmphotographer © Rocksweeper / Shutterstock

Printed in the United States of America

For Mum. Our sun-bleached island holidays have attached lifelong memories in the girls' hearts and now a story in mine. Thanks for always listening, loving, laughing with me over rosé wine, over white sand, over balcony sunsets over Rottnest.

AUTHOR'S NOTE

I wish to acknowledge the traditional custodians of Wadjemup, the Whadjuk people of the Noongar nation and their Elders past and present. I acknowledge and respect Wadjemup, meaning 'the land across the sea where spirits are', and I respect the Whadjuk people's deep, personal and significant connection to this land and island.

As a frequent visitor to Wadjemup – Rottnest Island – I am aware that some of the facts, names and settings within this story are fictitious and have been altered or written to fit the narrative.

PROLOGUE –
SATURDAY

Eloise, 7.40 p.m.

They say nothing bad ever happens on the island. Only twenty minutes by ferry from the mainland, this popular chunk of lime-stone, sand and reef has a way of transporting visitors back in time, reminding many of their idyllic childhoods spent here, burning all day in the sun with the freedom to roam until dusk. They say they've never seen a bad thing happen here. I say they're wrong.

The balcony groans with too many adults, a trestle table over-flowing with stale crisps, empty glasses, an opened bottle of rosé and a lone peanut slowly drowning in the hummus.

We're all buzzing because it's that kind of vibe. Holiday sunsets, endless villas strewn along the ocean crammed with loving families, comfortably drunk adults and frying seafood.

Someone inside starts singing Whitney Houston and a group of Penny's friends are gathering like they do, shoulder to shoulder, blasting out the song, getting the words all wrong. I'd hate to clean this villa in the morning with a hangover.

I'm leaning over the railing, wondering how many more kilo-grammes it would take before this balcony collapses beneath us all, into the sand. I don't want to join the singing, or the conversation about boats and fuel prices. My vision is blurred, hazy, and for the first time since I arrived, I finally feel less paranoid. I'm warm, even in my slip dress and bare feet. Taking another sip of tepid wine, I then stop.

On the beach, under a mauve sky, some of our party have formed a teenage-type bonfire circle, with beers, towels and scattered snacks. They haven't left their clique since the sun set thirty minutes ago. Their voices echo over the still water.

And Penny is there. With my husband, Scott.

She's standing and storming off as though she's annoyed with him. And he's scrambling to his feet to chase her. *Chase her.* I can't hear what she's saying, because she's whispering, and I can't hear my husband either, but then someone bumps my shoulder. It's Penny's brother, Brett, and he doesn't look good. He sways, holds in a burp, then speaks with beer breath, saying, 'How many kids are supposed to be in the villa next door?'

'Four,' I tell him, turning back to the beach where Penny and my husband have disappeared, probably up the side steps. And someone on the beach laughs as a dinghy drones by. And Whitney Houston stops singing. And then Brett calls out to everyone around me, 'The party has to stop.' He's been to check on the kids next door. Next door, where they watch movies with bleary eyes, high on sugar, the oldest looking after the youngest. It's the safest island, they said. Nothing bad ever happens. And then Brett tells us one of them is missing. One of the kids is missing, and no one saw a thing.

FRIDAY

Penny, 11.03 a.m.

There are dangers on Rottnest Island, but we don't tell the kids that.

Our villa overlooks the bay with a balcony hanging over sharp spinifex grass that detaches in the sea breeze. Their needles are covered in the sand, ready to prick your bare soles. You have to pull them out and limp quickly away, especially in October when the dugite snakes start mating and hide shyly in the bushes.

Bluebottle jellyfish wash up on the shores, their pearly cobalt crowns able to pop then smother a toe with a stinging rash. Sharks have been spotted haunting the reef off the beach at Thomson Bay. Rays glide under dinghies, matching their girth. The meeting of currents, the swirling offshore rips, suck the unwary out to sea.

If the kids knew about this, knew about the dangers, they'd never leave us alone.

'There's nowhere else in the world you can leave your kids unsupervised,' Mum and Dad used to say. This was code for, we can drink all the wine we want, neglect the kids and no one will bat an eyelid. It's simply island tradition. Kids cycle off exploring and parents gift them five dollars to buy all the sugar they need to keep them quiet, entertained, while the parents grow louder, entertaining themselves.

Our villa is the most sought-after accommodation on the island. In the afternoons, the sun blasts half the balcony, so you can choose whether to toast your legs or cool them off in the shade. The balcony faces the ferry jetty. Every so often, the ferry arrives, disgorging hordes of noisy tourists and regular visitors who ride around the island like they own the place.

There's a certain possessiveness that arouses visitors here. A sense of ownership over the island.

If you've spent your childhood here as the privileged offspring of 'boaties', then you've earned bragging rights over those who haven't. They are less than you.

You see this superior attitude all the time. In the zigzagged riding around the island without a helmet. People bare-footed with a few stubbed toes. In the order of Pimm's at the pub, the rebellious dragging of chairs on to the sand, away from the rest of the crowd.

Children of 'boaties' are entitled on this island, separate and proud to be. As adults, they stroll around the village with the newspaper stuck under their arm, knowing exactly which meat pie to buy, where to order the best coffee. You often hear them reminiscing about their days spent here as kids, when they'd cycle around the island until dusk. When they became too hungry to keep playing, craving a sausage in a floppy bun.

I guess you could say I'm one of them, the child of a 'boatie', knowing the island like the creases on my hand. I've got scars from falling off my bike and painted freckles from my childhood spent unprotected by sun cream. I'm comfortable with the stench of rotting salty seaweed and boat diesel, the wafting fat of hot chips and powdery seagull poo.

Our villa is the best because I wouldn't have it any other way. If you book the ones behind us, then you may as well not come.

This prime spot allows me to gaze at the guys flinging their fishing lines from their boats and the sunbathers flipping like seals on the sand. I can predict the weather from here, identify when the wind is about to switch, chopping the sea into sharp waves. From the balcony vantage point I get to be in control over the island, the comings and goings of everyone.

◆ ◆ ◆

Holidaying on the island comes with a sexual obligation, a silent contract most couples ignore. I don't ignore it.

The salty air resembles sweat, while stiffened hair prickles against receptive skin. Everything feels bare and sun-kissed, heated and hot. It just makes me feel youthful again. Makes me want to fuck him. Kav. My husband on the beach with the awesome arms.

Other, regular couples can invent excuses to dismiss intimacy. The heat's giving them a headache, they've exhausted their limbs from swimming, the bike-riding has chaffed their inner thighs. But not me. When I'm here, I'm thirsty for it.

Kav's talking to my brother, Brett, and beside them – stuck in the sand – the champagne bottle has developed tears. Over here, too much wine gets sploshed around. Hot glasses are dotted with sand from kids' kicking feet. Wine makes you boozy and light and free enough to rip your bikini top off and run into the waves, frothing and foaming around your nipples.

I dive under the relaxed wave, a wave that's too lazy to develop into anything forceful and rumbling. It collects my hair up into its current and I kick like a frog under the turquoise water, opening my eyes, and surface laughing. Even the water is on holiday here.

'Come in,' I call to Kav, falling back into the water's embrace. The men keep talking. Brett's sipping on Moët with the cheese platter beside him as my son, Edmund, builds sandcastles. And Kav's been mentioning how he wants to go surfing before the others arrive. But this is my first swim and I want to feel it. The foam feels like Kav's flicking tongue.

The sun's out and high, whitening the beach, and we've only just begun. This is the way all beach holidays begin. Happy, laughing, cheese, Moët, tanning skin.

Paradise island.

Eloise, 2.02 p.m.

She owns the island. That's why she chose this place. With her long salty hair under a hat, Penny can weave in and out and around and over the hills, people, trees and bays like only *she* has the right to be here.

But that's not the reason I didn't want to come. We've only visited the island once before, when Penny and Kav weren't here, so for a slice of time we could pretend the island was ours. And only because Scott, my husband, begged me. I remember relaxing at the beach bar, ordering cocktails and hot chips, and beer for Scott, with our legs propped on the low wall and our eyes on the cool bay. We were silent while Levi played on the sand for hours, dipping in and out of the sea and dripping water over the plate of pizza.

But I could never relax, not fully. The whole trip, I found myself squinting over my shoulder, checking faces, feeling triggered by the memories of this place. And then I never wanted to come back again. If I couldn't relax then, how will I relax now?

This is the city's island, the holiday island every family boasts about visiting. *Why can't we go back?* This is what Scott used to ask me. *I just hate the island*, I'd say.

Scott wonders why and I can never tell him. So, I lie instead and say I hate islands, being trapped and isolated away from hospitals and police stations and shopping centres. And he says nothing bad ever happens here, but he doesn't remember what I remember.

Now, we're in a queue, about to disembark the ferry. And as for all queues, time stops when I seriously need to pee. Nerves have this effect on me. Thank God I didn't get seasick on the way over, but my bladder is pressing against my toddler, Coco's, knee.

'We should get the bikes first,' I tell Scott as he collects Coco on his back with one arm. Like a pro. He doesn't speak to me, so I do what I normally do when I'm feeling rejected, pull out my phone. Get ready to take pictures of the milky water. If I focus on my photos and Instagram account, I'll focus less on faces, people noticing me.

Also, I'm going to try and think positively, use this setting and holiday to reconnect with Scott. I'm staring at the back of his hat while Levi bumps into me, gazing down at his phone. My son's neck is unusually lumped at the back with poor posture. It's a problem I have to keep reminding him about. 'You're only eleven now but come fifty and you'll be the Hunchback of Notre Dame.'

The water is cloudy, like the inside of an oyster shell. Trust Penny to get the good weather for the weekend. I don't know why I hoped it'd be shitty weather today, rain or even wind. Not to spoil things for Kav, just to spoil the atmosphere for Penny. She gets everything the way she wants it – the villa, the dates everyone can make, the pale sea. How she even scored The Bay Restaurant and Grill during wedding season is beyond me.

Behind me, a smelly English woman is perspiring heavily, her muggy breath dampening my shoulder blades. She's almost treading on my sandals. I step closer to Scott, finding myself wrapping my arm around his waist. A deep yearning to be held like he's holding Coco has me leaning my forehead into his spine. But I feel his stomach muscles tense, so I step back.

If anything, I'm trying to be upbeat and pretend this holiday will do us both good. We need a break and this is a forced one. But Scott pulls away, readjusting Coco on his hip and gifting her blonde curls a quick kiss.

His profile is sharp when he turns and says, 'I still have no idea why you don't want to be here, but at least try and have fun.'

The ferry doors open and a gush of hot salty wind blows across my face. Holidays and coconut sun cream, the shameful smell of my past. I hold my breath, trying not to inhale it, and tell myself I'll only 'try and have fun' for him.

Penny, 2.03 p.m.

Everyone's in a holiday mood. I'm out the back of the villa, bending to the peg basket and hanging my drenched towel on the line. Two kids wheel by on bikes and a bunch of guys meander by, holding fishing rods.

Across the road, beside Eloise and Scott's villa, they're starting a late lunch barbeque, sizzling onions in oil. They have the radio playing, an ad blasting about a sale on lounge chairs, and the scraping spatula reminds me of summer. The man at the barbeque waves to me. I wave back. People are happy here. I'm suddenly conscious of my dress and the way it lifts up when I bend to reach the pegs. I crouch instead of bending.

Tomorrow night, down at The Bay Restaurant and Grill, we'll be hosting thirty of Kav's closest friends in a seafood and champagne soiree. It's cost us a bomb, but it's money we can afford to spend. Most of the guests are arriving on the island tomorrow and staying at the Beach Hotel for one night, and the weekend has to run smoothly, because I have a surprise for Kav.

A woman laughs across the road as the man at the barbeque drops the spatula with a noisy clang. The man spanks his wife on the bottom with the spatula and a horn from the jetty echoes across the island, loud and intruding. They've arrived. Eloise and Scott.

I shade my eyes with my hand as a swarm of tiny moths fly in the afternoon sunlight. Sun cream, frying sausages and beer hover in the warm air, pressuring me to remember it's a holiday. That's all it is.

Shoulders stiffening, I peg my towel, brushing my hands down the wet fabric. I really can't let Eloise get into my head this weekend.

◆ ◆ ◆

I've been scanning the blue horizon, waiting to spot the white dot of a ferry churning over. Out on the balcony, I see it. The three-levelled ferry, the passengers spilling out like vomit, ready to sprawl over the tranquillity of the island. Eloise will complain of seasickness, even though the ocean is swelling smoothly. She'll get everyone's attention. Painkillers will be offered, tea brewed and the kids whisked away. That's if they've brought her nanny along. Her husband, Scott, will give her nothing though. He'll give her distance and a tired look.

We're not friends, but Scott and Kav are, which is a shame because it means I sometimes have to associate with Eloise, a 'sexy mummy' influencer with sixty thousand followers. I can imagine her followers are regular mothers who are doing it tough, without the help, without the cleaners, nannies and assistants, all staring at their screens wondering how they failed at motherhood when they look at how well Eloise is faking it. She's a liar and a fraud, getting paid to post pictures of her immaculate stone kitchen with cakes and coffee displayed, wearing a cherry apron without a smudge of butter. No one sees the housekeeper who baked the cake and polished the kitchen.

And then there's Rosie, my daughter, who likes to gush about following Eloise for her luxe fashion, make-up routines and modern home. I try to ignore the comments she makes about *having a mum like that*. She doesn't mean it. It's all coming from spite.

◆ ◆ ◆

Kav calls out from the back courtyard, 'Are Scott and Eloise here?' He's been for a surf.

'Just arrived.'

Leaning his board against the back wall, Kav then steps inside the villa. I love him like this, all salty and dripping.

My greetings to my husband are much more delicious than those of typical wives. I never greet Kav with *how was work* or *what do you feel like for dinner* or *how was your day?* No, those questions prompt the death of a marriage, make the marriage routine and predictable. I often pride myself on how unique my greetings are. Not that Kav knows. And I wonder if I'm weird or just clever. Do other wives plan their moods the way I do? Like a scratch and win ticket, Kav is rewarded or punished, depending on what mood I choose to conjure.

'How was it?' I shake his wet hair with my fingers. Bits of sand flick off.

'Weak.' He reaches for some bread crust on the chopping board and shoves it in his mouth. 'No swell.'

Kav's back from his surf because he knows the guests will be here soon. He's good like that. Considerate and responsible. He's about to shower off the sand, but I don't let him go just yet. I pull his cold arm.

'Wait.'

His eyebrows have grains of sand stuck in them and a white coating of salt runs under his hairline. When he's been surfing, he looks like the teen I briefly remember back at high school. He was

16

tall and graceful then and he's tall and graceful now. Only hairier and more tanned. More rough.

Grabbing the back of his wet head, I whisper over salty lips, 'Suck my nipples.'

Raised eyebrows and throaty laughter mean that once again, I've nailed it.

'Naughty,' he says.

We sneak into the pantry in case the kids return and Kav brushes the dress straps off my shoulders. Cold lips circle my nipple. I groan. And this is what keeps us together, unlike other married couples.

I push Kav slightly away, to tease him. 'I better tell the kids to come up from the beach.'

'No time for a quickie?' His lids are lazy.

I shake my head. 'Scott and Eloise are here.'

This is what keeps our spark and love alive and spontaneous. Tease, fuck, come. Tease, tease, tease. This is what I look forward to while we're here. Dragging him out of bed one night and cycling to The Basin, a beach that's renowned for sex in the dunes. We'll romp on the sand and skinny-dip in the water and return to bed heaving and spent. And across the road, Eloise will be asleep with her husband Scott, wanting love, yet never getting close to experiencing it. Because I know he's fed up with her, he told Kav they aren't happy, and something about that makes me skip.

Down on the sand, Rosie, my seventeen-year-old daughter, is not being herself. She's being lovely. She and her little brother, Edmund, are building massive sandcastles, attracting two other kids. Rosie involves the little ones, handing them a spade. They've collected shells, seaweed, cuttlefish bones.

Even the way she's playing with Edmund, who's digging a hole with his bright yellow rake, makes me stare. Rosie's forgetting all the issues she has with him, and Edmund, being six, is relishing the attention. I can hear what they're saying, something about building a moat, a channel where the water can flow up. Edmund says thank you to Rosie. I swallow.

He's our adopted son, but if he knew who birthed him – a young druggy called Pearl who's been in and out of jail – I don't think he'd ever look at himself the same way. I know what shame feels like. It's not something you can just shrug off.

Edmund was a ward of the state, found in a cot covered in shit, with a bone-dry bottle. He was taken from a mother who never wanted to give him up. Fifteen she was when she had him. *Fifteen*. Pearl. A now twenty-one-year-old woman who both frightens and repulses me. A person who thinks it's funny to post up-close pictures of her nose piercing, so you can view and wince at the pus coming out of it.

My hands are gripping the railing and I don't want to release them. I haven't told Kav that Pearl's recently contacted me via social media. She found me, said she's been searching, and I have no idea how. What started as a semi-open adoption for the sake of Edmund rapidly led to it being closed. Pearl became worryingly unstable, threatening and stalking us, and we really should have seen this coming. We never should have kept it semi-open for Edmund's sake. It wasn't as though he could safely build a relationship with his messed-up biological mother, even if the adoption agency promised a semi-open adoption could help 'heal' Edmund's trauma. We closed it, with the agency finally agreeing that this was in the best interest of Edmund. And then we moved house, which is what scares me most – Pearl's gone out of her way to track us down and it should be impossible. In the text, she said she wants her son back. And with hands trembling, I instantly blocked her like a bad memory.

But who knows how long she'd been scrolling through my social media, pinching the screen with nicotine-stained fingers, zooming in on the new house, the landscaped garden, pictures of Edmund everywhere, the leafy area in which we live. Our identity on social media is a stain I can't seem to scrub out.

I've accidentally chipped the railing paint. Pearl has done this once before when we first adopted Edmund, often threatening to find us. So, we changed the rules of engagement, with police telling us to change our social media profiles to private. But how on earth has she found us again? Telling Kav will make it more serious than it needs to be though. I know what he's like and this will worry him. She's blocked, she's been removed and she'll never find us.

Now, Rosie notices me on the balcony and gives a hesitant wave. So, I finally release a hand and wave back. I call out, telling them both to come up. Our guests are arriving. She nods and starts packing up the spades.

We're all here and it's all good. I knew the island would do it, make Rosie normal again. She's usually on her phone, posting photos of her pouting lips to her friends. Now, in this sunshine and fresh air, vitamin D coats Rosie's bare shoulders, returning her to childhood, back to the little girl who used to play for hours with her sunhat on, babbling away while I read beside her on a soggy towel.

Sometimes I can't look at her because the guilt's too strong. So, I just watch from afar like a stranger in a park. I pretend we're okay. And I think she knows that and hates me for it. That's why she tries to meet my gaze by burping, pulling her shirt down to reveal cleavage and a pink nipple before snapping the picture and posting it to whoever. To get a reaction, to incite a conversation, a fight, *anything*. But she never gets a reaction, because her mum is numb and Rosie's the first to know that nothing shocks me anymore.

Eloise, 2.10 p.m.

Arguments erupt about the stupidest things. *Why do you let Coco run off when there's crowds of people? Tell Levi to get off that phone and help carry the luggage. What the hell have you packed in here, your face creams?* I smile and allow it, trying to temper my own jolting thoughts. When you're paranoid, it's hard to stay focused. So, the noise coming from Scott's belittling abuse gets blurred and distorted like a bad radio signal.

Scott wheels the suitcase away from me, over the concrete, and I grasp empty air. I want to hold his hand and rest my cheek on his shoulder, the way the girl and boy behind us are doing. Because they're here on the island for love, and the sand is blinding, and the sun is crisping our arms, and everyone everywhere is already craving that first sip of frothy bitter beer. Coco's hand is sweaty, and she's whinging about the fly that keeps sticking to her lip. Levi helps to carry her, but she's a squirmy toddler who just wants to walk and take a year to get to the villa, stopping every second to inspect a pine cone, a shell, a dollop of bird poo with her chubby finger.

'Yuck,' Scott snaps. 'Eloise, don't let her touch that.'

'It's only bird shit.'

'Don't swear.'

His luggage is rattling heavily over the gravelly path, so he has to shout to be heard while the people beside us glance at our family. I know what they're thinking. Because I'd be thinking the same. Those poor people. Too many responsibilities, not enough time, not enough love. Their marriage is crumbling like those cliffs on the bay and not even the romance of this island can save them.

◆ ◆ ◆

Terracotta villas are shaded by pine trees that bleed sap. At night, the pine cones drop and pound the tin roofs like grenades. I'm surprised no one's been knocked out by them. I hate that I know this about this place. I hate that everything looks the same and smells like memories. It's the pine's blood that makes up Rottnest's smell. Some say it's the sea, the doughy bakery, the yeast from all the beer that hovers over the island like a haze. To me, it's the pine cones and resin, similar to marijuana, making my mouth water. This little habit of mine that no one knows about is my coping strategy. And sometimes, when I feel insecure, the smoking leads to a greater wanting, a pull towards a stronger substance like cocaine or painkillers. For now, I feel assured that inside my suitcase, rattling behind Scott's thick calves and tucked inside a sanitary pad, is a stash of curled green weed that I will fill my lungs with tonight. Coco holds up a pine cone and I take the knobbed nut and sniff it deeply.

'This,' Coco says, bending to another one. Scott hurries us along.

I'll see if Kav wants to join me. He's always been up for a puff.

◆ ◆ ◆

Steep rotting stairs run down to the sand alongside Brett and his girlfriend's orange villa, 212. We're opposite them, 211. We don't have the view, but I don't mind. From here, we could be in Corfu.

21

The blinding blue sky above the sharp needle pines and white sand. I take a picture of the colours, remembering a time when all I wanted was to stay in these villas.

Try to forget, try not to look at every face passing us. Rosie and Edmund are tramping up the steps holding yellow buckets, striped towels and flip-flops.

'Oi,' Levi shouts out to Rosie, who looks up under her palm and then waves with a smile. My son's young eyes fix on her athletic body.

'Hi, Eloise.' Rosie almost does a jump at the sight of me, not Levi. I give her a wave.

And then there's Edmund, a solemn, unhappy little boy who carries the look of sadness on his face like a black-and-white photo. Coco jumps, squeals, claps, does all the excited things kids do when they've seen someone on holiday, while Edmund stands with his spade dangling, black flopped hair covering one eye. Horrible little boy. Suits his name.

Coco runs towards Edmund, chubby legs getting too far ahead of her body.

'Coco,' I call. 'Let's get settled first and then we'll see Edmund.'

She waddles back to me. My little fluffy duckling. I press her against my stomach and watch as Edmund dawdles off. Rosie stares at me, a half-suggestive smile. She twirls a wet lock of hair around her finger and then leaves Levi gawping. She's always looked up to me, had this funny fascination towards me, liked every story and post on my social media. I don't know why, but it fills me with something I'm too embarrassed to admit.

◆ ◆ ◆

Scott's making me get the villa keys from Kav. *His* friend. Best friend. Work friend. I swear he puts me through tests just to see

22

how I'll react around his friends, men in particular. It's obvious in the way he'll casually slip in a man's name every now and then while I'm stacking the dishwasher, making a tea, pulling tights on, then watch me intently to detect the changing colour of my skin. It's either to catch me out or because he's jealous. Both are crap, but I'd like to believe it's the latter.

So, while Scott rests the luggage against the door and I place Coco down beside Levi, I smile. Casually. I'm only getting keys. Scott folds his arms and watches me, but there's nothing for him to spot. No blushing, no awkwardness. It's him testing me that's awkward.

'Come on, bubby,' I say to Coco. 'Let's go and find Edmund.'

Stepping through our sky-blue gate of 211, we cross the road to 213. Kav's surfboards are tilted, salty water droplets evaporating in the afternoon heat. A fishing tackle box, a pair of sand-encrusted sandals and a scooter are positioned by the door, making their villa look lived-in. Owned.

Voices echo from the kitchen area. Laughter. She's laughing. And he follows suit. Happy together. Someone's making toast. I clench my teeth and Coco's hand too tightly so she pulls it away.

'Hello?' It feels like an intrusion stepping into their back courtyard, like I've entered their life and their love. I still feel Scott behind me, watching me from our villa as though I'm about to jump on Kav and start kissing him. But at least he feels *something*, even if it *is* jealousy.

The back flyscreen flings open and Kav steps out holding a toasted crust. 'Ah, the Walters have arrived.' He grins and wraps his heavy arms around my shoulders. A glistening smear of peanut butter from his mouth greets my cheek and I'm tempted to nestle into his neck, let him hold me there a while. I'm tempted to close my eyes and press myself into him. Not because I'm attracted to him, just because I need to be held by a man. And then Penny steps out with a bottle of French champagne and those eyes measure my appearance against hers.

I wipe the crumbs of toast off my cheek and think about the odd combination of champagne and peanut butter.

'Just here to get the keys.' I smile. 'How are you, Penny?'

'We heard the ferry dock,' she says. 'Fancy a drink?'

'Starting early.' I nod to the booze as Coco peers through the doorway. Edmund and Rosie are out on the balcony, eating lunch.

'It's a holiday.' Penny seems to flinch. 'It doesn't matter what time you start.'

'I'll get the keys,' Kav says, hand cupping his wife's elbow as he pushes past her.

Wiping my cheek again, I feel the stickiness of peanut butter. 'I'd love a drink. Just need to get the kids settled first. Do you want to come to our villa?'

She looks back inside. 'Ours has a better view. Get settled and then come over.'

'Sure.'

The conversation is polite yet abrupt, terse with a sprinkle of smiles. I hate it. I hate the flakiness of it. We're not friends. Our husbands are friends, that's all. Have I ever wanted to be more than the husbands' wives? Yes. Do I think Penny wants to? No. I don't know what she has against me, but there's a concrete wall between us and she'll never lug over a rope.

Kav steps out with the key dangling on a blue chain and presses it into my palm. He's crunching into the crust and grinning. And I can't help but smile back. Because he has that effect on people, and I know she's looking.

'I'll follow you over and see Scotty,' he says.

'What about the champagne?' Penny says.

Kav starts towards the gate. 'Bring it over when you come.'

There's a fascination in watching Penny and I don't know if other women feel it the way I do. For a few years I've tracked her Instagram accounts, and seeing her on holiday like this is a bit strange. Like spotting a celebrity at a gas station. And because the relationship didn't stem from friendship – a school yard connection, a college study mate, a mothers' group confidante – I've always observed Penny from a distance at our husbands' parties and business dinners. Adjusting his tie before kissing his lips and curling her fingertips around his lobe. Her body, fit and youthful and without a hint of plastic. The fruit platters she arranges for the kids at a family day barbeque. I guess you can say I've become quietly addicted to watching her. We're not friends, far from it. That doesn't mean I don't know everything about her.

Never imagined her mouth up close when she ate or the way she laughed. Never pictured her flicking a flake of dandruff off her coat. She seems more than human to me. Not like a real mum.

But still, I watch her and wonder if she watches me. I want her to comment on the colour of the dress I'm wearing. Emerald green to bring out my eyes and Mother Earth nature. But her eyes evade me like she's used to being around lots of people who like her. There's only one person in her sights and that's Kav.

I don't compete with any other woman I know, and in fact with Penny I'm more of an observer, interested in her and what makes a woman so strong, assured, not needing anyone but her family. She doesn't have help, no nanny tailing her, and she seems to do everything just right. Their secure, unbreakable marriage, their close group of high-school friends, her dinners out on their patio I know for a fact she's cooked. She's the perfect mother. The mother I probably pretend to be. I just can't seem to get close to her. Either that, or she will not let me in.

Once you hit thirty, it feels harder to make friends with females unless you've grown into adulthood, motherhood, together. Shared the gruelling newborn timetable of sleep, feed, repeat. Connected through past lovers. With Penny, it's a polite hello and a how are the kids, but the bond was never established, therefore it's fake and forced, yet required. Like completing a Pap smear, a breast exam. Painful, but necessary for our husbands.

I suppose the need for her to accept me has been there since day one. Two handsome men, both doctors, introducing their two potential partners. I came later and of course that puts me a foot behind Penny, who's known Scott longer. I've been playing catch-up ever since.

But Penny, she likes to leave me in the dust.

Penny, 2.40 p.m.

I'm not opening this bottle of vintage champagne while they're setting up. No. Kav's already strolling towards their gate and Eloise is following him and I'm balancing on the doorstep with a fury in my gut that's eating me up.

You know what? I have things to do anyway. There's a list with blank tick boxes on the counter. Most of it can be done tomorrow, but I may as well get it done now before everyone arrives. I need ice for the drinks tonight, some extra vegan cheese for Rosie, and to pay the caterers down at The Bay Restaurant and Grill.

The champagne shifts back into the fridge alongside the smoked salmon and cream cheese. Edmund's crying outside about something Rosie has done and I shake my head. Please, please don't fuck this holiday up for me. A hurtful thought about my daughter creeps into my head and just about grabs a hold of me. I flick it away.

Outside, she grinds her chair back, leaves her plate and her younger brother with his roll on his lap. She's whacked it off his plate. This is what she does. She turns aggressive like the breeze on the sea. One minute calm, the next, ripples start up, and any loveliness I witnessed from the beach has now evaporated.

'What did you do?' I ask Rosie when she steps inside. Her shoulders are burnt. Already. New freckles patterning her skin. I told her to wear cream. I told her I'd put it on her.

She stops, glares at me. 'What did *I* do? Ask your golden child.'

When she passes me, I viciously grip her wrist. 'Don't you speak about him like that.'

But the thing is, Rosie enjoys this. Her eyes dance with taunting pleasure, a sickness that churns my stomach. The confrontation, the pain of my nails biting her slender wrist bring her to a state of guilty acknowledgement about me. It says, *you are a bad mother and don't you forget it.* 'He *is* the golden one, though, isn't he, Mum.' And this statement carries more meaning than one.

I release her wrist. 'Come here.' I go to hug her. There's a smirk, a smack of empty air. I'm left standing while her agile, once-baby body marches out of the front door. Edmund picks up his roll and bites into it, sniffing away his tears.

The villa feels cold. I need to put a jumper on.

◆ ◆ ◆

We ride. Down the road that's never been resealed. He rings his bell at a strolling seagull that takes flight. We ride. Shade to sun, sun to shade. His black mop flaps in the wind like raven feathers. His bike swerves in front of mine, sun to shade. Another ring of the bell, another hot gush of bitumen filling my nose. If I lick my lips, I taste salt, an ever-present flavour that sticks itself to everything, corroding everything, hardening everything.

Rosie's comment lingers through my body and it's hard to pedal it away. Edmund's furiously riding.

'Don't get too cocky,' I call out to him. He's thinking he's clever as he swerves like a snake from left to right along the road. But one pothole, one pine cone, one cyclist pulling out from their villa will send him falling, grazing every inch of his knees. 'Slow down, bud.' I never want him to get hurt or be hurt. He had enough hurt in the first three years of his life, an infanthood his brain has smartly boxed away. All he knows now is me, and love, and kisses in cosy beds with storybook reading and cut-up apple. Clean sheets, fluffed pillows, milk when he wants it, not when he cries for it.

But I get it. I get the way he feels right now. A childhood rush that leaves you breathless as you ride under trees that are pregnant with berries, catching the filtered sunlight that blinds you a little. So I let him ride with foolish innocence.

When we get to the village, Edmund is a pro at skidding to a stop, lining his bike alongside the others, unfastening his helmet with squinty eyes, dangling it on the handlebars and stuffing his hands in his pockets to fish out a gold coin for lollies.

'I'll get a lollipop for Coco,' he says, holding the coin to the sun. 'This one is from the year I was born.'

The year we don't discuss. We don't discuss any years prior to three years ago. Edmund doesn't understand this. He can't know about Pearl and how much she wants him back. I turn his attention to a seagull gagging on a chip.

'You don't have to pay for anything, buddy.' I kiss his head and unclench my helmet. Over by the playground, there's a man leaning against the trunk of a pine tree. Ankles crossed, he's biting an apple, hand in one pocket, staring straight at me. Even with sunglasses on, I know he's staring because as we walk, his head follows us. He's dressed in black. Black sneakers, jeans, hoodie and cap. And I find it odd because it's warm and it's Rottnest. I find it odd, but I let him stare anyway.

Eloise, 2.45 p.m.

Amazing how my shoulders hurt from tensing while Kav's slouched against the wall. I'm packing the fridge with staples we brought in a cool-box. Milk, beer, butter, cheese. Scott has the buckets and spades out for Coco, while Levi's already left to go and grab a meat pie with sauce and that's fine. I want him to go and hire a bike and be a kid again. Squirt red sauce over the pastry and stuff his face while gazing out to sea. He'll look at this place with innocent eyes, the way all kids should.

While Kav speaks about the small surf breaking on the other side of the island, I have my head in and out of the fridge, peeking at the door, waiting for Penny to arrive with the champagne. She hasn't come. I have four glasses set on the dining table, ready for pouring. Kav fingers the stems while lamenting the sluggish swell. Scott pulls a beer from the cool-box and offers it to his friend. But Kav says no. He should go back and help Penny with tonight's drinks.

In fact, I've just seen Penny cycle past with Edmund. She doesn't even glance this way, doesn't even call in to explain why she's chosen not to drink champagne with us. My heart thumps.

'What should we bring tonight?' I ask Kav.

'Absolutely nothing.' He straightens, about to leave. 'Pen will be annoyed if anyone messes up her cheese platter.'

'I know how she is.' Because I do. She's one of those people who likes things *just so*.

'What time?' Scott asks, swigging his beer.

Kav checks his watch. 'Come when you're ready. Brett and Sal are over the road, probably shagging. Haven't seen him since they arrived, but I guess that's what it's all about.'

We all laugh but there's a tightness that clenches my shoulders even more at the mention of sex, the scent of it. I can't look at Scott or Kav. I busy myself with stocking the veg compartment with celery, carrots, spinach. It's the ease in the way he utters it, as though he's comfortable with the subject, like mentioning war to a soldier, crime to a cop.

And it only suggests one thing: they have sex.

And my awkwardness in handling the courgettes that I'll never steam, the busying myself in the fridge, stems from the fact that we obviously don't.

My youth was wasted and in a blink of an eye, I'm thirty-five and no longer sexy. No one admits it, but it hurts like a needle above the eyebrow, like a scalpel to the lip. That's why I've turned to implants of all kinds to tighten the skin and make me appear desirable.

It hasn't worked. Scott looks at other women like they're a meal to devour. He wants to spread their legs and pound them and he doesn't notice my own legs, spread and inviting.

We treat growing older with humour. The discussion of age spots and grey pubic hair and sagging tits that touch the belly button generates laughter among groups of women.

But what happens if you've only ever based your identity on how beautiful you are? Then what's left? I'm a crisping shell, an exoskeleton. And instead of maturing into beautiful, I'm simply maturing.

And I watch the way other women, women like Penny, go about their days not focusing on that. But that's because they're whole people. Whole women. Formed with personalities that make up multidimensional identities.

They're career women, studying to become physiotherapists. They're party women, constantly hosting friends' brunches. They're women with hobbies, aspirations, wanting to set up refuges for homeless pregnant mothers. They're the family builders, each with supportive parents who they take on holidays and picnics with chequered blankets. They're the home decorators with money to spruce up their modern kitchens. They're the fitness women training for half-marathons.

They are not just their long legs and long hair. They're not just their pretty lipstick smiles and black fanning lashes. No, these women are whole. Real. Unfussed about ageing. They don't have thousands of followers to make themselves feel relevant.

These women scare me. Penny is this woman.

Eloise, 4.14 p.m.

Scott has been over there with Coco since Kav invited him. I told him to go, leave me to unpack everything. I just needed a moment of quiet and calm. To open the windows, letting the squawk of seagulls float in on the hot wind, airing out the dusty muskiness of the villa. To rehearse affirmations in the mirror. *You are safe. No one knows you. No one will ever find out what you did here.* The guano smell and breaking waves activate a sense of time travel that has me hurting inside. Even as I busy myself, setting my toiletries up on the bathroom counter, arranging Coco's travel cot with teddies, attempting to pop the cot beside our bed, it's there. Because nothing on this island ever changes, and only two streets behind me, in the cheaper accommodation with no views, I'm wondering if what went on back then still goes on now?

I've needed to pour myself a large gin with lots of ice and a splash of soda and swallow it in a gulp. Once the gin swirls around in my bloodstream, I inspect myself in my new bikini, jutting my hips out, bunching my breasts up. I've needed to try on a few clothes hopefully Penny will comment on when I join them.

I've lathered myself in coconut oil, which will infuse this place. And, in a nicer tipsier haze, I've prepared myself for the intimate occasion across the road.

I needed to.

A cheese platter with a plastic container of olives swimming in oil, three cheeses, wafer crackers and three strawberries wobble as I walk over to Penny and Kav's villa. I don't know what I'm doing without Freddie, my nanny. She's so good at arranging platters and this looks pathetically shit. But I also don't want to go over there empty-handed, no matter what Penny makes of this embarrassing clutter of snacks.

Penny and I have never hung out, just the four of us. While Scott talks to Kav, I'll be expected to speak to Penny. Unless the kids interrupt, which I'm sure they will. I better just make sure Coco doesn't go off with Edmund and leave me. My two-and-a-half-year-old is so bubbly, so joyous, so unlike me. My toddler knows how to converse and socially engage better than I do.

When I open the door to their villa, it already feels like an interference. I don't belong here. It's got a different, cheerful, holiday vibe. Jazz music playing with a sexy Italian singer crooning, aqua blue views outside each window, the aroma of meatballs, something garlicky wafting from the oven. She's even collected pine cones, shells and spinifex that are arranged in a bowl on the table like something from a home and garden magazine. There's a pitcher of ice-cold water with sliced limes, tumblers, crystal glasses, which she later tells me are cheap and okay to break. She naturally does what I try and fake. I blow the hair from my eyes and step out.

Outside, Penny lazes in a chair with her legs catching the sun, large straw hat covering her face. On the table is the French champagne in a wine cooler, a cheeseboard overflowing with salamis, sausage, crostini, caper berries, honeycomb, pâté and grapes.

When she sees mine, she laughs. 'Oh God, you didn't need to bring anything.'

So, I leave mine inside for the kids, who are playing on an iPad, who don't even look up. Edmund's sulking about losing some online game and Coco's just standing there watching him. Levi's opposite them, watching YouTube. When I kiss his hair, I smell meat pie.

'Champers?' Penny says as I step back outside.

'Yes, please.'

After she pours me a glass, it fizzes over the edge, and she tells me to hurry up and suck the bubbles before I waste it. I feel told off. I'm five again. My glasses shade the water in my eyes.

She sits on Kav's knee and he kisses her neck and I perch my bare bikini bottom awkwardly on a stool beside Scott.

'How's this view?' Scott says.

'Best on the island,' Penny says, sucking her teeth. 'We always get the best.'

Penny, 4.16 p.m.

Wow. Just wow. I have no idea what Eloise is playing at, but I am deeply embarrassed for her. It's like watching someone slipping on an ice-skating rink. I want to laugh. I can't actually look at her because then I might. I think Kav feels the same. He's averting our attention to a fisherman on the sand, yanking his line. Scott tightens his jaw, fingers clenched around the neck of his beer as though strangling it. Poor fucking guy.

Her white see-through bikini top is one thing, showcasing the fake roundness of her breasts, the erect nipples, which I assume are plastic. She has a large, faded butterfly tattoo at the base of her spine and we all know what that means. She likes to be taken from behind. But her G-string bikini bottoms are next level. We are not in Ibiza and I feel like saying it, feel the words just there, right behind my smile. This is a family holiday island.

'Is anyone going swimming?' I say, pouring Kav some more champagne. I can't help myself. 'I'm quite cold, to be honest.'

'I thought I might go and take a dip,' Eloise says, from the stool. She's trying to balance her naked arse on the aluminium and perhaps that's what's attributing to the goose bumps that cover her arms like prickles. She's freezing. Get a shirt on. I take Kav's arm and wrap it around me, leaning back into him. Lucky, so lucky to have him.

'Take Coco,' Scott says to Eloise. He barely even glances at her. And it's an order. And Kav doesn't speak to me that way.

'Let her finish her drink,' I playfully scold Scott. It's always been that way with him and me. Familiar, friendly. Scott treats his wife like a stranger. To me, he smiles.

When Brett and Sal call out from inside, I stand to greet them. I can't stay out here on the balcony with Eloise, but I'm certain she and Sal will get on like best friends. Both blonde, both tanned, both full of lips and lashes. The only difference is Sal is twenty. Youthful, pretty and doesn't have to try. When I embrace her small figure, it's like cuddling a younger sister. She smells of shops, the perfume department and coffee. I tell her to help herself to the champagne.

While I'm in the kitchen pulling the meatballs out of the oven, I'm also watching how Eloise reacts to Sal. Will she smile, look her up and down with an insecure gaze? Will she watch Scott watching Sal? Sal is in tight ripped-denim shorts and a flowing flowery top. Her hair is up in a bun and the strings of her pink bikini top hang down her olive back. She shakes Scott's hand and pours herself a champagne, with no choice but to bend right in front of him. And Eloise notices and looks to her husband. And it's then that I laugh into the tea towel. You see, there's something so amusing about insecure women. Just the smallest sight of someone pretty, and they're rattling like crystal glasses on a tray, ready to shatter.

Preciously pretty, see-through and empty. I only hope Rosie doesn't come home while they're all here.

◆ ◆ ◆

My daughter hates me. And she probably has every right to. But last year, while Kav's work colleagues were over for dinner and Eloise and Scott arrived and Rosie raced towards Eloise, flinging her arms around her shoulders as though she was a relative when in fact they barely knew one another, gushing over Eloise's extensions, her nails, her diamond ring, her designer shoes while Eloise showcased it all with a look of glee, as though craving the accolades from a then-sixteen-year-old Rosie, I couldn't help but want to keep them separated. It's no different now.

She's a fake mother and I'm a real mother and Rosie can't tell the difference.

And this obsession with Eloise is Rosie's way of punishing me for her childhood and it works a treat. She gets a medal in it. Purposeful punishment.

So now, when my daughter enters with a bucket of chips and a creamy ice cream, and runs towards Eloise, I find it hard not to comment. After she slapped Eddie's roll off his lap, she cycled off down the road in a huff and I'm guessing that's where she's been for three hours. The general store. On her phone. Eating junk. But to see her excited reaction to Eloise makes me yank back her wrist.

'Have a nice ride?' I say, my fingertips brushing her hair. She shakes my hand away, ignores my question and spots Levi on the couch with his ear buds in. Rosie pops a chip in her mouth and then licks her finger like she's licking a lollipop and I look away, back to the meatballs, which I slide off into a bowl.

'Wanna go riding?' she says to Levi.

'What?'

Rosie laughs. 'Take your buds out.'

'What?' Levi says again. His voice is breaking. He's somewhere between squeaking boy and gruff man. It'd turn Rosie off. She's deliberately ignoring me. But with her, I've learnt the best way to act is indifferent.

'Let's go riding to a bay and swim,' Rosie tells Levi. He goes to stand up while his baby sister, Coco, smacks the iPad out of Edmund's hands. Eddie starts crying.

I leave the meatballs and go to him, crouching down. 'Are you all right, darling?' I glare at Coco and firmly say, 'No.' She doesn't flinch.

'She always hits,' Eddie screams, fists clenched, teeth bared. I don't know this look, this anger, but it's becoming habitual and it frightens me. I hate that there are parts to him that are not a part of me. The way his ear joins the curve to his neck. The way his hair is jet black instead of blond. Edmund swipes a stack of magazines off the coffee table while Coco watches, blinking. I want to slap her face. She's staring at Edmund like he's imbecilic.

'Are you hurting Edmund, Coco?' I quietly say.

'Mum, we're going riding,' Rosie tells me. But I don't look up. This little girl is always upsetting Edmund and I'm getting tired of it. I don't like to see him hurt.

'No.' Coco turns away. She's not afraid of me. Precocious. And Eddie is wailing and running off. Eloise pokes her head around the door frame and asks if everything's alright. Because it's typical of her. Leave me to look after the kids.

'Coco needs her nappy changed,' I say. A thick stench fills my nose as the toddler waddles past me to pick up the magazines. 'Are you toilet training her?'

'Um,' Eloise says.

'Coco, how about you pick Edmund's iPad up?' I smile down at the little girl who made Edmund cry. 'I'll get you some nice garlic bread and you and Edmund can watch a movie.'

Eloise picks up Coco, with her bikini between her bum, and doesn't say a word. But she's pink in the cheeks and sucking in her lip. And her butterfly tattoo waves its wings as she moves her hips, sashaying out the door. I've embarrassed her. Good.

Eloise, 4.30 p.m.

The trees overhead block the hot sunlight, creating a cool oasis of shade. Attached to my bike is a rolling, bumping buggy that Coco sits in, quietly gazing out at the surrounding bay. The bike shop was just about to close, and I managed to hire this bike and carriage before the guy pulled the shutter down. I flashed him a smile, and perhaps that's what did it. I do tend to sway men easily. Although it's a shame that's there, right beneath the surface of my skin. Like remembering when you used to pick your pimples and the scar pots your skin. Any time a man looks at me, smiles at me, winks or whistles, I'm reminded of this island.

The only man I don't sway is Scott. My foot leaves the pedal and almost catches in the chain. I used to dink around on the back of these bikes, without a helmet or flip-flops. Used to fly around corners, visit the bays, sunbathe naked on the sand. Used to stub my toes and catch my ankle against the chain like I have now. It's bleeding and a flap of skin opens up.

I stop. 'Shit.' Sucking my finger, I press it against the red cut.

'Mumma, boat,' Coco's muffled voice squeaks behind me.

I could kiss Coco. Her poo nappy was the perfect excuse to leave Penny and Kav's villa. My limbs were shaky as I carried a stinky Coco back to our place. It sounds silly, immature even, but

Penny's presence feels greater than mine, a presence I just can't shake.

Now, I feel like I've rolled my shoulders free of her.

'Need a hand?' a voice asks behind me. Peering up, there's a tall man dressed all in black, head to toe, behind Coco's buggy. 'Looks like you've cut it nasty.'

I can't see his eyes at all. But he's gaunt and pale, looks afraid of the sun.

'It's fine. It'll just need a plaster.' I suck off the blood, tasting copper, and watch as he nods over and over and over. Staring. Then swivels on his heel in an exaggerated fashion, hands in pockets, and wanders off towards town. It's bizarre the way he does it. But also quite eccentric. The way he moves, swaggers off, reminds me of a magician.

'Mumma, boat,' Coco says again. She points to the beach, the white boats glinting in the afternoon sun.

My ankle is still bleeding so I'll have to buy some Band-Aids. 'Yes, boat.' I smile at Coco before climbing back on the bike. As I ride along the road with my girl trailing along behind, hair out and flicking, lips drying in the wind, in a way I wish it was just me and Coco here. A lot of the time, Levi mirrors his father; disinterested and distant, plugged into a fantasy world of touchscreen technology. Barely speaking, barely listening. I think even Scott's given up telling him to look up from his phone.

Coco is still at an age where she wants me, needs me, relies on me and loves me. My skin-to-skin contact comes from her. My tight cuddles and sloppy kisses. I glance back at her and smile. She's quiet, sitting there holding on to her belt buckle. My baby. So light and blonde and smiley and carefree. So unlike Edmund. He's bleak and grizzled, with a wide face that already tells you what he's going to look like when he's older. Like he popped out of his mother an old man. Never smiling. Never happy. Always crying with that whiny screech. I wonder if Penny regrets her decision to adopt him?

◆ ◆ ◆

The bay's filling up, boats clogging the space, some moored up against one another. Music's thumping across the water, backed up by excitable voices and popping corks. It's a party weekend. *Her* party weekend. It's always been a place of parties. Trust me, I know. But I don't feel like partying, I barely even want to be here.

All I feel like doing is crawling up to the bar, away from everyone, ordering Coco some chips and myself a Pimm's. Should I? Would Scott even care or notice? I just needed to get away from that constricting atmosphere. Coco playing with Edmund, Penny treating me like I'm invisible as soon as Brett and Sal arrived.

Steering the bike towards the town, still bursting with tourists, I decide to grab Band-Aids and bits and pieces for dinner. However, I avoid faces, I avoid the workers, I avoid how little the scenery has altered. Same colours. Orange, tan, white, blue. Same sounds of dinging bike bells and laughter. How can I hate such a beautiful place?

Over by the general store, Levi's hanging out with Rosie. She's leaning against the wall, provocatively posing with her jutting hips, welcoming my innocent son. And there's smoke curling up from behind her back. Rosie draws the cigarette into her lips and then offers it to Levi. But he shakes his head and flaps it away, and a strong mix of pride and love fills my chest as I watch on.

He refused her. He doesn't need her. He doesn't need drugs or nicotine. I suck my bottom lip in as I slide the front wheel into the bike railing. My habit isn't a reflection on Levi. Like swearing; just because parents do it doesn't mean the kids have to follow suit. No one knows about my smoking, the way it helps soothe my limbs, my frantic thoughts, spreads an oozing lightness through my body. If I didn't do it, I wouldn't be the mother they need. Some mothers need yoga, meditation or running. Some drink herbal tea. I just happen to smoke weed.

'Eloise,' Rosie calls out. She flicks her cigarette butt on the ground, exhales smoke and saunters over. She doesn't seem to mind that I caught her smoking, and something about that makes me stand taller. It's like I'm privy to a secret that Penny isn't.

'What are you two up to?' I smile as Levi glances away. He's nervous he's been caught out. 'Coco is under all this mesh.'

As I zip open the carriage flap, Coco reaches out for Levi, little fat fingers opening and closing. She looks up into the glare, eyes closing.

'We were going to go and have a swim at The Basin,' Rosie says, bending to unclasp Coco. I don't like the name, *Basin*, the way it casually rolls off her lips. *The Basin* is a bay with coloured waters mimicking the Mediterranean Sea. And when she says it, I'm triggered like a soldier with PTSD with a memory funnelling in. I'm a little older than her, riding to *The Basin*, dunking my head under the water, wishing I could leave the island but knowing I'm not allowed to.

Nicotine floats from Rosie's hair and Levi stands back. I want him to know that I'm not mad at him. He didn't accept the cigarette and I'm proud of him. I fish a twenty-dollar note from the carriage side pocket and a bundle of one-hundred-dollar notes fall out on to the pavement. Rosie crouches to help me collect them and stuffs them back in the pocket.

I hand a twenty to Levi and a twenty to Rosie. 'After that, why don't you go and hire one of the paddleboards.' Even if I don't want to be on this island, I can't let Levi and Scott see this fear in me.

He grins and kisses my cheek. 'Thanks, Mum.'

'Wow, I absolutely love your watch, El.' Rosie is standing with Coco on her hip and smiling. I bet Coco will stink of cigarettes now.

Twisting my wrist, I tell her, 'It's Cartier.' And then I watch her forehead lift. She's impressed by me, by my things, and truthfully, I like when people notice the watch. It was my first big purchase after getting paid through my social media.

Rosie moves around to my back and checks the tag on my bathers without asking. 'You have such a great figure. Where did you get these?' She's always been up front, anytime I've seen her. A cocky confidence that comes from age, naivety or bad manners. 'These are the nicest brand,' she says. 'I've seen so many celebs wear them.'

Weirdly, having her compliment me makes me suck my lip into my mouth. And when she utters, 'I wish my mum could be as cool as yours, Levi,' I almost want to sob.

I almost have to stop myself from hugging her.

Penny, 5 p.m.

The village is buzzing with tourists about to depart the island on the five-thirty ferry. Some load up on jam doughnuts from the bakery and souvenirs from the general store, with a glum look pasted on sunburnt faces. They're going home. Leaving the freedom of this idyllic getaway and bracing themselves for humdrum suburbia. The sun is setting on their brief time here, and I can't help but puff my chest with smugness as I park my bike up against a Moreton Bay fig tree and drag my sandals past the lot of them. I get to stay.

'Excuse me.' I push between a couple arguing over where their tickets are and notice Eloise at her bike, leaning up against the bakery wall. Fuck. I check my watch. The bakery will close soon. I have to go in to get dessert, at least a cake for Kav. Eloise grabs something from the bag at the back of her bike, and then goes into the bakery. Coco's in the back buggy and of course Eloise leaves her unattended. I wait a minute before following.

Inside it's freezing, even in the heat of summer. You feel it on your bare toes and pink shoulders. Rob, the owner, is behind the till, serving a line of tourists. He looks up and flashes a cigarette smile when he sees me. Shit. I didn't think he worked on the island anymore. It's been years since we've seen him here.

I've still never forgotten the time he invited me and my ex-husband back to his house on the island, a dilapidated thinly built house of corrugated iron and pale-yellow boards that gave the illusion of stain rather than colour. Foam mooring buoys hung from the sagging rafters and salt rotted his three bikes. We'd been drinking at the pub, pre-children. My ex-husband and I had met him in there with a six-pack of beer and later stopped at his home's flyscreen. On the coffee table, six powder lines were measured equally by a bank card. And I remember backing away and urging my husband to follow. I've never been one for drugs or anyone who dabbles in them. Over the years, we'd see him here and he got to know Rosie, and then he got to know more about me and my past life before Kav. Things only close friends and family should know. I wish he wasn't here. I wish he never came back.

I'm aware of my see-through sun dress, the one I've thrown on because it's too hot for proper clothing. I'm aware of the way it sticks between my thighs and clings to my breasts. Avoiding Rob, I'm hoping the other cashier will serve me.

Eloise's perfume lingers in the air like a hippy's and I use it to locate her. She's bending over the freezers, pulling out an ice cream and examining it. I tiptoe past her into the bread aisle, hoping she won't look my way. I'm pretending to read the labels on the shelf, keeping an eye on her. She's too absorbed in selecting ice creams for Coco or Levi.

Quickly, I dump a loaf of rye and hotdog buns on the bench, not bothering with the cakes. To choose a cake means going past Eloise. Too risky. The kids can eat sweets. Or fruit salad. Or a couple of biscuits for dessert. I'll buy Kav a cake tomorrow. Rob serves the last customers, a young couple, and makes a sucking sound with his teeth when I'm next. Nicotine has coloured his fingers mustard.

'Well, well,' he starts, like a sleaze from a bar. 'Haven't seen you in a while, Miss Penny.' He scans the buns and I quickly smile. 'What brings you here? Family holiday? Romantic getaway?'

'My husband's fortieth.'

He frowns. 'Your new bloke?'

I can't be bothered explaining how Kav and I have been together for eleven years now and I've been divorced for thirteen. 'Yes.'

'Wish him a happy one for me.' He barely smiles and places the bread in a plastic bag. 'He doesn't know how good he's got it, does he?'

But I don't acknowledge Rob. Eloise is coming up behind me in the line. I smell her perfume deep, like an incense stick. Two people I greatly want to avoid. I beep my card against the machine and rush out with my head down.

Penny, 5.31 p.m.

We've got an adult ambience on the balcony, especially now Sal's gone to nap before dinner. Funny the way women without kids go about their day napping, nails, no responsibilities. I remember being like that. I never felt quite complete until I had Rosie.

Since Sal left us, the men have settled. When she's here, they're like three dogs aroused by a bitch on heat. Once she goes, they calm down and resume eating, lazing. Brett, Scott and Kav are quietly discussing the merits of owning a home versus renting.

I'm quite content here, eavesdropping on their monotonous drone, the last of the sun's bite on my legs. My hand has a way of constantly cupping my stomach. I don't need a wine. I'm drunk with happiness here on this balcony, legs on Kav's knees, eyes semi-closed under my straw hat so that I can just make out the blurry blue sea.

Energetic voices inside dampen the easy mood we've created out here on the balcony.

It only takes me a second before I'm sitting, flipping the edge of my hat up to peer through the window. Rosie, Levi and Eloise clomp along the floorboards, hanging helmets, clumping bike keys on the counter. And Rosie is smiling, *smiling*. She's gazing up at Eloise as though she's just made a new best friend. She laughs, squeezing Eloise's upper arm, and I bite my teeth together.

'Well, you'll have to come and babysit Coco sometime,' I hear Eloise saying. 'We have the pool house, you could even come and sleep.'

My tongue finds a bit of bitter olive stuck in a molar. I flick it out and chew on it, watching this woman bonding with my daughter.

Right, I'm over hosting the afternoon drinks. They can all go back to their villas. We were supposed to have the first of the guests over here tonight. Kav's college mates, a few of my mothers' group friends. But I don't see why we can't just meet at the pub for dinner? Lively music, kids running amok, hot chips, drunken boaties.

'We should go to the pub for dinner,' I say, hoping Scott will get the hint to leave us. I don't want her to come out here. I don't want to hear her chatting animatedly with Rosie.

Kav nods. 'I'm easy, Pen.'

'I thought we were eating here tonight?' Brett asks me. His cheeks are flushed and shiny. I've always loved my brother. He's easy to please, easy to love. I think he's Mum and Dad's favourite. He's like a big kid who has never grown up and people don't expect him to.

'It'll be easier meeting everyone at the pub, don't you think?' I say to him. As children, Brett would stay here for weeks on end with Dad while Mum and I stayed home to let the boys have some time away. I've noticed the way he talks about the island to Sal. With a sense of authority, pride, a belonging.

Scott sits up, swigging his beer. 'Yeah, we should probably see about getting our kids ready.'

Eloise steps on to the balcony. At least she's covered up now. A sheer cloth hangs off her bony frame. I don't even bother looking up at her. My straw hat shields me from her, so she won't think I'm deliberately ignoring her.

Brett stands, placing his beer bottle down on the table among the cheese that's starting to sweat. 'Pub sounds good. Sal's never been.'

'To a pub?' Kav jokes. 'Still underage?'

Brett punches him playfully on the arm. 'Jealous?'

My husband pulls my hair like reins and kisses me straight on the lips. Beer breath hovers over my nose when he says, 'Sorry, mate. I scored your sister.'

Brett makes a spew sound, and when I glimpse Eloise, she's staring straight at Scott. I can read that expression anywhere – an awkward tightness. A telling sign. You don't kiss me like that.

I'm the woman who has it all. They say you can't balance work, life, kids, husband, self, sex, exercise, nutrition. But they haven't seen *me* do it. I'm the woman with schedules pinned on the fridge and office door. I'm the hoarder of notebooks, the checker of lists, the reminder-keeper, the organiser, the pantry stapler. If you don't know where the long white socks are, they're in the top tallboy drawer. The coconut milks are stacked in threes and when one gets used in a Thai red curry, I'm ordering another in the next shop. We never run out of toilet paper. I'm that kind of woman.

The business shirts are ironed with starch, the college blazer dry-cleaned weekly. I have boxes for shoes, cupboards for guests' coats, every type of tea you can imagine. You can't catch me out, and no one has, because if someone wants almond milk in their latte, I'm frothing that milk for them. I'm known for it. I'm proud of it. There's no badge, but people recognise what I represent. I hear their comments behind my back and pretend not to. That Penny, that organised Penny. How does she do it? I don't know how she does it.

She just does. How can any woman or mother not? In fact, it really irks me when a mother at school proclaims to the group that she can't make béchamel sauce for lasagne. They call it *white sauce*. I like to correct them about that.

Mothers these days are quite hopeless and ignorant, unknowing how to French braid, sew a button, apply nit cream to hair and give their husband a decent blow job. They think that requires a special occasion like his birthday or anniversary. But do it every second day, and he'll look at you with desire, no longer needing porn or his office assistant's cleavage on show to help him along while secretly masturbating.

A woman who does it all, has it all. It's lesson one. I learnt this a long time ago and I'm determined to keep it that way. And that's why I don't like Eloise. She fakes it. She fakes everything.

Eloise, 6.20 p.m.

The pub is brimming with holidaymakers, and we're back to this again – Penny at a distance, chatting to a group of women all dressed the same in nautical stripes, hessian shoes and red lipstick. This is what we're used to. Safe distances. Brief conversation. Different groups. People everywhere to hide behind. I never used to come here, to the pub. I was underage and kept to the other side of the island, where the parties went on all night and the sheets were never clean.

The dim pub lights hang on strings across the courtyard, making everyone appear bronzed. The beach is white, the sea is milk and boats are facing all different directions, meaning there's no breeze and no current tightening their mooring ropes. It's a perfect night and yet paranoia blemishes the scene. I've taken so many photos of this evening, my data is almost full. And Scott looks so good in his white shirt, chest hair curling under the V of it. He's showered, sprayed cologne, run a brush through his thick hair and now laughs at Brett's jokes. He hasn't said anything about me agreeing to come to the island and I'm grateful.

The temptation to reach under the table and take his hand is strong. I touch my tongue to my lip and stare at him. He's like a prize that'll never be possessed. I only own him from afar.

I glance around at the women surrounding us, each of them flicking their hungry eyes at my husband. They'd wonder how he feels, like I once did. They'd wonder how he kisses. How big he is.

I inhale deeply and smooth my hand down my thigh and under the table, where it rests alongside Scott's shorts. Just this. Just my bunched fist against him makes my heart thump. One second, two seconds, three seconds. I go to place it on his thigh, and he moves to allow Sal to sit down. My hand gets squashed under his bottom and I yelp.

'What?' he frowns.

'You sat on my hand.'

A smirk. 'Relax.' And his conversation resumes.

And I'm biting my tongue until I taste pain. If Scott needs me to relax, then I need something to relax me. When Kav steps up to the table with his pint and gives me a quick wink, I finger gesture to come closer. He's the perfect accessory to easing my nerves. Chilled, carefree, lovely Kav, who knows how to make people smile. His head tilts as he steps around the table, as though considering me, as though curiosity killed the cat. My tongue skims my upper lip again. I dig into my handbag then uncurl my hand, displaying a thick, fat joint. And I nod my head over to the dunes. And he laughs, head back, so I stand and leave my husband, leave the group, leave Penny and her party.

The dunes are white bed sheets, soft and silky. I kick my sandals off and sink my toes into the grains, still warm. And when I twist my head around, Kav's there. And he's following.

◆ ◆ ◆

There are rumours of a tragedy happening to Penny. Before Kav, before Edmund. When she was married to her ex: a banker, or butcher, I can't remember. But there was an incident and Rosie was involved. But even Rosie's probably been sworn to secrecy.

That's the thing about Penny, she's as tight-lipped as a clam.

And who knows if the tragedy is even true? I wonder if I can ask Kav? Would he even tell? I've tried before to ask Scott about their relationship, but he's only ever grunted and shrugged. Besides, it's hard to discuss couples and love and marriage when your own is on the rocks.

I think rumours are spread to make Penny seem tarnished because she's not. We all want to cut down and slice up the tall poppy, don't we? We all want to find weakness in the perfect vase. We all want to shit on people's happiness. Penny is perfect. People can't stand that. She makes us stare at what we aren't.

Eloise, 6.45 p.m.

We've spoken about his birthday, about the kids, about his job, but I want to know what makes them happy. Handing over the joint, I shimmy my bum further into the dunes, picking at a piece of sharp grass, which I prick into my palm. I want to know how long they've been happy. Is it just a front? A show? I bet it isn't. There are some couples who genuinely feel content.

'We better get back,' Kav says, exhaling into the purple sky. He passes the thick papery cocoon to me and I drag it into my lungs, feeling settled and blurred. This has been too good, sharing a joint with Penny's husband without her knowing. Children's laughter floats on the breeze. Sand sifts between my toes, a ruffle of wind between my thighs. I finally like this setting, this island, this night.

'Just wait,' I say. 'Finish this.'

He eyes the joint. The smoke curling up. 'You're bad, you know that?'

He's not saying it in a sleazy way, more like a guilty way. He's accepting the joint, loving it, and he probably shouldn't.

'What would Penny say if she knew?'

He laughs, coughing the smoke out in splutters. 'She probably wouldn't mind. It's my birthday, after all.'

'You two seem so happy.' My voice comes across tainted. He nods over and over and smiles down at the hole he's been making with his thumb in the sand.

'We are.'

'How?' I lick my lips, desperate for knowledge. And perhaps he notices how personal my questions are when he frowns up at me.

'How what?'

'How does she make you happy?'

A smirk. 'I don't know what you mean.'

And he wouldn't. Because happy people don't question why they're happy. They just are.

'Do you argue?'

'Not really.' That wasn't the answer I wanted to hear. I hoped for a different response. A *sometimes*, a *once a month when she's on her period*, an *all couples fight* kind of response.

I inhale until the paper crinkles red.

'What about you and Scotty?' he asks, watching me. I don't like when people watch me. It reminds me of when Mum put me in front of a therapist all those years ago. Being scrutinised, prodded and poked only heightens my anxieties. I draw the joint deep into my lungs. They fill with heavy smoke, but my brain remains light.

'We're fucked,' I admit with a shrug. I can't believe what I've just said. This is the way all affairs start. One person admitting their marital troubles, the other consoling with patting shoulders, raking fingers through hair, shuffling closer, and in this sickness, a bond develops. But I don't want this with Kav. Don't want his affections or attention. I just want Scott. And the tears escape without me even realising. God, I feel stoned. 'He hates me.'

'That's not true, El. Why are you saying that? Come on.'

56

And then it comes, just like I'd anticipated it. Kav shuffles closer, arms wrap around me, and I feel like a thirsty baby in need of milk, in urgent need of nourishment.

And his arms are the thing to quench my thirst. The weight of them, their warmth, his hairs prickling my skin. The *there there* in my ear. So, I let him embrace me for a while as the joint burns on the sand. And I imagine he's Scott, loving me like he used to.

Penny, 7 p.m.

Sucking on a bitter orange, I eye Kav over by the table of blokes. He thinks I didn't notice, but I did. I saw him returning from the sand dunes, kicking his flip-flops free of sand before heading back over to the group. His eyes are bloodshot and happy. And it's not from the booze, the beer, the buddies. I bet if I stare over to the dunes, I'll spot her blonde hair like a tuft of weed behind a sandhill. She's nowhere near Scott or Julie, her little sidekick, who she's managed to befriend since tonight. Her daughter is running wild on the sand with a dirty, smudged nappy under her sun dress. I've been keeping my eye on her with Edmund, who's burying himself into a hole with a blue spade. Other kids have joined the group and it's like a day-care centre with only one supervisor. Me.

I leave the ladies at the table, leave the prawns with creamy dip and jugs of Aperol spritz, and sashay over to Kav. My hands dig a little too hard into his collarbone.

He peers up at me and smiles, an unfamiliar earthy musk coming from his breath.

'Having fun?' I say.

'Sure am.'

'Come with me.' I smile, pulling the back of his shirt.

I step away and Kav follows me out of the pub entrance until we're standing underneath a row of peppermint trees. He places his hands on his hips, slightly smiles, slightly frowns.

'What's up?' he says. I enjoy seeing him nervous. Nervousness displays how much I mean to him.

'Where's Eloise?' I ask.

He sniffs, a gesture he does when he knows he's about to say something that scares him with my reaction. Then Kav laughs like a teenager in front of his class, trying to contain himself, and I place my hands on my own hips, like a teacher, with raised eyebrows.

'We just smoked a joint together,' he blurts. 'But don't get all shitty.'

'Why would I get shitty?' That makes me shitty, that he expects me to get shitty.

'Because I know you can't stand her.'

'That's not true.'

'And it was just a few puffs in the dunes. She obviously feels out of place here with all your friends.'

'What do you mean?'

He laughs again and points lazily to my group of friends at the table, flowing dresses a mix of colour, jugs of Aperol and oysters glistening like sweaty vulvas. And the way he laughs at them has my neck turning hot. He laughs at them, he laughs at me. It's an insult. And he chose to go with Eloise. But that's not what I'm upset about.

'Eloise is the most irresponsible mother I have ever encountered. Off taking drugs and leaving her toddler alone to pick at dirty cigarette butts.'

'Calm down—'

'No, I'm not going to fucking calm down.' Because I can't. I'm fuming now. And I don't know how to gather myself and return to the table happy and vivacious like they all expect.

I turn away from Kav, who has disappointed me greatly, and walk behind a tree trunk, picking bark off it.

Our marriage is the kind people envy. In fact, so is our whole family.

Sunday mornings are pancakes in bed and newspapers under crinkled sheets. Thursday night is for romance. Edmund gets babysat by Kav's parents, Georgia and William, and we're free to love and laugh. We may eat at our local Italian restaurant with big bowls of garlicky spaghetti and goblets of shiraz. Or we might choose the bar on the beach with its black-and-white umbrellas. Sometimes we recreate the night of our first date at a quaint wine bar and flirt with our legs rubbing under the table.

Friday nights are family movie night with popcorn, chocolate and wine.

While Edmund and I arrange cushions and quilts for the three of us to laze on, Kav and occasionally Rosie are up at the kitchen bench, popping corn. I can't quite believe it when she joins us, but on the rare occasion when she does, I make certain to take extra pictures to remind myself just how wonderful our family life is.

Our beachside home is our sanctuary; a refuge from people and buildings, a quiet place to soak in the views and put our minds at rest. At times, I see our home as a public place, a place for entertaining greedy guests who stay too long and expect too much. French cheese, Moët, the kids to be fed with home-made pizzas. Our home lacks privacy because we let too many people in it. Kids, teenagers, business associates, mothers' groups.

It just takes these movie nights to bring us back together.

But Kav and I know movie nights aren't really about movies. We are a family, continuing a bond we've crafted after a loss I suffered so great, it threatens the very essence of the word. Family.

Edmund is here to improve me. To paint over the tears and cuts and bruises I've spilled and endured. He slotted into this family three years ago like a missing jigsaw piece beside his new older sister, who also used him for that very purpose: someone to share the popcorn bowl with, someone to watch cartoons with. He's a replacement puppy, a new car or a planned holiday. A symbol that gives us hope, a bright outlook, and fills a very deep gap. The fact that he's too young to notice helps with my guilt, makes it justifiable. Makes me less of a liar.

Rosie doesn't see Edmund the way I do anymore. Rosie sees her brother as a threat.

But Edmund is the healing salve I crave.

Sometimes, people have to be used as necessary.

Eloise, 7.28 p.m.

Penny and the Peacocks flutter around the table, gulping champagne like overexcited teens, loose with the freedom this place supposedly offers. The men congregate at one table, jugs of beer sloshing into pints, slapping shoulders, laughing deeply, bonding over masculine jokes.

I'm stoned and my make-up needs a touch-up.

Coco's on Scott's lap, sucking her thumb and nodding off. A bowl of fries sits in front of her. Every now and then she plucks a chip from the bowl. She's happy, content, unbothered about where I am. I have no idea where Levi is, but I'm sure he's somewhere on his phone, watching YouTubers with his ear buds in. I probably should go and look for him. But my make-up. I'm certain my mascara is running.

I scan the tanned bodies and bleached hair, sweaty and soaking in the atmosphere of the pub. There's drooping fairy lights, café lounge music and the briny scent of sea mixed with boat diesel. I've just spotted that man who tried to help me with my cut crouching down and speaking to Edmund on the beach. Penny's too busy talking to notice. Whatever. Part of me feels lazy, sleepy, like Coco. But I'm also drained. It's hard pretending to fit in here, to be watching over your shoulder. And with Kav, he let me be vulnerable.

I swallow, tasting weed, needing a mint or a drink to wash the smoke down before someone smells my breath. Skirting around the party to the toilets, where a mother and her daughters exit with dripping hands, I notice the middle cubicle's occupied. Someone's in there, crinkling a packet. I hear scuffs on the toilet lid, like dragging plastic. Chopping sounds. And then a snort, followed by a long sigh. Pretty brazen, knowing two little girls were just weeing in the cubicle next door.

The reflection shows my sunburnt shoulders, my running mascara. I dab cold water over my face and under my eyes, wiping the black ink with my fingertips. I'm a mess. But at least I look different. Anyone who's been on this island for over twenty years will not remember me. My hair now blonde, my breasts a larger size. I rehearse the affirmations in my head then cup some water in my hands and suck it down. I dry my dripping face on a paper towel.

After this, I'm going to take Coco home, back to the villa. I can sleep with her in the second double bed. I probably shouldn't have packed the travel cot. Scott and I never sleep in the bed together without Coco squashed in the middle. Her chubby body between us dried up the sex, the touch and any chance of reconciliation. Most mothers use this as an excuse to not be intimate with their husbands. But me, I want Scott so badly, I'd happily do it beside her.

I glance at the cubicle. The sniffing continues, followed by a nose blow. Who the hell's in there? I'm actually intrigued to see who exits. Like the stranger and I share a bond: stuck on paradise island and caught up in the bathroom, stoned and separate from the holidaymakers. Fumbling through my handbag for lipstick and concealer, I stop when the door swings open and Rosie steps out.

Penny's daughter.

Penny, 7.32 p.m.

I'm done with the party, the pub, the parenting of Eloise's kids. I want to go back to the villa now, have a shower and make a cup of tea. People are slurring, drinks are being spilled and the plates are empty with pizza crusts, oyster shells and stale chips. And Rob from the bakery has just parked his bike outside the entrance. Which means he'll spot me and want to join our group. I stand behind a pillar and wait for him to pass and mesh with the crowd of islanders inside. I don't want him getting chummy with Kav, asking about our relationship and kids. Each time we've been to Rottnest Island, thankfully Rob hasn't been working, so there's never been an opportunity for him to leech on to us, settle in and gossip about old times. It's been a while since I've seen him here, so I figured he'd left the island for good. But now he's here and he knows about my ex, my past, a secret trauma only Rosie and I are privy to.

Anyway, this is the perfect time to go. We told Rosie we'd be back to meet her at seven thirty. We've got a long day tomorrow with Kav's birthday celebrations and the rest of the guests arriving. Edmund is playing with other little kids, climbing trees just outside the entrance. He'd be tired.

I glance at my watch, kiss the ladies goodbye and pull Kav from the table. He's still got the red-eye look and he's barely talking. Too stoned. Immature, like a teenager. I'm turned off him and I think he knows. That's why he keeps stroking the back of my neck, hoping to make up for it. And he will. He will make up for this. But I still can't believe he went with her.

Scott glances up at me with Coco on his lap, sucking her dirt-creased thumb. Poor man, having to deal with all this while his wife is off smoking pot in the dunes. I'm so tempted to tell him, but then I'm only tarnishing Kav with the same brush. If she does something like this again though, he'll be the first to know. He means a lot to Eloise. I know how little the feeling is reciprocated. She doesn't want any added judgement coming from Scott.

Coco is sticky, saucy, in need of a bath. I want to take her and shower her. Perhaps I should. Perhaps I will. Yep, I will.

'Let me take her,' I say. 'You enjoy your night and I'll shower Coco and get her and Edmund into their pyjamas.'

'You don't have to do that,' he smiles. 'Eloise will take her home.'

He's handsome, in a Clark Kent kind of way. Not my type, not my style. She doesn't match him though. I'd be better suited. Scott looks around for his absent wife.

'I saw her head off a while back.' Taking Coco off his lap, I hold her chubby, sweet body on my hip. 'Coco can sit beside Edmund in the buggy. Have you got your villa key?'

Scott tucks his hand into his shorts pocket and then dangles the villa key. 'You're a superwoman, you know that?'

'Our kids are young and tired,' I say. 'They need a bath and bed. I'm only doing what any mother would do.'

Any mother who's not Coco's own. Scott's eyelids flicker and it fills me with a deep satisfaction to be taking his baby and taking care of her. It's what people know me for, it's what they love about me. It also accomplishes a need to hide the truth: what kind of mother I am *really*. Only Rosie knows. No one else needs to find out.

What happens when you block a memory out for a long time? It steadily rises like a lump under your skin. You can cover it with make-up, bronzer, skin glitter, fillers, but it comes up eventually and everyone looks at it.

Memories can be so grotesque that your mind will cleverly find a way to adapt the memory in shape, size, colour. You can shrink memories, blur them out, add a clown to make them funny. You can change the setting too, so it's no longer where it once was – on a steaming hot summer night, with the doors to the house open, letting in mosquitoes that'll soon feast upon your naked skin. You can change the drink in your hand from raw grapefruit gin to orange juice, maybe even a peppermint tea, just so the blame doesn't feel so bad. You can change the circumstances, the reasons, the people involved.

Thank God the mind protects itself from itself. Thank God I can shun most of my memories.

Eloise, 7.33 p.m.

Rosie's eyes widen and she mumbles out an excuse. Looking into her bag, she's trying to distract herself from me, because she's been caught out. And I don't know what type of role to adopt – a concerned parent or a young, hip, modern mother? I still feel the compliment Rosie gave me this afternoon on my skin. It's the first time someone has complimented me in a long time. For this, I feel fond of her, like I shouldn't be too hard.

'I didn't know anyone was in here.' Rosie laughs, sniffing again.

I shrug. 'Well.'

'Love this dress.' She fingers the golden sheer material and I feel it again. A tingle. Like being noticed in a tight skirt by a van of tradesmen. Noticed at a restaurant when I saunter in with my hair done. Noticed by the mothers at school for how youthful I look. Rosie complimenting me sends me back to high-school toilets where I'm a teenager again, being accepted into the group.

'Thank you.'

'It's a designer dress, right? I've seen it on this supermodel I follow.'

I nod. It was a couple of thousand dollars for something that looks like it should only be a couple of ten.

'You're so trendy, Eloise.' It's a distraction, a ruse. I remember being the same way when I was young and caught out. And it feels good, great in fact, to be noticed. But I also have a responsibility. If I'd seen Levi step out of a cubicle, sniffing, wiping his red raw nose from drug-taking, I'd be livid.

'Rosie, I know what you were doing in there.'

She looks up at me and laughs, a chiming, bright laugh. Swipes her red nostril. 'Do you want some?'

I step back. 'What?'

'I've heard Kav say you're a bit of a party animal.'

'He did?'

She smiles and pops gum in her mouth. 'Said you're heaps of fun.'

'That's nice of him. Don't know whether it's true.'

She glances back to the toilet bowl, lid shut. 'I promise I won't tell Levi.'

I hate that she's mentioning my son. She's always been much older for her age, able to suck you in like her mother does. But Rosie's only seventeen. Too young to be doing this. Too young to be peer pressuring me. Still, my eyes are stuck on the toilet.

'You don't have to have it now, but if you want some, I've got some.' She opens her worn brown shoulder bag and presents two little packets of white powder. It's so scarily tempting, and I don't know why. She's found my weakness. The joint has only made me emotional, soppy and insecure. Perhaps this white powder would lift my mood, create a spontaneity in me that the other women out there would pick up on and enjoy. I could be the life of the party, the guest they're happy came along. Scott could look at me differently, see me as attractive and confident like Penny always is.

But then Rosie interrupts any notion of agreeing when she says, 'I was never going to offer Levi any.'

Inhaling, I face her in the mirror. 'I really hope not, Rosie. He's a child who doesn't know about any of that yet.'

If I took it and they found out what I'd taken, Levi would be disgusted with me, Penny would probably have me arrested for buying drugs off her daughter.

I ignore her staring gaze on me as I fish inside my bag for lipstick. And then a woman walks in and Rosie clips up her bag, adjusting it on her shoulders.

It's one of Penny's Peacocks and she gives me a wary look as she whispers *excuse me* and slips into the toilet with the remnants of cocaine on top. And it's then I want to rip Rosie's bag off her shoulder and run away with it. But instead, Rosie heads out. And I drag fresh lipstick over my quivering lips.

Penny, 7.58 p.m.

Rosie's phone rings and switches to the voicemail she recorded with background teenagers squealing and carrying on. While I head to shower Coco over the road in Scott and Eloise's villa, I ask Kav to keep on trying, keep on calling until she picks up.

Their villa lights are off, but the front door is open. They must have let Levi come home on his own. In the lounge room, Levi sits cradling a bowl of barbeque crisps in his lap, scrolling through his phone while *Escape to the Country* blares on in the background. I ask him where Rosie is, and he shrugs and says he has no idea. Great. The one tween on this island I thought would be following her around like a puppy and he's already lost interest. Or she's lost interest in using him as her plaything.

My daughter is quite mature for her age because she's been through things I don't like to admit.

Rosie's the type to hang out with older girlfriends and talk with confidence to the teacher. She's not your typical insecure, gawky teen at all. In fact, a few weeks ago I met the guy she's started seeing, through the driver's seat window. He barely grunted hello, didn't offer a name and Rosie told him to hurry and drive off. He wore shades, a beanie, and looked older than Rosie. The fact I couldn't read his eyes annoyed me, but then again, he could've said the same about me. I was coming back from a run, and I didn't want to slip mine off. Behind the lenses, I was squinting, judging his black four-wheel drive with tinted windows. Show pony. I'd estimate he's in his late twenties, unless he was driving his parents' car. But when I asked what his name was, Rosie told me to mind my own business. Later, when I warned that she'd be made to stop seeing him, Rosie promised she'd bring him around for dinner once we get back from this trip.

I once heard a mother from school say it's best if your teenage girl gets a boyfriend. It distracts them and stops all the dangerous nonsense like drugs, partying, hopping in the car with drunken friends.

No, I'm not too worried about why Rosie isn't back in the villa, because it's a safe island, but I *am* annoyed. She knew we were meeting back at seven thirty and this rebellious flouting of the rules just has me feeling as though the attachment between us has severed completely. I can't feel warmth towards her. I just can't. And it makes me feel ill to admit it. I'm sure she senses it, too, but it's better to push all those emotions away for now. Besides, I have kids to shower.

Levi doesn't even ask where his parents are, and maybe all kids his age are the same. Distant. Grim. Provocative. But then I know that's a lie because Rosie has always been this way. Ever since . . .

I blame her, I really do. And at times I've wondered whether I should see someone about this horrible coldness that has me staring at my daughter like a murderer. But then life just gets so busy. Edmund has his after-school sport, Kav needs his shirts ironed, Book Club is held at mine once a month.

Now more than ever, I'm too busy. I smooth my hand over my belly and smile, enjoying the bubbly scent of peach coming from the bathroom.

Coco is playing in the shower, squealing and giggling about the bubbles spinning around in the drain. I can't wait to wrap her in the towel and pull clean pyjamas over her fresh, squishy body.

In Eloise and Scott's room, I find a nappy bag and tug out a fresh nappy, holding it against my nose and closing my eyes.

It's been so long. Thirteen years too long. I can barely swallow.

There's a bottle of baby powder, which I twist and sprinkle on my palm, breathing in the milky, baby scent of it. This makes me want to cry. And her bottle – hopefully sterilised and BPA-free – sits snugly in the side of the bag. Perhaps I'll feed her on the bed and at least lie with her a while until she's full and sleepy. Kav won't mind putting Edmund to bed while I go about settling the little girl.

She needs a mother like me. Someone to heat up milk, place her in fluffy socks and stroke her head to sleep. I think she enjoys that I'm here with her.

'Levi, have you eaten dinner?' I ask, turning my attention back to the living room. I have Coco's pyjamas and toiletries ready to brush hair and teeth. But Levi needs the same attention. Poor kid.

'Nah. I had a meat pie before. And I've got these.' He stuffs a mouthful of crisps into his mouth.

'Are you hungry, though? We have some frozen pizza across the road. Would you like me to heat some up for you?'

Looking up from his phone, he nods. 'Alright. Thanks.'

I smile. 'No problem.'

Returning to the bedroom, I then stare over their private belongings. There's a lot you can learn about a character from their luggage – what they pack, what they deem as valuable. Just from Coco's nappy bag alone, I can build a picture of Eloise. The perfect pretend mother with her bamboo baby brush and eco-friendly wipes. Her Instagram posts are centred around the concept of 'Pure Earth mothers' being the best mothers. As though those who allow their kids to watch television and eat fish fingers from time to time aren't.

From the outside, looking in, you'd believe that Eloise is a perfect mother with her linen, sandy-coloured photographs. Coco

72

naked on her lap with amber teething necklaces hanging down her tanned body. Coco in a white pinafore dress, running through long wheat grass. A picnic rug, complete with a vase of daisies, healthy fruit and vegetables and loaded wholemeal sandwiches. She gets the comments, the likes, the endorsement products sent to her. But it's all a lie. And looking in this villa now, I see it.

Her technology-addicted son consuming crisps for dinner, her toddler left awake and tired and hungry, her bags packed with unfolded clothes, a hairbrush and charger cord stuffed in between the socks and beach hats. She's actually no different to Pearl – neglectful and hopeless. Her life is chaotic, like this very suitcase that I'm searching through. It brings me great joy to catch other people out.

Eloise, 8.15 p.m.

Where is Coco? She's not at the table with Scott. The Peacocks are rowdy, now enmeshed with the men in their multicoloured silk fabrics. But there's no ringleader, there's no Penny. There's no Kav either. There's a table filled with beer jugs and cocktails with sour cherries.

Beyond the gates, Rosie's on her phone, heading under the shadows of the peppermint trees. I edge around the table and tap Scott's shoulder.

'Where are the kids?'

He blinks at me and slams his beer down hard. 'Have a nice smoke with Kav?' His voice is cold, hard and straight to the point, highlighting his absence of affection towards me. It's a sadness I often try hard to ignore, just like our splintered memories. Our European holiday before Levi arrived unexpectedly. Sex on the beach, under the umbrellas and rising moon. We were passionate, all over one another, fingers in hair and tongues in between lips. I swallow something thick. 'Where is Coco, Scott?'

'Having a nice warm shower. Being put to bed.'

I frown, shifting my feet. He's not making sense. Levi? Did Levi come and grab her? When I don't respond, he stares up at me with glassy, drunken eyes. 'Penny's taken her back to the villa . . . for you.'

A wild fury tenses my leg muscles and when it comes, it's almost shocking. I want to bolt to the villa and slap Penny across the face. I want to kick Scott in the gut. It's unreasonable and harsh but I understand where this anger hides. It's been simmering in there and now it's reaching a point that's hard to overlook. Scott thinks Penny is better than me. Of course he does.

'Why would she take Coco?' I shake my head. 'She is so weird. That is such a weird thing to do.'

'It's quite hospitable actually.'

'And you just said, *sure, go ahead*?'

He glares up at me. 'Why wouldn't I?'

'You didn't think to come and get me?'

'Where?' His voice rises. 'Where have you been? Her mother is absent half the time.'

It's then we both realise the rest of the table's listening. So, I speak louder. 'And her father is fucking useless.'

Turning on my heels, eyes stinging and blurry, I march off in the same direction as Rosie. Into the shadows, under the flowering peppermint trees, deeper into darkness. I call out and see her silhouette stopping a few metres ahead. And then I ask her for a bag of that stuff, paying her whatever I have in my purse, stuffing it into her eager hands.

Eloise, 8.20 p.m.

Riding down the dark island roads with the ocean view to the right, I savour the boats floating on the black water, the yellow dotted window lights spilling out on to the ink surface. The colours of the city, twenty kilometres away, wink back, a reminder of how far removed we are from civilisation. The cosy villas with people in their kitchens, making cups of tea or coffee. It was a lifetime ago since I was here. Some people are out in their courtyards, radios playing, deep in mumbling conversations. I ride past all this. I ride with my dress almost tearing at the bike chain, grease up my leg.

But I don't give a shit.

Because Penny is with my baby, in my villa, taking over.

Rosie's sweet little packet is tucked in my bag. I've decided not to use it yet, no matter how distraught I feel about Scott and my argument at the table, the group listening in, him vocalising how absent I am as a mother. I want to sniff it all up into my brain and leave. I want to take the kids with me. I want Scott. I don't know what I want. Wind smears the tears to my cheeks.

Arriving at my villa, I slide the bike against the gate and hop off. It crashes behind me, the pedal whirs, because I've forgotten to kick the stand down. Again, I don't give a shit.

I kick the gate open and barge through the unlocked front door. The lounge room is empty, a half-full bowl of crisps and crumbs scattered around the cushions. But the air is infused with soap and baby powder, so what Scott said is true. She's washed my baby. But where has she taken her? They're not in the bedroom, yet a towel lies spread out over the bed sheets, sopping wet and soaking through. I shake my head, bundle up the towel and take it to the bathroom, where I hang it over the rail. She must be over the road in her own villa.

Leaving the door open, I allow my fury to crest and stride out of the gate, towards Penny and Kav's villa. I don't bother knocking. I push the door open and see them all there. Coco drinking a milk bottle on Penny and Kav cradling Edmund while they watch a family Friday night movie. Levi at the dining table with a slice of pizza. And when they see me, they look up and smile. As though I've entered their family home and everything about this is normal.

'What are you all doing?' I say.

Coco stays on Penny, playing with her curls as she sucks her bottle. This infuriates me.

'What are you doing, Penny?' My voice is low and aggressive, and I can't help the way it comes out.

'I'm glad you came home.' Penny smiles. But it's a smile that doesn't meet her eyes. And she's patronising and petty and parenting me. 'The kids needed to go to sleep. Coco needs to.'

'I know what my daughter needs,' I snap. And then Kav looks at me as though I've somehow crossed the line. And I probably have, because she has this way of scolding me, making me feel in trouble. I hate myself for reacting to this.

'Are you okay, El?' Kav frowns, standing.

'I'm fine. Let's go, Levi. Coco, come to Mummy, please.'

I can't look at Penny. I don't want to watch how she's observing me. I feel the energy of judgement in the room, the awkward silence I've created. Levi is clearing his plate in the kitchen like a good boy who's been roped into this. The family movie plays a silly circus song and Edmund sits like a preppy schoolboy with his hair perfectly washed and combed. No one washes their kids here on this island. It's the law. Kids run wild with sandy bed sheets and bits of seaweed in the suitcase when you get home. They don't look like Edmund. They're not supposed to look so neat.

'Coco,' I say again.

Coco glances up and Penny helps her to her feet. 'They've been showered and fed—'

'I don't understand why you feel the need to do this, Penny.'

She pulls a face and laughs.

'No, I mean it,' I continue. My heart is pumping. It pumps whenever I'm met with confrontation. I hate fighting, hate arguing. But my anger, stemming from Scott, is raw and real. 'Why would you take Coco for a shower? Don't you think that's a little weird?'

'Weird?' She says it like *I'm* weird. 'We were coming back anyway.' She smirks. 'I thought I'd help out so you and Scotty could enjoy yourselves a bit more.'

She looks to Kav, who shrugs. 'There's nothing weird about this, El. Pen was just trying to help.'

'She's always trying to help.'

Penny places her hands on her hips and glares at me. 'I didn't know that was a fault.'

'It's . . .' I'm left feeling stupid and unknowing what to say. Because, no, it's not a fault. It's perfection. It's what more people should be like, what I should be like. And now I'm coming across as selfish in Kav's eyes. I'm coming across like a lunatic who's just barged in here and accused them of kidnapping my kids.

'It's lovely.' I tightly speak and smile, throat lodged with shame. 'I'm sorry. I'm just tired and felt a bit shocked when I couldn't see Coco with Scott.'

Penny shrugs, thinly smiling, and Kav places a hand over her shoulders.

'That's understandable,' he says. 'But we just wanted to help out.'

Coco reaches up for a cuddle and I collect her. A strong perfume of baby powder wafts off her hair. I kiss her warm cheeks.

'I know. I'm sorry. I overreacted.'

It's all I can say. Because I'm about to burst into tears and I don't want them witnessing it. 'Levi, what do you say to Penny and Kav?'

Edmund ignores us all, fixated on the television with his ice lolly. Levi thanks them and walks outside.

'You're welcome, darling.' Penny smiles genuinely. 'I loved doing it.'

It sends a chill up the back of my legs. It's a pointed statement, passive aggressive, and Kav can't see it. I'm humiliated and backing out of the doorway with Levi trailing behind when I'm certain I hear Penny mutter, *poor woman*. But when I turn around, they're discussing bedtime for Edmund, so I can't be sure, can't accuse. But a darkness inside me feels like getting back at Penny, playing her twisted game.

I want her to suffer. I want the upper hand. I want her to feel like I do.

Penny, 10.15 p.m.

There are traditions people undertake while holidaying on the island that we compare with others. Some families go fishing at Salmon Bay. There're the delicious jam doughnuts from the bakery islanders consume for breakfast. At night, kids watch the fishermen at the end of the ferry jetty with the rays and dolphins gliding underneath the bright spotlights. Families run around with torches, playing hide-and-seek. People cook bacon and eggs each morning on the crappy barbeques while someone collects coffees. It's the little things that make this island not just a moment in time or a memory, but a custom. In the way we celebrate Christmas each year with its ceremonial events, holidaying on this island is no less serious, no less planned with expectations.

And one of those expectations, traditions, moments Kav and I must meet is our sex at The Basin.

After the kids are asleep, and Rosie has been told off for returning an hour later than we'd planned, after the kitchen tops have been sprayed with disinfectant and the dishwasher moans in the darkness, Kav and I sneak out of our villa, quietly close the door and climb on to our bikes, excited and aroused by the forbidden act of it. I feel like Rosie. A teenager again. It's after we've been entertaining and the haze of sleepiness and relaxation loosens our limbs, making me want to press down harder on my bike seat. I follow my husband through the empty roads, past darkened villas with only the mainland lights winking back. The boats are sleeping, the island is heavy with the burden of gifting visitors with sunshine beaches and photo-worthy scenery. Tomorrow, it will awaken and start over. Introduce more people. Show off its brilliance. Seep into the memories of anyone who's lucky enough to experience it.

Kav pedals in front of me, and we don't speak, just ride.

And the air is filled with sex and salt, an earthy rawness that provokes us to push harder up the hill, down the hill, up another, down again. We crest the final hill, his breath, my breath, panting and gasping until we reach The Basin.

Its jagged rocks and smooth sand and lapping waves are like our bodies. I lean my bike against the trunk of a pine tree and finger the folded papery bark as Kav takes my hair and bunches it in his fist. His lips are on my neck, his chest pressing against my back. And the waves slap.

It's eerie but pleasant and majestic being here on the ocean, stars dotted like spray paint. We make it to the sand, toes cool and grainy. We make it to the dunes, where I collapse on all fours. And the waves roll. I love watching them as I come. I love screaming down the hill, knowing only the waves can hear my pleasure. It helps Kav come.

With his fingers gripping my hips, pulling me back on to him, I open my eyes and everything is clear. And I swear I see someone down the hill, stepping behind a thick pine tree. Shit. How long have they been there, watching and listening to us? I quickly push Kav back and roll my dress down. 'Someone's there,' I whisper, going to stand.

'Where?'

'Down by the pine trees. I saw them step behind the trunk.'

But I can't see anyone now. A dull yellow streetlamp spotlights a bike rack and a garbage bin with its bag rustling in the sea wind.

Then beyond that, shadows sprawl to the beach and cliffs. Kav zips up his shorts and pats my bottom. 'I can't see anything.'

My eyes don't leave the pine tree because I know what I saw. 'They were probably watching us.'

'Come on.' He pulls me up and kisses my forehead. 'You gave them a great show.'

We hop on our bikes and chuckle like teens as we zoom down the hill. Yet, despite my laughter, I can't seem to loosen the way I normally would after sex. I'm not drowsy, wanting to cuddle, or curl my limbs around Kav's. We were being watched. Are we still? Slowing down, I turn my head, staring at the crest of the hill. Nothing. No one. Our spot, our tradition, our sex has curdled. But Kav calls me on to keep riding.

◆ ◆ ◆

After a ride along the beach track, we return to the villa dozy, in the mood to cuddle. I check the kids. Rosie's snoring, with wet hair from the resort pool. Chlorine fills the stuffy room. At least she was with Kav's parents. Even if she was late, at least she was safe with them, lapping up the free mocktails and salt and pepper squid.

Sometimes I stand over the bed and stare down at Rosie, wondering what she dreams about. Sometimes I hover my hand over her face, too scared to touch it. Sometimes I have to leave the room before she hears me crying. She and I are the only ones who know our past.

Kav showers quickly while I apply thick dollops of cream to my face, rubbing it in until I'm satisfied my lines will lessen come morning. Our bedroom faces the ocean, so I open the window, coaxing in the beachy soundtrack of tumbling waves, seagulls disturbed by one another. In the morning, the seagulls will wake us up with their feet tapping over the tin roof. Crows will wail from the pines. The dinghies will motor across the bay as boaties head to town, collecting the newspaper and hot pastries. The ferry will arrive. The horn will beat the island. People will cycle by, ringing their bells. And our weekend will begin, well and truly.

I'd glanced into their villa on the way back from The Basin. A small blue light from a device hovered through the curtains. Someone was in there awake. Possibly Eloise, feeling foolish about her erratic display tonight barging into our villa. Clearly, she felt threatened by me looking after her kids. Maybe she does know she's a useless mother after all.

After switching off the light, Kav sinks into bed with his skin still damp. He's sprayed cologne under his arms and when he gathers me against him, I breathe in the zesty scent.

'Still think she's really strange,' I whisper to Kav. 'All uptight and over the top. I didn't think she had that in her. She always pretends to be so calm on her socials.'

'I think she was just pissed.'

I scoff. 'Pissed off.'

'Nah, just pissed.' He tells me what she was like in the dunes, crying about Scott and her relationship. And I want to laugh. The tickle is there in my chest. Because I have love, I have Kav. And this news is fresh and beautiful, like the salt breeze whipping through the open window. She presents herself as perfect to the world, but now I'm privy to the truth: her marriage is a sham.

We lie a while in silence. I think Kav's slipping into sleep. I want to keep discussing Eloise. She's a topic I've never wanted to broach before this weekend. To discuss Eloise means I care. And I don't. But I despise lying, because she's *not* the caring mother people follow her for. She is *not* the ideal wife. She's *not* what Rosie thinks she is. Rosie's just attracted to the glamour of Eloise and the number of followers she's probably paid to attract. If we ever switched places as parents, Rosie wouldn't get the ironed underwear and the hot chocolates I bring in when she wakes. She'd be forgotten about, like Coco was tonight.

Once Kav starts snoring, I roll over and take my phone from the bedside table, flicking on to Eloise's profile page. It's the first time I've really studied it. Sixty thousand followers. Who are these people? I scroll down, squinting as I absorb the pictures of their pretend life. Eloise in the garden with an apron, planting bulbs. Coco in the sandpit. An apple pie, which I'm certain she's bought from the store, sits on top of a chequered tea towel. The comments all stem from bored housewives living vicariously through Eloise, praising her beautiful life. The words *nature, earth, spirituality, motherhood, divine, blessed, grateful* and *love* are captioned across the posts, with Eloise at pains to persuade her fans about who she wants to be. But only I know the truth. She's a phoney in an insecure marriage and I would love some more dirt on her.

Flicking away from her profile, I notice a notification. I haven't posted any stories while I've been here, but tapping on the heart shape, I spot a whole grid worth of likes from an unknown user. Hju_7856

Each photo has been liked, extra hearts to the very bottom of my grid, going back to three years ago. All seven hundred and eight of them. I blink and roll on to my back, scrolling back up. That would have taken a while. Who is this person? I click on their profile and there's nothing there. No profile picture, no pictures, no followers.

They're only following one person. Me.

Eloise, 11.58 p.m.

The waves have gone from languidly lapping the shore tonight to a hard dump that bores into your head like a throbbing pulse. A restless energy keeps me awake and Scott's snoring doesn't help either. It's not the waves, which are picking up strength, with a strong easterly blowing in. At the pub, the water was so flat it looked like you could walk back to the mainland. Now, it's churning and chopping.

It's still not the reason I'm awake beside Scott and Coco. It's not her chubby arm, sticky and hot on my skin. It's not Scott's murky breath hovering.

It's a sense that there's trouble around us. On the island. One of the guests. Inside this house. Across the road. Down by the beach. The island doesn't feel happy.

Lifting Coco's arm off me, I lower it carefully so I don't stir her deep sleep. I roll off the mattress and stand in front of the window, naked and open to the stinging wind. All is well. And yet.

Pulling on Scott's shirt, I decide to check on Levi. He's curled up on his side with his back to me. His breath is heavy, gurgling and rested. Sand sticks to my soles and I carry it with me across to his window, which I open to let in some freshness.

The air is thick, suffocating. I need some cool night silence. I need to feel safe.

But this island, it's a sanctuary for some and a bad dream for others and that's why I never wanted to come back.

Something bad always happens here.

SATURDAY

Penny, 6.17 a.m.

I like to start my mornings here with a steady jog. Sun visor on, zinc over my nose, hair tied tightly in a ponytail that'll flick the flies away as I run. I'm doing up my laces when Eloise steps out into the courtyard clutching a steaming coffee, with Coco at her feet. I don't know whether to acknowledge her with a wave or keep tying my laces with my gaze down on my feet. Over the road, she clears her throat. I ignore it and put my ear buds in, pull my sunnies down and push open the gate, before running in the opposite direction. It's a nuisance because I'd like to run past their villa, and down to the town, but to do that means I'll have to wave. I flick a fly away from my nose. I feel her gaze on me, so I run faster up the hill, calves burning, dodging a little girl on her bike.

At the top of the hill, I veer down the back lane, under pines and shade, and blast my music. I need it to clear these stupid thoughts that have started cropping up about Pearl. The user who liked my profile page last night could've been a bot. Probably was a bot. I slap a fly away from my face again. But I blocked them regardless and I don't feel the need to tell Kav. Nothing has happened. They didn't leave a message and if it was Pearl, then it would be likely she'd type something. My breathing is out of sync and I need to slow it down into a perfect rhythm. I wish I didn't feel so rattled. I blame it on Eloise last night.

'Penny,' a voice calls behind me. It's Kav's parents, William and Georgia. The interruption is annoying, especially considering now I'll have to walk with them. They arrived late and we were supposed to be catching up with them for breakfast this morning. I wave and stop, flapping at another fly that's decided to befriend me.

'How's the accommodation?' I ask, regaining my breath and waiting for them to join me.

William's dressed like a golfer or yachtsman, whichever you'd prefer. Pastel clothing with the hues of peach, lemon and pale blue are the only colours I ever see him in. Boaties' shoes, white brimmed hat. They belong in a country club. Georgia reaches out and cuddles me, smelling of Chanel and coffee, and I'm suddenly embarrassed by my own attire. I hope I don't stink.

'It's a lovely room.' Georgia smiles, holding a hand up to shield the sun. Even now, at 6 a.m., she's dressed like she's going for dinner. Perfect coiffed hair and lipstick, gold necklace on her thin neck. 'We're facing the ocean.'

'What more could you ask for.' We walk slowly down the hill in a line.

They're partly the reason I married Kav. Not that I'd admit this to anyone. My own family are wonderful and supportive, but the Cliffords are a next level up. And I need good in-laws. Not the type who I'm going to visit once a month for a cup of tea in front of the television. No, the Cliffords represent what it means to be a traditional family. Christmases with all the trimmings out on their terraced garden with the aqua pool sparkling. Mother's Day high teas with layered cakes and women who run wellness clinics milling around. Georgia is all about family roast Sunday and holidays to their vineyard, where we're all invited. William is about teaching Edmund to sail and play golf and cards. They're sensible upper-middle-class people who fit perfectly into my life like the antique furniture she's gifted me over the years.

'We're looking forward to breakfast,' William says. With one hand in his pocket, the other clutches a stone, which he throws up and down.

Georgia pops up an umbrella and I'm thankful for the shade. 'We've booked the Beach Club overlooking the lighthouse,' she says.

'How was Rosie last night?' I ask. 'Behaving?'

'She didn't get out of the pool,' William grumbles.

'I wondered where she'd got to.'

Georgia nudges him. 'She's a teenager.'

'She had her phone in there,' he adds.

'Will she come along for breakfast?' Georgia looks to me and I can't see her frowning behind her glasses, but I know it's there. It's in the hesitant way she asks. My daughter is the outsider of the family and she's not their granddaughter, even if they try to accept her as such. She just doesn't seem to suit. Not when we're there for breakfast and dining on grapefruit with sugar or French pastries. Not when we're there for anniversary parties, dancing to swing bands and jazz crooners. Rosie will eat Vegemite on white toast and play on her phone. She will sit at the edge of the dance floor, feet on the white chair beside her, sipping on Coke with her nails chipped and red. I get how Georgia feels. I feel it too.

'She'll be there.'

'And what about her boyfriend. Is he here too?'

My cheeks redden and I'm thankful I've been running. Georgia won't notice them as an expression of shame. 'Who told you about him?' I laugh to mask it.

'Kavan,' Georgia says tightly. We pass a group of kids drawing chalk monsters on the street.

I cannot believe Kav told his parents about Rosie's boyfriend. I wonder what he told them? About the flashy car, the grunting welcome, the rude behaviour of staying behind a car window? How we don't even know his name? 'He's not here. They've only just met.'

91

I'm gritting my teeth when William says, 'Kav tells us he's a lot older than her.' They're not Rosie's real grandparents, but I like pretending they are. And this is not coming across as loving and concerned, it's coming across as disgust, as though they expected nothing less from Rosie. An older boyfriend we've never officially met. And I'm starting to sweat, because I feel it too. My daughter disappoints me and now she's disappointing the two people I'm constantly trying to impress. But Rosie's actions and personality are a horrible reflection of my past, of what the Cliffords don't know. So even though I blame Rosie, I also blame myself. Constantly.

So, there's only one way to make this all better again. 'I have the best news I can't wait to tell you tonight.'

And Rosie's behaviour is dropped and therefore our damaging past is too. We can't have her screwing up our future. I've worked too hard to get here.

Eloise, 7.11 a.m.

Smoking weed makes me hungry, so last night after the kids had gone to sleep, I'd snuck out into the kitchen and noticed the cheese and olives in the fridge, ready for our platters. I'd scoffed half a circle of Brie with half a packet of seed crackers. Then I ate a ham sandwich and snuck another three crackers back to bed. Coco slept soundly beside me as I scrolled through Penny's social media, zooming in on her life. But then indigestion followed, burning acid up my throat, and I found myself vomiting in the toilet like I usually do after smoking and bingeing. Thankfully, Scott didn't hear. Thankfully, Levi stayed sound asleep.

Scott's gone surfing with Kav. I didn't see him go. I doubt we'll talk again for the rest of the trip. Coco is out in the courtyard with me, eating bowls of cereal. Levi has gone to get a meat pie, while I sit reading a magazine on the sun lounger. Each time a person walks past, I find myself lifting my gaze above the magazine, hoping to spot Penny returning from her run. She ignored me again this morning. And I still can't get over her showering Coco.

I may have overreacted in front of Kav, something I'm not proud of, but there was a real smugness to it. A reason behind why she chose to make me out to be a bad, absent mother. The one Scott claims I am. I pick on my thumbnail and sigh quickly. It hurts. My stomach hurts. I'm not an absent mother.

Taking my phone, I hold the camera up and swipe to a better, grainy filter, where I click a dozen photos of Coco eating her cereal and swinging her legs. The pine trees are in the background, framing Coco like a Christmas shot. And the orange villas with blue doors are working well to present a beachy, holiday vibe. I post the picture of Coco with the words: *Beach* and *Sand* and *Fam*. And then I place the phone down and lay the magazine on my chest. It's probably wrong to make out we're a happy family. People comment on how lucky I am to look as good as I do with two children, one a teenager. Our family is so photogenic. Blonde, tanned and bleached. I smile when I read those comments; they make my heart swell. But then I remember the truth, remember the cold bed sheets beside me, the untouched skin, the unshaved legs, because what's the point?

And I have to stop myself from crying. Have to show the kids how happy I am. Have to ignore the villa across from us with the family inside it, curled up on the couch last night watching movies.

If I don't pick myself up soon, I'm afraid I'll do something I'll regret to Penny. Because it's the only way I'll feel better about myself.

Eloise, 8.01 a.m.

Scott arrives back from his surf with his wet suit peeled down to his waist like a second skin, and I'm so tempted to run my fingers down his chest and stomach that I clench my coffee cup instead. What would he do if I did it, touched him, fingered his chest hair?

'Do you mind if I go for a walk?' I ask him. My thighs are turning warm from the sun. He shakes his hair and nods as Coco waddles up to him with a lollipop that Levi's brought back from the shop. He scoops her up and kisses her neck, tickling her with his dripping hair.

'Go,' he says. A muffled statement that comes from inside Coco's neck. I really want to ask about last night and why he chose to fight at the pub table, in front of Penny's friends. But now is not the time to ruin the weekend. If anything, I want to make it better.

I ask Levi if he wants to come walking, but he says Scott's promised to take him fishing. I love that Scott bonds with the kids. But I wonder if Levi notices his father never bonds with me?

The walk down to the town is pleasant and just what I need, although I'm still always checking. Is someone watching me? Does someone recognise who I am? I shake my head and just walk. Walk with intention, purpose, and no one bats an eyelid. Still, I will not go down the back streets where the villas are made of wood and the beds are bunks and the hot air penetrates through. Where you hear everything from a person farting to a person fucking. I will not go there and relive it all.

I inhale the clear, fresh day. The sun nips down on my shoulders. When I don't have Coco hanging off me or the responsibilities of motherhood waiting for me, I feel alone. In fact, I feel alone most of the time now. Without Coco and Levi, I'm nothing, nobody, a person with no identity. What is my purpose? What's my reason for being here? I don't like these questions. They're questions I'd ask myself as a young woman, only ever receiving the answer in the wolf-whistles and derogatory comments about my tits.

That's why when I spot Georgia, Kav's mother, browsing the boutique windows, and she notices me and invites me back to the resort for a coffee, I can't help but do a little skip. It's a distraction, like everything in my life – the Netflix series I'll binge on through the week, the new novel by Claudia Wylde, the shopping, the renovations. Without these distractions, people would have to stare at what they are and what they hate. The only difference between me and other people is I'm aware of when I do it and need it.

Pulling away from myself is a coping strategy I've learnt to do well since Scott and I have started arguing. Before this, I studied yoga, meditation, hung out with women who spoke about our demons. You see, there are two versions of me, the self-aware me I haven't met in a while, and the version I'd prefer to be.

I've often wondered what it'd be like to live in Penny's shoes for a week, even a day, an hour. How would it actually feel to be her? To have her husband look at her the way Kav does Penny?

'How's your beautiful husband?' Georgia asks me on our walk back to the resort. She's the sort of woman who doesn't expect an answer. She likes talking, smiling, being the vivacious storyteller. 'You know, when Kav and Scott were in university, they used to come back to our house and invite all their med friends and host ping-pong parties with their beer cups that would spill all over the pool house floor.' She pops an umbrella up.

'I can imagine that,' I laugh.

'And your lovely husband used to offer to pay for the dry-cleaning bill. Because he never liked those games.'

'He would have found them immature,' I say.

'He was always so grown up and responsible, even back then in his twenties.'

I remember. Scott was the reliable, protective type. As a teenager, he'd be the one to make certain you got home before your curfew and that's what attracted me to him. He was the safety and security I craved after a whirlwind teenage life and wild young adulthood. The yoga women always said he was the anchor to secure me.

But Scott doesn't know who I was before.

We met in a café when I was hungover and sleep deprived, coming down from drugs I can't remember ingesting. He accidentally spilled his coffee over my purse and bought me a large coffee with a sugar cookie in the shape of a love heart. My hands were shaky and clutching the coffee for warmth. The cookie was sweet and just what I needed.

I never told him where I'd been the night before or what I did for a living.

When we chatted, I discovered he was a doctor, so I lied and said I was a relief teacher about to change careers. And after our first date, it was like play-acting from then on.

'Let's have a drink,' Georgia says when we sit under the feather umbrellas beside the resort pool. 'Would you like a cool juice?'

'I'd love one, thanks.'

And it's just like now – play-acting Georgia's daughter-in-law. Sometimes it's fun to pretend for a little while.

But if Scott – ever loyal, ever reliable, ever ethical – finds out about my past, knowing him, I don't think he'll look at me again.

Penny, 8.45 a.m.

They always choose the table closest to the pool; that way, they can enjoy an oblique view of the ocean without the howling sea breeze messing Georgia's hair. The pool makes them feel like they're on a secluded tropical island and not on what William likes to call a hunk of limestone covered in seagull droppings. Georgia often slaps him when he insults the island. She, like me, was a child of a boatie, appreciating the unique qualities that no other island can compete with. But William is from England. He doesn't quite 'get' what the beach and sun and surf is all about. Give him a sailing boat up the river any day and he'll be happy. That's why they choose to stay in the resort when they come. Compromising is what's kept their marriage alive and fertile.

I squeeze Kav's hand as we stroll past the pub, and my wedges clomp over the shelled footpath. He kisses my head and Edmund skips in front of us, dressed in a white linen top and beige shorts. We could be out of a catalogue for an expensive clothing brand; only Rosie is the odd one out, trailing behind in a bright yellow bikini top and ripped shorts, hair wet, salty and tied messily in a bun. I told her to change. I told her not to bring her phone. She never listens. That's why I'm happy she's behind me, where I can't see her.

'Looks like Eloise is joining us for breakfast.' Kav nods his head over to the restaurant area where Eloise is in fact sitting with my mother-in-law. I frown and cough away an uneasy tickle in my throat. What the hell is she doing here? 'Mum's always loved Scotty,' Kav adds. 'Nice of her to ask El.'

I hate when Kav calls her El. Makes him sound like they've been friends for life. I drop his hand and squint through the sun at Eloise. She hasn't seen us yet. Surely she must feel embarrassed. I'm so tempted to tell her, 'You're not a part of this family, sweetie. I think you've lost your way.' Especially after her rant last night.

Rosie perks up when she spots Eloise and runs up the steps to wrap her arms around her. Eloise seems taken aback, but pats my daughter on the head and grins. My jaw hurts as I watch them both, biting my teeth together. My daughter asks about Eloise's clothes, her expensive running shoes, her huge gold watch, while Georgia waves to us.

'This looks cosy.' I smile, taking my seat beside Georgia and opposite Eloise, who shifts in her seat. Her cheeks are pinched and pink, but she does a great job of showing Rosie the watch face. I shake out my napkin and place it on my lap, helping Edmund with his.

'I saw Eloise while I was shopping in the boutique.' Georgia smiles, patting my hand. 'It's been years since we've all caught up. If only Scotty were here.'

'Where is your husband?' I blink at Eloise, adjusting the knives and forks.

'He's taken Levi and Coco fishing,' she says, sipping her drink once more.

I sniff. 'He's such a great dad.'

'What are we ordering?' Kav slaps his dad's arm. 'A full brekkie?'

'I want their pancakes,' Edmund tells us, swinging his legs under the table.

'I think we can arrange that.' William tickles Edmund's cheek.

And it's in this familiar family environment, with our nuances and reliable conversations about who gets the coffee and who enjoys extra bacon and what cocktail are the others having this time, a Bloody Mary *and* champagne, that I can't help shaking my head at Eloise, who sits awkwardly, quietly, sucking on her straw. It's infuriating to watch. *Why are you here? Don't you feel like an idiot? I certainly would.*

'Eloise, are you staying for breakfast with us all?' I ask as the waiter fills my sparkling water. She looks up and then looks to Georgia for an answer. Judging from the table, they've already had a coffee each and now a juice. How long does she plan on staying and role-playing happy families with us?

'Stay, El,' Rosie says.

I laugh to myself and everyone hears.

'No, I'll probably head back,' Eloise says.

Sipping my water, it bubbles on my tongue. I don't want her here. I don't want this intrusion while I'm buttering toast and talking to my family about home decorations and Edmund's school fees. This woman needs to take a hint. Leave us alone.

But when Kav and Georgia tell her to stay and Eloise smiles and nods, and Rosie claps, I can't help but stand to go to the toilet. I need to breathe and calm down, but I'm staring at myself in the mirror and shaking my head. Over and over.

And when I go back out, she orders fruit salad, a typical dish that you order when you want to be healthy but don't know how to be. She orders another juice and I wonder about her children. She sits like a squatter, eating, in between Georgia and Rosie, and the whole time I'm clenching my teeth. Rosie posts a picture of the two of them, tags Eloise in it. They look through an online shop together while the rest of us try to chat. But my gaze keeps flicking back to Rosie. Animated, bursting with admiration, wanting another mother's advice on what skincare to buy. She never looks at me, not even once. I've hurt my daughter so badly, and this is her way of punishing me.

Eloise, 9.11 a.m.

These people fit together, running like a machine of understanding. Hands are reaching across the table, passing jam, croissants, pouring juice in each other's glasses like they know. They just *know*. Georgia knows to cut Edmund's pancakes while Penny cuts his sausage and William knows how to slosh the champagne around the glass and hold it under Kav's nose. And Rosie knows to pour her grandparents extra sparkling water, avoiding her own Coke, which Georgia ordered for her. With a lemon. Don't forget the slice of lemon.

Envy gnaws at me and won't stop until I leave this island. I can barely talk now. It's numbing my mouth. And it was my fault, because I chose to stay here and endure and put myself through what I knew would hurt. A happy family. A loving family. A forever family. I know I self-sabotage, I've been doing it for years, but I just wanted to feel it for a while, feel what it's like to be Penny.

I suck on my straw like it's giving me air. And my fruit salad comes out drowning in white yogurt and I'm too nervous to ask for less, too nervous to speak. So, I sit like a fly on the wall of Penny's world and listen, watch, observe someone else's happiness. They speak about the party, why they chose to have an afternoon event, how it'll give everyone a chance to come back to their villa afterwards while the oldies can retire early. And both Georgia and

William laugh at that. And then they discuss home renovations while Rosie snaps pictures of us both.

'But what about the kitchen?' Georgia begins, slicing into the pink flesh of watermelon. She places the fork into her mouth like a food judge on TV. Perfectly, pouted and no mess. I want her to be my mother-in-law. 'I thought you were going with the honeycomb tiles?'

'Well, it's the colour, you see,' Penny says, sitting back and brushing a lock of hair behind her ear. 'Kav adores the marble. I like the cream.'

'Kavan, let Pen decide.' Georgia winks. 'You can renovate the outdoor kitchen.'

Kav grins, lips greased. 'Gee, thanks, Mum.'

They're the family you see in American movies. The one whose sons go to med school and whose daughters marry rich and breed white-teethed children who play frisbee with their fluffy-coated dog on the thick lush lawn. I rub my hands down my shorts and chew quietly.

If they just push Rosie out of the scene, pluck her from her seat and drop her down on the beach, Penny and Kav and pristine Edmund make up the image of what it means to be family. Rosie is the odd one out and I bet Penny hates her for it. I sit up and scoop my fruit salad, dragging the dregs of yogurt to the side of the plate. I know something Penny doesn't know. I'm smiling and chewing and Rosie looks at me and beams. Penny's daughter takes drugs, and the memory of our little bathroom rendezvous changes my attitude. I'm suddenly feeling a little brighter, the heaviness in my gut disappearing.

Eloise, 2.45 p.m.

The afternoon sun glows and everyone remarks on the colour of the water, how nature has displayed its art just for Penny and Kav. They've spent a lot on this soiree. And that's exactly the name I'd give it. Not party, not gathering, not fortieth birthday. An Afternoon Soiree. The word is meant for people and occasions like this. I want to sit beside Georgia and have her mother me again like she did at breakfast. I'm in the awkward in-between setting of not knowing where to be. With my husband, who ignores me and speaks to the men on our table, or with my son, who plays on his phone and occasionally lifts an eyelid to speak to Rosie?

I just sit while others mingle and chatter and giggle and chink glasses. I down my first champagne. Nibble on some bread without butter. Down another champagne. Scoff two smoked salmon canapés. Check my watch. The babysitter will be feeding Coco afternoon tea now. Watch the people on the beach, couples strolling, with flip-flops dangling and towels over their shoulders. Idyllic setting. Idyllic sunset. Everything so fucking idyllic.

And there's that guy I've seen before in black, strolling along the boardwalk, peering into the restaurant while on the phone. He's not taking in the ocean view, he's staring in here at us, but with his glasses on, I still can't see his eyes.

I down another sip. And another. Half a glass left. I better leave it a while. I'm not good with crowds or speaking to people I don't know. I just don't know what to say. My mind sometimes feels like it's empty and useless. You know blonde Barbie? I'm her.

I take a snap of the white table setting and post it. But shit, I've caught that guy in the photo. He's a distant shadowy figure on the beach. I go to delete it, but can't be bothered, because I've already written out the hashtags. *Holidays, sunshine, party vibes.* I'm happy. That's what the post means. I'm happy, not scared, not paranoid, not checking the manager's face.

Rosie stands up from the table on her phone, brings it to her ear, and I hear her say, 'I'm coming.'

Buttering Levi some bread, I then hand it over, and he shoves it in his mouth, rudely, and I forget to tell him off. Because my gaze is now outside on Rosie, running in heels and flicking her head left and right, looking for someone. And when a man steps out from behind a tree, arms covered in tats so dark you think he's wearing a shirt, I swallow my bread whole. It slides uncomfortably down my throat and I down the rest of my champagne to dislodge it. She flings her arms around his shoulders, they kiss passionately, and then she backs away, brushing her hair from her face like a little girl looking up at Daddy. He's rough. Black jeans on a heated day. Shaved head displaying more body art travelling up his skull. I can't see his eyes, the way he looks at her, but it's the body language. The grabbing of her arse, the slapping of it, the cocky side swagger, making me ill. The way he yanks her hand and pulls her down the path, away from the party, makes me shift in my chair.

This guy doesn't look good. And I've been around plenty bad.

Penny, 3.03 p.m.

It's a scene out of a romantic movie, the type you'd watch where Diane Keaton plays the main character. It's completely what I envisioned for Kav. Everyone keeps telling me just how divine the food is, the setting, the ambience. I've always loved that word. It's a feeling I attempt to create in everyday moments. Ambience at the breakfast table with the aroma of coffee, browned toast with all the condiments, soft jazz to wake the household and set the mood for the day ahead. It's the same here. Georgia has taught me how to be, how to live. I know she appreciates this so much for her son.

The seafood is fresh, succulent, and served on trays of ice with wedges of juicy lemons. The cocktails are elegant and sharp. The decorations are simple; white roses, white vanilla-scented candles and white shells with coral, hidden in front of porcelain, rimmed in gold. It's like a wedding. And that's the way we've always entertained. That's why people want to come to our house. Because the hospitality and ambience invited them there.

I'm dressed in a gold sparkling dress and I'm ready to tell Kav the incredible news. This baby is going to change our lives. It's what we've always wanted. Our own. Not someone else's. Not half of someone else. Our blood mixed.

I'm only eight weeks pregnant and I'm surprised he hasn't even noticed. The tiredness, the mood swings, the craving for citrus fruits. But then, why would he? It's his first baby and *I* only just realised a week ago. My periods are irregular at the best of times, so I took a test and had my first scan a few days ago. This is a huge surprise for Kav and I've planned to announce it for that reason. This is his first baby. I know people wait until the twelve-week mark to announce, but that's just not me. Everyone needs to hear it tonight to congratulate him, because this weekend is ours.

I'm swanning around The Bay Restaurant and Grill, and I'm so satisfied with my life and how things have turned out that I honestly don't think anyone or anything could pop this little bubble I've built. And that's how I see it – I've built this. I've earned William and Georgia's trust and the stocking on the mantelpiece at Christmas time with my name embroidered in curly gold writing.

'Can we talk?' Kav says, pulling me aside to the front of the room.

I'm starving and this sparkling water in the guise of gin just isn't hitting the spot. It's been difficult staying sober while everyone else around us has been pickled this weekend. Including Eloise, who's sitting beside our family friend, Julie, at their table in a dress that shows off her midriff. I honestly cannot believe she stayed with us at lunch, through the entrée, the wine, the main course, and downed three glasses of Bloody Mary. She must have been drunk then and she certainly is now, chatting Julie's ear off.

Following Kav to the front of the restaurant, he cups my back. I kiss his cheek. 'What is it?'

He turns my shoulders to face the party and chinks his champagne glass with a knife. And I can't believe he's about to do this before me. He must have figured it out somehow. I smile and put my hands up as if to say, I have no idea what he's doing. But when the crowd falls silent and Kav kneels down with his hands holding mine, I eventually realise. He doesn't know about the pregnancy, and it looks as though he's proposing again. I can't help but giggle with how sweet he is. His thumb rubs my knuckles and we stare at each other.

'We have had the most incredible years of marriage.' Kav raises his voice so the people at the back can hear. 'And I've loved every minute with you.'

'Are we getting a divorce?' I joke, and the crowd laugh. Georgia is by William, pressing a napkin to the corner of her eyes.

'I want to remarry you,' Kav says, looking up at me. He licks his lips and smiles. 'I want to renew our vows right now.'

The crowd gasp around us and Kav motions to an older woman behind the bar with a folder in her arms. She has short auburn hair that's been styled for this occasion and wears a blush trouser suit. She's tilting her head, smiling at the surprise. 'I've brought along our very own celebrant.'

I shake my head. 'No way.' I was not expecting this at all. Kav stands again and presses his mouth against mine. His lips are warm and his breath smells of lime, and I hate to take the attention away, but it's going to make this moment even more special, more memorable. 'You won't believe this,' I tell him, leaning my forehead against his.

'What?' He squeezes my hands.

Staring at the crowd around us, I tell them, 'I too have an announcement.'

Everyone looks at me and I ask them to raise their glasses.

'Not to steal your limelight, honey,' I beam at Kav. 'But we're having a baby.'

Eloise, 3.20 p.m.

When you're trying not to display emotion and yet it courses through your body, it's very difficult to hold on. We're viewing a moment in time that these two will remember and look back over in the albums with their children and grandchildren, and I can see their whole life displayed before me like a predictable Hallmark movie. Inside my heels, my toes are scrunched.

The party guests, all dressed in their floral patterns and expensive beachwear, are smiling, beaming up at Penny and Kav, who stand together on the stage, exchanging their vows. Under the lights, Penny's gold sequin dress makes her appear like a champagne glass, bubbling and bright and ready to burst.

Scott's half-smiling. That's one thing I'm noticing, he's not overly happy. We're the only couple in this candlelit room, with white roses infusing the summer air, who isn't gushing over the loved-up couple. I sip my gin and suck on my lips, watching him. His half-smile fades and his chin is tense, jutting out like a dog about to fight.

I look away to the family table, where Georgia is dabbing her eyes on a thick linen napkin while William holds her other hand on the tablecloth. Gold rings glinting on their fingers. They're so happy it hurts. The room just stinks of happiness, of love, of pathetic emotion. I down the rest of my gin so the ice chinks against my teeth.

And Julie notices and looks at me, before resuming the gushing over the couple now kissing.

Rosie is back in the room with us, with red eyes from drugs or crying, and she's the only other guest who's faking a smile. She sees the joke in it all. She's not happy about this reunion and I'm itching to know why. Perhaps she feels me staring at her when she flicks a look to me and then gazes down at her fingernails, avoiding eye contact.

When it's all over and the sweat under my pits starts drying, some of the guests go to congratulate the couple, while others swivel back around in their chairs, ready to discuss the shock of it all. Julie, Kav's family friend, is the first one to enthuse over Penny and Kav, plucking a third slice of thick bread from the basket and slathering it in butter.

'Amazing,' she says. 'The most romantic thing I've seen in a long while.'

Scott remains silent and I want to know why that is. Besides, the gin is giving me a sense of false confidence. One where I can tap his hand and glare at him.

'Can we have a word?'

He raises a brow and uses his tongue to pick at his teeth. 'What about?'

'Outside,' I say. I kiss Levi on the ear while he watches a video on his phone. 'We'll be back in a moment, Levi.'

Scott doesn't have a choice anymore. He doesn't get to. We need to talk. He has to follow me past the circular tables cluttered with shells, coral and feathers and past the people lining up to embrace the happy couple.

When we get outside on the decking, the wind has picked up and it's cold. It pulls my hair to one side and shocks my dress, so I have to clench it between my thighs. I hold myself, waiting for Scott to close the door. There's no one out here. Just us, the milky sky and choppy waves, pummelling down on the sand in quick succession.

'What?' He raises his hands, palms up. I'm fuming now. I've had enough.

'What do you think when you look at them?' I ask.

He scoffs. 'What?'

'Penny and Kav.'

'I don't want to play games, Eloise—'

'This is not a fucking game,' I hiss, stepping forward as he stares at his shoes. 'Do you know what I see? I see happiness. Love. Respect. Appreciation. A future.'

The look he gives me when he looks up. It's like he's smelling shit. I hate him for it. I hate him.

'I see the complete opposite of us,' I whisper. And it comes out squeaking. I'm trying really hard not to cry. If I cry, my make-up runs and she'll know. Penny will know.

'I see that too.' He nods.

'Why?'

'Because we're nothing like them anymore.' It's so matter-of-fact that I can't help myself when I slap him. My palm stings. He stays standing, disgusted, unmoved.

'Then why don't you leave me?' The tears are coming now. Gushing down my cheeks in childish rows, spilling into my lipstick. 'You only stay for the kids.'

He looks down at his shoes and shakes his head. His cheek where I slapped him tenses in and out. 'No, I don't.'

'You do. Because you're that type. You'll stay for them, not for us.'

'That's not true.' He glares. 'But you think I should forgive you after what you did to me?'

I nod, sniffing the snot that's starting to leak from my nostrils.

'You're crazy.'

'I'm hurting,' I scream. 'We never talk about this. We've never got help—'

And the door opens and Rosie steps out on her phone, light casting blue across her face. She sees us and sees me and stops, pulls a face, apologises and quickly pushes past us, out on to the sand.

'I'm not doing this here,' Scott says, turning and marching back inside. He leaves me like this, in the wind, shaking. He enters the warm golden room with the tinkling music and the pearl balloons. He enters the life he wants, kisses Penny on the cheek, shakes Kav's hand and smiles. And I can barely breathe, I'm hurting so much. So, I turn my attention to the only other outsider. Rosie. And I can't stop myself from following her to escape this mess.

Penny, 4.05 p.m.

It's happening again. I wasn't expecting it to coat me here, now, among the sunburnt party guests and jazz band. But I've just seen Rosie out of the large windows, walking off with Eloise. And my daughter didn't congratulate me, doesn't even care that she's having another sibling. And it's during these perfect times, when I have everything I want, that I don't want any of it. I only want Rosie. There's an emptiness inside me I fear can never be filled. Not with this movie-style life, this romantic love, this doting mother-in-law, this baby. It's at these times I'd like to collapse and give up. It's an undeserving that I feel. And it isn't welcome when others are around. It comes, coating me in thick black paint. It constricts my neck and tugs at the corners of my ever-smiling lips. It's not anxiety, it's not depression, it's a little piece of me dying, being smudged out, erased. I'm no longer colour and light, I'm sepia tone and then grey and then nothing.

Georgia is laughing, champagne wobbling up the sides of her glass, and Kav is hugging Brett, slapping shoulders, squeezing them, and Edmund is dancing on the dance floor with his old great-auntie, who's swinging him around. It's a scene from a movie that's only been created to make the audience hate their lives and wish they could live this one. It's always a scene from a movie. This is when it comes the most. And nobody notices. I'm glad this party will be over soon. It's only meant to be an afternoon and evening thing. After this, people can come back to our villa and we can continue without the pressure to be *on*.

'Excuse me.' I smile with a twitch and push through a group of Kav's work colleagues. One grabs my wrist to pull me back and congratulate me and I want to cry and instead taste salt on my upper lip. Sweat is a part of this scenario. But usually I'm alone, not around bubbly guests. 'I'm bursting. Sorry.'

They make a joke about pregnancy and bladders and I catch Rob from the bakery sneaking into the party with his own beer bottle. Usually, I'd care and ask him to leave, or at least ask why he feels entitled to be here, but I feel my wrist being released and used for better things like shoving open the bathroom door. A quick scan to check I'm alone. I am. Only the tangy scent of a pine infuser lingers. I lock the door, a final, clunking sound that means I'm safe to release this black tar crawling up my throat. It bursts out of me in gasps and I finally collapse against the door, biting my forearm as I let it come.

You do not deserve this, Penelope. This happiness, this love, this party is not for you. You are a liar, a killer and a horrible mother. You'll screw up this baby's life the way you screwed up Rosie's, Edmund's and the one before. You will be left with nothing. And only then will you know your worth.

I know I don't deserve anything, I have to say. *I know I'm a liar.*

And only then does it retreat, back from wherever, when I've agreed. And only then does the bathroom become a bathroom with pine-infused fragrance and a dripping tap. Only then do my legs become my own, bronzed from the sun, bruised from the bike stand. And colour returns to my cheeks. Out there, it's all a show, scenes from a theatre performance, meant to prove happiness. And I'm the leading lady, fooling my co-star, adjusting my dress, smoothing back hair, checking for leaking eyes before stepping back out into the spotlight.

But my daughter is the missing piece in the picture.

Eloise, 4.05 p.m.

We've found a spot where Penny will never find us, behind a hill peppered with dying paperbarks. No one ever goes here besides wasted teenagers and snakes. Trust me, I know.

We lean up against the papery trunk, its bark dusting our arms in white powder. And then we decide to sit and get comfortable. Rosie's breath is sweet like champagne, but she won't shut up. She thinks this is all so funny. And I guess it is. It's also illegal and I'm wary of getting caught here with an underage person. But I'm drunk and I'm fucked and I also don't care.

Across the road is the beach and the party – now wedding – and soon people will leave the bar and wander down the road. I don't want to draw attention. I cover her mouth with my palm, while she goes to bite it.

'We're going to get caught if you don't be quiet,' I tell her.

'Sorry. Sorry.' Rosie bursts out laughing again and then covers her own mouth. 'I'm going to be so hungover tomorrow.'

Part of me twitches to hear her say it. She's been secretly drinking champagne while her blissfully unaware mother ties the knot for the second time, and I should be responsible. Levi's vacant face springs to mind. *If this were him*. It's not him. It's Rosie, the adult child. Levi is happily inside with his father.

I scan the dim area in front of us. At night, this would be like a spooky graveyard. A place where the island authority dump junk like rotting wood, old broken slabs of cement, boulders, parts of jetties and tin dinghies. No one would come here.

Distant laughter resonates around the island, along with a changing wind. There's the smell of frying seafood in the air, reminding us of where we are and what we should be doing. Enjoying this holiday destination.

We've brought our packets of powder and Rosie lights up a joint that she's hidden in her pocket. She offers it to me and at first I make a face. I feel bad to be doing this, taking advantage of Penny and Kav's daughter to appease the dread that's lodged itself in my gut. But Rosie seems so upbeat, so carefree, so what I remember being. I want to impress her. I want to grab a quick hit of validation. So, I take a deep drag. This starts Rosie up again, laughing at me. Such a herby, piny flavour. The movement of smoke has an impact that knows exactly where to go – straight to my head, where it belongs. To dull the ache and rejection. I don't want anyone catching us smoking, but Rosie is nice and smiley and having someone cool and young like her offering me a joint makes me ease against the tree trunk. She blows smoke in my eyes.

'I knew you'd be fun,' she says. Just her saying that makes me feel better about myself, more so than the drug. At school, I bet she's the cool girl. Distracted in a confident way, chatty with gum in her mouth, someone you want to play with. Someone her mum would hate.

'What's your story with your mum?' I ask.

'She's just a bitch.'

A tingle up my spine. 'Were you ever close?'

She smirks like a teenager. 'For the first four years of my life.'

Okay, so something bad went down with them. I wriggle and a stick penetrates my thigh. I tug it out from under me and heave it towards the pile of rocks. She offers the joint and I take it, squinting as the smoke curls into my eyes.

'What happened?' I asked.

'Don't want to talk about it.' She changes the subject. 'What do you think of Kav?'

'Lovely.' I take a long slow drag of the joint. It instantly loosens me up. 'Scott loves him.'

'Well, he's the perfect husband, isn't he? If only he knew what Mum was really like.'

I blow the smoke so it billows above us. 'What's she really like?' If I was sober, this topic would have me leaning in and perked for information. But I'm sleepy and drunk and closing my eyes.

'Don't ask,' she says.

Passing the joint back over to her, I shrug, feeling envious. It's true, Kav is the perfect husband. Doting, affectionate, loving. Everything Scott's not anymore.

'Mum looked far and wide for someone like Kav. Someone who ticked all her boxes.'

'You know, you're very smart for someone your age.'

Rosie smiles with her teeth showing and jiggles her shoulders in a childish manner. She has a way of switching topics like shuffling cards. Just when I'm on to new information, she hits me with another ace. And because of the drug, the drink, the dread, I'm finding it hard to keep up and slow the conversation. She mentions Kav and the adoption of Edmund and my tongue is heavy against my teeth. Too languid to form words. I close my eyes.

'I hate my mother,' I hear her say.

'Why?' I open one eye. 'Does she favour Edmund?' I'm not sure why I said that. It's probably not even true. Penny would be perfect at sharing the love. 'No one hates their mother. They just hate the way they were mothered.'

'I wish you were my mother,' Rosie says.

My face heats up and I don't know how to react. I can't even look at her anymore with the way she does and says things. Rosie is too familiar, like we're long-lost friends. She's treating me like I'm someone she can trust and it's also deeply weird how she's happy to tell me. I want to confess how often I've wanted to be like Penny. How perfect her mother is.

But no one can ever *be* Penny. She's unique in her standoffish way. A jewel who won't be collected, worn or admired. Not by Kav and not by friends. I am plastic, a pearl that'll only smoothen if you grind it between your teeth. No, Penny is tough and rare, like this island.

Footsteps approach from behind and we stiffen. And all I can think is, I really don't want to be found. I've avoided this island for so many years, but I'm sure they'll smell the marijuana. They'll know we're here. We need to find another spot, like the public toilets down the road. I hold my finger up to my mouth and Rosie obeys, staying silent. If she fucks this up, I'll be pissed. If someone catches me with an adolescent, it's over. My kids, my husband, everything. And I'm already too close to losing that.

◆ ◆ ◆

We've moved from the open area and paperbarks to a deserted public toilet block with more light, more isolation and less chance of getting caught. Rosie snaps a happy selfie with us without me realising and I'm telling her to delete it, which she says she will. I'm awkwardly beguiled by the prospect of 'belonging'. She giggles, I laugh, but my attention is stuck on the lines she's chopped up over the toilet seat.

I don't admit I've seen people doing drugs, shooting up. Heaps. It was just the way back then. People become pros at it. Like popping open champagne with a knife, like using your teeth to twist a bottle top. Rosie fumbles around, chopping the cocaine, and I watch, still undecided. I'm wasted from the weed, floating in a strange world of sleepiness and the need to be awake. And I'm wired for something more, to fill my empty, neglected cup with a boost of dopamine. But Rosie's young and I'm supposed to be responsible.

I pick my nails and ask, 'Who was that guy you were with this evening?'

She blows her nose to clear the passage. The way she blows it reminds me of Coco. She's wearing her jumper over her dress, and I know Penny would hate to see her like this. Grungy, black, squatting by a toilet seat with germs and urine smudging into her forearms.

'My boyfriend.'

'Looks quite old for you.'

'What are you, my mum now?'

I ignore the dig. 'He looks—'

She gives me an eyeful of arrogance. 'I know. That's why I fell for him. Someone my mum would hate.'

I lean against the tiles. 'Why is he here?'

She rolls her eyes as though she's getting impatient with me or the bank card, which has fallen off the toilet lid twice.

'I think he senses I'm about to break up with him. This is what he does. He likes to assert himself.' That explains the red eyes. I think they've been arguing.

'Is he staying here?'

She shrugs. 'I didn't even ask. He comes over here quite a bit with mates. I think he came on a boat.'

'Why are you breaking up with him? Besides the fact he's too old for you and looks like he rides motorbikes in a gang.'

She looks at me like I've caught her out and I stop smiling. 'Probably for that reason,' she says. 'He's not a *nice* guy. He's too aggressive. I saw him bite a guy's ear off once.' She looks at my reaction and then nods when I wince. The image is too vivid and unsettling for me. And I want to be happy, not disturbed.

'Are you serious, Rosie?'

She nods. 'I mean, he's dangerous. Always thinks people owe him.' She chews her lip as though remembering. 'He has a list as long as my arm with people he needs to "get back" and he always manages to.' She gives a small sigh and tells me how she texted him, telling him she wanted a break. 'That's why he's come. He doesn't want me having a break.'

'Did he do something to you when you told him? You came back looking upset.'

She lifts her shoulders. 'He likes to be violent.'

This isn't good. Rosie swipes the card, lining up the powder, and fumbles around. I don't think she's done this very much before. It makes me feel ill to see her right now. Knobbly knees pressed together without the lines from sun damage. Perfect white teeth clenching her sleeve. Smooth skin. She's a child. A confused one. I can't let her do this. Her nose hovers just above the white line, her finger pressing the right nostril.

'Rosie, wait.' I pull her hand back. 'This is really disgusting.'

She stops. 'You wanted to do it.'

'I know I did,' I say, grateful she's leaning back on her heels. 'Who gave it to you? Was it your guy?'

She doesn't agree but it's obvious. 'This shit is addictive. Trust me, I know. And if you're going to get rid of him, then get rid of this too. Start fresh. Meet someone nice, someone who will love you more than your mum does.'

The toilet light flickers on and off. Her eyes are dark and tired. This is a bad dream I've dragged her into. And I suddenly feel

121

nauseous with a dirty guilt that has me turning to wash my hands. The cheap soap can't even create foamy bubbles. Just releases a chemical scent in a weak lather. Rosie nods once, yawns and stands.

'Go home,' I tell her. 'Go and watch a movie. I promise I won't say anything.'

She gives a small smile, almost relieved, like I had her trapped in here. 'You're fun, El.'

She cuts my name in half because she needs to show me that she's rebellious, in control and unafraid of authority. And I get that. I was her once upon a time.

When Rosie pushes the toilet door, a fresh salty burst of air collects the rank stench of the cubicle. I'm left with my reflection, and I see how little I've changed. There are lines, weak sunspots beginning to develop around my upper cheekbone, and my once fair hair is now a mousy blonde. Lips have lost youthful fullness and streaked skin above my breasts can't be smoothed by creams. But I'm the same pathetic girl. Needing drugs, needing attention, needing to be loved because I can't find it within myself.

There's only a footstep between me and her white lines. Only one snort.

I've seen how it's done, I've seen men like Rosie's. The past can be conjured in an instant.

Penny, 6.45 p.m.

Guests are starting to pedal up to our villa carting beers, wine in backpacks, with the glow of the sunset giving their skin a luminous tinge. The party at The Bay Restaurant and Grill is over and the relief is here. It's an 'after-party' and it's what Kav wanted – a never-ending birthday day. It's what Georgia always did for him. Special breakfasts, sumptuous lunches, fancy dinners and after-parties. It feels like the night's only just beginning. The music is pumping, the kids are cycling up and down the road in pyjamas with ice cream dripping over their fronts. It'll be a late night, but that's okay. I'll allow it. Sal is sitting on Brett's lap and he's jiggling her up and down like a child.

Coco is with Edmund on the road, making a horrible caw-caw sound like a raspy crow, and I tell them both to behave. We're not the only ones on holiday. About twenty other villas with hanging balconies line the beach. All types visit the island, young and old, retired and married, single and ready to mingle. We have to be mindful of not being antisocial. I turn the music down a notch and step inside to grab Edmund's teddy and Rosie some snacks.

'Are you sure you're going to be alright putting them all to bed?' I ask Rosie as she taps away on her phone from the couch. I've noticed Rosie has changed her appearance since we left the party. Glossy lips and hair unusually brushed. Which makes me feel slightly ill because I think she's trying to impress and dress like Eloise. Tonight, she's going to babysit the kids next door in Brett and Sal's villa. Levi's beside her on the couch, mirroring my daughter, head dropped, shoulders slumped, typing. He doesn't need looking after but the little ones do.

'Coco's still only a baby,' I remind her. 'So, she'll need to go to bed early.'

She looks up at me, dazed, only just noticing I'm speaking to her. She still hasn't said anything about the vow renewal, the baby, her new brother or sister. And I've been waiting.

'What?' she says.

I throw the plastic bag of cookies, chocolate and crisps into her lap, causing her phone to slip between her knees. She tuts and I stand taller. 'Edmund can have two biscuits and a row of chocolate,' I tell her. 'Maybe a handful of crisps. Don't let Coco have any. And if anything happens—'

'We're right next door.' She snatches her phone from the floor and stands. 'Seriously.'

Ripping the bag of cookies open, she shoves two in her mouth and stares at me. Wanting a fight. I look away. Her angry eyes are watering and red.

'Right, then have fun,' I say as Levi follows her out. 'Call if you need anything.'

I sniff and head back out to the guests who are gathering on our balcony. She hates me. I hate me.

Penny, 7.05 p.m.

The kitchen window is a peephole I can use to spy on the kids who are next door in Brett and Sal's villa.

I'm at the sink – I'm always at the sink – washing five fresh glasses for the guests who are still down on the beach, with sand in their wine.

Through the window, I spy Rosie on the couch, her face glowing by phone light. Coco's pointing to Edmund and laughing about something. I'm assuming they're watching a movie. I'll go and check on them shortly.

If Rosie stays in that position, she won't know where Coco is or what Coco's doing, but do you know what, Coco is not my responsibility. If the little girl wanders, then let her wander. Eloise really should have her two-year-old attached to her hip instead of socialising outside on the balcony with Kav and the others.

Dipping the glasses into the bubbly hot water, I'm almost scorching my skin as I run the sponge around the rim. But my attention is stuck on the guests out the back, huddled around the hissing barbeque, cool-boxes like bricks piled up against the wall.

Rob, the bakery owner, cycles up and sits, leaning against the gate. He's been hanging around too much this weekend. In fact, after I spotted him at the party, I forgot to check back on him after my panic attack, forgot to politely tell him to leave. But I don't recall seeing him there after that. How long did he actually stay? He used to be attractive; now he's aged and gone sour. I bet it's drugs. Drugs have damaged his sagging skin, browned his teeth. The shirt on his back, emblazoned with the island logo, is the only new thing on him. I wish he'd leave us and our guests alone. Wish he'd stop asking for Kav.

'He's out the back, I think,' I hear Brett say.

And Rob takes that as an invitation to join the party. He kicks his bike stand down, dismounts and pushes open the gate. I should have been watching what I was doing, because I've smashed a wine glass and my finger's bleeding, and I'm at the sink, and Rob will have to walk past me, so I pull my hand out and wrap a tea towel around it with the glass still stuck in and sidestep around to the bathroom, where I close the door and watch him through the gap.

He asks to see Kav, 'The birthday boy. The one who's married to Penny.'

Penny, 7.10 p.m.

Sometimes things just get too much for me. Like now. Holed up in a tiny, steaming hot bathroom with a creep outside. I'm going to escape Rob and head down to the beach with the new glasses. But first, I need to get the shards of glass out of my skin. I've locked the bathroom door and I'm using tweezers to scrape against the splinters, wincing whenever I feel one move inside my skin. Then I pluck it out and wash it down the bloody drain.

I'm sweating. Salt beads above my top lip and between my breasts. A faint waft of onions leaves my armpit and I ignore the cut and furiously spray cold deodorant under my shoulders. Laughter outside the door. Someone's smashed a glass. Things are getting messy. That's why I want to go to the beach and sit on a towel. I need space, air. Why is Rob *here*?

This is the side most don't see in me. It's the side I hate in myself, only revealing it every Sunday when Kav takes the kids out for their routine milkshake. When it appears, it's alarming, like I didn't see it coming. Every Sunday, though, it comes. And when the three of them return – chocolate around Edmund's mouth, sweet milk on his breath – my eyes are puffy, made over with concealer, bronzer, fresh mascara that pulls on my lashes and makes them appear big. And Kav's eyes flitter a little, linger too long on my blotchy face. And I turn away from him, too shy to present it. And he never asks, never asks. If he did, things wouldn't be so perfect.

◆ ◆ ◆

With my hand bandaged, eyes redone, face splashed with water, I open the door and peer through the gap. Rob's still out there on the balcony with Kav, laughing, while Sal sweeps up the broken glass. I hate that Rob knows me from before. It's like reading a character from one book and then suddenly noticing they're in another. He doesn't belong here now. He belongs in the past. If he spots me, he'll call me over in a familiar way that'll encourage conversation about my ex and how it ended, and how Rosie has coped ever since. And Kav will think Rob's just referring to the divorce, but he won't know the truth. How it's much more than that.

When the living room is clear, I slip out of the bathroom and leave the soapy sink, grab the few glasses that I've washed and dart to the back courtyard, where Eloise lingers beside Scott, talking to the only woman she's befriended at the party. Julie. One of Kav's parents' friends. A chatty, overly friendly woman who accepts anyone. I've noticed how Eloise sticks to her, using her as a social Band-Aid.

Scott looks up when he sees me walk past. 'What happened to you?'

I lift my hand. 'It's nothing. Just a cut.'

He puts his beer down beside his foot and stands. 'Let me see,' he says, taking it. And it's too intimate, too close with everyone around. So, I pull it away.

'It's fine.' I flap the air as though I'm laughing, as though it's no big deal. I just want to get the fuck away from this villa and down to the beach. I think you can read this on my face, this panic, this alarm at the thought of being caught out. 'I'm heading down to the beach.'

Through the window of Brett and Sal's house, Levi's on his phone, ear buds in, with TV light flickering over his pimply face. There's no sign of Rosie or the kids; however, they're in there, squealing and laughing.

'I'll join you,' Scott says, staring at me. He's picking up on my anxiety because he's a doctor and anyone who looks hard enough at me can see through the facade.

But I walk away, clearing my throat, pretending not to hear.

Eloise, 7.13 p.m.

Inside, a group of Penny's friends are gathered in the lounge, singing to eighties music, clicking their fingers to the beat. Julie rolls her eyes at their behaviour. She's a lot older than the rest of us. A family friend of Kav's parents, apparently. She's alone, unmarried, and likes to be around the young ones, she told me. Kav's parents are staying at the beach resort and wouldn't bother coming here tonight. Kav's mum and dad are the country club type. The golfers. The cruise-ship travellers. I can picture them right now back at the resort, sipping expensive Riesling by the pool with their other proper friends. They'd also roll their eyes at the eighties singing, the stale crisps, the sand on the floor, needing a good sweep.

This villa looks nothing like the villa I entered when we first arrived. Penny's table display has all but rolled around, with pine cones scattered everywhere.

'How long has your hubby known our Kav?' Julie asks me, leaning against the fridge, making it wobble. She's topped up our drinks.

'Since they were in med school.'

'How about her?' She says the word, *her*, in a tone I can't quite decipher. Halfway between bitterness and jealousy. But I can't understand why. Julie is so lovely. I've only seen her being nice. To the waiter who forgot her burger at the pub. To the guests at the party this afternoon.

'You mean Penny?'

'You two don't get along.' It's a statement. How does she know? 'His parents love Penny like their own daughter – in fact, probably more than Kav.'

I almost can't believe what this woman is saying. I have never met anyone who doesn't love Penny. I can imagine Penny has all sorts of admirers. The school mums, the wives who gather around her, fishing for her approval and compliments, needing her advice on how to pack a healthy lunchbox. I know that if I can be like Penny or if Penny likes me, then my husband will too.

I find myself leaning in closer, wanting Julie to divulge all Penny's dirty little secrets to me. I feel nasty, bitchy, yet also excited. The key to unlocking her secret. A little magic I can sprinkle on myself, to turn Scott's attention back on me.

'They'll be happy to have a child of their own though,' Julie says. 'He needs a baby. You know Edmund came from bad blood,' she continues. 'Dodgy parents who apparently tried to lure him back a couple of years ago. It was a horror for the family. They had to get police involved but then the mother went to jail and I think it's given them some peace of mind.'

This would be a stain on Penny's reputation. I almost can't believe what I'm hearing. I take a big gulp of wine and try to hide my smile. Everything about their life looks peachy and yet they've been through this with Edmund. I wonder if Scott knows about it? 'You mean the parents found where Edmund was placed?'

Her breath is sour as she speaks into my face. Her skin is flushed and shiny, hair slightly wet and sticking to her forehead.

'Back when Edmund was first adopted out to Kav and Penny, it was an open adoption.' She nods and slurps her red wine, and it coats her lips in cherry. 'But then things went sour and they reversed it. They haven't heard from the parents since though.'

Julie was so different before the booze hit her. So friendly, cheerful, upbeat, a younger Mrs Claus. But now she licks her upper lip and the tip of her tongue points, dabbing at the sweat below her nostrils. She enjoys this gossip session and enjoys spreading the dirt. But what Julie's saying sounds fabricated and intense. Dodgy parents luring him back?

'I can't believe I didn't know all this,' I whisper. 'Scott's never said anything.'

'Oh, there's lots more you don't know about that family.' She nudges me with her elbow. 'About Penny. Just don't trust her, whatever you do. I think she's learnt how to manipulate everyone around her.'

It's never occurred to me before, but perhaps what Julie's saying is right. What if everything Penny stands for is fake? To keep people at bay, to keep people believing that she's good. But why? Why would she bother?

Julie heads out to the courtyard and I gaze past the women singing in a circle, drunk and loud and unfazed by their screeching voices. Out on the balcony, I peer at the beach, the gang of people drinking. Scott's down there chatting to a colleague and Penny's laughing with one of her friends. I wonder if what Julie said is true: Penny's learnt how to manipulate everyone around her. But you only manipulate when you're scared, right? I sip my wine, eyes on her.

So, what are you afraid of, Penny?

Penny, 7.18 p.m.

We all sit with knees touching, as though about to hum a campfire song. Everyone's drunk now, talking loudly and animatedly, rudely forgetting the rest of the sober island guests observing from their villas. Because I'm sober, I'm noticing. And because Rob is up on the balcony, I'm shivering.

There's a conversation going around about how children screw up marriages. I don't like this subject. It's a topic that men prefer to bang on about. Kav and I must be the exception.

Small waves lap the beach, pulling towards our campfire circle. I stare up at the stars and breathe. We're so lucky. Everyone here together. Just try and focus on how good this is and forget why Rob's there with Kav.

'Pen, you've done such a great job this weekend,' my friend Sarah says.

'You really have,' her husband adds.

'I think we should make a toast, actually,' Scott pipes up. I sit up, brushing the sand from my stinging palms. Glass must be stuck inside the skin.

'There's no need,' I say.

'You're too humble.' Sarah smiles. I must admit, it does feel quite nice to be recognised for my efforts. From the party this afternoon to the accommodation and food we've provided, no one can compete with this weekend. The group of seven around me are smiling and happy and enjoying the warm evening together on the beach. Singing voices and bad eighties music echo from our villa behind us. And this is why I do what I do. Because if people really knew what I did before meeting Kav, before meeting them, this circle would not be around me. There would be no cheering, no chinking of glasses. And that's why I wish Rob would leave our villa. My gaze flicks up to find him. I can't see him anymore.

While Sarah hands around the champagne bottle, Kav's friends pour extra bubbles into their clean glasses. They raise them and I laugh, rolling my eyes.

'Cheers to Penny.' Sarah smiles, chinking her glass against mine.

'To Penny,' Scott says.

'To Penny,' they all chime.

And while the others take a sip, Scott adds, 'I think we need to nurture Pen a little more. She's looking a tad stressed tonight.'

Everyone looks at me.

'No, I'm fine.'

Leaning back on one hand, he tilts his head like I'm one of his patients. 'I know a panic attack when I see one, Pen.' Scott's drunk and forgetting social etiquette. He's forgetting how embarrassing this is. 'You looked frazzled before. How's your hand?'

My heart loses its rhythm, and I don't know what to do. Laugh it off? Tell him I agree? Make a joke? I'm not used to this. I'm used to being an actor on stage, with audiences watching and applauding me. If I fail in front of people, friends, family, then I'm failing what I've built. I wait for someone else to step in and take the reins, but they don't. They all just listen and watch me with creased brows.

Scott is acting like such a dick and I want to bury myself under the sand. Instead, I stand, dusting off my bottom.

'It's okay, Scott,' I say. I shouldn't be angry. Anger only makes it worse, more dramatic, more attention-grabbing. But I'm livid. My face is hot. I tip the champagne out of my glass until it fizzes and bubbles into the sand. As if I'd drink it anyway.

But no one answers. And I can't look at them. They've dropped their gazes and the only sound left is someone singing up in the villa. So, I leave the group.

Scott follows. 'Pen, are you okay, I didn't mean to embarrass you—'

'You need to leave me alone,' I whisper harshly. 'You're making me out like I'm a bad—'

'What?' he says.

'It doesn't matter.' I start running back to avoid him, kicking sand. He's created a scene, created a narrative I didn't want. People don't see me like this, out of control, impatient and frazzled.

The balcony above us acts like a podium and Eloise is leaning over the railing with Brett and the others. It's dark, I can barely make out her face, but she's arched over and staring. She must know something's up. How will I defend myself?

Stepping under the balcony's shadow and away from view, I let Scott pass me as he stalks up the beach track. He doesn't spot me here. Good. I can only imagine what the group on the beach are thinking. *Poor Penny. What's up with Penny?* And then Kav will get word of it and wonder why I'm panicking on an occasion like this. And then he'll probably mention Rob. Boisterous voices boom from the balcony above me and someone asks where I am. I can use pregnancy as an excuse. I'm tired, hormonal, overwhelmed.

Leaving the safe shadowy sand, I jog up the steps and push the courtyard gate open. But then I stop. Our guests are talking urgently, and the music's been turned down. The mood reminds me of a nightclub closing. And their words are clear and pressing: One of the kids is missing, that's what I hear. One of them is gone.

The news lands like a kick to my gut and my voice cracks as I ask Julie to repeat what she just said. Am I hearing wrong? I must be hearing wrong. 'What did you say?'

It's horrible and painful to admit, but my first thought is Coco. She's wandered. And now Eloise will understand how irresponsible she is as a mother, to leave a toddler while she parties here. I lick salty lips and scan the pale, worried faces. Where *is* Eloise?

But then what Julie says next is a blur. The blinding lights of the courtyard switch on and the music completely switches off. Brett steps out, breathing heavily, and Rob cycles off on his bike. Kav pushes the back door open with a force that almost knocks Julie in the back.

'It's Edmund, Pen.' Brett. My brother. Clutching my shoulders with sweaty palms. 'Edmund's missing.'

Penny, 7.52 p.m.

My son is missing. Rosie said that twenty minutes ago, he was playing inside Brett and Sal's villa with the other kids. Monopoly Junior was spread open on the coffee table with toy bank notes piled beside fizzy lemonade and crisps. Twenty minutes. Rosie was on her fucking phone and Levi was on his, ear buds in, unable to hear how Edmund left or who came in. Twenty minutes. That's all it took for him to leave or be taken. Taken? I highly doubt it. Not on this island. Not here. Not ever. No one saw a thing.

What starts out as a quick search through their villa, under beds, behind shower curtains, in the toilet, grows into accusations, with the beat of hearts surging. His bike has gone. He can't have gone far. But it's gone, which means he's ridden off.

'Well, what were you playing?' I ask Coco.

'Hide-and-seek?' Kav asks.

'Chasey?' I add.

'No.' Coco shakes her head.

'Rosie?' I can barely utter her name. She isn't talking because she feels guilty and so she fucking should. She can't stop staring at her hands. Shock, guilt, fear etched over her pale face.

I scan the lounge room, hands on hips as our guests linger outside. They should be starting to search. But they're trying to stay upbeat, unalarmed. Kids do this, they go out and run around and they get in trouble afterwards. I know that's what they're thinking. Half of them are still on the balcony, still drinking.

'He's probably gone for a ride.' Levi shrugs and I'm so tempted to slap him. I turn and storm out of the villa.

But of course, the panic builds up slowly from *why wasn't anyone watching him* to *where the fuck is he?*

Kav informs the rest of our guests and starts off in one direction while I run in the opposite, screaming out his name until my voice scratches. And there's no response, no matter how many of our guests are now searching under bushes, down on the beach. So, panic meets me head on, because there is no response, there is no Edmund.

A neighbour who I've never seen before steps out of their kitchen, clutching a ginger tea, and I grab them by their shoulders and beg them to tell me whether they've seen a little boy riding by.

'Black hair and brown eyes. Only six. He's snuck out the front gate. Please tell me you've seen him.'

'I'm so sorry,' the woman says in a tone that conveys helplessness. But she doesn't just go back inside. She places her mug on the low wall and says she'll join us. 'I'll knock on doors and see if anyone else has seen him.'

'Thank you,' I blurt. 'Thank you so much.' I'm about to kiss her because she's a good person and she's right. If anyone had seen a boy riding the streets in the dark, they'd take him back to the villa or call the police.

I run down the dark road, phone casting a light, urging myself not to cry just yet. You only cry when you know something bad has happened. And yes, something bad has happened, but he'll be found soon and then we'll laugh with our neighbours and guests and have a cup of tea and I'll feel like a bad mother, and the neighbour will probably bad-mouth me to her husband in bed tonight, but it will all be okay. I'm not a neglectful mother. My son has been playing in a villa next door where we can see him. And I was going to check as soon as I'd returned to the villa. I'm the only sober one here. I'm the only one not drinking.

Fuck. I mouth the word over and over, scaring a few people in their courtyards, finishing their dinner, scraping their plates with cutlery.

'Have you seen a little boy walking or riding past here? Six years old. This high,' I say, realising how bad it sounds. 'I'm his mother. My son has taken off from our villa.'

I say that as though it excuses me for neglecting my boy. But no one has seen him. No one has seen my Edmund.

When I turn and head back to my villa, I'm running, proper panic propelling me. I've only ever felt this level of fear once before. Only once. And it's familiar and dirty and I don't know how to stay calm now. Where the fuck *is* he?

The neighbour helping has recruited another group of people from a nearby villa who are off with torches and phone lights doing the rounds, door-knocking, and Kav is nowhere to be seen. But he's got Edmund. Somewhere down the road, in the opposite direction, he'll see Edmund collecting pine cones, or out with a torch searching for owls or bats in his pyjamas and slippers. Because that's what he loves to do when we come to the island. Go out with a torch and search for nocturnal creatures. But he shouldn't have gone out alone. Silly boy. He's going to be in big trouble after I've kissed him a thousand times. He's probably become distracted by a bird call or a boat out on the water droning by with a loud engine. He likes to explore. He likes to be independent.

Fuck Scott for making me run away from him. Fuck the group for cheering me. But I'm not crying yet.

When Kav comes back down the road, empty-handed, holding his arms up as though surrendering to the fact that my son is missing – not his son, my son – that's when the tears start. I slap his hands down. Slap them and slap them and slap him hard across the face so an instant rash appears on his cheek.

'Where is Edmund? Where the fuck is he?'

'Calm, Pen. *Calm*,' he says, one hand on his cheek, the other out, as though I'm a creature about to kill him.

But he doesn't know this has happened before. I can't lose another son. Not another. I collapse like they do in the movies and someone lifts me up from the hard footpath and I slap them away also. I'm not together, can't be put back together. My son is gone. My second son. My son will never come back, because my first one didn't. And it's all Rosie's fault.

It's always been her fault.

Eloise, 7.55 p.m.

We only ever get to see the put-together Penny. I've never seen Penny act like this to her daughter, or to anyone for that matter. In fact, watching mother and daughter go at each other through the window of Brett and Sal's villa is not only sickening, but fascinating. Like watching a couple arguing in public or a waiter being abused. You can't stop staring, even though you know you shouldn't.

I'm hovering in the dark with my fingertips collecting dust. They can't see me out here because they're too caught up in what's just happened. And Penny is angry, raging with wild hair and wild eyes and telling her daughter to 'Get the fuck up'. Rosie stands immediately from the couch, eyes staring down at her bare feet. Her arms dangle limply by her side, reminding me of Coco when she's in trouble.

Levi took Coco back to our villa to bed. I couldn't have them witnessing all this. Guests bolting from the beach, quickly sobering up by the announcement of a missing child. The whole situation has restrained the guests in a scary instant. Lights have switched on, music's turned off and the streets are now busy with people cycling around to find Edmund.

I run my sweaty fingertips down my shorts, dirtying the fabric. I lick my bottom lip, tasting sweat and garlic from the kebabs we'd eaten earlier. From the shadow of the fig tree, I watch. No one knows I'm here. Not Scott, not Kav. They're all searching the streets for Edmund. So I guess this is my private viewing. I guess that's why Penny feels she can let loose and react with a normalcy that finally encourages a different perception of her. No one is present to experience such venom.

'It's you,' Penny screams, with a finger pointing at her daughter. 'You did this to punish me.'

'You are a crazed person,' Rosie shrieks back. 'Do you know that?' Her young face is wet and blotchy, with mascara running down her cheeks. And Penny is a mess. Eyes like she's on drugs. When she shoves Rosie against the wall, I jolt back, almost bumping my head on the branch behind me. I look away and then back up as Rosie stumbles and Penny whirls around to escape her daughter. I would never react this way to my kids, no matter what has occurred. This rage and reaction pulls Penny down a notch in my book.

When the back door slams, I linger by the window, staring at Rosie, feeling what she's feeling. I find myself reaching to touch my back the way she does. It's a sad sight to see a daughter and mother fight like this. Her lip quivers while she slumps on the couch, covering her face. Her shoulders shake and I hear the sobs and that's when I back away from the glass.

This is not her fault and I suddenly feel helpless and bad for Rosie, like I want to rush in and comfort her. But what would Penny say if I did?

As Penny enters the street, I hide further behind the tree. She's crowded by Kav's friends. I hear them mentioning the police and Kav's parents. Someone goes to phone them just in case Edmund's gone there. It's like watching a documentary, both real and separate. A real-life story I don't want to be a part of. It's best if I stay here, stay put and stay out of the headlights.

I don't want Penny's accusing eyes on me. I don't need anyone accusing me of anything.

Penny, 8.05 p.m.

The island police are now involved and these are not your big-city police. They live here, so they're used to drunken idiots falling off boats and cyclists without helmets. They've never dealt with a missing child. They're novices. One looks only as old as Rosie. The other looks like an old horse put out to pasture.

Georgia and William have joined the search in their matching tracksuits. We've alerted the whole street, asking residents to help search for my baby boy. I'm demanding the police alert the whole island, but Kav keeps reminding me, it's only been half an hour, and Edmund's a wanderer. He can't have gone far in that time. But they don't know the whole story: who Edmund used to be connected to and how I've watched him like a hawk for years. And Kav doesn't know about Pearl, or my social media likes from an unknown person. She's out of jail and he doesn't know that. He doesn't know I often check her social media profile to scrutinise her life. Not that she gives much of it away in her random, erratic photos. A plastic bowl of orange crisps with the word: *dinner*. A tattoo of a pouting mouth, etched above her nipple. *Lick my kisses*. An empty flask of wine that's floating in a lit-up pool. *Lit*. A picture of a salivating bulldog with a chain around its neck. *Pup*.

I know I can't jump to conclusions, but I have to tell Kav now. I've been desperate to hide this information from him, to protect this blissful life we've built. Any drama, any problem could cause a crack. And I know first-hand what happens when a crack appears in a marriage.

We're standing outside our villa when I say, 'I need to tell you something.'

Kav shifts from foot to foot and sniffs, waiting, and I wish I'd told him sooner. All this lying, all these secrets only hammer a wedge into our smooth, loving marriage.

'Pearl contacted me recently on social media.' Kav frowns, sucking in a lip. 'She's out of jail and I didn't want to tell you before because I instantly blocked her and that was that. Also, mentioning it to you and you getting worried would only freak me out even more.'

He crosses his arms and I suddenly feel sick for slapping him. Crack, crack, break. 'What did she say?'

I fiddle with my wedding ring. 'She said she misses Edmund and we never should've taken him off her.'

'But then you blocked her?'

'Yep. Straight away.'

He squints at me. 'I can't believe you wouldn't tell me.'

Twisting the ring around and around, I watch him watching me. 'I hate negativity coming into our lives.'

'You should never lie to me,' he says, shaking his head.

'It's not a lie—'

'It doesn't mean anything though.' He uncrosses his arms and twists around to the street at the party guests mingling. 'I think we should tell the police, but I truly think he's just wandered off.'

We tell the police, just in case, and the young cop says they'll get authorities in the city to follow up on Pearl and Edmund's biological father. That's if they're even still together.

'But we're still assuming he's wandered,' the older cop says, adjusting the torch in his belt. 'It's important we stay calm.'

And I know I need to remain calm, but it's very difficult. Where would he wander, and why? The only hope I have is that he's got lost while exploring. And he *is* the type of kid to just leave and wander off. Especially on his own. But not in the dark.

We've questioned the kids. Levi and Rosie were on their phones, watching YouTube, and Edmund was playing Monopoly Junior, with no one really joining in. Coco was watching an inappropriate family movie filled with violence and practical jokes and gorging herself with sugar. Edmund was halfway through the game when he apparently went off to the bathroom.

And didn't come back.

Coco was too preoccupied by the movie and lollies and the teenagers weren't even aware of anything other than their screens.

But he still didn't come back.

More needs to be done. Julie has placed a jacket over my shoulders and Georgia has made me put on some sensible shoes so I can continue looking for him. I'm a shaking mess and I want to throw up. I do. In the bushes. It's small and bitter and mostly fruit juice mixed with garlic kebabs. Wiping my mouth on my sleeve, I look up to see Eloise standing by her villa, holding herself and watching. It's a peculiar expression, one I can't accurately describe. Intrigue?

'We've got a group of people down by the cliffs,' Kav whispers in my ear, pulling my attention away from Eloise. 'Just in case he went exploring down that way.'

I'm nodding, but not really absorbing what he's saying. Someone hands me a tissue and I wipe my mouth, smelling sour garlic.

'At what point do we alert the island?' I ask the older police officer, who's speaking to his colleague about which direction they'll take. They don't seem too alarmed by this. They look like I've just interrupted them from a gripping series on TV and this is really all a nuisance.

He gives a short smile and tucks that torch in again. 'I'd say if we don't find him by ten, then we'll phone the city police. Remember, it's only been thirty minutes, ma'am.'

'And in that time, he could be drowning.'

The young cop has a smear of acne on his forehead. Way too young to deal with this. 'Your husband says he likes to wander,' he reminds me.

'He does. But not at night, never at night.'

'Let's give it a while, Pen,' Kav says, taking my hand and squeezing it. 'He can't be far.'

I want to scream. And cry. And vomit again. 'I'm so angry at Rosie.'

Georgia rubs my shoulders with warm bony hands. 'Now, now. We've got the whole road out searching. Someone will find him. Let's take a breath for a moment.' She has a wobbly voice, as though she's worried too, yet wanting me to calm down. She doesn't want me to get into a bad state, she keeps saying. Not now that they all know. I'm pregnant, I'm vulnerable, and they love me more because of it. I'm now officially part of their tribe. If I lose this baby due to stress, then I've lost three altogether.

And maybe losing Edmund is my punishment for what I've done.

Eloise, 8.45 p.m.

Penny *is* actually human when she's suffering. It's the first time I've seen her like this. She doesn't care about the running mascara, the vomiting in the bushes, even with everyone watching. This situation is making her real. I'm no longer looking at a celebrity I can't touch or get near. Although I'm choosing to stay clear because she looks like the type to flip in an instant. I've seen her now with Rosie. I've seen what she's capable of.

I've joined Julie and Sal to search for Edmund by the lighthouse. A couple of minutes ago, the police brought out a map of Rottnest and we've chosen to trace sections of the island with torches, in groups of three. While the cops spoke to the group, I hung back, scared their eyes would land on my face. We've all dispersed in every direction and, through Penny's persuading, at 9 p.m. the whole island will start searching while the mainland police are contacted. I guess that's when things will get serious.

People are really worried, pale-faced and rugged up in jackets and sneakers to begin searching properly. We're going to be searching the town areas and popular tourist spots, beaches, caves, golf course and playgrounds. And after that, we're doing the rest of the island.

'Does he like lighthouses?' Julie asks Sal and I as she cycles in front of us, puffing with the exertion. I can't imagine she'd do much exercise.

'I don't know Edmund that well,' I say.

'I do,' Sal says. 'He loves anything out of the ordinary.'

'He's a strange kid,' I say. And then wish I hadn't. It's not the right thing to mention, but it's true, he's always had a darkness to him, a face with no expression. I can imagine him as a baby lying there on the rug, people smiling, trying to coax a grin, a laugh out of him. I can imagine him like someone from *The Addams Family* or a horror movie. A child no one wants.

'Julie said his biological parents are dodgy,' I say, riding beside Sal.

Her blonde flowing hair smells of peach and teenage skincare. Her bum is tight in expensive activewear that looks like she's packed it just for this occasion. It bobbles ahead as we ride up the hill. She shrugs. 'And?'

Perhaps I'm the only one being morbid.

When we reach the top of the hill, we rest our bikes up against the rough wooden fence and start walking up the rocky path that winds against the ocean. It's so much bigger at night. A blanket of never-ending black. The stars are much brighter out here. The wind stronger. I hold myself. It's an eerie place to be. Waves crash against the cliff to the right of us, pounding like a warning. Up ahead, the white lighthouse looms over the cliff like a sheeted ghost. Yellow light fans around and then disappears. But you can hear the whir of it. You feel the ship-wrecks out there. It's a desolate place. I'm glad the women are here with me.

When we get to the top of the lighthouse, I've almost forgotten why we're here. It's not until Julie shouts out 'Edmund' and the wind carries her strong soaring voice out to sea that I hold in a breath.

'What if it's his real parents?' I say to the waves. Julie and Sal can't hear me. 'What if they've come to take him back?'

Penny, 9.03 p.m.

I fear it's all going to come out and now there are witnesses here, ready to watch me fall. As the police officer hops into his car, radios back to the city and the search for Edmund becomes serious, I'm paralysed by the wall outside our villa. Pearl and Edmund's biological father can't be found. They're either out partying on a Saturday night or they're here. But they aren't answering their phones and I don't know how long until officers visit their home. Kav is the only one who knows what I'm thinking, the only person who worries like I do.

'I think someone took him,' I utter in a voice so small it sounds like Edmund. Kav runs his hands through his hair and looks at me. We've been searching for an hour, calling out Edmund's name. Scouring the main beaches on the bay, the caves, the cliffs, the lighthouse, the campsite, the town, near the pub, down the three roads that run adjacent to the ocean, one behind the other. But he's gone. Without a trace.

'And if it's not them, then it's someone else,' I say.

'What makes you say that?' Kav says as the younger police officer looks up from his phone. He's communicating to someone back on land but trying to listen in to me. The rest of the party guests have left us alone to keep searching, while Kav and I have returned to our villa, coming together in a moment of messy hugs and crying.

'I saw someone strange staring at me,' I tell him. 'Yesterday in town. He gave me the creeps and I don't know why.' I say this to Kav and the police officer hangs up his phone and tells us back-up – police and forensics – are coming over by helicopter. There's no need to ask the island tourists to search.

'They'll be here in twenty minutes,' he says, stepping out of the car. 'And we'll be searching all the villas along here and in the other bays.'

'Good.' I stare at him, blinking. 'Because I think someone has taken my son.'

'But who would Edmund leave with?' Kav says. 'Someone would have seen him leave.'

I shrug, lip wobbling, staring into Eloise and Scott's dark villa. Her kids are in there, sleeping. 'I don't know. What about that person I saw at The Basin last night? They were watching us.'

'You can't be certain you saw someone—'

'But I know my son,' I snap. 'He wouldn't tell the kids he was going to the toilet and then just leave and ride away to go exploring.'

'He does like to wander—'

'Not at night,' I shout, turning away from Kav. 'He wouldn't ride off at night.'

Kav doesn't reference the 'my son' comment. He lets me say it because he knows where that comes from. Kav and I aren't so different. Ignorance is paradise and he appreciates that as well as I do. How often do we choose denial over truth, silence over conflict, sex over arguments? How often do we kiss over unsaid words and smile away the glares? To cuddle instead of push, to laugh instead of cry, to drink wine over water. Pleasure is the only driving force of life.

Pain is too constant if you allow it in. Much better to bandage over the weeping cuts. Much better to dose ourselves in lies.

We've become that way now. Better liars than saints, better lovers than liars.

'This is karma.' I speak into my hands. 'All karma.'

'Don't be silly,' Kav says, going back to his bike. 'There's still twenty minutes until they arrive. That's twenty minutes where we could be looking.'

'It's my fault,' I say, hanging my head.

He starts to ride off. 'Okay, it's your fucking fault.'

And he always lets me win. It's just easier that way.

On Sunday mornings I collapse in a heap by the washing basket full of folded clothes. I don't know why it happens in that spot, but I figure it has something to do with the laundry sink. Most mothers use them as baby baths.

The washing machine becomes a change table with the towel spread out while the baby soap rests on the edge along with the nappy. New parents fill the basin, testing the temperature with their elbow, and gently lower their fat, wrinkled babies into the basin, where they kick like frogs and make cooing noises. I have my back against the washing machine and that's where I lose it.

We built our first house without baths. Edmund only ever has showers. So that basin, large and silver and deep enough to hold a new baby, stirs the rage and guilt inside me.

I wait until no one's home. I lock the laundry door and go about folding the washing, humming and pretending as though it's not going to happen this week. But it does and has happened every week for thirteen years. Life just gets too much and the mental exhaustion of trying to keep this family happy, afloat and loving is too much to balance.

I now have everything I'd ever wished for. An expensive house most people envy, a healthy son who loves his school and friends. I have a happy husband who goes out of his way to care for and love us all, even Rosie. I pray she'll return to normal soon. But overall, there is no sickness, no poverty, no addiction, no toxic people surrounding us. Kav's medical practice is flying. We have it all.

But once upon a time, thirteen years ago, I'd been in the same situation. Another loving husband, a happy daughter, a beautiful house, an eight-week-old baby boy. And then it all came crashing down around me. That's why Kav can't know anything about before. He has to believe what I've been showing him since we first got together. In my previous marriage, if I'd been better, cooked better, looked better, fucked better, birthed better, mothered better, it never would have happened.

It was my fault then and it's my fault now.

Eloise, 9.13 p.m.

We return from the lighthouse the same time as the others, who are congregating on the street with their bikes. It's like an eighties school camp, a meet-up where one of us has dared the other to go night cycling. I expect to see backpacks and torches and some dinking others on the back. But it's not camp, it's not fun. This Edmund missing business is serious. I see it in the wrinkled face of Brett, in the dishevelled hair of Georgia, who looks like she should be in bed with a novel and a nightcap.

Scott's had to stay here with Coco and Levi, but he now wants to switch places with me, mutters a jibe about being more useful and knowing where to look.

'Like where?' I whisper, poking my head around the bedroom door. Coco's in my bed, with her teddies bunched under her arms. Imagine if it were her. I grip the door frame, my nails marking the paint. 'How will you know where to look?'

Scott plucks a jumper from the suitcase. 'Kav said he's an explorer. Likes wandering off at the park.'

He pulls a cap on as though a hat in the dark will be the key to finding Edmund. Really, it's just habit. He wears a cap most days and shorts even when it's cold. I love and hate that I know that about him.

'I heard Penny say she thinks someone's taken him,' I whisper. Coco's stirring. We need to leave the bedroom and the milky sweaty smell of her. But I don't want to open the window. Not now. Not now Edmund's missing. 'What if it's his biological parents? Have you heard about them?'

He ties his jumper around his waist and nods. 'Yes. A little. Kav doesn't really like to discuss it with me.'

I find myself sucking in air. 'Do you think they'd come and take him?'

'I don't know,' he shrugs and looks back at Coco. 'Let's hope he's okay.'

We're both looking at our baby. 'What if it'd been Coco?' I say.

I don't see it, but I feel the back of his hand stroke my cheek and it makes me flinch unexpectedly. 'We'd get through it,' he says. We stare at one another and for the briefest of moments, his eyes land on my lips. Like he's about to kiss me. But then his lashes flutter and he looks away, stepping back from the door and from me.

I'm holding my breath, watching him gather his phone and villa key off the table, and my cheek tingles with absence. How will I ever get him back again? What will it take? Not a blow job. Not even a night out together without kids. I can't remember the last time we ever had a night like that, with oysters, thick menus, a candle between our glowing faces. *I want you back*. But how? *How?*

'I hope you find him.' I sniff.

'It'll only take one person to figure out where he's gone.'

And this is what we do. Often, our words provoke and harm in roundabout ways. We manipulate and prod each other beneath monotone voices. Just the rise in pitch, the rise in volume will hint at the emotion we carry for each other. So, we speak levelly, evenly, purposefully wanting to damage the other for the hurt we feel, the absence of touch, love, sex, partnership. And as soon as Scott leaves the room, the house, the car, the table, the yearning for his affection, attention, is so great, I feel I'm drowning. And no matter what I do, I'll never resurface, never be back the way he wants me. So, we remain bitter and sharp with barbed-wire words that cut and slash.

As I gaze out of the window at Penny and Kav, hands forged together like steel, the strangest thought teases and scares me. Because Scott has just touched me for the first time since forever. So, will the trauma of Edmund missing bring Scott and I back together?

People need a wake-up call to be healthy. Cancer, diabetes, a death in the family, a divorce. It always takes trauma to heal a part of yourself. If you don't get to suffer then you never get to heal. I've suffered, but never got past the healing part. And it's the same with our marriage. At what point do you start to mend? Move forward? Forgive and forget? At what point will the image of my legs gripping the tradesman's shoulders as he's pounding into me leave Scott's mind?

He walked in one lunchtime when Coco was a baby, sleeping soundly, and I'd just fixed myself a salad and the tradesman a coffee and it happened so quickly, so out of the blue, the shock of it sexually aroused me. Up on the bench, legs spread, hair in the mayonnaise, skirt pushed up, zip down, hands gripping my calves, plunging. And it had been a long, long time since I'd felt Scott's fingers in my hair, his stroking thumb on my hand watching a movie, his smiling eyes and licking tongue. Because that's what happens when you have kids and get married, right? Sex stops. Fun and friendship and affection stops. Right?

The mayonnaise went flying off the kitchen counter, smashing against the wall in white globs as Scott leapt over his briefcase, face pallid and grey with a flu. It didn't matter how sick Scott felt, he punched the tradesman so hard I heard the crack of his cheekbone. And the poor guy let him. Because he knew he deserved it.

But I got nothing. No slap, no roar, no saliva on my face from yelling. I got the cold shoulder. The freezing silence. The absent husband that became even more distant, more unloving, busier, and even more career-orientated than he had been prior to that moment.

And that was my punishment, still is. Still will be. Because we've never healed even after all the suffering.

Eloise, 9.23 p.m.

Kav and Scott ride off together and I linger by the door while Kav's friends decide to search back down on the beach. As she bends to the gravelly road and cries into her hands, Penny doesn't know I'm watching, but I feel her pain. It's a soft child's cry. And I want to hold her.

There's an idea I've been toying with for a while now, not just on this holiday. Now, in this private interval, with no other guests around, I feel as though the universe has offered me a magical moment. Here, it says. Take it, it says.

Kav and Penny are like family to Scott. If Penny and I become close friends, we could become a frolicking foursome, sharing spring holidays at the vineyard and Christmas Eve dinners. She'll appreciate and respect me, educating me to become more like her. And then Scott will see us as twins, setting the tables at dinner parties, shopping for birthday presents, getting manicures together. I'll become the sort of practical, efficient, responsible wife he wants.

So, I do the unthinkable, my legs jittering as I step out of my gate and stand behind her. Our shadows morph. We're the only ones here on the dark street with one flickering dodgy streetlight attracting a cloud of moths.

Crouching, I wrap my arms around her quaking, bony body. It's foreign, stiff like concrete, and when she gasps and quickly turns to me, my face glows hot. I feel like an idiot.

'You scared me to death,' she splutters, wiping her nose and tears on her arm. She looks up at me like I'm a monster from her childhood. And perhaps I am that. But I need to get into Penny's good books, so maybe, just maybe, I can get back into Scott's.

'I'm so sorry.' I shake my head and offer her a scrunched-up tissue I've had in my jacket pocket. 'What can I do?'

She takes the tissue and dabs at her nose, still crouched. I offer her my hand. She looks at it first like it's crawling with disease before taking it. And I'm clammy and trembling. It's like touching royalty. Silly thought, but true. I want to kiss her hand like a prince. Instead, I smile.

'I can't leave Coco,' I say. 'But I can wake Levi and get him to help search.'

She flaps my words away. 'No, it's okay.'

'I'm so angry at him,' I lie. It's not my son's fault. 'For not looking up from his phone.' Penny shoving Rosie earlier and their argument springs to mind. 'I feel like it's their fault in a way.'

She quickly nods in agreement. 'It's more Rosie's,' she says, glancing over the road at their villa. It's lit up. I assume her daughter's in there, sheepishly shying away from her mother. I want to mention the boyfriend, but don't. I just need something that'll bring Penny and I closer and not completely destroy Rosie's life. The boyfriend would be pushing it.

'She's just a teenager,' I say. 'But I know what you mean. I saw her leave the house at one point—'

'What?' Penny jerks her head as though what I said hurt her. 'She left the villa?'

'For a decent period of time too.' I find myself lying too easily. And then I can't stop myself. Helpful information could be used to bond us. 'I wondered where she'd gone and wanted to ask Levi. But he was there with the kids, so I guess we had one of them babysitting and didn't bother.'

'How long was she gone?'

'I'd say about thirty minutes, but she really shouldn't have.'

'No.' Penny sniffs. 'She is going to have a lot of explaining to do.'

'And they're so good at lying.' I shake my head. 'I can't believe Levi most of the time.'

Penny nods. 'I'm glad I'm not the only one.' It's as though she's forgotten about Edmund and the horrible situation. But for a glimmer of time, a small moment, we're just two mothers, discussing our kids, and it feels natural and real. Perhaps Penny feels it too when she sighs and shrugs, displaying vulnerability and trust. 'What if we don't find him?'

I touch her arm and this time she doesn't flinch. 'Penny, we will.'

'This is my worst nightmare,' she says, with heavy tears landing on her cheeks.

Grabbing her shoulders, I pull her into me and hold her there. At first, she stiffens, unsure and threatened like an injured animal. But then she relaxes, sinking into the embrace.

In that instant, my heart shifts, swells, thumps with life. It's like Penny's touch has replaced the need for Scott and any addiction to him. *If only you knew*, I want to whisper, *how long I've wanted you to like me*. To have Penny this close, allowing me to mother her, melt into my arms, accept me, is too much to bear. I close my eyes, press my cheek into her hair, breathe in her scent. It's not how I imagined. Peppermint gum, body odour, masked with fruity perfume.

I expected washing powder, coffee and sun cream. And I wonder what the Peacocks will think when they see us both having lunch together at the yacht club and barbeques on the river with the kids? I freeze, holding her sobbing body, and open my eyes. Because now that I have Penny here, accepting me, I don't know how I'm ever going to let her go.

Penny, 9.24 p.m.

This is a moment I never thought would occur, me being held and comforted by Eloise. Oddly, it doesn't feel wrong either. I let her. The scraping back of my hair, the gentle shushing takes me back to my childhood and I'm unaware of how strange we must look, sitting here in the middle of the road. If only Mum and Dad were here. Instead, they're cruising the world and I'd never want to bother them with this. Their once-in-a-lifetime dream retirement holiday. They've never been to Europe and when Kav offered to buy them their cruise for their anniversary, they jumped at the chance. Only now, since having Kav in my life, have I been able to do that. Splash out on friends and family. Offer holidays, pay for dinners out, buy lavish gifts for Mother's Day and birthdays. My life is ruined, but I don't need to ruin theirs. Besides, it hasn't been too long. Edmund will be found. Surely.

'We should keep looking,' I say, sniffing and going to stand.

But Eloise won't let me. She supports me under my arms and says, 'I think you should come inside for a tea and let them search for a while.'

But I can't stop searching. Edmund needs me. He'll be lost, scared and tired.

'You've had a huge night and you're pregnant,' Eloise adds. 'Come on, just for twenty minutes. By then, someone will find him.'

She says it with such conviction I almost want to kiss her. Like she knows. Why can't I be that confident? I let her take my hand and lead me into her villa. It's dark and quiet and I'm tempted to close the door, draw the curtains and snuggle beside the little lump on the bed. Coco is sound asleep. I frown as my throat tightens. To think I've been so cruel to Eloise. Her children are here, safe, alive and sleeping. I'm the neglectful parent. I can count the neglect on three fingers. Rosie, the other one, and now Edmund. To touch my stomach is a curse. I'd rather pretend I'm not pregnant. I want to sleep. I want to cry. I want Edmund.

Eloise flicks on the kettle and plops a spoonful of sugar into a mug. Watching her from the lounge room falsely provides a sense of quiet calm. I could be back in holiday mode with her and the kids, travelling together. I could be about to have a cup of hot tea, settle down to watch a movie and laugh with a lapful of biscuits.

'I should go and look,' I say again.

'There are fifty guests out there looking,' Eloise says with a warmth about her. I'm looking at her differently now. Her voice is no longer sharp and harsh, gravelly and uneducated. She speaks with a breathlessness that lowers my pulse. Her hair extensions are now threads of satin gold. Her revealing shorts are longer than once thought and similar to a pair I own. Her nails are a pale pink, soft and matching her cheekbones and lips. She's angelic. Mother. She passes me a sweet tea, which I sip and love. It heats my neck, loosening the suffocation I keep feeling.

'After you drink this, we can go looking.' She smiles again.

I speak into the mug. 'Thank you.' Steam puffs against my nose.

'You're welcome.'

We stare at one another and suddenly I have an urge to tell her how maybe I've been wrong about her. And how jealous I am of my daughter's admiration for her. I want to ask her how I can do it, get Rosie's approval again. But Eloise speaks first and tells me she hates this island. Has never liked it. Always felt like it's tainted. She reveals how she didn't want to come this weekend.

'And not because of you.' She laughs quietly into her cup and slurps the tea. 'I used to come here as a teenager and I believe bad things happen here.'

'Funny. I have the totally opposite experience. This island's my childhood.'

'I know.' She nods. 'I know you've had a great life.'

But she doesn't know. Not really. I sink my lips into the tea and drink a hot mouthful.

'What bad things happened here?' I ask.

She chews her lip, then shakes her head. 'You don't want to know.'

But I do. I really do want to know. 'A kid has never gone missing here.'

'No, they haven't.' Eloise considers this for a moment and then asks, 'Do you think it's Edmund's biological mother?'

I place the cup down on the table. 'I didn't know you knew about that.'

'I only found out tonight, from Julie.' She rolls her eyes and sighs. 'Because Scott never tells me anything.'

'He didn't?'

She shakes her head and it looks like she wants to cry. To someone, possibly to me.

'I wish he would let me in a bit more—'

A group of bicycles skid up outside with voices, hurried and loud. I run to the door. It's Kav, Scott, Brett and Sal. But no

Edmund. And for a second I thought they'd found him, but they haven't. I got my stupid hopes up and I'm not shocked by anything anymore. He's never coming back. I kick the door and feel bad because I've probably woken Eloise's kids. And then she comes up behind me, squeezes my shoulder, and lets me sob once more.

Eloise, 10.27 p.m.

There are rolling hills, swathes of bushland, expansive salt lakes, numerous caves and fifty-something bays. The island takes an hour to drive around. It's not a small island, even if as a young woman I thought it was. Finding a missing kid here won't be easy. The fact it's almost midnight adds to the worry. Searching in the dark only compounds the difficulty. But it's better than just waiting for daylight.

The authorities have stopped boats coming and going. But really, how can they detect who comes and goes on an island this size? Five of fifty bays are fully occupied by boats. And they've started door-knocking on villas, motoring around on dinghies with flashlights skimming across the water, waking sleeping boaties to check inside their vessels. And we all want to sleep, our brains tired and twisted with lingering hangovers and dwindling drunkenness. But the tension to keep searching yanks us out of exhaustion. Must. Keep. Searching.

Scott joins another group, who decide to ride to the south side of the island. Really? Would a little boy ride thirty minutes away? So much of this island is uninhabited, barren, thick with gumtrees, paperbarks and scratchy bushland that's harsh enough to survive the salty winters, the scorching summers. I think he's been taken.

By the creepy mother, or by that weirdo I saw stalking through town. Actually, maybe I should mention that guy.

One of us has to stay here with the kids. And Levi is finally asleep after wanting to join in on the search. I've got my two babies tucked up in bed, where I can watch over them. It would be cruel to fall asleep while the rest of the island panics. It would be harsh to make myself a tea and butter myself some toast. But I'm starving, thirsty, tired.

Our street's suddenly empty. Police who were scouring through Brett and Sal's villa have left to head down to the beach and Penny's gone off in the crew-cab ute with other police, demanding that she be allowed to search with them. I guess one piece of toast wouldn't hurt? One cup of tea? I need comfort and nourishing as much as anyone.

It's not until I'm reclining with the toast rested on my stomach, crunching into the buttery goodness with my feet up at the end of the couch, that I hear someone outside. Our front door is open, with the flyscreen locked. I can see out. No one can see in. Who is it?

I use my elbows to lean up and peek out. Across the road in Brett and Sal's villa, a tall man opens the front gate and ensures it doesn't swing back and slam. He's deliberately trying to be quiet. Wearing a hoodie, the man is tall, lean, reminding me of a shadow. It's something about the way he's creeping in. A prowler? Or someone to do with Edmund's disappearance? He reminds me of the guy I've seen around the island. Setting my plate down, I can barely swallow my toast. I let it just soften against my tongue. I want to shout out, *Who are you? What are you doing in Brett and Sal's villa?* But then Rosie opens Penny and Kav's back flyscreen door and the intruder gets a fright, slips over the fence and disappears down the side of the house towards the beach. What the fuck? Why was he about to enter Brett and Sal's villa? The villa where Edmund went missing?

Penny, 10.27 p.m.

I believe someone has taken Edmund. I don't think he's wandered. And I think the police and detective sitting behind me agree. How could a child go missing in front of everyone he knows? That's what I keep repeating to the constable beside me who's driving the crew-cab ute across the causeway that cuts through the salt lakes. We were all there, out the front, out the back, on the beach, in the villas, crowding the balcony. No one saw Edmund leave. No one.

The causeway is narrow and corrugated, vibrating the cabin. I've never been out here at night. And why would anyone? The smell for one is a pungent sulphur that reeks of eggs. Foam balls roll across the road in the headlights from one lake to another, piss-coloured froth. Why the fuck would Edmund wander or ride out here? No, he wouldn't. That's why I think they're treating this suspiciously now. Especially with the city cops here. Not the homicide team or forensics yet. *Yet*. I don't know whether that reassures me or makes this worse. If they come, then they'll suspect he's been kidnapped, killed even. If they don't come, then they're not doing enough, and they aren't using enough resources to look for my son. They've still heard nothing from his parents, they still can't find the loser druggy who birthed him. It's her. I know it is. But where has she taken him? There are only so many places she can hide on the island. And someone would have seen her with a screaming kid.

Police have started combing the beach in front of the villa, Brett and Sal's villa, the boats moored in the bay and the villas around us. Have they found anything? I keep asking those four words. When my phone rings: have you found anything, have they found anything, has anyone found something? Something. Someone. Edmund. What are they looking for? A lost shoe? Pyjama bottoms? A strand of his hair?

I'm chewing my lip.

We exit the causeway and travel down a bumpy, rocky road that edges around the largest of the lakes. On my side is a barren hill of spinifex. In front, a derelict-looking house that could be made of cardboard. I thought we were driving to the next bay.

'Why are we here?' I ask the officer. Detective Wallis. He's about my age, dressed in tight trendy jeans and a black polo shirt. How high up is he in the ranks? It's strange that I suddenly care. The higher they are, the more they'll know, which offers greater chances of finding Edmund. The constable sitting behind me and next to him is in uniform. I wonder how she keeps a straight face during situations like this. Does she have children? I bet I know what she's thinking: *Thank fuck this isn't me.* I shift in my seat.

'We need to speak to someone,' Wallis says.

'Someone suspicious?' I ask.

Wallis side-eyes me and the female constable and driver step out.

'He's the longest-residing resident on the island,' Wallis says. 'He was also the longest-serving police officer here through the eighties. He's coming with us.'

'Has this happened before?' I ask Wallis.

I go to follow, and he holds up a hand. 'Wait here.'

I don't get my answer, but I know cops. I've been on the bad side of them, investigated and interrogated. If the three officers aren't thinking *thank God it's not my child*, then they're potentially thinking something worse.

She did it. The parents are always the guilty ones.

Eloise, 10.39 p.m.

Across the road, Rosie's on the phone, pacing in the back courtyard. I go to call out and then stop. Because Rosie's voice shrills over the road, 'No, I can't do that, you know I can't.'

Sitting up, I watch. She's getting aggressive, whispering in harsh tones with the words *bitch* and *arsehole* bouncing off her tongue. And she doesn't wear a look of fear. No, there's nothing fearful about this kid. Lips clumped together, swagger purposeful and decisive, knowing where she's heading and what she's doing.

I must be holding my breath the whole time, because my abdominal muscles are tight and sore. Waiting a while, breathing calmly, I question what to do. Go over and console her? Help her through this distress? But before I can help, Rosie kicks the gate, swivels on her heels and marches back into Penny and Kav's villa, slamming the door behind her. Her muffled cry gets blocked from inside the villa.

I could go to her and find out what's bothering her, but I also want to follow that man who just jumped Brett and Sal's fence. He could be a suspect and I'm sure it's the guy who's been watching us all weekend.

In the next room, Coco sleeps heavily, wrapped in sheets and her blanket, thumb slipping from her open mouth. I'll have to lock them in. And I think it's probably worth it.

Levi's sleeping when I nudge him a little. He moans *what?* and I tell him I'll be back in ten minutes. I have my phone, keep the door locked. He mumbles *okay* and rolls over to sleep up against the wall.

And then I push the front gate open and jog down the sandy steps beside Brett and Sal's villa. Energy tickles my calves as my bare feet sink into sand. There's something energising about this. Potentially catching or identifying Edmund's abductor. That's *if* he's been abducted. I can't really jump to conclusions, although why was this individual slinking in black through the courtyard? To cover tracks? To collect evidence left behind? Was he a party guest? Someone we know?

The beach is deserted. Both ways. Tin dinghies have been pulled up on the sand. Someone's left a towel down here. I disturb a few sleeping seagulls. And my shadow has disappeared. Crap. The sand dunes spread into grass and large fig trees and there's no one walking underneath the branches. At one end of the bay, the cliffs and the steps leading up the hill are vacant. Down the other end, the ferry jetty is cast in an orange, gloomy light. Yachts chink. Waves lick the sand. The lighthouse spotlights across water. Empty bottles from tonight's social circle remind me of how altered the night, the weekend, the holiday has become. Where did he go? Where did he go on this sacred island, this family playground?

I'll have to tell the police about this, even though I don't want them recognising me. Screwing my toes into the sand, I nod. Too bad, I have to tell. And Penny will appreciate me more than ever for doing so. It's an offness, a grim gut feeling that has me typing in her number to call her.

This person has something to do with Edmund's disappearance.

Penny, 11.01 p.m.

It's been three hours now, but I've watched enough crime shows to know that the first twenty-four hours are the most crucial when children wander off. Toddlers who live in homes backing on to bushland go missing all the time. Kids go missing at parks. I once lost Rosie in a shopping centre and had to have her name called out over the PA. Then there are royal shows and fetes. Children go missing there too. This isn't my fault. This sort of thing happens all the time.

I've said this to the old man who's been searching with us since we collected him from his cardboard house. He was dressed in a grimy singlet, with a bulging beer belly and sunspots as large as coins splodged over his face. He was wrinkled, not just from sleep, but from years of sun trauma and island living. He came into the car with a grunt, squeezing beside the female constable with his floppy flip-flops dropping out the side. He wasn't dressed for searching, but he told us he only ever wears flip-flops nowadays.

'This sort of thing happens all the time, right?' I said to him as the car meandered back down his rocky drive. 'You've seen this before?'

He cracked his knuckles and undid his window and gave a long 'ah' sound.

And then he said he hadn't. That most parents knew where their kids were.

◆ ◆ ◆

Most parents find the newborn stage challenging. The number of high-achieving corporate CEOs we know who would rattle off about the rearing of a newborn, the sleep deprivation, the torturous cries being worse and harder to handle than any job, any deal, any competitor they've ever encountered, used to fill me with a tingle of acknowledgement.

New mothers love to hear this. They feel validated. My stinging, chapped nipples, my stretched, throbbing vagina, my constant sweating is testament to the hardest and most underrated job in the world. I should be paid five hundred thousand more than those CEOs. I have to listen to a lamb-like cry for hours at night, testing my sleep, frustration and patience.

The mothers who lied about it being easy were the enemy. Really, mothers like that should be ripped away from their newborns. They should be shoved out of mothers' groups and whipped. How dare they claim this to be easy. Whenever I heard a mother saying they loved the newborn stage, they felt blessed, they wanted ten thousand more of them, I seriously had to stop myself from spitting in her face.

This rubbery pink creature stuck on my bleeding breasts and sucking the life out of me could never be loved. But I had to pretend it was. To keep up with the other mothers, carting their newborn babies into the mothers' group with cooing voices and soothing behaviour. They were skilled in swaddling their creatures, flopping out a tit and plonking them on it. They spoke about loving the feel of it. The gentle tugging, the sucking noises, the curled fist pumping for more milk. Look at that, how nature designed such a flawless being.

Mine was lying in its pram, clumsy in its wrapping, fists out and cold. As soon as it wakes again, I'll have to deal with it.

And then Rosie, all curls and blonde hair. All red cheeks and cute comments. How did I love her and not it? How did I become such a monster?

Eloise, 11.01 p.m.

Penny won't answer her phone and I'm heading back up the steps when I see Rosie's silhouette at the top. Arms hung by her sides, fists balled in anger. That determination I saw earlier in her court-yard is now directed at me. And it's the image of her standing there, higher than me. The outline of her body, face in shadow, has me stopping mid-step, has me stepping back. Has me clutching the railing, nails digging in wood. I don't know why I sense it, but I do. In the same way ants sense rain, building a pyramid of sand around their entrance hole. For protection. For survival. I sense Rosie is about to harm me.

'If Mum finds out you were giving me drugs, imagine what she'll tell the cops.'

It comes out so bluntly, it almost pushes me over. Does she know how much I value my children? Does she know how terri-fied I am of losing Scott? She probably doesn't know that, but I'm certain Penny does and if I get on Penny's bad side, so will Scott and my kids. Rosie doesn't realise how much ammunition she has against me. I will lose my children, my husband, and any friend-ship that I could have developed with Penny. But why? Why is she stating this now?

I feign a smirk, a silly laugh. I'm not nervous. 'I don't get it?'

'I need fifty thousand dollars by two a.m. Monday, or else I'll tell them everything.' She holds something up on her phone, but I can't see it. I can only see a manipulative devil.

I squint. 'What is it?'

'A picture of us in the toilet cubicle.' She steps down to join me and holds the phone up to my face. The drug packet behind us on the toilet. And she pockets the phone before I can grab it. Then she climbs one step and I can barely see her face.

'I thought you deleted that?' I swallow. I could grab the phone from her and delete the photo, but still, the proof circulates in my bloodstream. And she's probably saved it to the cloud.

There are cops here too. Cops who would arrest me in an instant for dabbling in drugs, and doing so with a minor. Cops on the island who probably remember my face from before. There are drugs in my blood. One test, one scrape of saliva off my tongue and I'd be locked up. Possibly even suspected for Edmund's disappearance.

'Fifty thousand,' she repeats.

Some call it blackmail, a bribe, or a payoff. But I don't. I call it cruel. It's only then that I realise just how clever, how conniving, how intelligently manipulative Rosie Fisher is. The rebellious teen who fobs off her mother and any form of authority is now coming for me. I should have known last night that the toilet episode would bite me in the arse. But why the hell does she want money?

'I don't have fifty thousand dollars, Rosie.' I say it calmly, as though I'm not really sweating under my pits.

'Bullshit. You wear thousand-dollar dresses and you live in a bigger house than we do. Your watch is worth that. That's why Mum hates you so much. I hear her bitching about you all the time.'

I shake my head at her. I can imagine Penny bitching about me. I knew I wasn't imagining it. 'Why are you doing this to me? Did you plan this?'

'Mum called earlier and said you called me irresponsible, and that I wasn't looking after Edmund well enough tonight.' She steps backwards, up another step. Ah, okay. This is where it's coming from. I've stood in the way of her and her mother. But surely she wouldn't go to these lengths for revenge. Fifty thousand?

'Why do you need the money right now?'

She ignores the question. 'You'll have to transfer it into my bank account.'

'I think my husband would realise. So would my bank.'

'I swear I'll send this picture to Mum right now.' Her voice rises in hysteria. 'And they'll get you arrested. There are cops crawling all over this island.'

'Wait.' I hold up my hand as she goes to prod her phone screen. I just heard her on the phone ten minutes ago, screaming at someone. This can't just be about me lying to Penny about her leaving the villa. 'Has someone threatened you, Rosie? We can go to the police if they have.'

'You have no idea.' She pockets the phone again. 'There is no other choice. You have to give me the money, Eloise.'

'Just wait,' I say. 'We can figure something out here. I know you're scared right now.'

She buries her face in her hands and her body jerks. Very scared. Of whom though? And of what? She's covering her face like a child who's responsible for breaking a vase, for being caught stealing money, for hiding cookies in their room. Not only in fear, but in shame. And then I understand.

'Was it you?' I lick my dry lips. 'Did you take Edmund somewhere?'

She shakes her head, continues shielding her face. I step up to her. I pull her wet fingers away from her face. 'Did someone kidnap Edmund?'

Stepping backwards, Rosie turns away, running up the steps, and I'm worried that if Penny or Kav turn up now, they'll wonder what the commotion is about. This is the last thing that needs to be happening right now. I follow behind, searching the street for any sign of the guests, cops or the island community. She's being too loud, starting to cry into her hands with angry gasps. Coco could wake or, worse, Levi. But we're the only ones here.

Then Rosie tells me something I haven't even considered. This blackmailing me is one thing and the consequences of me taking drugs with her is another. But when Rosie speaks down to her feet, I almost don't hear her voice.

'They're probably watching now,' she mutters in her palms. All the nerves in my back twist as I gaze around the empty street. The flickering orange light, the whispering air through the pines. *They? Who is watching us?*

'Oh my God.' I cup my mouth. 'I saw someone peering through Brett and Sal's window before. Is it Edmund's biological parents?'

'I can't say anything,' she cries. 'And we can't tell the cops. But if you don't give me the money, that'll be the end of Edmund.'

Penny, 11.20 p.m.

We leave Geordie Bay because Barry, the island's old cop, says we need a plan. He's no higher than Wallis in rank, but his age, experience on the island and demeanour demands a level of respect that Wallis seems to respond to. I don't. The man is arrogant, an old wanker who I can imagine never lasted in a marriage because he drinks and farts too much and spits out derogatory comments. Maybe he doesn't. I haven't heard him say anything disrespectful. But he's hinted at my bad parenting, he dresses like an Australian cliché, and he continues to avoid my questions like he doesn't suffer fools. And I'm no fool. I'm a panicked mother, trying to remain composed, smartly realising if I show my true feelings, they won't permit me to search here with them. So, I don't like him. Even if he's helping to look for Edmund. I asked if he has children, he says he doesn't, therefore he doesn't understand the intensity of emotion one experiences with their offspring. When Edmund has a headache, I know to feed him 5 ml of paracetamol and to lay a cold flannel on his forehead. He won't want bright lights, loud noise or pungent smells. He'll want to rest until the painkillers kick in. This man knows nothing. How can he earnestly search for a kid without any emotional attachment to him?

That's why when Barry says we've had enough in one bay, door-knocking, scouring the beach and sand and rocky cliff, disturbing partying families who sit on their balconies with beer bottles, bathers and hanging towels flapping over the railing, presenting his photograph to the pitying faces, asking them to contact the station if Edmund shows up, I don't believe him. It's not enough of anything. I could spend five hours in this bay and still not be satisfied.

I hate that this bay is on holiday. I hate their drifting laughter. I hate the water and moon on it, portraying a picturesque setting. *What if it was your kid?* I want to yell at the mother who I glimpse quickly checking on her sleeping baby. I'm envious of this party, this family, their sunburnt, peeling shoulders and reggae music. This was us only four hours ago. And I want to return to that moment.

Instead, we're stuffing our bodies into the ute and Wallis is starting up the engine and I'm no longer in the front, I'm in the back beside the constable, whose starchy uniform is scratching my arm.

'Once we've got a plan, the guests can be useful,' he tells Wallis. 'There's no point in random searching. We need a coordinated grid-pattern approach to save time. Most of these people have probably never even visited the island. The toffs prefer to travel to Europe than their own backyard.'

He's talking about my guests, referring to me and Kav as snobs, and I'm starting to get beyond tired and cranky. We're travelling along the ocean. It's calm when I expect it to be choppy.

'That's true actually,' Wallis chuckles. 'I've only been here a few times myself.'

'See? You need a true local to show them around.'

This casual chit-chatting makes me grit my teeth. The laughter from Wallis, the disregard for what's happening. The constable beside me smells of stale coffee and spray-on shampoo and the female constable is a mute. I lower the window, breathe in the salt and sigh.

'Well, I grew up here,' I tell Barry.

'Yeah, but to live here. To know the island, the visitors, the way they think. I didn't end up here for no reason. You lot treat this island like a nightclub. Nah, it's a lot more than that. It's a sacred place.'

My heart thumps. 'You lot? You mean *me*?'

'It's become a party island for rich families who can't be arsed caring for their kids—'

'Let me out,' I snap at Wallis.

Wallis glances back at me. 'No, wait. Barry, I think that's a tad harsh, considering.'

I jiggle the door handle. If he doesn't stop the car, I'll jump out and graze my knees and hands and palms and face, but I don't give a shit. I'm not sitting in this confined space with this bastard. The car is only allowed to go thirty kilometres an hour at most. It's not dangerous. I'm hopping out. I open the door and it swings out, bouncing on the hinges.

'Just wait, would you?' The constable grabs my arm and Wallis slows to a stop.

I unbuckle the belt and jump out, tears starting to swell. And I start running. The door thuds behind and the car rolls up beside me. I hear the window whirring down.

'Penny, please come back in,' Wallis calls from the driver's seat. I keep running. Past the ocean, the dark boats, towards the giant hill of spinifex. I can run forty kilometres and I have done before. I'm not afraid of running. 'That's not what Barry meant, did you, Barry? You didn't mean Penny.'

I hear a grunt and I squeeze my eyes until a few tears drop out. But I keep running. Up the hill now, and I'm puffing more from anger.

'I am a good mother,' I yell, looking onwards up the dark road. The car lights detail the curve of the hill, the steep incline. 'A *really* good mother.'

'We know you are,' Wallis says.

'No, you don't.' I stop with the ute and point my finger at Barry, who sits like a smug bastard, his chin jutting out, his eyes in front. Chauvinist. Never had a woman pointing at him. Or maybe he has. His mother. Maybe that's why he hates mothers. 'You don't know anything about me. And that's why this man here sits in front and judges. Because he knows nothing.'

A few seconds go by and the spinifex beside me rolls across the road like tumbleweed in a western. The car ticks and the constables in the back wait. Barry can apologise and then we can move on. But until he does, I will stand my ground.

'Do you want to find your son, or not?' Barry mutters, folding his arms.

I don't take it as an apology, nor a sign of regret. But he mentions what matters most and what matters most is Edmund. So, I open the car door and squeeze back into the warmth of my seat, brimming with anger, brimming with fear. Someone's caught me out. Someone knows the truth of what I run from.

Eloise, 11.20 p.m.

Rosie stands before me, tears dripping on to her big toe. Fuck. 'They'll kill Edmund and it'll be all my fault again, just like before,' she says. 'Mum will disown me for good this time.'

I have no idea what she's talking about, *my fault again* and *Mum will disown me for good* and *this time*. A ringing in my ear has me wobbling slightly. And she's never told me what happened between the two of them. But I know a serious person when I see it, and Rosie is dead serious about dobbing me in. I see it in her eyes, scattered with fear, unknowing where to focus. She's left me standing on a step with the weight of the world on my shoulders. She's handed me an ultimatum I'll have to agree to. And does she care? I don't think so. But she's scared, with full black eyes, and now crying. Surely she must realise what she's doing.

And here I am, swaying slightly, grabbing a trunk of a pine tree for stability. I'm stuck. And poor Edmund. Who has taken him? It must be the parents.

'Who's *they*? Who took Edmund, Rosie?' I shuffle forward, reaching for her. 'They're threatening you. And perhaps you helped them take Edmund,' I say ever so quietly, going to reach her dangling arm. She's like a ticking bomb, about to wreak havoc on my life, my future, the future of my kids, my husband. I can't let her do this.

Once she realises my hand is holding her wrist, Rosie viciously pulls back. 'You really think I'm going to tell you, Eloise?' she blasts. 'This will be my fault.'

The way she uses my name, as though she's the mature adult and I'm the child, trying to get me to understand the bigger picture, slaps me across the face. And now I do understand. Someone has kidnapped Edmund and Rosie is a part of this.

She's sobbing into her hands, but I tell her to shush, because I don't want anyone hearing. Does she understand this situation we're in, that she's now dragged me into? There are cops everywhere and everyone on this island is searching for the same kid. And now we're a part of it. *I'm* a part of this. Fuck.

'Do they know who I am?' I cringe, waiting for her response. She nods. 'They know my name?'

'Yes. They know you've got money.'

Which means if and when these people get arrested, they'll not only blab about Rosie, they'll blab about me. I'll be called in for investigation. I don't know what to do, but I lower my hands and nod. To appease her? I'm not even sure what I'm agreeing to. The fifty thousand? How will I do this? Scott controls everything. I get paid an allowance, a decent amount that I keep in the safe at home, but I don't have fifty thousand dollars just lying around. There's probably a few hundred, max, in my purse.

'Okay,' I say. How long can I bluff? Rosie stands upright, shoulders back, and stops sniffing. 'Okay,' I say again.

'Yes?' She gives a nod, wiping her eyes, like a kid throwing a tantrum and finally getting the lolly.

I close my eyes. 'Yes.'

'You can do this?'

'Only if you tell me who has taken him.'

She shakes her head. 'I can't do that.'

There has to be another plan, another solution. I don't have the means to do this. But there are people riding back up the hill, a rumbling threat of voices. They see this, they hear this, I'm done. Chewing my bottom lip so hard my eyes water, I nod.

'Fine, I can do this,' I lie. 'We'll get Edmund back.'

Eloise, 11.44 p.m.

When the group returned, I made certain I loitered by Rosie, hoping my presence would prevent her blabbing. And it's only now Scott's left the villa again, after stopping for a quick drink and a mouthful of ham, cheese and crackers, that I can experience the weight of this without anyone witnessing. To maintain composure and swallow up the secret we're keeping is too hard to handle. Eventually, the pressure has to escape. And I need to let it.

Rosie's run back to Penny and Kav's villa and I'm pacing the villa lounge room, rubbing my pounding temples as I figure a way out of the disaster she's put me in. I've allowed myself a cry, a pathetic muffled one in a damp bathroom towel, sliding down the wall in a heap. I don't want the kids to wake and hear me, but it needs to come out.

Pouring myself a large glass of white wine – Chardonnay, wooden and oaked – I then take three gulps of it. Its acidity burns my throat, but the effects should soon numb this tension. There's no pot left, no drugs, and I'm itching to soothe myself. On the way back from searching the lighthouse, I made sure I used the public toilets to flush the contents. There are police all over and eventually guests will be interrogated and searched. The impact of wine will have to do for now.

As soon as Penny and the others return, it'll be back to pretending nothing's happened. Only Edmund. Edmund missing, and I'm a concerned friend. I'll have to relocate the worry over my jeopardised life to the worry over Edmund's. Which I am, deeply concerned for his welfare. It must be his biological mother, but then who was the man at the window? The father? A party guest? Someone living on the island?

I don't know how he got taken without anyone noticing, and I also don't wholeheartedly blame the immature callousness in Rosie. Her rational brain hasn't developed, she's terrified and rightly so. At her young age, she doesn't comprehend what she's doing. However, her immaturity is what makes Rosie more dangerous, more prone to slipping over the edge with her stress showing in her high-pitched voice, the fear over her brother's life, and the guilt over not caring for her brother. Not me. She couldn't give a fuck about me. I know we're in deep shit. I know how bad this is. I'm old enough to foresee.

Eloise, 11.54 p.m.

The road's become a restless swap-meet as party guests, police and now Penny and Kav consider their next step. It's not ideal, this crowded road, bikes leaning up against the walls, the dim street-lighting, and our lead detective, Wallis, telling the young island constables to prepare their police station for incoming investigators.

'It's where we'll need to conduct interviews,' Wallis tells his colleagues, and I tighten, biting my thumbnail. Interviews means interrogations and blunders. Rosie meets my eyes, and I can read them like a private diary. *Don't tell. Don't say a word. Act normal.* I look away.

I have a plan I haven't told Rosie yet and I can't establish whether I feel relieved about it, or more apprehensive. My plan is to get Edmund back without anyone knowing, so I won't have to transfer the fifty thousand dollars. She won't know that's the reason I'm planning it, I just have to make her realise it's achievable.

Rosie's on the wall, holding her legs, and I can already picture her yelling at me for lying. *I don't have fifty thousand dollars. Well then, say goodbye to your family.* This makes my gut wrench with nausea, makes my headache start up again. She has to agree. I have to make her agree. I have to assure her that it's possible. But first I need to discover who took him.

The only assurance I have is knowing that while we search, so too will everyone else. While we frown, fiddle with our hair, bite our nails, so too are the group. We won't look suspicious; we won't look out of place. We just have more riding on this than anyone else does. We know Edmund's been kidnapped. We know Edmund hasn't wandered. We know far too much. But I don't know who's taken him and that's the piece I need to get Rosie to admit to. Full disclosure, or no money.

I swallow, flicking a glance to Scott, who's in need of a shave and hair-brush. If only he knew the shit I'm in. *I'm doing this for us, Scott.* I want to take his hand and hold it the way Penny and Kav are holding theirs, their fingers bound in a tight secure lock of love. I lock my own hands together and squeeze. He never should have married me.

We're being briefed by Detective Wallis, a man who arrived with two other plain-clothes detectives and a group of uniformed cops. They've flown in from the mainland. But I don't know cops and I don't know their business. All I know is that once upon a time, I used to avoid them. Unfortunately, here I am once more, a lying, guilty accomplice, knowing *precisely* what's happened to Edmund. And now I feel like I can't mention the man who was sneaking around Brett and Sal's, because what if he's the kidnapper demanding the fifty thousand?

'We're all in this together,' Detective Wallis keeps saying. 'It's look out and watch, and I mean for anything. Things you may not have noticed before. This island needs to be on high alert.'

He doesn't say suspicious behaviour, people acting flighty, abnormal movements, but we all know that's what he's referring to. Apparently, a child of Edmund's age usually only disappears within one kilometre of their home. Is this a hint that Edmund's been abducted? Are police considering this yet? No one is mentioning the obvious, so I fall back beside Scott, picking my thumbnail, ignoring the palpitations that keep jerking my pulse from fast to slow, irregular to normal. I've never felt so out of my body and I'm certain Rosie feels the same. She's sitting on the low wall, sleeves covering her fists and biting on her shirt, creating a hole in the fabric. But Rosie *gets* to act like this, because she's a teenager and they always act guilty and awkward.

There are other things being passed around too, such as colour-coded island maps, and photos of Edmund that have been printed in sepia tone. He already looked like a missing person picture prior to tonight. The dark hair, the solemn face, the unsmiling eyes. His face belongs on this poster. Why do they always pick the worst photos anyway? Not the kid who's cute and smiling. No, Edmund's photo tells a story. It says, *help me, I'm already as good as dead and I'm just as scared as this photo suggests.*

'We get that it's late and you're tired,' Wallis says. Although he looks fresh and crisp, like he's going for dinner in the city with his partner. 'More will be done as soon as that sun comes up, but we need to keep positive. We will find Edmund—'

'You sound so certain,' Georgia interrupts.

'I am.' The detective gently grips the old man standing next to him on the shoulder. 'We've got Barry Mullins.'

At first glance, I'd guessed the old man was a holidaymaker, a neighbouring guest. The way he's dressed had me assuming he wasn't anyone Penny or Kav should know. Thick plugger flip-flops, wiry white brows, singlet and parachute-fabric shorts.

And that's when it arrives, like a court order in the mail. I *do* know him. And he knows me. I slink further behind Scott and clench my toes. Fuck.

'Barry's the island's longest-serving cop and resident,' Wallis tells us. 'He knows the island well. He's seen it all.'

And I believe him. Julie mutters something about boats. Something about sailing off. And Barry overhears.

'Boats have been checked, love.' Barry speaks with a drawling Aussie accent, just like I remember. He tucks his swollen hands in his pockets. 'We know some of the boaties really well. Boaties who've lived here their whole lives. We've spoken to them.'

'There are others we aren't too familiar with,' Wallis adds. 'Those have all been checked out.'

Penny's chewing her lip and staring at her feet. How many of the guests are suspecting abduction? Does Penny believe Edmund's been kidnapped? And by whom, his biological parents? Wallis's voice diminishes as I stare at the pine cone at my feet. This is a seed that must be planted. His parents have come. This is the seed to steer them away from me and Rosie. Resting on the wall beside Scott, I avoid Barry's direct eye contact and try to breathe normally. Barry's presence is another dilemma I can't handle. It's going to be like putting out spot fires. When I feel Scott's hand on my hip, his unexpected affection towards me makes me want to cry.

'The more people searching, the quicker he'll be found.' Wallis ends his monologue and the questions start up. The crowd is restless and paper maps flap in the cool midnight breeze; they want to keep looking, but they also want answers.

'Do you think he's wandered and fallen asleep?' Brett asks Detective Wallis.

'We're hoping.' A short smile.

'Could someone have taken him?' Georgia asks. She suddenly appears frail and older. I imagine her looking like this in her coffin. Grey, wrinkled, without lipstick. I wish she hadn't asked this particular question. 'After all, if he hasn't been found with all of us searching . . .' She trails off and William massages her shoulders.

'There's nothing to suggest he's been taken, but we keep an open mind,' Wallis says. 'That's why we're looking at CCTV footage from the pub and general store and we're door-knocking along the bays.'

'When will you bring the dogs over?' William asks. 'Wouldn't it be quicker and easier to find him with them? I feel like we're wasting time here.'

'More resources will be arriving if we see it as necessary.'

'What resources?' William barks. 'Water police?'

'They're already out there.' Wallis nods to the bay. 'They've been checking around the rocks and beaches, but again, it's much easier in the daylight.'

So then where has Edmund been taken? I look at Rosie chewing her sleeve. Only she knows the truth. And I'm sure this flurry of questions, the anxiety in everyone, is eating her alive.

'Helicopters?' William continues, growing louder. 'Search and Rescue?'

'Most of these cases end in the child being found. Most children get lost and fall asleep,' the detective says. 'But every resource will be employed at dawn if necessary. The ferries will be cancelled, no one will leave this island until we've found Edmund.'

'For now,' Kav cuts in, and he steps away from Penny. He eyes each of us. 'We've got fifty guests, holidaymakers wanting to help and the police. We'll find Edmund if we all work together.'

When Penny suddenly stumbles beside Kav, crouching and holding her face, he quickly bends to support his wife. Georgia tends to her frail, tired and frightened daughter-in-law and I hate that I know about Edmund and there's nothing I can say to Penny. Rosie turns away, unable to face her mother's strain, because this poor woman is about to break. But I wait for Barry to hop back into the ute, wait for his attention to be redirected. And then I can go and support Penny like I want to, without the island's eyes on me.

Penny, 11.59 p.m.

It was only a stumble, a wobble against Kav, initiating a crowd of people to fuss. Brett swings around to me, Kav pulls me up. And I'm known to faint from time to time from heat, exhaustion or stress, particularly during the first trimester of pregnancy, but this was nothing.

Wallis has ordered everyone to join groups, pick a section from the map and search for Edmund in a deliberate fashion, rather than aimlessly riding around, calling his name.

Rosie has stormed off into our villa and I don't have the energy or patience to follow her. She needs to feel guilty about not caring for Edmund the way I wanted her to. I can deal with her later. Our guests are joining forces and now they're urging me to rest. I'm pregnant, remember? Like I don't know this. They're telling me to rest in Georgia's room at the hotel, with her there for comfort and company. It's Eloise who's begging me. She'll take me there herself. She jokes about dinking me on the back of her bike. I force a tired, fake laugh and she tells me she'll wake me later, around 3 a.m., when it's closer to dawn. She tells me she'll personally come and wake me, that she probably won't even have to, because Edmund will be found by then. I think she's trying too hard to be nice.

'Eloise is right, darling.' Georgia rubs my arm up and down in soft grasps, as though I'm dough to make cookies. It feels good and I lean into it. She looks just as exhausted as I feel, but I imagine I'm looking worse. Mascara running down my cheeks from crying, face red and dehydrated. Still, I'm betting Georgia would like to rest her weary limbs with me. But I can't be tempted. Edmund needs me. I'm his mother.

'I can't.' I shake my head, gazing back down at the map. 'I don't want to stop looking.'

'Honey, you have to think about our bub,' Kav reminds me, taking the map from my hands. It's his precious package and I've always expected he'd be more protective over me once we fell pregnant. But I'm not leaving, even if I want to collapse in a heap. Not until I've found my son.

'There are so many of us out searching.' Eloise smiles. But I care more than any mother. I'm not resting.

'He'd want to see me first,' I say. 'If he's lost and scared, he'll want me.'

'And we will wake you the minute he's found,' Brett says with a tight smile. My big older brother, always looking out for me. He's asked me why we haven't called Mum and Dad yet, but I've made him promise we won't until tomorrow. Edmund will be found by then. We don't need to ruin their cruise.

Kav kisses my ear with hot lips and whispers, 'But you almost fainted, Pen. We've got our hands full as it is, without you causing another problem.'

I run my fingers through my greasy, sticky hair. They need to back off. I know what I'm doing. 'I just need some water and maybe a bite to eat and I'll be good to go.'

William is already on his bike, joining Sal and Julie with a backpack on and a map under his arm. And if a seventy-eight-year-old man can ride his bike when he's tired, then so can I.

'How long have you been awake?' Georgia frowns.

I shrug. It was a long time ago. Five a.m.? I couldn't sleep much last night. I hold my breath and flick a look to Eloise, who's standing with her hands on her hips. Her hair is straw, tied back in a messy pony. She looks pale. We all look pale.

Kav pats my bottom. 'Just go back to the hotel with Mum for an hour. Just an hour's rest, how about that?' He's just as shattered, if not more. Hungover and seedy.

But it's not in me to give up on my child. 'I'll be awake worrying the whole time.'

He smiles. 'But at least you'll be off your feet for a while. Come on.' He leads me over to the ute, where the island police are climbing in. And part of me wants to keep arguing, keep riding, keep searching, but they're wasting time and Kav's annoyingly right. I could end up being a liability. He asks them to drive Georgia and me back to the hotel.

Smiling weakly, I climb into the back seat beside Georgia. Brett knocks on the roof above my head, satisfied with my decision, and joins Sal and the others. Instantly, my hips loosen and soften. 'If you could make sure Rosie's okay?' I ask Eloise. 'She's disappeared inside our villa and I'm sure she's locked herself in there.'

Eloise blinks a few times. 'Of course I will. I'll be the babysitter and stand guard.' She then gives an awkward wink and steps back to allow space for the tyres to roll.

And then the door thuds, the noisy chatter dims, and our guests are no longer guests but hunters, riding off in front of the ute, torches glowing, backpacks swishing from side to side. And Georgia slumps beside me, groaning with relief, taking my hand and smoothing the skin over my knuckles. The pressure is soothing, calming and needed.

And it hits me then. Maybe I can't be the perfect mother all the time. Maybe, just occasionally, I need to be the one being mothered.

SUNDAY

Penny, 12.08 a.m.

In normal circumstances, this would be a setting to post about on social media. Georgia and William's suite is lavish and cool, decorated in pearl fabrics, with wicker furnishings, natural earthy perks such as sandalwood soaps, organic liquorice teas, local coffee and salted caramel chocolates. She instructs me to shower, and I do, stripping my clammy clothes off and kicking them against the deep bath. Under the hot beads of water, I lather my hair in lemongrass shampoo and burn my face until I can't feel the tears. And when I step out, I wrap myself in a fluffy white robe like I'm cuddling myself.

When I'm with Georgia, I feel homely, warm and safe, like I never want to leave.

She just has this way of transforming regular mundane tasks into cosy, satisfying rituals. A cup of tea isn't just a tea with Georgia's tinkering. Strong and hot, Spode cup and saucer with an embellished silver spoon, and a butter biscuit. Sleepovers at her and William's house come with their own traditions for the kids. Toast with real butter, cut without crusts and placed on their own plates. Treats after dinner, sprinkled with fruits, jelly lollies and biscuits. She cuts flowers on a Monday and spends time arranging them in heavy crystal vases that cast diamonds in the light. Sunday is roast dinner with all the trimmings and her olive-green apron tied in a neat bow at the back. Shopping for presents before Christmas turns into an occasion, not a nuisance. We meet for brunch in a city patisserie, where Georgia orders croissants with jam and baguettes with butter; we get our presents gift-wrapped, we have champagne lunch in a hotel lobby and then continue shopping well into the evening with coloured-foil-wrapped chocolates in the trolley, ready and open for when we require a sugary hit.

That's why I knew I needed to come here with her. To be looked after and babied.

Now, we lie beside one another on the king-size bed with, between us, a tray of herbal tea, oval chocolates, sandwiches with chicken, dill and curried mayo, a bowl of blood-red strawberries immaculately arranged on white china. With the double doors open, the ocean wind pushes the sheer curtains out like swaying ghosts. My damp legs bristle in the breeze and Georgia turns a romantic movie on very low, so we can barely hear the dialogue. I eat three chocolates, she pours me a steamy tea and I cup my fingers around it, breathing in the aniseed and sucking on the chocolate. It coats my tongue in milky sweetness.

'Thank you,' I breathe.

A pat on my thigh, a tired sigh. 'We'll find him.'

◆ ◆ ◆

I guess I had a problem. I guess no one noticed. I guess that's what happens when you pretend to be perfect.

My son, Harry, just wouldn't sleep. Wouldn't feed. Wouldn't connect with me in the same way Rosie had. She was such an easy, beautiful baby, full of smiles and sweet gurgles. And all of Harry's constant wailing meant my attention on Rosie was stolen. As my four-year-old daughter chirped outside in the pool with her father, Greg, diamond droplets spraying into the sunny sky, pink and purple polka-dot bathers dripping in summer delight, the inside couch became my prison. It'd developed a dip in the foam from my fat bum sitting there day in and day out, feeding Harry. Outside was warm and happy with Rosie. Plates of cut watermelon, radio music, rubbery sounds of pool toys being jumped on. Inside was cold, isolating, with a screaming baby. Sour vomit coated my shoulder, a lukewarm tea with skin on top, a cramping calf from all the rocking.

And time was ticking. Soon Rosie would be four and a half and I wouldn't get to be with her. Soon she'd be at kindy and we'd lose our time together. Our precious time. Of lazy mornings, pre-Harry, where I'd make her cheesy toast, cut in squares. We'd eat it together under the orange tree and plan our day. First breakfast, then music class, then a scoot along the river, then lunchtime nap, then Daddy will be home. Life was sunny, like the colour of Rosie's hair.

But Daddy barely came home until after bedtime now. And when I'd complain, he'd selfishly mutter something about being second to Rosie. So, when Harry came along, wailing and pink, needing to be burped every fifteen minutes, needing my every moment, Greg stayed away. I couldn't tell anyone that. From the outside looking in, everything was perfect. The television got all of Rosie's attention. And my mum. And Greg's mum. And Brett. They'd whisk her off me like *she* was the problem. Let's get Rosie out of your hair so you can be with the little man. But it was the opposite. I wanted to hand back Harry. I wanted Rosie in my bed for morning cuddles and bedtime stories.

Time was ticking, this is what I remember, the passing of time. Hours, days, nights, feeding, another feed, another burp, more rocking, Rosie going off with Mum, more feeding, the evening growing crisp, enrolment forms being sent off. Time just abandoning me.

But I couldn't tell anyone. The need to be perfect, to be loved by Greg, to be admired by the mothers' group, the playgroup, my mother who'd done it so well with me, came before the honesty of hating my new baby. I needed help, support, someone to trust. But how dare I complain when my life was so great?

Plus, I was Perfect Penny. Penelope Perfect. That's all I ever heard growing up.

And it's a label that's stayed with me ever since. That's why it became such a problem. Isn't that why most people turn to lying?

Eloise, 12.08 a.m.

And just like that, the road's silent. The wind rocks the pines and the needles scratch together, shifting above. Beyond this, the waves clap, seconds apart. The road sighs and I swallow a thickness in my throat. It's a hard lump and I know it's anxiety because I remember as a teen getting my throat checked. The doctors found nothing, but the other symptoms – the tingling arms and heavy chest – all pointed towards a panic attack.

I know what I have to do, and I don't want to do it. But with everyone out of our way, riding in their groups, maps in their baskets, torches in their backpacks, we have time to plan alone.

Rosie just needs to be convinced.

Inside, Levi lies in bed with one leg out and dangled, arms up, exposing a slight tuft of underarm hair. My growing boy. I wish I could keep him young like Coco, bottled up in powder, nappies and milk. We were so happy when we fell pregnant with Levi, as young newlyweds needing something more. When Levi came along, soft and pink and mewling, I needed another. But Scott was too busy working, training to be a better doctor, so I had to time our sex strategically. A quickie before Levi woke in the morning, before the alarm had him rolling off me, a quickie as soon as he crawled into bed, stinking of antiseptic and old coffee, a quickie in the shower with him complaining about being late for his exam.

After years of trying, it finally worked. Along came Coco. Was Scott happy about the second child? Not overly. His career took over, which consumed him. Passing exams with flying colours, moving up the ranks, being adored by the nurses and his old uni mates, that's what hardened his erection. Not me.

And this wasn't something I was used to. A drought in sex for a year. No, I was used to sex every day, sometimes four times a day when I was younger. You see, once upon a time, I came with a price tag, something to be paid for, desired and earned. What was once a deep-rooted shame became something to question. If men paid for me then, why can't I turn my husband on now?

Tonight, he touched me. There's that. And that touch is enough to keep me going. Besides, there is no other choice, I need to get Edmund back and convince Rosie. Old Man Barry's eyes lingered on mine a touch too long while I farewelled Penny. While he stared, rubbing his chin, I got the notion his brain started piecing together a memory. Summer 2003, an island bursting at the seams, villas and the campsite overrun with unbathed families, squatting friends, wedding parties screeching around on bikes with matching pink T-shirts, belated Christmas holidays. If he notices me too much, that will be the end of everything. This is the reason I've avoided the island for so many years. And my past has shown up like fate, pressing the mirror against my face, saying, *Look at it. Look at you. Address your shit.*

Last chance, otherwise you'll lose it all.

Penny, 1.13 a.m.

Georgia's snore wakes me and for a minute I have no idea where I am or what's happened. I just want to hang in this blissful dream state consciousness where nothing can hurt, where the sheets protectively drape my shoulders, and the pillows support my head. I blink. The lights are out, but the corner lamp is switched to dim, illuminating a fanned collection of home and style magazines. Another movie's playing, one I don't recognise. B-list actors driving through a snowy scene. I must have been asleep too long. An hour max, that's all I promised Kav.

The tray of food rests on the bedside table beside Georgia. She's facing away from me, the satiny sheets pulled up to her neck. I don't want to wake her. She needs to sleep, but I'm different. I'm the mother and sleep's a luxury. An overwhelming wave of guilt has my heart leaving its restful, sleepy rhythm. I reach for my phone and check the time. My battery is only on one per cent and there's a notification that's sprung up from an unknown number above Kav's messages:

Aren't you having a lovely holiday.

Holding my breath, I sit up and stare at the number. What the hell. I can't stop staring at the words riddled in bitterness. It has to be her. Pearl. It can't be anyone else. How does she know we're here and how did she find my number?

I go to call Wallis and tell him about the text, but Kav's messages are there, unread, and my battery is going to die on me right now just when I need to call them.

1:03am: No luck around our villa and road. Kav.

1:13am: Cops seem interested in the bakery owner. We're at his house.

Rob. Rolling out of bed, I push my feet into my flip-flops and hold my breath. Rob. It's Rob or Pearl. My heart picks up the pace. Was that Rob messaging me? Was that him liking all my photos on my social media? While Edmund's out there, afraid, possibly with a deranged person, I've been asleep and it's so selfish of me to come here and shower, lie back on the bed and rest, so utterly selfish.

'Pen?' Georgia's voice is croaky. She leans on one elbow and blinks away the tiredness. 'What's the time?'

I turn to her. 'They think the bakery owner might have something to do with Edmund. But I also think it could be his mother. I think she's come for him.'

Georgia sits up straighter and reaches for her glasses. 'What? What do you mean? He's taken Edmund?'

'I don't know.' I shrug the nightgown off and pull my clothes back on. 'But I can't just stay here. Kav said they're at Rob's.'

She flaps the air. 'Wait a minute, wait a minute, I'll come.'

'No, you need the rest.'

She swings her veiny legs out from the covers and waits a second, holding the mattress before standing. Her back cracks. 'Nonsense. I'm coming.'

There's no stopping Georgia. She opens the closet and I notice how perfectly she's hung her and William's clothing – folded trousers, starched white shirts and floral dresses are beside one another, like at a boutique. She reaches in the shelves and takes a fresh pair of tracksuit bottoms and a hooded cashmere sweater. I'm staring at her, only because I'm so tired my eyes don't have the energy to move. I yawn and wish she'd hurry. The phone's up to my ear and I'm dialling Kav, but he won't answer and then my phone dies. Shit. How am I supposed to know where he is or whether Edmund's been found?

'I always knew he was a weirdo,' I mutter to Georgia as I slip my phone in my pocket and drink the dregs of herbal tea.

'Who, the bakery owner?'

'His name's Rob. He's always had a strange way of speaking to me.' In other words, I found him to be sleazy, too interested in me, my family, our boats when we were growing up. 'But if they don't find Edmund there, they'll find other things on him.' Drugs, porn, other illegal activity. My father always told me he was bad news.

Eloise, 2003

It was summer, and this was the third time I'd been invited on to the island. Of course, we weren't staying in one of the front villas. No, they were booked out years in advance for families who holidayed together. Our villa was one of the back weatherboard shacks with the lattice veranda that allowed the heat and flies in. And if I cycled by the front villas, balconies hanging over the beach, families eating their cereal and toast as collective groups, I'd pedal harder and faster past them. That would never be me. That had never *been* me.

Frank, my older boyfriend, invited me here – no – *ordered* me here, and I was getting sick of it. The heat, for one, had a way of sucking the air from the island, smothering your limbs in sweat that dripped and soaked into bed sheets and against hairy skin. I couldn't breathe here in the summers, and yet the summers is when they came.

Boats unloaded stag groups, riled-up men who were here for the weekend to celebrate and go nuts before they lost themselves and their independence to their fiancées flicking through bridal magazines at home, oblivious to the fact that their soon-to-be husbands were going to have a last bit of fun. One last hurrah. One last shag. One last woman before they resigned themselves to fucking the same one for the next sixty years. That's what I'd hear when I'd arrive with Frank to do my bit for the weekend, serve the men beer, run drugs, be their ultimate 'party girl' while remaining hidden behind the lattice in case any families disagreed and reported us to the island police. But the heat. The sweat. It was hard to keep fresh and upbeat, on show. The men would hover outside the villa in singlet tops with bare feet, drowning their souls in beer. And once they knew that I was there, not only as entertainment and fun, for drinking games and flirting, but as the chick who carried the drugs, they'd line up like schoolboys at a canteen, cash in hand, ready to pay for their chips.

Frank loved it. He left the island cashed up and eager for the next time. And at first, as a naive and insecure seventeen-year-old, I think I loved it too. Or maybe he led me to believe it. The attention, the comments about my tight bum, my incredible physique, my smile, God, my smile. It drove them wild, they'd say. That smile will get you anywhere. I was fussed over, stared at with tongues licking lips and eyes following me across the room. Isn't this the purpose of a woman? Isn't this all that we're meant to be?

There was only one groom who didn't want me to be there. When offered, he blushed too red and got slapped by his groomsmen and when he didn't want me, the groomsmen did. He watched Frank like Frank was an alien. He also stayed out of my boyfriend's way. Frank was like that though. Beefy, intimidating, persuasive. I'm guessing the groom's friends were the ones to organise this party.

I remember watching the fair-haired groom outside while his friends laughed like hyenas, flicking bottle caps on to the road to deliberately pierce a bike tyre. The groom sat, almost alone and to the side as though he'd been coerced here. I could picture his pink-cheeked dimples smiling at his wife as he said 'I do' without a glimmer of doubt.

His leg jittered up and down as he twisted his beer bottle now and joined in on the laughter every now and then. And every now and then, I'd catch him staring at me. And not in the usual hazy, sex-driven way. He stared at me as though watching someone being beaten. A kind of shocked and saddened gaze. It made me uncomfortable. Made me arrange my hair over my bikini top. I felt exposed in front of him, like I would around a brother or a father.

Two hours later, when the men had gone to the pub for dinner and a game of pool, a policeman knocked on the lattice and told me to let him in.

'I know you're in there, sweetheart,' said a voice. I climbed up from the floor, dressed in a cool nightie, and stubbed my bare toe into a nail jutting out from the boards. I swore, then bit my lip to stop myself from crying.

I'd been caught. I'd be kicked off and Frank would be pissed off. I opened the wooden door, and a policeman shook his head at me like a disappointed father. It was Barry, the island cop.

'Someone told me you're in here,' he said. The groom. The pink-cheeked, dimpled-faced groom. 'They're concerned for your welfare. Get your things, we're sending you home.'

'But my boyfriend,' I said, closing the nightgown across my chest.

'You mean the older feller with the tattoos? We've arrested him for drugs.' He shook his head again and I'd never felt so embarrassed. 'How old are you?'

'Old enough.'

'Too young,' he corrected me. 'This is a blessing in disguise, trust me. Get yourself cleaned up. You deserve a better life than this.' He phoned the police on the mainland and told them to meet me at the ferry terminal. Which could only mean one thing, I was about to be arrested or charged.

Barry waited outside for me to collect my small suitcase and dress back into my bikini top and shorts and then drove me down to the ferry with country music playing. Up on the villa balconies, smoke curled from barbecues and kids and mothers chatted. A pink sunset gave the water and sky a strawberry tint. Families rode past wearing helmets. Fathers took their sons fishing. And I stared down at my toe, weeping blood.

Penny, 1.20 a.m.

The staff on the island live in eco-friendly shipping containers that are spruced in black paint and decorated with click bamboo flooring. Once they've done their shift for the evening, they sleep there until the ferry arrives the next morning to collect them and sail them back to the mainland.

But Rob doesn't lodge on the island. Like Barry, he lives here with about twenty other people who have never shifted from the rock. For twenty years, they've relinquished city life to be at one with this landscape. Any normalcy or hint of metropolis has vanished from their character and that's why they don't see their homes as squalors of rust and mildew. They aren't fussed by the paper-thin walls, the pine-covered tin roofs splattered with blobs of bird poo. They can't remember what it's like to step inside a white-tiled shower, tasting water without metal. They are salt-crusted and worn, harsh and dry like this island.

'He couldn't possibly live out here, could he?' Georgia asks as we meander under sagging gums, following the light of the moon. The path hasn't been redone in fifty or so years. Shells, chunks of limestone rock and gumnuts now form a path through the darkest, eeriest part of the island. To the right of us is a golf course and to the left, the salt lakes. We're under a forest of eucalyptus and Rob's tin shed is out the other side.

'I've only ever been out here once, many years ago.'

She doesn't ask why on earth I would come here and I'm glad about that.

I don't see any commotion in front though. No voices echoing under the gums, no lights. Are they even here?

'Perhaps we should have gone back to the villa first, got our bikes and seen whether they were there?' Georgia suggests, almost rolling her ankle in a ditch. I grab her arm to stabilise her. Perhaps we should have done many things. Perhaps Georgia and William should own two phones, instead of sharing one, so I could be using hers. But when you're in this frame of mind, you don't think logically. And Georgia's right, we should have gone back to the villa, but we're here now and I want to see whether Rob has been taken away.

He's been hanging around too much, lurking in the shadows like an intruder, just waiting to take my child. He's always been seedy, so he fits the character of a kidnapper. Drugs, porn, booze. Always had an uncomfortable manner about him, chatting to me like we're long-lost friends. Too familiar.

'I can't see anyone,' Georgia whispers, as though afraid she'll awaken something evil.

It's dead quiet here. Through the gumtrees, Rob's rectangular boxed house is dark. My heart thumps. If they've found Edmund, perhaps that's why they're not here anymore. Perhaps they're medically examining him, feeding him water and salty crackers like they do on crime shows.

'If they've found him, they'll have taken Edmund to the nursing post or police station,' I tell her. 'Let's go there and check.'

But when Georgia states *I knew we'd find him*, something doesn't sit right with me. I thought I'd lost Edmund. Lost him to the sea, the sharp boulders at the base of a cave, the rip currents that tug the water out from the bay. And there's a haunting reason for that.

I still don't believe Edmund is ever mine to keep.

Eloise, 2003

I've been an imposter in our relationship since the day Scott and I met. Six months earlier, after Old Man Barry kicked me off the island, I'd deserted my whole life. Friends, habits, behaviour, flat. I moved back in with my mother, a waif-like woman, who chain-smoked, binged daytime soapies and lived weekly off a measly pension. My mother was the absent, neglectful type. She never asked about where I'd been for three years or who I'd been seeing. Had I finished high school? Was I working? No. She just accepted me back into her flat like I'd only just stepped out for milk. She asked me what I wanted for dinner, meatloaf or sausages? I told her I'd cook. This new-found me hated meat, it would be vegetable stir fries and salads from now on.

I'd left my no-hoper friends, my drinking, my drug-taking, my self-destructive behaviour, and joined a yoga class with three older women who believed I was training to be a teacher. They taught me how to hold a handstand scorpion, to interpret the Tao and to drink green tea to aid digestion. I got a job there cleaning the bathrooms and yoga mats. I worked at night and saved what I could, scrubbing sweat off the pastel-coloured mats with a coarse brush.

When Scott met me, he never asked about my 'teaching role' or my 'changing careers'. I was twenty, able to lie freely, and his medical training was far more important than what I did, therefore we carried on that way. Me not needing to work, me spending days at Scott's river apartment, cooking him vegetable pies and curries, practising yoga on the balcony as the yachts sailed by. I had a key to his spare car. And soon, my toothbrush had its own holder. This was a life I never anticipated living. Those families on the island, balconies hanging over the spiked grass, this was now me. My blessed life.

I vowed to myself I would never, ever, not in a million years would I ever return to my old life. Scott would never see that in me. Scott would only see what I aspired to become. A green tea, flexible, clear-skinned, white-nailed, natural blonde, soon-to-be-bride that I was.

Our honeymoon to Europe was a gift from Scott's parents. Five weeks in London, Paris and Italy. Five weeks in his Christmas break from med school. He'd be graduating mid-year, and the party at his parents' was planned six months ago. His mother had sent out invitations, booked the caterers and redone the guest bathroom. Things like graduating from university were a big deal to Scott's family. His sister was a dentist, his older brother already a doctor. They were a family of high achievers.

London was crisp, hand-holding weather, arms-around-shoulders weather, cosy cuddles in cafés kind of weather. Christmas lights blinked around us as Scott and I picked a spot for dinner, just down the road from Harrods and our hotel. It was a busy restaurant, with waiters dressed like penguins, balancing silver trays on their palms. They had no tables. They were fully booked. But Scott had a way of coaxing a table from the maître d', a glass of champagne from a crowded bar, a candle from the flushed waitress.

He just had a way about him. People liked to accommodate him. And he lived to accommodate me.

'Is this nice?' he asked as we sat at our round brass table by the frosted window.

The candle glowed warm yellow across his cheekbones. We held hands and he kissed mine and the huge diamond on my finger sparkled like the Christmas lights outside.

'This is perfect.' I smiled.

'Good,' he said and kissed my knuckle once more. 'Our whole life will be as good as this.'

And I believed him.

Penny, 2006

I wasn't perfect enough for Greg, wasn't living up to my title. And what would my mum or friends say if they knew? To be a perfect wife means a myriad of checklists that should be accomplished well before the husband comes home from work. You can't be slack in your chores, or appear to be lazy in slippers, even if your baby has been screaming for four hours straight. Before putting dishes away, you have to scrutinise extra carefully for smudges around the rim. There should be enough milk in the fridge for his coffee, a fresh loaf of bread ready for lunch. The bed should be made with seven pillows arranged like a Bed and Bath catalogue. Your pussy should be waxed, your eyebrow hairs plucked, your legs shaved to baby-bottom standard. If you're accomplishing this each day, only *then* can you say you're doing a perfect job.

But it was five to six and Rosie was still finishing dinner, a simple spaghetti with store-bought sauce and grated cheddar. Spaghetti hung down her fork, flicking red juice over her dress and cheeks. The dress Mum had bought her. Fuck. And the floor hadn't been vacuumed since breakfast. A peanut-butter crust had jammed itself under the stool. And my underarms weren't shaved, and the baby was *again* starting to fuss on the bouncer while the cartoons irritatingly screeched about kindness and respect towards others. There were diced onions still on the board, burning my eyes, and not enough pasta for Greg's bowl. He usually liked garlic bread, but I'd forgotten to get to the shops that day. I'd poured myself my fourth glass of red wine and my lips were stained, my teeth were stained, and a perfect round dollop of red blush had stained into my white dress. The one I planned to fuck him in later. He liked me in dresses. Said I had a youthful quality about me. But now I'd have to change.

And by the time we were in bed together with the baby asleep for all of forty minutes, max, and Rosie asleep with the fairy lights spinning around her pink room, I was exhausted, dry between my thighs and nowhere near wanting to be touched, kissed, thought of as sexy, nor youthful.

But I had to do it. Because we hadn't had sex since the baby was born and to be perfect meant pleasing your husband.

'What's up?' Greg asked, unbuttoning his business shirt. It wasn't a kind *What's up, my darling?* It carried a cold tone. Like I was already pissing him off.

'Nothing. Come here.' I reached out like a baby needing to be picked up and he softened into the mood I was pretending to create. Nuzzled down into my neck. I did not want to have sex with him.

It started with sticky kisses, below my ear, trailing down my neck to my leaking breasts. And the whole time, my jaw was clenched tight, gritting with unease and awkwardness. I was stiff, trying to relax, because he'd notice and not want me. He'd already been showing signs. I'd caught him wanking in the shower one morning. And then there was the secret porn-watching at his desk. His fingertips felt like spiders crawling over my body. His breath was hot, too hot, and my face had a way of turning left and right to avoid his lips.

And that's when he sat up, knees either side of my hips, and folded his arms across his chest.

219

'We're done,' he said.

'No, we're not.'

'You're not into it.'

'I . . .' I wasn't. But I needed his support, not agitation and disappointment.

'And you're drunk again.'

'I'm not.'

'Smell it on your breath.'

I turned my head away and he climbed out of the bed. 'We're done.'

But we weren't, not just yet. Eventually, though, if I didn't lift my game, we would be.

Eloise, 1.20 a.m.

Rosie's hiding inside her villa, cross-legged against the wall, staring down at her phone with a box of cookies in her lap. The villa's dark. Just her glowing blue face. She crunches loudly, like she's never been taught manners. *That* or she's too involved in what she's watching to care. When she sees me, she gasps, flinching so her head knocks the wall like a coconut.

'Who are you afraid of?' I start. 'Who's watching you?'

She drops a cookie back into the box, sucks her middle finger. 'Can't say.'

I crouch beside her and fish in the box for a biscuit. 'I have a plan.'

Rosie looks at me and raises an eyebrow. I tug out a cookie and sit against the wall beside her. Our elbows touch and I take two bites. I'm really hungry. Sick with nerves, but empty in the stomach. I act casual, in control, and eating this cookie is helping with the guise.

'We find Edmund before anyone else does,' I say, like it means nothing.

'Why?' Her breath is chocolatey. 'What's the point?'

I shrug, looking out the back down to the ocean. A cool breeze flushes the mugginess out of the villa. She needs deodorant. 'I was thinking about it,' I say. 'If you tell me who's taken Edmund, we can find them first and get him back.'

I wait until she's not looking at me before I offer myself a sneaking glance. Rosie pokes her tongue against her cheek while I chew my cookie, waiting for her response. I'm acting calm, casual and in control. Inside, my throat constricts. I need her to trust and listen to me. I almost have her. I see it in the way she picks her toenail, deep in thought.

'Eventually, your mum will find out what has happened,' I add for greater emphasis. 'And these people will return for more money, more threats.' I swallow the biscuit and brush my hands down my thighs. 'So, we need a plan.'

She quickly turns to me and she doesn't look happy. 'We *have* a plan. Fifty thousand dollars.'

I inhale and hold it. *Fuck.* I exhale and say, 'I can't get it for you. Not until you tell me who's taken your brother. Or maybe you don't want him to be found? Maybe this money is for you too.'

She scoffs, pissed off with me, and swipes her phone. 'Well then, you know the deal.' She's about to finger the buttons, so, snatching her phone, I ditch it across the floor, until it slides, banging up against the kitchen chair leg.

'I have our photo backed up, Eloise.' She pouts her lips for a second. 'And if you smash or damage my phone, how will I communicate with them?'

Twisting around, I press my hand against Rosie's mouth, pushing her head against the wall. It's forceful, but I'm not intending to hurt her. I just want her to pay attention and listen. She doesn't get it, but Rosie is as threatening to me as these kidnappers are to her. Teenagers don't care about adults and their problems or families, they only care about themselves. And I can't make this about me, I can't mention what I could lose if she goes against me, because making this about me will only fuel her fire.

But my little girl is over the road, tucked up in bed with her teddies and sweet dreams. She *needs* me. My cuddles and kisses, our river picnics and playdates. And my beautiful growing boy, who's as angelic asleep as he was as a baby. I need a future with him, to watch how he'll turn out, to be more present and attentive. To guide his attention away from technology and back into sports, to champion him and watch and support him.

And our home, I can't lose our home. Stone benchtops, fresh flowers, lap pool and shaded garden. There's all of this and Scott. I've worked so hard to get him back and now maybe, after all this, I finally feel like he's responding to me.

Rosie doesn't see this, and because of her age, she won't. But if she turns against me, I'll lose everything.

Her eyes widen, terrified by my sudden aggressive behaviour. And maybe she needed this all along. To be scolded for what she's doing. I lick my salty lips, as tears prickle my eyeballs. Her mouth is sweaty under my palm. I push her head harder against the wall.

'Tell me who took him, and I'll help you get out of this mess, whatever it takes.'

She blinks and nods and I release her mouth. It takes a while for her to compose herself. To wipe under her nose. And then she agrees and says, 'Okay, I'll tell you. But one word to Mum or the cops and they'll be seeing that picture.'

Penny, 1.37 a.m.

My toes sink into syrupy sand, cooling my hot feet. Gentle waves ruffle over my ankles. It doesn't matter what time of night it is, the lights from the mainland are always there, golden and twinkling. But because my eyes are swollen, my vision hazy, the lights spread as though they're zooming by. The boats are black, the breeze has dropped, and they face various directions, as if confused and needing guidance. All the unfamiliar ones have been searched, apparently. And now, their owners sleep. I hold myself and shift further into the water until my calves are submerged. I want to just drop into it. So, I do. Water fills my lap and startles my tummy. I gasp, holding my breath, and then allow it to cool and soothe me. My dress floats around my ribs like a jellyfish and I wonder how long it'll be before I hear the wings of stingrays flapping in the shallows.

Rob was not found with a kid. I sigh and throw a palmful of water over my face, splashing away the tears and tantrums. Gossip led us all to believe bullshit. I know everyone's just trying to help, but sometimes having too many cooks spoils the broth and, in this case, too many 'detectives' are spreading rubbish theories.

The neighbours beside Brett and Sal's villa are to blame. An old retired couple who are passionately eager about helping with the search. I'm sure she watches too many Agatha Christie shows. Their lives are so boring, they needed something like a missing kid to spice up their routine. Apparently, they spotted Rob walking the streets in the dark with a boy, who Rob later told police was his boss's son. It's been confirmed. That kid wasn't Edmund. And anyway, Rob was at our villa at the time Edmund went missing. I should have known it wouldn't have been Rob, but I grasped the gossip, hoping to have Edmund back.

Pearl and Edmund's biological father still haven't been found, which makes me think it's her. Them. In it together. Apparently, police are now searching far and wide for them back in the city. But they're here, I know it, the text they sent proves it.

Another palmful of water pools over my face, dripping down my neck and into my cleavage. Police have checked out the number and it's been sent from a city payphone. But what if they've already taken Edmund back to the mainland?

I've asked for some alone time and told our guests to go and get some sleep while Wallis, Barry and the island police take care of things. I'll stay here on the beach and wait until I see the police boats from the mainland arrive at the ferry jetty. They're coming in earlier than planned because it's real now.

Behind me, scrunching sand makes me turn. It's Kav. I thought he was with the search party. I sift the sand between my toes.

'Skinny-dipping?' He makes a joke.

'I'm hot. Bothered.' I don't want him to see my eyes. If he sees them, he'll know how crazed I feel. 'I'm waiting for the police boat.'

'They won't be here for at least an hour,' he says, standing beside me in the water.

'They may come earlier.' I lean against his hairy shin. 'This is an emergency now.'

'But they won't look in the dark.' His palm presses down on my head. 'I'm worried about you.'

'Don't.' I swallow. 'Be worried about Edmund.'

His fingers scrape back my hair. 'Are you just going to sit here in the water like this?'

'I just feel so fucking helpless.' I scrunch my eyes tight. 'Feel like no one's taking it seriously enough.'

I hear him sigh. 'There's only one plan, Pen, and that's to keep looking out further.'

'That is such bullshit,' I snap, splashing my fists into the water. 'Edmund wouldn't walk five kilometres away, not even one.'

'But ride—'

'You heard what Wallis said, most kids are found eight hundred metres away from their home. He's been taken, Kav. By boat. Back to the mainland by his mother.'

He stares out to the city. 'The boats on the island were told to stay put.'

'But it could have happened before we even realised Edmund was missing.' I'm exasperated now. 'It's his real parents. They've snatched him.'

I look up at him and he rolls his eyes. 'You're just too paranoid about them. You always have been.'

I stand out of the water, dripping like a waterfall. 'This isn't paranoia, Kav. This is feasible. You know how crazy they were and what they've threatened in the past.'

He laughs falsely. 'They are two obese derelicts who live six hours away from here. They wouldn't own a car, let alone a boat. And why would they pick now to take Edmund and why in this place? How would they even know to come here?'

'Because she's obsessed with getting him back and finding me.' I wring my dress out. 'We should've got a restraining order on them.'

'For God's sake, it's Edmund.' Kav raises his voice now. 'He's always been like this, never listening to instructions, always defying.

It's about fucking time he learnt his lesson. Eventually, if you keep on wandering off, you're going to get lost—'

'How dare you say that,' I scream, dropping my dress.

'You know what I mean.'

I point to the end of the bay. 'What if he hasn't been taken? What if he's fallen from one of those cliffs, his body washed out to sea. You would feel really guilty then.'

Kav shakes his head and rubs his face, done with arguing.

Holding myself, I look away. 'I never should have left him with Rosie.'

'You know, you've got to stop blaming her for every one of your fuck-ups.'

My teeth bite my tongue, and I turn to my husband and slap him hard across the face, delighting in the retaliation. But it only lasts momentarily before my palm stings and I gasp, realising what I've done, who I've hurt. I didn't mean to hurt him, but his words are what burns. It's too late. Kav holds his cheek and shakes his head like I'm the biggest disappointment in the world. And then he leaves me standing there, alone, cold and shaking.

Eloise, 1.40 a.m.

Soon, Rosie and I will *both* carry the heavy cargo of a horrible secret. She knows who took him and she's finally ready to share her burden, to offload the responsibility on to me. I hate her for it, I can't stop glaring, and yet I need to know.

Her breath rattles as she sighs, speaking down to her hands in her lap.

'Nico, my ex, took him.'

I'm surprised. I guess I thought she'd say that she and Edmund's biological mother were friends. Or perhaps Brett, Penny's brother, did it for some sick reason. Or even a party guest I haven't noticed yet. But her boyfriend? 'The one I saw you with here?'

She nods. The second I saw Rosie and her boyfriend, Nico, out the front at the wedding, his tattooed fingers grabbing handfuls of her arse, it triggered me. Black jeans and black Converse shoes. At first you'd think he was wearing a long-sleeved shirt, but an armful of tattoos inked his skin, crawling up to his skull. Her boyfriend, soon to be ex, she'd said. No, men like that weren't exes. They'd kill before letting their partner break it off with them.

'He's kidnapped Edmund, and you helped him?'

'No.' Rosie's voice cuts deep through the air. Final and genuine. 'Nico has a price on his head. He's a bikie and he owes money. This is his last chance. He won't let me get away with it, trust me,

I've seen him at the bikie club rooms.' She inhales and shakes her head. 'Worst of all, he said if police find out about this.' She stops. 'Mum will be next.'

Holding my knees, I'm shaking with this revelation. Rosie's involved with bikie gangs and Edmund has been taken, but knowing Penny could be harmed if we don't get the money to this criminal is another level of danger I'm not ready for. Dropping my head between my knees, I ask, 'How did he take Edmund?'

'He rocked up while you lot were all partying. Threatened to introduce himself to Mum and Kav if I didn't get back together with him and give him money that I owe him.' I lift my head again and see Rosie picking at a corner of fingernail. 'Edmund was hovering around and I thought he may have been listening. Levi was inside with his buds in and didn't hear a thing, so I told Edmund to go and get an ice cream from the general store. I didn't want him hearing and seeing Nico and telling Mum.'

'So, Levi never actually saw Nico?'

'No. I never thought Nico would take my brother. I just suspected something like that'd happened.'

It wasn't until Nico phoned Rosie earlier with two simple options: your brother's life or the money. I heard the conversation between them, the screaming agony of Rosie's voice.

He's taken little Edmund. But where? Where on the island would he hide him? Surely someone would have seen the two? He can't be that good at hiding a kid on an island swarming with searchers. I don't think he's taken him to the mainland, either, because as soon as he has his money, he's promised to return Edmund to the beach. That was the condition Rosie smartly asserted. Which means only one thing.

Surely, he must still be here. *He's still here.*

I nod to myself, staring out of the doors to the balcony and black sea beyond. If he *is* still here, then why can't we find him ourselves? What's stopping us? We don't need to give Nico *any* money. What we need is to get Edmund back, on our own, without him knowing. Without anyone knowing.

'Before you came over tonight, I saw someone about to creep into Brett and Sal's villa. It didn't look like your man. This guy was tall, really lean. And you said, *they're* watching. Is it only Nico who has Edmund, or is he working with someone else?'

She shrugs. 'I don't know. He could be.'

It's going to be harder to retrieve Edmund if Nico's got an accomplice. And I have to make Rosie agree to finding Edmund before I can even start planning this. Right now, she's still believing that giving into him by passing over a big lump of money is the only option. But I know the truth: I can't get a lump sum of money for her.

'Nico's never going to leave you alone,' I tell her, knocking my shoulder against hers. 'Once you give him the money, he'll be back for more. It's called power.'

'No, he won't.' She turns to me. 'He's promised to leave Edmund on the beach.'

'And then what?' I shrug. 'You think he's going to let you get away? He wants you for himself. You leaving him will be the ultimate betrayal. He'll keep blackmailing you. These men are dangerous and relentless, trust me. I've been around men like this.'

And that's not a lie either.

'You need to listen.' I take her hands in mine. They're cold and small. 'Trust me, Rosie, I know these guys. You give him the fifty thousand and he will be back for more. He has nothing to lose and everything to gain. You've fucked him over, you've made a bad decision and I get that, I get that you're scared. But you need to trust me. I can make this all go away.'

'How?'

My throat is dry. 'I can get Edmund back.'

'Yeah. By depositing the money—'

'No, I mean I can get him back without giving Nico anything.'

Her eyes track to the left of my face, as though finally contemplating my words.

'Let *me* handle Nico, Rosie.' I squeeze her knuckles. 'What he's done to you and now Edmund, he should pay for big time.'

It's like staring at myself at her age. Scared, submissive, losing control of my values, childhood and identity and giving it away to scum. She stares at me, finally listening, yet wary and quiet. So, I loop a strand of hair that's fallen in front of her eyes back behind the ear where it belongs. It *could* be working. She's not talking. But I need to deliver a statement so deep and convincing that Rosie will jump up to agree. So, I consider what she needs most, what all teenage girls need, what I lacked and needed more than ever. I touch her cheek with the backs of my fingers. She's sticky and hot, reminding me of Coco. I actually hate that Nico's done this to her. I'm sure she would have been a beautiful child, especially with a stable mother like Penny. I know something happened between them, I've heard the rumours, but she had the foundation of love, support and guidance – something I lacked.

'Can you imagine your mother?' I say ever so gently. 'God, Rosie, she will love and adore you for bringing back your brother. You'll be her hero.'

Her throat gulps and I hear the swallow. Jackpot. She doesn't need to say it, it's a clear indication that she's decided. A great conflict happened long ago between mother and daughter, something Rosie can't get over. But the mental image of her mother hugging and kissing her, *being her hero*, is the key to unlocking Rosie's black-and-white mindset. And this tender image overwhelms her. That's why she nods and agrees. And I embrace her teenage body tightly and smile.

'We *will* get him,' I whisper.

There's the photo that hangs over me, bearing down on my urgent need to find Edmund. And I can't mention it now in case she unpredictably changes her mind about this new plan. But I do understand one thing: if I don't find her brother and Rosie gets caught, then she'll readily flash around that picture and my whole life will be over.

Eloise, 1.50 a.m.

Rosie needs to sleep because she's still a kid. At that age, my bed-time was whenever I felt too tired to keep drinking with friends. But Rosie's different. She needs to be rested, to get herself back on track after this, to make new friends and paint her nails nude instead of black. She met him through one of her drug-selling friends, apparently, and he charmed her seventeen-year-old mind. Bought her watches and gadgets and everything he knew a girl that age would want. Part of me wishes Penny knew what her teenage daughter was up to. How much trouble she's got herself into. She needs to be guided back down the correct path, away from drugs, crims and bikies.

I leave Rosie over in the villa, rested and assured that we'll start looking for Edmund and Nico once she's had at least two hours' sleep. In that time, my job is to figure out where to look, and whether he's with someone else. A friend? Someone working on the island? A tall, lean guy? We assume they're still here on the island based on his promise to deliver Edmund instantly once he gets his money. To make certain, Rosie texted him asking for confirmation.

As soon as the money comes, will u let my bro go?

Yes

On the sand in front of the villa?

Yes. Tick Tock . . . 24 hours

Rosie decides to sleep on the couch with the doors locked, with the television playing old nineties movies that no one would pay to watch. I place a bed sheet around her and even stroke back her hair before leaving. I think she likes the sense of touch. I can tell by the way her eyelids lazily shut. When was the last time Penny kissed her daughter? I want to ask what happened between them, but now's not the time to get personal.

I leave to go back to our villa, worn and teary.

When Scott stumbles off his bike and pushes the villa gate open, he asks if I want to swap with him. He's been off on his own, searching for Edmund, and he's exhausted. He kicks off his flip-flops and they slide across the concrete. Even though I've been stuck here minding the kids, I haven't been able to nod off. For thirty minutes, I've paced this lounge room, drinking glasses of water, chewing at loose skin on my lip, trying to conjure up a plan.

But I'm not a natural problem solver. I've watched the occasional crime show and thriller movie; however, my personal connection to crime in the past means I avoid any glorified version of bad guys. I'm really in over my head here. Wherever Nico's taken Edmund, it's a good hiding place. The police and guests have been searching for hours now and with the emergency services and more police arriving at 3 a.m. from the mainland, Nico's either oblivious or stupid. Either way, I'm certain he'll be caught and when he is, he'll spill the beans on Rosie and me.

My brain is fried, my mouth dry, and my hands don't seem to stop shaking. So, I can't sleep, even if I wanted to. It's better if Scott does. He steps in, yawning, and I gaze over the road to Penny and Kav's dark villa.

I promised to wake Rosie at two thirty. I promised I'd have a plan. But I have nothing. Just an aching head and stinging lip. Maybe it's exhaustion settling in, tilting me off guard and murmuring to Scott like we're happy. I need companionship and a shoulder to cry on. My ideas and thoughts are rambling in circles. I wish I could confess to him.

'You should lie down,' I say, brushing my hand over his abdomen as he walks in. Normally we'd tiptoe around one another, avoiding our skin like fire. But tonight, I'm not worried about touching him. My husband. He doesn't even tense, or suck his stomach in. Like me, Scott's drained and overwhelmed.

'Might take the couch.' He ruffles his hair before slumping down, legs out and straight. I pour a big glass of water, add in some ice cubes and pass it to him.

'Here. It's got ice.'

'It's hot out there. The breeze has stopped.' He takes it off me. 'Thanks.'

The ice rattles and chinks against his teeth. He slurps it all down and I refill it.

'Any luck?' I ask, passing him more.

'Thanks,' he says again, and he drinks half and stops so the water shimmers over his top lip. Stubble grows below his nose. He looks rough, manly and sexy. 'It's funny, you know. I don't want to be the one to say it, but I think something bad may've happened to Edmund. I don't think he's asleep somewhere. I think we would've found him.'

'I agree.' I swallow and watch as he downs the glass. Once he's finished, I take it off him, setting it on the dining table. Scott flops on to the couch and rests his hands on his chest. I hate that I'm lying to him. I pinch my lip between my fingernails.

'I reckon the cops think so too.' He closes his eyes. 'But they don't want to alarm Kav. They're talking about the bakery owner.'

My hand drops from my lip. 'Really?'

'It's probably just hearsay, but someone saw him with a kid tonight.'

I frown. 'He was at the party with us.'

'It was later. Someone saw him after dark.' He shrugs and rolls on to his side. 'Or maybe it was someone else. Who knows? I haven't heard from Kav in a while.'

Only I know. That's the problem. And I don't want Edmund or Nico to be found. If they find Nico before we do, we're in trouble. If they're suspecting Rob, or someone else, then good. The more misdirection, the better. Process of elimination is the only strategy I've worked on while pacing this lounge room.

Nico doesn't strike me as the type to hire a hotel room, nor rent a villa. He came intending to kidnap Edmund to pay back his debt. He's not going to risk parading Edmund in public. No, I think he's stashed him on a boat. But with water police searching them, surely they would have found Edmund? And now there's Rob. What if they were connected somehow? Was Rob the tall guy I spotted creeping around Brett and Sal's courtyard? I'm straining to recall what he looks like, and yes, I do think he's tall and lean. If the police find Rob and Nico together, then Nico will blurt everything he knows about me, the drugs, the fifty thousand. He'll have kept all the text messages from Rosie, my name being mentioned. I stop pacing and stare.

Scott is quieter on the couch, eyes closed. It's horrible to be lying to him, but I'm doing it for our family. *I promise to never let you down again.* My hand hovers over his head like he's untouchable. He can either turn away or knock my hand back. But we've been talking, talking nicely, and this momentous occasion could be the glue to fix us. I lower my hand and stroke my fingers through Scott's thick hair, sucking in my bottom lip. And he lets me. There's no flinching, no rolling away, no slapping me back. There are only soft snores, escaping his parted lips, and there is only my heart, filling with blood.

I lie down beside him and he lets me. And then I accidentally fall asleep.

Penny, 2.31 a.m.

There's no sea breeze out here. The hills block it from cooling the barren landscape. So, it's hot, steaming, stinking strongly of sulphur and lake birds. During the day, the sun bakes your arms, thighs, as you pedal over melting bitumen, cycle past pink lakes and pray for the nearest bay. Then you can skip over baking sand, yank the sweat-soaked shirt off your back and dive into the water that's as blue as it is cool. That's the regular routine. Cycling up and down hills that make you gasp for breath, perspiring between shoulder blades, testing the water, the silicone sand in every bay until you arrive back to the villa hungry and thirsty, in need of a wine.

Kav's in front of me, hat backwards, pushing his calves strongly down against the pedals as we funnel towards a large hill. I lick the salt below my nostril. Brett and Sal are behind, and nobody talks.

They've found Pearl at a friend's house, pissed and sleeping on a couch. So, she can't be here. Doesn't mean she didn't send me the text from the payphone. Edmund's dad and her aren't together and police have tracked him down in Sydney. I don't know whether this news reassures me though. Yes, it means Edmund hasn't been taken by Pearl or his father, but where the hell is my son? Has he been taken by someone else, or is he simply lost and alone out here?

As soon as Wallis told Kav and me the news about Pearl, I wanted to ride out here with my brother and husband to search the place we often ride to with Edmund. He loves this big hill, so maybe this is where he's come with his bike.

We're taking this route while the others take theirs. Halfway up the hill, a track that can't even call itself a track winds to the left of us, displaying an old tree-brown sign without a name. Once upon a time, this track would have been named. Once upon a time, rocks and shells would have formed the path. Now, it's grass – growing shin-high; scrub – covering the path; branches – falling across the trail. It's not a path, track or trail. And yet there are many, many, many tracks like this one. Some leading to a bay, a cliff, a lake, to another road running adjacent. Some leading to nowhere. Most edge beside gumtrees, spiky bushes, salt-stained limestone. Too many hidey-holes, too many places for a kid to get lost, go missing, get hidden, get trapped, get hurt.

Brett hops off his bike first, kicks down the stand, and we all follow suit. Swinging legs, kicking stands. He crunches on to the path, head moving left and right, and I know what he's searching for. Dugites. This is their habitat. And if Edmund got bitten, he'd have half an hour to get to the nearest emergency department before the poison inks his veins. I hold in a breath.

Sal before me, then Kav, then me, holding my backpack, blinking the sandy puffiness in my eyes. I want to say, *why would he come along this path?* But I don't. Because you don't give up unless you've searched every cave, every cliff, every limestone boulder, every shrub, every lake on this island. And of course, the track fades like a memory. Trees arch over and shrubs grow higher. Who knocked the sign into the dry dirt? Who decided to build this track? Who decided to give up on it?

Brett faces us and gives a shrug. A determination spurs me on and although my legs are weak, ready to collapse, I won't give up on this son. So, I turn and walk back the way we came, gripping my backpack, ready for the next slog up the hill.

Eloise, 2.45 a.m.

Rosie knocks the lounge-room window with her knuckles and my eyes ping open, heart thudding. I must have dozed off beside Scott, because I'm met with a queasy hungover drop in my stomach. Dread over what's happened. Dread knowing it's not a nightmare. I need more sleep, more rest, but this problem isn't going away. When I raise my head off the couch armrest, Rosie motions to come outside and mouths the word 'quick'. So, I leave my babies asleep, creep back away from Scott, who's now facing the couch backrest, and gently push open the door.

'If your mum sees you awake—'

'Let's go somewhere and figure out what we're going to do,' she says, holding the gate open for me. 'When Mum comes back to the villa, I won't be able to leave.'

Her statement reminds me of her age, and how much she still values her mother's rules. She has round cheeks and long lashes. Still a child. A child who's facing a dilemma and needs to be led. I almost want to put my arm around her and ask her to tell me what happened between Penny and her.

'Come on,' I say. 'This way.'

We walk briskly, listening out for voices, guests who have returned from searching. I don't want anyone spotting us together.

'Sniffer dogs and probably Forensics are arriving at three,' I say. 'So, we need to think fast and hard about all of this. Can you think of where he might hide Edmund?'

'I've told you,' Rosie says. 'I have no idea.'

That's not good enough. 'They'll find him before we do unless you think hard.'

'*You* were meant to be planning.' She glares, quickly reverting to her immature tone. 'What happened to that?'

'I fell asleep.' I scratch the sweat on my scalp and ignore her insolent teenage tone. The blame. The whingy voice. 'But I *have* been thinking. You said last night he comes here sometimes. Where does he usually stay? The hotel or a villa?'

Rosie shrugs. 'I don't know.'

I shake my head and exhale into my hands. She's not helping. It's like she's deliberately given up. I want to shake her, but she steps in front of me, leading the way down the stairs towards the beach and undercover pavilions. There's a gentle breeze gliding off the ocean, cooling the sweat on my neck.

'We need to check the hotel, I guess,' Rosie finally says, as though that's the only option. 'Ask for a guest with his name. Assuming they even give it to us.'

'And what if he's used a fake name? He's not exactly going to store Edmund under the bed or in the shower, is he?' I look at Rosie and she shrugs again. I stop walking and choose a seat under the beach pavilion. I drum my fingers on the seat and say, 'Or does he ever come on a boat? Has he ever mentioned a boat and going out fishing, or skiing or anything?'

She shakes her head and we're joined by a seagull, squawking over its territory. We both sit there a while, staring out at the white boats, thinking. And then Rosie looks over at me, smiling. 'The ferry wasn't there.' Her face lights up and she claps so loudly, I jolt.

'What?'

'At the party.' She flaps her hands as if I should know what she's talking about. As though we're playing a game of charades and the timer is about to go off. 'When I saw him, he said he'd just arrived. But there's a ferry that departs at two thirty and I know this because it's the one we always leave on. And it wasn't docked at the jetty – it had already come and gone.'

I'm still trying to decipher what she means and how this is relevant.

She shakes her hands to expel energy. 'He couldn't have been on the ferry.'

I know what she's saying. I know what she means. I smile too, nodding. 'Which means he arrived on a private boat?'

'Exactly.'

'Are you certain he said he'd only just arrived?'

'Yes.' She nods positively. 'I asked him why he was here and how long he'd been here, because him turning up was so unexpected. He said, I came to surprise you and I've only just arrived. His shoes were all sandy, I remember now because he was kicking them up against a tree trunk.'

I want to jump up and squeal, but instead I stand, walking onward up the beach, fast, adrenaline kicking in. Rosie keeps up with me. 'It'd be too risky to hire a villa or room for the night,' I say. 'I knew he was still here.'

Rosie nods. 'And he'd have mates who'd lend him a boat.'

'I'm sure he does,' I say. 'No wonder he can leave Edmund on the beach once he gets his money. He's probably based right there off the sand.'

I stop directly at the entrance to the ferry jetty. There must be at least fifty boats out there on the bay. Is little Edmund being held captive in one of them? I chew the inside of my mouth, eyes inspecting each boat. Some are larger than others, modern, costing hundreds of thousands of dollars. There are smaller vessels too, eighties and nineties versions with ugly windows, creating sad and angry faces. Then there are yachts, their masts down and swaying slightly.

I swing back to Rosie and say, 'The only thing is, they've all been searched.'

'Every single one of them?'

'Apparently.' I shrug a shoulder.

'But what if he's switched bays. Gone over to Geordie Bay or something?'

'The cops said they were stopping movement.'

People on boats don't hibernate in summer. They dive off their duckboards and polish their windows and drink champagne and beer while sunbathing. The less activity on the boat, the more suspicious it becomes. The only way we're going to be able to figure out if Edmund is definitely on a boat is by spying on them during the day, making note of who's outside eating breakfast, who's cleaning their hull, who's fishing off the back and who's travelling to and from the shore. And there's one more thing.

'He may not be alone.' I frown, eyeing a boat with its cabin lights on. I can't be sure the man I saw at Brett and Sal's villa wasn't an accomplice. Or perhaps it was even Nico.

About one hundred metres in front of us, two silhouettes are at the window of a boat, walking around. They're the only ones with their lights on. Towels flap off their flybridge and a flickering light from a television tells me they're regular holidaymakers. Which reminds me. 'That old cop Barry said there are some boaties who practically live here. What if he's on one of theirs?' Rosie stares at me, not registering. 'Police may not look into theirs if they're reliable and well-known visitors to the island.'

'But then they'd tell the cops,' Rosie says.

'True. But we have to at least try.' I give her a smile. 'We'll start as soon as it gets lighter. I really think Edmund's on a boat.'

I tell her how we're going to accomplish it. Come morning, Rosie can say she's too sick to search, therefore she can keep track of the boats and their residents from the vantage point of her balcony. We'll take photos, track the activity, and eliminate which boats are holding holidaymakers and which aren't. We have a plan. It may not be flawless, but at least we have something, *something* to start with.

And this new information hurries my pulse into a quick, excited rhythm, leading me to ask her something I've been holding out on. In a small voice that won't go any higher, I ask, 'Can you delete that photo you took of us?'

And she stares at me and shakes her head, face falling from a great high to an obvious low. 'Nup. You're forgetting the deal—'

'I'm not. I'm really not, but—'

'Get my bro back and then I'll delete it.' She kicks the sand. 'Simple.'

And Rosie walks off and leaves me like a poor, stupid child.

Penny, 3 a.m.

We can't find Edmund and I'm tired, sick and needing someone else to blame. Unfortunately, Eloise is the first person I see, with my daughter, on the orange wall outside her villa. Hanging out like mother and child. Or teenager and friend. It's 3 a.m. and she's up with my daughter instead of telling Rosie to go back to sleep. What is Eloise's plan? To alienate me from Rosie? The night is stifling, my skin sticky, yet shivering with shock. No Edmund. No Edmund.

Rosie's doing that thing with her jumper, eating it, and I know she feels guilty about Edmund. And I can't help but smugly smile, because she deserves to feel bad, to own up to it, to apologise for not taking better care of him. My blood boils seeing the two of them together and when my blood boils, the fury I keep buried can only stay trapped for so long. Like a pressurised pipe, I soon have to release it.

'Go back to sleep,' I shout down the street. I don't care who I wake. They both look up at me. 'For God's sake, it's the middle of the night, and this isn't some party, Rosie.'

She jumps down from the wall and her sleeve hangs over her hand like she's Captain Hook. I've frightened her, them. They both appear caught out. Rabbits in the fucking headlights.

'I couldn't sleep,' she says when I approach them.

Eloise has a stiff smile. 'I thought it'd be good if Rosie helps us look for Edmund—'

'Why didn't you call me?' I snap at Eloise. She crosses her arms and opens and shuts her mouth. 'When they thought Rob had taken him, you failed to tell me, and I want to know why?'

'I didn't know—'

'Any *mother*,' I emphasise the word, 'would know to contact me.'

'Penny, I honestly didn't know. But even if I *had* known Kav said you needed sleep with your pregnancy and—'

'You're loving this, aren't you?' I smile, nodding at her.

'Mum,' Rosie says, attempting to make me stop or soften the tone or appease her new favourite woman.

'Shut up, Rosie,' I snap. 'And go back to the villa.' She hovers so I point and yell, '*Now.*'

Shoulders slumping, Rosie storms off, slamming the villa door behind her. It's a satisfying smack of a sound. I turn my attention back to Eloise, who plays with her necklace.

'Penny, I know you're really upset and—'

'And I know you're happy about seeing me like this,' I spit.

She frowns and gives a quick laugh. 'I have no idea what you're saying, but you're being really rude right now.'

'You're jealous of me,' I tell her, and she scoffs, perplexed, or at least pretending to be. 'You always have been. You're a shit mother and you love the fact that this has happened to me and not you.' She tries to interject, but I hold up a hand. 'All of a sudden you're the golden girl, doing everything right. You're even trying to get my daughter to fall in love with you.'

There are tears in her eyes when she says, 'How dare you speak to me like that.' She seethes, breathing heavily and stepping towards me, pointing towards my face. 'That girl is missing her mother, aching for you—'

'How do you know that?'

'She told me—'

'Told you what?'

'Would you let me speak?'

'No, I won't,' I say.

She quickly sighs. 'She's hurting.'

'Been trying to get the dirt on me, have you?'

'What dirt, Penny?' She cocks her head to the side. 'Do you have something to hide?'

The words form in my mouth, pushing against my urge to stop. I've upset her. It's clear by the water pooling in her eyes. But she's upset me even more with Rosie. I don't stop to hear what she says next. She murmurs something about *what happened between you two*, but I'm spinning on my heels and running, away, away, away from the villa, from Eloise, from my wounded daughter and my toxic, lethal words. I run past villas, under dying streetlamps, down the wonky wooden steps where I almost trip and fall. I clutch the railing and keep running until I'm down under the pine trees, palms scratched with splinters, ankles aching. When I hit the soft sand, I don't think I deserve it. It holds my body too gently and I am not a gentle person. I'm gasping for a breath that won't come. My chest swirls with tension. Sweat glistens above my lip and I'm bursting to cry, sucking it in, because I brought this all on myself. Rosie. What I did to Rosie. I crouch and let it come, because it can't be stopped anymore. My body is racked with guilt, trembles with a remorse that has me suffocating.

I hate myself. I really, really hate myself for not being a perfect mother.

Eloise, 3.10 a.m.

When I step inside the villa, Scott's still the same man on the couch, snoring, hands clasped on his chest like he's praying for us. I leave him to pray and close the bedroom door behind me, seeking space and solace beside Coco's spreading body. There, I lie, while Coco shuffles into my waist as though she's been expecting me. Mother and child bound by an invisible cord. And then, as if I were waiting for it all along, it arrives – an odd sense of compensation. I sniff Coco's sweaty, milky hair and kiss her forehead gently, leaving my lips against her skin. She smells of plastic nappies and rubbery dummies. I lie listening to her breathe and suck and I don't cry.

It's not Penny's fault. She's only held up the mirror to my face. Conflicted people can't stand to see what they are. But I know what I am, I know what I did to Scott and what I deserve. Rosie won't delete the photo. I'm really, really stuck. But this is my penance, and I'd known all along it would appear.

Turning Coco, I watch my darling sleep. *I promise to be better for you.* I stroke her chubby, sticky cheek. *You and Levi. And Scott.* But this whole predicament is my punishment.

Penny's hurting. She's disappointed about the false lead to Rob, but her words about my mothering cut deeply into my insecurities and now I'm scared. She's gone against me again. I'm no longer a friend. I'm now a threat and perhaps I was foolish to think we could ever be friends. Like a goddess befriending the devil, she'd soon see through me.

Eloise, 6.30 a.m.

There are croissants, two lattes, a bowl of grapes, and blueberry Danish pastries placed in the centre of the table, arranged by Georgia, who's ordered me and Scott to sit down for five minutes and eat. She leaves in a hurry, her and William's bike baskets filled to the brim with bakery goods, ready to deliver to Penny and Kav. She's become the mum of everyone, ensuring we all eat and rest before joining the emergency services in an island search for Edmund. I don't get time to say thank you. I'm stepping out of the bathroom, towel-drying my washed hair, body feeling cleaner and a bit more awake.

I'm trying to ignore Rosie's threat to disclose the photo if I don't get Edmund back. We have a plan. We have a plan. We have a plan.

My stomach growls at the sight of food and Coco and Levi are still fast asleep, meaning Scott and I get to enjoy this banquet alone.

The news blabs from the TV, a good distraction from the silence between us. Scott gestures to the table and my heart hurts as I face him. I need to fill this vacant space. I step towards the table and reach for the latte, un-pop the lid and add in two sachets of sugar. I use the plastic spoon to stir the froth and then press the lid back on, holding it up to Scott. It's the way he likes his coffee.

Two sugars. He's always had it this way. I cannot remember the last time I made him one. But it's there, as he takes it off me – a very subtle hint of a smile.

'Kav's parents have always been like this, haven't they?' I take the other latte and suck the hot coffee into my mouth. It's creamy and delicious and just for a moment I want to forget what's going on outside – the police, the dogs, the helicopters, the beginnings of media arriving after getting a whiff of this. I want to sit at this table with my husband and enjoy this breakfast and talk as though we're on holiday and in love. So, I sit and flick my wet hair back over my bare shoulder, cutting into a croissant. I don't want the kids to wake. I want to retain this moment. I feel myself holding in a breath.

'Jam?' I ask Scott.

He nods, dragging out a chair, and surprisingly, he sits opposite me. I remember learning once from the yoga instructor who trained me that life is all but a reflection. If you are kind, people can't help but be kind back. If you smile, they smile. If you frown, so do they. I feel it now. A mirror between us. Me scraping jam over the base of his croissant, me adding sugar, Scott sensing the sweetness and reciprocating. I suck the jam from my thumb and hand over his pastry.

'Much cooler today,' Scott comments. And perhaps he wants to pretend also. We're on holiday, we're happy and our children are asleep. It feels like a date and I'm tingling. I rip open my own croissant and butter it.

'I don't think we should come back here again in summer though. Too hot, don't you think?' I rub my lips together, noticing the ease with which I'm speaking. As though we have future plans together, holidays and family trips, and we always talk this way.

'Autumn and spring are better months. Better surf too.' He offers a small laugh and I smile. We still haven't made eye contact yet. Just me busying myself with breakfast and him chewing opposite me.

'Next time we should take Levi out surfing.' I finally bite into my pastry. Not that I ever want to come back. But I need to pretend for him. 'He'd love it with you.'

And it's then that we meet. My mouth full. I stop chewing. He gulps down his mouthful and wonkily smiles. His eyes are special. I remember the way he used to look at me. On top of me, inside me, staring with a deep intensity that can only be described as love. Imagine if he knows what I'm thinking? Or maybe he does. He blinks away and takes a swig of coffee and I resume chewing.

'Would you come too?' he says, eyes down at his plate. He presses his finger into the crumbs to collect them and my stomach swells with a deep breath.

'Of course.' I nod, trying not to tremble. I quickly glance once more at Scott and he's looking at me.

'Mumma,' a little voice mumbles behind. It's Coco, cuddling her teddy, hair blonde, ruffled and soft. Her cheeks are pink and creased. She's had a beautiful sleep. I move my chair to allow her on to my lap. Her bottom's squishy and padded as she wriggles to get comfortable.

'Good morning, my beauty.' I sniff her neck and she holds me.

'You had a peaceful sleep, didn't you, Cocs?' Scott stands and kisses her head. 'I'm glad someone did.' I feel his hand nudging my shoulder and I smile to myself. 'I better go and check on Kav.'

I nod, kissing Coco's warm cheek. 'I'll be over shortly.'

'No rush,' he says, collecting his coffee and his hat off the couch. 'Enjoy the breakfast.'

A gushing warmth spreads into the room like the first sight of sun after a long, dreary winter. No rush, he says. *No rush.* Accommodating me. Just like before. There's a fondness in his tone, a mellow lightness. It's not perfect and it's not like before – a kiss to the lips, hard and meaningful, a safety of knowing I love you and you love me – but it's a drop of renewable friendship. A connection. A moment I can never let go to waste. I now have more riding on finding Edmund than ever.

Penny, 6.45 a.m.

A blanket of darkness covers me and I don't know how to crawl out. Their voices are out there, timid and cautious as though they'll wake the bear if she notices them. They're burning toast and there's the bitterness of coffee. Toasted dough. One of the greatest aromas. They aren't disturbing me. There's coffee to be drunk, toast to be spread, showers to be had. Outside, the golden sun is rising over the mainland, spreading buttery skies over the island. Rottnest Island will live on. Minute by minute. Coffee by coffee. Hour by hour. It doesn't matter what's happened to Edmund.

Tourists will appear concerned, gathering by the general store and lining in front of cafés. A missing boy, they'll recount to other concerned holidaymakers. A widespread search. And they will discuss theories of kidnapping, possible parental abuse, and promise to search once they've ordered their long macchiatos and bagels. Then they'll find a sunny spot at the top of the town, where they will spread open their newspapers, cross their legs and enjoy their breakfast with the picture-postcard water views. They're not allowed to leave. They'll make the most of their extended holidays. They'll phone their bosses and families and pretend to care that they can't leave the island. The police told us. And then they'll resume flicking through the paper, glancing up every now and then as a group in bright orange suits walk past with the capital letters SES emblazoned across their backs. They'll mutter to their partners, *They must be here for the search*. And then they'll resume chewing their bagels, eyes zigzagging across the front pages.

I know how people act. Humans can be the most selfish creatures. I've seen it before and witnessed it first-hand. Concern followed by disregard. I bet most of our guests are pissed off and wanting to leave. They'll be jealous of the other islanders here, the ones who don't know us and therefore don't have to search. The ones who are waking to a gorgeous summer morning, meandering on bikes, planning their days.

My eyelids are heavy and swollen. The pillow's wet. Emptiness quickly leads to exhaustion. I've found myself bonded to the mattress, unable to open my eyes. It's better to sleep it all away, anyway. Better not to replay every detail of what I was doing while my son had gone missing. Scott on the sand, washing glasses, welcoming guests, being the perfect host that I am. I scrunch the sheet into my fist and a few tears slip down into my ear.

I only need an hour. When Georgia knocked on the door, asking if I'd like a tea, peppermint or lemon, ginger or chamomile, I squinted through the darkness. The living area light blinded me. The yellow walls were too bright.

'Nothing,' I said and waited for her to close the door again. 'Just an hour.'

But I know it'll be longer. I don't think I'll be leaving this room. This is what will worry Kav and Georgia most. This missing son is the link to my broken past.

Eloise, 7.15 a.m.

Rosie has texted me Nico's latest message: *Tick Fucking Tock. 19 hours*

And receiving it makes my cheeks heat with anger. She needs to delete this message and stop sending me more. No links to me, no links to her, no links to Nico. But I don't know whether she's following my orders and that dangerous photo taunts my memory. If she has these messages *and* that photo, then I'm more fucked than ever.

Coco's hair detangles as I collect it in my fingers and brush it down her back. This simple routine steadies me for a moment, counteracting the anxiety over the tremendous act I have to perform. Ever since Rosie came to our door last night, pulling me into her mess, I've gone through rushes of adrenaline, crippling fear, to this – a block on emotions. I think it's the only way the mind can cope with trauma.

Right now, I only have to focus on the wisp of hair, the silken ends, the brush dragging lines through her damp, strawberry-scented locks. Coco has been fed and washed, thankfully oblivious to the horror of the night. She's just wanting to get on with her holiday here. Bike rides, sandcastles, swims. And Levi sleeps in until ten thirty most mornings, so I don't have to worry about entertaining him for now. Scott and I have agreed to me keeping the kids here and away from the search. I can't very well go off tracking the salt lakes with Coco complaining in the buggy. I don't think Kav or Penny would expect me to either. Which is good. It means I can stay near the villa, walk the beach, snap photos of boats and eliminate the ones with usual activity. Across the road at 213, Rosie will be doing the same.

Scott comes inside with his empty coffee cup, cap shading his face, and shakes his head. Penny's stuck in bed and won't leave the villa.

'She's having some sort of breakdown,' he says. 'Kav's really worried about her.'

I frown, finishing Coco's pigtails. 'Is there anything I can do?' Not that she'd want me anywhere near her after last night's confrontation.

'Apparently, she just wants to be left alone.' He clears his throat and waits for Coco to wriggle off into the bedroom. Then he whispers, 'In the meantime, the police are starting to question guests about where we were when Edmund went missing. Are you good to stay here with the kids while Kav and I go?'

I nod. I anticipated the questioning, but it scares me. Means they're indeed starting to suspect abduction. 'Sure. Have the police found anything yet?'

'The dogs have,' he says. I lick my lips and pick at a grape. What if they're closer to finding Edmund than Rosie and me are? I crunch into the grape, accidentally biting my tongue. 'Apparently, they've discovered a strong scent down by the beach.'

Good. That makes the most sense to me. Nico would have put Edmund on his dinghy and taken him out to the boat.

'But because the kids were down there in the afternoon playing, it's likely his scent will be everywhere along here,' Scott adds. 'And they're saying that he may've walked to the cliffs and fallen. So, they've got divers going down to search the reef.'

I wince. 'I hope not. But what about his biological parents?'

Scott's brows pull together and he adjusts his cap. 'They've been found.'

Part of me wishes they weren't. At least having the spotlight on them for a while meant Rosie and I could go about planning without scrutiny.

'What about a boat?' I ask Scott. 'What if someone took him before we knew he was gone?'

'That's what I asked Kav. He said the yacht clubs back on the mainland have been contacted with their CCTV footage being checked. But he doesn't understand why someone would go inside the villa while the rest of the kids are playing and take Edmund.'

That's the missing piece that has them all believing Edmund rode out alone. And he did. But with Rosie's permission and money to buy an ice cream. How can no other person on the island have seen him walking off alone at 8 p.m.? How can no one have spotted Nico taking him?

'So, what's Kav thinking?' I ask, reaching for another grape. 'Edmund's lost?'

Scott mimics my actions and snaps a grape from the bunch. 'Kav said he's the type to do this. Wander off and not think about the repercussions.'

We're talking like before. Before Levi, that was the best part of the day. Me up at the kitchen bench, wine glass in hand, Scott flipping vegetables in a heavy copper pan, our favourite music softly serenading us, garlic and soy and ginger infusing our new home and the daily gossip rattling off our tongues. I'm determined to change it, to fill him in, to include him in my daily life.

'But how far can a kid ride?' I'm asking questions as though I don't know what's happened to poor Edmund, and perhaps it helps me to stay sane. If I remember I'm involved, I want to vomit. *19 hours.* Scott shrugs, crunching on the grape, and a group of bikes roll up outside our villa. The rest of the guests have arrived to search and soon we'll all be called in to be interrogated. Coco is on the floor, dressing her baby doll and mumbling incoherently. I hear her say Mumma, which grips and twists my gut. I cannot lose her. Scott steps out again and the sun disappears. And I cannot lose him.

◆ ◆ ◆

It feels shameful to be down here on the sun-streaked sand with Coco beside me, digging with her ladybird spades and buckets. Sand flicks over my thigh and I brush it off. Her little sunhat is a gleaming daisy and Coco squints into the brightness and finally asks, 'Where Edmund?'

'Good question, little one,' I say, snapping twenty or so photographs of the boats in front of me. I hover the lens over the turquoise water to the boats further out. The bay is flat like ice today. Zooming my camera lens in, I thank the latest version of my phone, allowing me to view and capture the names, the faces, the colours a naked eye wouldn't be able to distinguish. Small yacht with orange stripes has a man in underwear taking a piss off the side. He's older. Not Nico. Streamlined white catamaran hasn't had anyone outside yet. I make a note in my phone to check on it later. A boat called *Lucky* has two lovers eating breakfast, so I can swipe that one from my photo album. And it continues like this, a process of elimination, until I'm left with fifteen inactive boats who haven't yet presented their occupants. Sleeping? Morning sex? Breakfast inside? Or hiding a young child? Rosie, who's up behind me on the balcony with a bowl of cereal, is also keeping track.

'Look, Mumma,' Coco says, pointing to the sandcastle I built for her. It's decorated with shells, bits of seaweed and spinifex grass. Coco kicks it with her chubby foot and giggles.

But her giggling isn't distracting me. My phone pans across to the cliffs. A few divers bob on the surface of the ocean like seals. They're wasting their time and resources and I quickly look away.

Coco waddles off to the water's edge, where she collects a bucket. 'Look, Mumma.'

'I know, sweetheart. Clever girl.'

I zoom on to a boat further out.

'I want Edmund,' she calls from the water.

The boat has a black shade over the back. It must be quite old. A build-up of rust and barnacles spreads over the hull like a disease. This owner isn't boat-proud or concerned about its appearance, which is rare. I can't catch the name, with the wind direction pushing the boat towards me, and I haven't seen anyone on it. For some reason, I have a funny vibe. Most of the boats moored here are well maintained. This one is not. Why? Do its occupants only use it for quick trips, fishing? It doesn't look like a fishing boat. It'd be about forty-five feet long, but the black covering conceals the back of it. Why? Most boats are open, allowing in the sea breeze, sunshine and views. I snap a picture and lower my phone into my lap. I don't know why, but I feel like this one is a possibility. Far left of the bay. Behind the large yacht. Looks a tad dodgy. We'll have to swim out later. Night-time is best, when he least expects it. I don't know how Rosie will feel about swimming out at night, but it's the only way we can do it without getting caught.

Glancing up at the balcony where Rosie sits, I know that inside Penny is suffering. I can't even imagine how this must feel for her. That's why we have to get him back. For her, Rosie, and most of all, for me.

Penny, 9.38 a.m.

Most of the guests have been questioned by police and I'm starting to lose hope. CCTV of the general store frontage, the shops around the village and pub show nothing but sandy, salty tourists. No Edmund coming, no Edmund going. It means Edmund's probably wandered to the north side of the island. But according to Georgia, who keeps texting with news, the dogs didn't strain on their leads in that direction. There are fewer bays with villas on the north side, more scrubland, more dangers such as higher cliffs and choppy seas with a strong current. The helicopter hasn't found anything and after hours of scouring the island, the bays, the reefs, the water, it whirs back to the mainland to refuel. I've been slipping in and out of restless sleep, freezing with shock one minute and boiling with hot sweats the next. I've kicked off the bed sheets and replaced my soaking pillow.

Kav asked the police not to interview me yet. I'm too fragile, apparently. More than twelve hours since Edmund was found to be missing and I'm allowed to be fragile. It's not looking good. Yacht club and boat ramp CCTVs along the mainland coast are being scrutinised for any sign of Edmund. That can only suggest one thing. Abduction. Here. On this quaint island.

I bunch the blankets into my fist and haul them back over me. The ferry remains stranded on the edge of the rocky jetty. No one is leaving until Edmund is found. At least, until a trace of him is discovered. I squeeze my eyes and let out a moan. A trace. DNA. They've even checked out our home. Why? Do they think we have something to do with this?

Another helicopter's been hovering around too, the throbbing whine of it circling the bay, rattling the windows. Media. Hanging above us, reporting on my missing son. I pull the blankets over my head. I've been offered painkillers, sleeping tablets. I've received a knock on my door, an unfamiliar voice of an English woman calling me *Miss*. She's the island nurse, coming to check on me. I've told them all to go away. Water gets left outside the door, a plate of toast, a cold coffee. I want nothing. I only want Edmund. And then . . .

'Mum.' A voice, so distant it doesn't sound real. 'It's Rosie.'

Three tears trickle into the groove of my right eye. The neglected daughter. I can't bear this pain. She calls me again and her voice is diminished, young, riddled with a tone of guilt that leaves her words shaky, defensive, always wary.

'Come in.' I almost don't recognise my voice, deep and hoarse from crying. The door widens and a shaft of light blinds me. I squeeze my lids shut and she apologises. 'Don't,' I say. I've encouraged this ongoing apologetic nature in her. And now I don't want it. She makes me realise how much of a failure I am. How much a mother can screw up a child.

'Can I make you a tea?'

I lick my rough lips and blink my eyes open. She's shut the door and I can barely see her now. Only the outline of Rosie. But I wish I could see her. Once she was four and the love of my life. Where have all those in-between years gone? Our connection has dwindled, reduced to animosity, regret and guilt. We've been drenched in an oily substance where love can't stick.

'No, thank you.'

'Mum,' she says again.

'Yes?'

'I'm worried about you.'

'Don't,' I repeat.

'I'm sorry for Edmund.' I hear her voice cracking and I feel my body tense with control. If I let this come, this abundant grief, I'll never get over it. I've been keeping it locked inside and yes, every now and then it presents itself to me. But I'm good at sticking the broken parts back together and wrapping it tightly. This is one thing I'm good at. But Edmund missing, this reoccurring nightmare of losing a child, is setting me back, and I can no longer be perfect or pretend to be. I've given up and given in. I don't care who sees.

And when I hear Rosie sniff, a snotty snort, I can tell she's been crying.

'We'll get him back, Rose.' I use her nickname. 'And I'll be back to normal. Everything will be back to normal.'

'It's my fault,' she cries, bursting loud sobs into her palms. I can't handle this. Her self-blame, my blaming on her. Kav's words from last night ring in my ears and it's then I realise why I'm stuck to the mattress. It's this. Rosie and the burden I've placed on her young shoulders. She's carried my mistake for years and years and now the situation has repeated.

'I don't want anyone to hurt you,' she cries. 'I'm scared someone will hurt you.'

'Why would you say that? No one is going to hurt me, silly.' I pat the bed. She's clearly scared about the disappearance of Edmund. 'Come here.'

She doesn't have to be asked twice. In two steps, Rosie is on my bed, slouched over and crying like a four-year-old whose life has shifted in a second. She doesn't want to touch me and why would she? I'm the person who betrayed her trust. I'm a danger to her mental state and she's learnt to keep away, stay clear and watch her back. But once upon a time, I was soft kisses, tight embraces, snuggles in bed and love. I was the face she mirrored in the pram, kicking her legs and smiling. The arms who gave her aeroplane rides, jiggling her into giggles. I was the warmth she needed after jumping in puddles and the hand to stroke her when she was ill. I was it. *Mother*. Belonging to Rosie. She owned me and I owned her. And now. What am I? A stranger. A disappointment. A reason for her to see a therapist every week for the rest of her life. I'm bitter like orange peel and sharp like a shock. And it's then it hits me front on, forcing me to face it and say it. *What the fuck have I done to her?*

So, it comes before I can stop it, the control releases the grip it's had for years.

'It's not your fault,' I say. 'It's never been your fault.'

And my lip just won't stop quivering.

Eloise, 12.18 p.m.

Pressing a finger into my shoulder, I watch the skin transform from pale to pink. Sunburnt. It's bright and burning out here now. Coco is out of the sun, with Levi taking her to town for a sausage roll. But she really needs her midday nap and I'd like to see what's happening with the others, what the police are considering and how Kav and Scott handled the interviews.

It's time to leave the towel, the beach, the fake serenity, the scrutiny of each boat, and return to the villa, Penny's grief, the stress and tension from guests. It's been nice down here, considering how tight I've been feeling. Away from everyone, with only Coco's babbling voice nearby. I've taken a dip, wet my hair, floated for a bit on my back, pretended I'm on holiday. And the police haven't asked me to speak to them. *Yet.* Have I managed to sneak out of this while I've been down here, out of sight, out of mind? I'm hoping I'll be left alone. I scoop up the spades, towels and buckets, shaking the sand off them. I don't want to go back up. I could sit here all day until the sun sets and wander in and out of the sea.

But I know sooner or later I'll be called in to the police station for questioning. And luckily, my alibi is tight. At the point Edmund went missing last night, I was innocent, well and truly. On the balcony of Penny and Kav's villa, eighties songs behind me,

Penny and my husband leaving the group on the beach in a huff. I don't know what went down between them, and I don't want to know. Scott and I are talking, being civil, and the only way from here is upwards. Onwards.

There's only one thing pulling me back on to my sodden towel, to avoid greeting the conflict up on the road behind me. Barry, the ex-cop.

Would he be a part of the interviewing process? I highly doubt it. Just because he's been called in for his knowledge of the island doesn't mean he's now the leading officer. There are other bigwigs here now, taking over. I'm hoping Barry's returned to his hovel on the island, away from the investigation, away from the villas, away from me.

I've been down here for two hours, and out of the fourteen boats we've spied on, eight have now displayed activity. Dinghies carting people to the shore, families sitting on the deck for lunch, diving, snorkelling, guests arriving back on their boats after spending the night on the island. Only six remain and out of the six, the grimy boat furthest out continues to stay silent, gently changing directions, canopy down and shielding the deck. My eyes won't leave it.

The other five are stylish boats, three with rubber dinghies roped out the back and two without. The two without dinghies could be staying on the island. Families tend to do that. Sail over to the island to save the ferry cost.

But the three with dinghies tied to the back surely must be occupied. Hungover, maybe? Or perhaps they shared a lift to shore with someone else? They're clean, streamlined and luxurious. The type a family would own and possibly share. I can't imagine Nico being on board one of them. Then again, wouldn't a boat of that type be the perfect guise? Barry said there were boaties here that practically lived on their boat. But which ones?

Police searched the boats last night and this morning. I'm not sure whether they managed to inspect each and every one, but the maritime police boat has been out there today, edging around with busy two-man boarding parties. People have graciously granted them access. Their laughter has carried across the water. Even in a crisis, no one can stay stressed on the island.

My phone vibrates as I'm collecting Coco's soggy towel. It's Rosie. I tut to myself.

'You shouldn't be calling me,' I snap. But her voice is rushed and breathy and I know something is up.

'He just texted saying if I don't get the money to him by the exact time, he will keep drugging Edmund until he's dead.'

'Okay, calm down, calm—'

'So he's been literally drugging him. With what? What if it kills him?'

'He won't kill Edmund.' I face the boats and sigh. 'He wants the money too badly.'

Rosie starts to whisper, controlling her tone. 'Mum's finally up and we're going to go searching for Edmund. I'm trying to get her to relax and rest, but she's not listening. I won't be able to keep watching the boats.'

I look up to her balcony, but Rosie's not there anymore. 'That's okay. She needs you.' Pacing the length around my towel, I tell her Nico's getting impatient but we still have time. 'There's only six boats left. All the others have people on them. We will get him back.'

'Did you see the police boat?' Rosie says.

'Yes. I don't know whether they got around to all of them last night.'

'Even if they did and they've been on the boat with Nico, he could still be hiding Edmund somewhere they haven't looked.'

'Hmmm,' I say. It's unlikely. 'There's only so many places you can hide a kid on a boat.' I think Nico's boat has been left unattended. My eyes flick back to the boat with the black canopy.

'Nico came here prepared, knowing where he was going to hide Edmund,' Rosie says.

'I agree. You think he knew you'd never tell the cops?'

'Of course he knew.' I hear her snort in disgust. 'He's threatened to hurt Mum. And he always knew about what happened between her and me.'

I frown. 'What happened?'

'It doesn't matter,' she answers impatiently, which annoys me. After all of this, the least she could be is honest. 'What matters is he knew what happened and I think he planned to do this eventually. It was the only way he'd get his money back. I'm such an idiot.' I hear her slap something. 'I've got myself into such a mess.'

'And me, Rosie.' I flick away a fly that keeps sticking to my lip. My skin is burning under the sun. 'You dragged me into it by mentioning me to Nico. By telling him I have all this money lying around.'

She's quietly contemplating my words. Is she regretting this now? Ready to come clean? It would be so much easier for me if she did. The buckets and spades are digging into my fingers and the fly hovers around my eyes.

'It's not too late to tell your mum, you know.' *And leave me out of it*, I want to say.

'No.' It's stern, sharp and final, reminding me that I can neither fool nor persuade Rosie. 'No. Not now. We've just had a . . . Mum and I just spoke. No.'

I don't know what that means, but she's determined to keep me involved in her shit. I drag my feet through the warm sand.

'You and I have a deal, remember, Eloise. If you're chickening out now, I swear to God—'

'I'm not.' I squint through the sun, out to the boat with the black canopy. Six more hours until the sun goes down. Six more hours of interrogation, police interviews, searching, speculation. Six more hours of media camping down the road with their cameras ready. Six more hours of reporters trying to get an interview. Tonight, when we sneak out, I'll leave my phone in the bedroom. And if they wonder where we are, I'll have left a short, casual note telling Scott we've gone searching.

> *Rosie feels bad that she hasn't helped all day. I do too.*
> *We've gone for a bit and we'll be back soon. x*

And that's when we'll swim out there. 'I'm not chickening out,' I mumble. She hangs up on me and I stand there with the phone still up at my ear.

I've already planned how we'll do it and I don't feel great about the plan. In fact, the whole scenario fills me with a sensation of falling. My stomach flips and I swallow the taste of bile. But there's no way around it because Rosie's not ever going to budge on this. And part of me simply accepts this now.

Penny, 2006

Yes, the brain protects itself from itself: a beautiful paradox. It can block out a memory and distort it, erase it, sharpen and focus it. You only need your imagination, and the brain doesn't know the difference. Visualise a different ending, twist the story, muddle the memory and you can live with yourself forever.

But beware the triggers, the triggers are mines. You step on one, and you're brought right back to the past. Triggers come in the form of scents, sounds, sights, and when they're collectively placed together, that's when you remember the most. A scent of lavender oil, the taste of grapefruit gin, the sound of mosquitoes, the kitchen air hot and fatty, Rosie's cartoons. The baby crying.

The bath is too hot, so I turn the cold tap, testing the temperature on my wrist. The grapefruit gin spills into the bath and I curse. I need to be more careful. Plus, I don't want Rosie noticing. Every slurred word, every bump into the kitchen cupboard, every spill of drink and my four-year-old sees, like a loitering conscience. Lately, I've had to hide the gin in a teacup and tell her it's herbal tea. *Why does your breath smell so yummy, Mummy? Can I have a sip? It's too hot, no you can't.*

The next morning, I'll wake in a pit of shame with Rosie bouncing on the bed, with Greg's wrinkled pillow cold beside me, the remnants of his cologne lingering in the air. But for now, the gin makes the night bearable, doable, achievable.

I squirt in some bubble soap and beside me on the bouncer, the baby cries. It's a default setting. It only stops when Greg picks it up. But Greg is late. Late again. Greg is always fucking late. And this gin is a coping juice, a friend, a warm hug. It blocks the baby cries and quells the chest pains.

I set the gin down on the bathroom benchtop and help Rosie to untie her shoelaces. The baby wails, face red and wet. Rosie's used to it now. We all are. The neighbours are used to it. The dogs down the street are used to it. The baby's cries are the soundtrack to our life. Rosie sings over it and wriggles out of her socks, swinging a leg into the bath.

'Ahh, a bit hot, Mummy.' She giggles, to not upset me. I'm hearing this little giggle more and more lately. A nervous tic when she knows I can't tolerate the baby crying and everyday annoyances. Like a bath being too hot. Like the laces on her shoes being too tight. Like Greg being late.

'I'll add cold.' I stumble over the words and turn the tap harder until a jet of cold water surges out. And then Rosie uses her little palm to mix the bubbles, the water and the rubber duckies she's plopped in there.

I need to call Greg again. I've tried him at least five times, but he needs to get home now. Our dinner is freezing cold out there, Rosie needs her bedtime story and the baby needs his father. I turn the tap off and Rosie tries again, this time telling me it's okay. She instantly resumes a game with the ducks. Mummy duck and baby duck and no daddy duck. And I grit my teeth, reaching for the gin. A mosquito purrs beside my ear and I flick it away, locating it in the air where I smack it into my thigh. Blood squirts out over my skin. The sound stops Harry crying. His cheek is slicked with milky vomit. I need to phone Greg.

'Rosie, I'm putting Harry in the bath with you,' I tell her, lifting his naked body from the bouncer into the bath, where his bath seat sits snugly suctioned to the bottom.

She nods and keeps playing, dipping the duckies under the water.

Harry starts up again, crying, kicking, and my phone rings out in the kitchen. I down the rest of my gin and leave it against the bath and my head whirls like I'm on a merry-go-round. *Just shut up*, I want to scream at Harry. I flick some water over his neck and arms. Out in the kitchen, it rings. Greg. Greg telling me he's going to be late. I go to stand and slip a little on the bubble gel, holding on to the towel rail.

'Look after him,' I tell Rosie. I hear her talking gently to her brother. Something like, *There there, Harry. Mummy will be back, it's okay.* The phone rings.

Out in the kitchen, I realise I've left the doors open. Tiny moths fly around the lights, bumping their heads into the globe. The phone stops. I blink, gazing down at the screen. It isn't Greg. It's Mum. Where the hell is he? My heart pumps with rage. The dinner is cold and the mashed potato is crusting. I shut the kitchen doors, slamming them, and catch a whiff of summer lavender air, making me ill. My head beats with dehydration. Too many gins tonight. He'll know when he comes home. I slide open the kitchen drawer and grab a fork and start digging into the potato, stuffing it into my mouth, swallowing without chewing, just to fill the gut, to fill a need. The baby isn't crying. Rosie's still in there, mumbling. I stab the sausage with the fork and eat the end of it, eyes out at the garden. I'm going to throw his dinner in the bin. Just like every night this week. A waste. A total waste of money and time and effort and care. I swallow mouthfuls of sausage and lean against the kitchen bench, chewing with my eyes closed.

And then a scream echoes from the bathroom and I'm back, awake and present in the kitchen. Potato mashed into my elbow and sausage meat crumbled at the hollow of my neck.

'What?' I drop the fork so it clangs against the plate and then stagger down the hall, into the bathroom. Rosie's in the bath, little starfish hands covering her face and eyes.

And there's my son, face down at the bottom of the bath.

Eloise, 3.13 p.m.

The questions fire at me like bullets and maybe this is strategic. The quicker they ask, the quicker you respond, the quicker you tell on yourself. There's no time to think, rehearse or plan. Question, answer, question, answer. I'm so put off by these two detectives surrounding me, I can barely gather my voice. It's shrunken and weak and they are like hyenas ripping into a fresh carcass. They aren't compassionate like Scott and Levi assured me they would be. They're barking for an answer, keen to return to the city with a lead and an excuse for a promotion. Meanwhile, I'm sweating under my bottom cheeks. The aircon is old, rattling and useless, puffing warm air out on to the table. And the smell in here. Body odour, pine spray and ancient threadbare carpet that's weathered salt storms and heat. Patches are frayed around my feet, catching on my sandals. This dilapidated police station reminds me of a western movie.

First question: 'You let your baby be looked after by Penny's daughter?'

I smile and nod. 'Yes. She's almost eighteen. We have a babysitter that we use—'

'And your son said he's heard you say that Edmund is a weird kid.'

'Ah.' I laugh. Good one, Levi.

'Weird in what way?'

I shrug. 'Just, odd. I don't know—'

'You like to keep your daughter away from him?'

'That's, that's—'

'Has Edmund ever done anything to hurt your daughter?'

'Not at all.'

'When did you last see him?'

'I'm not sure—'

'We *need* you to be sure.'

'I didn't go and look,' I say quietly.

'You mean you didn't check on your children?' The young detective eyes his partner and scoffs.

The older cop smirks and keeps staring at me, leaning against the tin wall with crossed arms and a bulging belly. At the desk down the end, a female police officer taps away at her computer. Why would she want to work here with these two?

'We'd only just left the children with Rosie and Levi an hour before and my son is responsible.'

Another smirk. 'Your eleven-year-old son is responsible?'

'We were right next door.'

'That's right.' He smacks the top of the desk, making me jolt. 'You were right next door. And yet no one saw anything. I wonder why that is?'

I shrug. 'I don't—'

'Do you take drugs, Eloise?' He squints. 'Is it okay if I call you that?'

'That's my name.'

'Drugs?' He raises his eyebrows.

'Not at all, why?'

'Perhaps that's why no one saw anything or even cared to check on their kids. Drugs tend to blur the need to parent.'

My heart beats so quickly, I wonder if he can see my pulse. In the vein running across my temple. In the sweat drop below my collarbone. Does it bump and wriggle with each frantic beat? Is this how he'll catch me out? He's accusing us of bad parenting, a taboo insult no mother wants to hear.

'There were no drugs involved last night,' I tell him.

'Only booze. The liquid kind of drug.'

Clasping my clammy hands in my lap, I swallow.

'We think someone's taken Edmund. What do you think?'

I swallow again and he notices. How do I stop this? I've never felt my throat tickle as much as it does now. 'I think so too.'

'You do?' A glance to his partner. 'Indulge us.'

'I think if he was lost, he'd have been found by now.'

I want to tell them about the man I saw creeping around Brett and Sal's window, but then it may have been Nico. And if they find Nico before we do, then he has all Rosie's texts about me, her, Edmund. So, I stay quiet.

He sits up in his creaky chair and rests his own hands together on his stomach. 'And who do you think took him?'

'I don't know. The biological parents?'

He inhales deeply, eyes boring into mine, and uses his tongue to fish something out of his teeth. He's young. Attractive, with long lashes and perfect hair. Wanting accolades. He's intimidating, and his attractiveness has something to do with that. I don't know what he's thinking and that's what worries me. I just have to know, *believe*, that whatever he's thinking has nothing to do with Nico, Rosie or me.

'They've been cleared. But on this island that everyone claims is so safe,' he says, leaning forward on the table. Minty breath and sickly cologne. 'You think he could have been taken?'

I nod and then shrug. 'Either that or he's fallen and injured himself. Maybe even slipped off a cliff.'

'Lots of theories, Eloise.' He raises those brows again. 'You could be a cop. It's like you've really thought good and hard about all of this.'

'I have.'

He arches one brow again, so I continue. 'If that was one of my kids out there, lost, injured or taken, I would be considering everything.'

'Just like us,' he finally says, eyeing me and nodding as though he knows it all. 'Just like us.'

I leave the station rattled, wobbly, and on the verge of crying. Hold it in. Stand straight, walk as though you're on holiday. They'll be looking out of the window at me, wondering why my hair's wet and tangled. I wish I've never gone swimming. I appear too relaxed, too at ease. Rewinding to everything I said makes me realise how guilty everything sounded. Why did I have to appear like a know-it-all? Why did I have to agree that he'd been taken? Stubbing my toe on the gravel, I recoil and stop, bending to push pressure on my toe. It's not bad, just a graze. Did they see that?

Scott said they'd be nice, there was nothing to worry about. And perhaps they were. Perhaps they're becoming desperate now, in need of answers. Perhaps they're tired and hot. If I was a policeman unable to find a solution to a sticky situation, I would be peeved too. But I can't help feeling as though they know something about me. They see through me, my linen dress, my golden bracelet, my designer sunglasses, to the seventeen-year-old girl being paid to party, entertain and run drugs. The girl who was arrested and charged.

And when I return to the villa, limping, spotting Penny through her kitchen window staring back at me, I can't help but wonder if she knows I know about Edmund.

Penny, 6.36 p.m.

Now a storm is on the way, the search has been called off until daylight tomorrow. Edmund has been missing for almost twenty-four hours. I was worried we'd end up here.

Police have brought over every search and rescue resource. Drones, thermal imaging, helicopters, fishery officers, divers, maritime police, volunteers, SES, and still – Edmund is missing. Our party guests have been interviewed, as well as the visitors down the street. More extensive interviews will be conducted tomorrow when additional police resources arrive to interrogate island guests about where they were at the time my son went missing.

SES have combed the south and north of the island. They say Kav and I will have to speak to media tomorrow morning. That's if Edmund isn't found. And Edmund *will* be found. I can't and won't front the media, even if they say it's beneficial. Viewers may recognise him; viewers may have seen odd behaviour. But I've been in front of leeching journalists before. They lack empathy, they only want the story. And my son will not be a story. He will not be on the front page of the newspaper and our story will not be viewed around the country. We will not be the family people feel sorry for, sending donations, flowers, cards and setting up charity funds on our behalf. We will not be famous for this.

It's getting darker, cooler, the heat finally letting go and allowing us some respite. The summer storm could jeopardise search and rescue operations. From the balcony, I sit with a herbal tea and watch the way the water unravels from pure clear blue to slate. Waves tumble and roughen the shoreline, every now and then crashing up against the cliffs at the edge of the bay. Boats are starting to switch on their lights, with the sky darkening the island. They're settling down for the night. None are allowed to leave. Brett and Sal are quiet next door. If they saw me out here, I'm sure they'd quickly retreat back inside. No one wants to be around me and I don't blame them. I'm a dark storm cloud dampening everyone's holiday. Even Eloise hasn't come to check on me. She's finally decided to leave Rosie alone too.

I sip my tea, attention out on the cliffs. The divers have been around there today, in and around the rocks and reefs. Did he fall in? Did he slip off the rocky limestone and crack his skull? Did a shark come and finish him off?

None of our guests saw anything and why would they? This was us parents' responsibility only. It was not all Rosie's responsibility to care for her baby. Levi is to blame, too, for his lack of attention.

'Can I get you something to eat, love?' Georgia steps out with a sweater tied around her neck. I shake my head. 'I'll bring out some cheese and biscuits anyway,' she says.

Inside, William chats to Rosie about the latest iPhone while Kav showers and Georgia sets to work, slicing cheese and arranging crackers around a plate. The canned laughter on the television sitcom grates on me. It's like we're all back to normal, forgetting that Edmund ever existed. And once upon a time, he didn't. Is it because we adopted him? Is that why no one cares? He's not blood-related and we know the old adage about blood being thicker than water. When Rosie goes next, off to university or to study abroad, will no one care about her either?

I gulp the rest of the tea and slam the cup down hard on the table. Then I push my chair back and storm inside, shove the bathroom door open and slide the shower curtain back. Kav's washing his hair and when he looks at me, bubbles slide into his eye. We've barely spoken since the early hours when I slapped him across the face. But I need him now. I need him to assure me that I'm not a bad mother. I'm not.

'You okay?' he asks, washing the bubbles off under the shower.

'What do you think has happened to Edmund? Tell me?'

'Can you close the bathroom door, please?' He nods towards it. I kick it shut and he stares at me.

'Where is he?' I say, hands on hips.

Kav stands under the shower, dripping, eyebrows puzzled together. He's staring at me like I'm crazy. 'I don't know, Pen.'

'You must have a theory. I want to know. Tell me.'

He holds up his hands. 'I – what do you want to hear?'

'Tell me where he is,' I yell.

'The cops think—'

'Yes?'

He slumps and sighs. 'I don't think you'll want to know this, Pen.'

'Tell me.'

The shower rains down and the fog wets my face. He's been using my soap. He smells feminine and pretty. I want him to help me.

'They think he's drowned.'

I shake my head. We stare at one another. He's helpless, standing naked and loose. I shake my head again. 'Tell me what *you* think.'

He doesn't answer right away. Just blinks the water from his eyes. 'I think he's fallen from the cliff and—'

I step into the shower fully clothed and press my face up against his wet, hairy chest. The water rains down on me, sticking the shorts and singlet fabric to my body, sticking the hair to my scalp. Kav's arms collect my elbows, and he holds me fiercely tight. He smells like me. And I pretend that he is. Me holding myself. Me accepting myself. Me forgiving myself. Me cuddling myself the way I needed back then. And I don't cry, no noise comes out, but my body shudders with grief, vibrating. And Kav also starts to cry. His sobs hiss through the shower, with his chest pumping up and down.

We both agree, he's fallen from the cliffs.

We both agree, we've lost our son.

Eloise, 8.11 p.m.

Scott pours me a big glass of red wine and the glugging sound slackens my shoulders.

'Thanks,' I say, taking a sip. The rich deep texture coats my tongue, working as a sedative. Half an hour ago, Coco fell asleep within a few blinks. The fresh air, swimming and sun helped to conk her out. And Levi is resting in his bedroom, texting his friends about the weekend, almost dozing off. I've kissed him and told him to switch off in twenty minutes.

Levi has to keep the weekend events on the downlow. We don't want rumours spreading, subsequently causing more pain for Penny and Kav. Ever since last night, Penny's been avoiding me, but Scott would hate for Kav to pick sides. The last time I saw Kav he was riding back from the village with a takeaway dinner bag swinging from the handlebars. He looked wrecked, almost falling off the bike as he unhooked the bag before staggering inside the villa. He's that type of husband though. The one who tries to steer the family ship through turbulent waters. A duck. That's how I'd describe Kav. Smooth and calm on the surface, with legs beating frantically underneath. If he breaks down, there will be no one left to lift up Penny. He's a good husband.

So is Scott, who's pouring himself a red. The best husband. Well, he used to be before I betrayed him. The father to take Levi outside and kick the footy under the evening skies, the father who bathed his children, reading them stories while he did it. The husband to collect the washing off the line, fill the dishwasher and iron my dresses. To buy me flowers just because. To organise a romantic dinner. Accommodating.

Now, he's been buried under resentment. But I only need to dig around the boulders and bring him back to light. Again, another reminder of why I'm helping Rosie. Another reason to get this done and over with.

I couldn't tell Scott about the police interview, nor the accusing way they treated me. I'm too worried it means they know something, and I don't want Scott getting a hint. But I *do* want his comfort and yet he wouldn't know why.

I want to go home now. To throw away my clothes because they remind me of this weekend. To cook our family beef stroganoff and eat by the pool and brew Scott's morning coffee – just the way he likes it – and borrow his favourite books from the library. I want to pack lunchboxes and make beds and be normal again. I take a deep sip this time.

'I might go and wander down the beach,' I tell him. 'To chill a bit.'

Scott switches the television on and slumps into the couch with his legs up. 'I think that's a good idea.'

'This weekend has been horrendous.'

Scott looks up at me from under thick eyebrows and rolls his eyes. 'The worst. But it'll be over soon.'

'When Edmund's found?'

He clears his throat. 'That's right.' Takes a sip. 'When he's found.'

'I can't imagine what they're going through.' I stare over at the villa where Penny and Kav remain, door closed and shut to the world. 'I can't help feeling like we should do more for them.'

'We can,' Scott says. 'We will. But tomorrow. For now, we need to rest.' He turns his attention back to the mindless cooking show. 'You go for your walk.'

We're all exhausted and done talking, thinking. But Rosie and I are the only ones who don't have time to rest. Soon, we'll be on our way, swimming out to the boat where we believe Edmund's kept hidden. Will Nico be there? We don't know. Will there be others? We hope not. But we have to be prepared for every situation. Before the rain starts, I want to head down and check on the last boat. I want to see whether their lights are switched on, whether there's any movement. I'm going to plot our route and plan how we'll board, unnoticed.

I take my wine with me out on to the street and slip off my flip-flops.

After Coco's midday nap, we wandered along the shore to collect shells. While Coco was busy dropping bits of broken reef, coral and shells into her bucket, I hid Levi's bodyboard near the cliffs for later and investigated the six unattended boats. Five were finally showing activity on board. A father and daughter jumping off the flybridge. A family of six hopping into their dinghies. A group of old women, playing cards out on their table, an elderly couple arriving back to their boat, and two children eating ice lollies on the duckboard of the fifth.

Only one remains now. The boat with the black canopy – its chipped painted name finally revealing itself to me. *Black Swan.* Ugly Duckling more like it. I knew he'd be on that one.

With my wine and flip-flops in my hand, I stroll past Brett and Sal's villa, catching them through the kitchen window, hugging. It's been a rough twenty-four hours. Beer bottles and packets of open crisps are clogging their kitchen bench. I look away as they start kissing and keep travelling down the wonky steps alongside their villa to the sand. The grains are warm and silky, retaining the day's heat. There's a strong breeze now, whipping my dress. The lights from the boat windows streak out across the sea revealing mini white caps, rocking between the hulls. In the dark, it'll be hard to locate *Black Swan*. Yet this is something I've accounted for. Earlier, I drew myself a map of each boat on a chequered board, detailing where they're moored in the bay. I can count the lights using the map: eleven boats on the left, and all the rest on the right. It's hard to see everything now, and it won't be until we're out there that we'll be able to see fully. But *Black Swan* stays moored to the edge of them all, further out towards the cliffs. And from what I can see, there are no lights. Would he keep Edmund out there all alone? Tied up? We know he's been drugged. It makes me shudder to imagine what kind of toxic crap he's put into Edmund's bloodstream. I sip my wine and decide this'll be the only glass I have. I need to be focused for our swim.

I've planned this as best I can, but really, we can't rely on Nico's predictability. And there's a disparaging thought that's been bouncing around and teasing me all day: What if Edmund's not there? What if he's in another bay? What if he's not on a boat?

I down the last of my wine, reminding myself to stay calm, but it's difficult to stamp out anxiety. So I go through the positive list, the valid reasons why Rosie and I believe Edmund's hidden on a boat. It's the only tactic I have to settle and soothe my rapid heartbeat and looming dread.

The sniffer dogs found Edmund's scent on the beach. Rosie said Nico arrived by private boat. Nico guaranteed to return Edmund safely in front of the villa. Plus, police, guests, SES and volunteers have found nothing on the island. If Nico had Edmund hidden on the island, someone would have seen or noticed something. Surely. Hopefully.

The thought of swimming out there in the dark doesn't thrill me either. Sharks, stingrays and whatever else lurks in the black water. Rosie will have the bodyboard, but I'll have to overcome my fear of night swimming. I have to do this for Edmund, for Penny, for Scott, and even for Rosie. I truly believe Edmund is on a boat. It's the only place Nico could safely keep him hidden. And if he isn't? I just really cannot afford to think about that yet.

Confidence, although wavering every now and then, sets me running back up the steps alongside Brett and Sal's villa. I need to get Scott drunk enough that he'll pass out. And we'll have to store dry clothes on the shore, ready to pull back on after our swim. And there's one thing I've got up my sleeve, should we need it.

I'm veering on to our street when I notice an overweight man with a beer leaning against our small wall, talking to Scott. I stop. It's Barry. The ex-cop. When Scott sees me, he nods and motions for me to come over.

'Here she is,' Scott says.

I laugh, looking down at my sandy feet, wine glass dangling. Fuck. Just fuck. And this is where everything goes to shit. The plan wasn't needed. This is my undoing right here.

'Bit windy down there for a walk.' Barry speaks with a strong Australian burr. I don't make eye contact just yet. It's dark out here, only a streetlamp. I step past him at the gate, catching a pungent smell of sweat and yeast. The sound of his beer bottle dragging along the limestone wall sets my spine tingling. Like nails on a chalkboard.

'I don't think I've met you yet,' he says. 'Know your husband and just about every other one of Kav and Penny's guests here.'

'Eloise.' I smile, dusting my feet and looking down.

'Where have you been today, Eloise?' He reminds me of an actor in an Australian drama. It's like he's putting the accent on. To sound harsh, dry, colloquial.

'Looking after our daughter,' Scott tells him. 'Two years old.'

'Ah, tough age,' he says.

I sigh, finally looking up. But I'm in the shadow of the porch, deliberately, and the shadow is my saviour. 'Sure is. They need their sleeps.'

Barry stares at me for a while, and I feel it instantly. Recognition. His eyes squint and he blinks. 'How close are you to Penny and Kav?'

'Kav and I are good friends,' Scott says. 'Studied together.'

'Yeah, I've seen you all day beside the poor bloke. Good thing he has a friend like you, Scotty.' He's still staring at me.

'I'm going to go and take a shower,' I say, banging my flip-flops together.

'Wash those blonde locks.' It's an inappropriate statement and I see Scott stand straighter. I've seen him do this before, in the past. When someone has attempted to strike up a conversation with me at a bar. When a tradesman working on our pool whistled under his breath at me. Scott's showing a protectiveness I haven't seen in a long while. And it's a good sign, *great*. But right now, I just need to avoid Barry.

I go to step inside, and Barry calls out, 'Hang on, sweetheart.'

'Mate,' Scott says firmly. 'My wife needs a shower.'

He ignores Scott. 'I'm one of those select few people who can remember a face and I know I've met you before, Eloise.'

Turning to look over my shoulder, I smirk. I need to fake a casual tone now. Can't allow him to hear the stickiness in my mouth. 'Really? Where? In town? I've never met you.'

'No, I know I've spoken to you at length.'

I laugh again, give my flip-flops a few more claps together. 'I don't think so.'

'But I do. Know your face.'

I shrug. 'Funny. Scott and I barely come to the island.'

Barry continues to stare deeply, squinting, and Scott steps up to the porch. For the first time in years, he touches me. He holds my elbow. 'Honey, go and take a shower. Barry, would you like another beer? I can see you're out.'

'Nah, mate, you're alright.' Barry flicks the air. 'I've just come from the pub.' This explains the inappropriateness. Scott wants me to get away and go inside and I don't know why and I also don't care. I walk quickly into the villa and into the bathroom.

Once in, I switch on the shower tap, but stand up against the door, fully clothed, fully shaking, unable to breathe. If he wasn't drunk, he'd remember me. If it wasn't night-time. But what about tomorrow, when the sun reveals the kinks, flaws and reality? What then? Barry will remember and Scott will be told and my past will be revealed and it doesn't matter about Edmund. I'm as good as dead anyway.

Penny, 9.44 p.m.

And so, the island sleeps. Kav's dead to the world, lying on top of the covers instead of under them. He's snoring loudly and I don't want to move or disturb him. I've rested today – not mentally, but physically – and he hasn't. Kav hasn't slept in forty-eight hours. I want to sleep, yet feel guilty. Even the shower felt wrong, using soap and caring about cleaning. Scoffing cold pizza felt wrong. Like these normal acts mean I'm forgetting Edmund's missing. But the baby in my stomach needs nourishment. It also needs liquid.

Filling a glass with water, I down it in three huge gulps and fill it again. The windows and door to the balcony are open and there's a rumble of distant thunder over the city. The sea picks up on the wind and weather, chopping and messing the reflecting lights from the ferry jetty. I cannot think of him out there in the water. I close my eyes, swallow the last of my drink and face Rosie's bedroom. It's dark. No strip of light underneath. She must be sleeping. Placing the glass down, I then step over to her door with my stomach sloshing. I imagine the baby doing somersaults. Twisting the old doorknob, I slowly push open the door and peer inside. She's on her bed, phone lighting her face. She looks up when she sees me.

'Are you okay?' Rosie's voice is groggy.

I nod and step closer to her bed. 'I'm going to sleep. You should get some rest, too.'

'I will.' She swipes her phone and places it beside her on the bedside table.

And I stand awkwardly under the door frame, watching her roll on to her side. When I don't leave the room, Rosie glances up again. 'Mum?'

Mum. Mother. Mumma. Do I deserve the title? My chin pinches uncontrollably and I mutter, 'I want to cuddle you.'

She sits up slightly and stares. And then I feel it coming, just like before. The grief paralyses me. I want her back, us back, what we had. Knowing looks, closeness, kisses, touch.

'Then cuddle me,' she says, voice cracking.

One, two, three steps and I'm lying on her bed, wrapping my arms around her bony shoulders, breathing in her teenage shampoo and . . . that scent. The one that's always belonged to her. My baby. The baby Rosie I used to breathe in, never getting enough, always craving that soft, warm scent of her. She smells the same. *Feels* the same. It's like she hasn't changed. I press my lips into her hair and kiss her over and over and over again, dripping tears into the strands. And I hear her sniff as she finally holds me back. And I swear I hear her murmur, *Mumma*. Just like she always did. And years crumble. And time shrinks. And anger pops like the bubbles in her bath. She's four and it never happened. Just her in the bath. Just her and the ducks.

'I am so, so sorry,' I breathe. Did I even say that? It's like smoke from my mouth. She squeezes me tight, squeezes the air from my lungs. Forgiveness from someone else sometimes makes the guilt even worse. Especially from your own daughter. But the pressure of her arms placates me. My head is heavy against her skin. It's dark, it's warm, it's forgiveness. And I'm falling, falling, into peaceful sleep.

Who sank first, me or my son? Couldn't Greg see me sinking? *I* needed to be lifted, supported and cradled like Harry. I needed to be rocked and sung to.

Three seconds. That's all it took for Harry to suck in water, fill his tiny lungs and drown.

And why hadn't Rosie heard or noticed him slipping down? Couldn't she see him kicking his legs, crying and slowly drowning?

Greg left the home and the marriage a week later, his car stoked with old records, business clothes and a few bits and pieces for Rosie, to set up shop somewhere else. Said he couldn't and wouldn't be able to look at me the same way. Said he couldn't be in that house. But I already knew he was on the way out. This was the perfect excuse for him to neglect me when I needed him most. This made me hate him even more, prevented the pain of losing him.

Did I deserve to be jailed? No, he didn't want to go that far. After all, Rosie still needed her mother, and he couldn't imagine being a full-time parent. Besides, it was an accident, that's what everyone was saying. A horrible, preventable accident.

Greg carried his shame like an embarrassing zit you don't want anyone noticing. The truth was, he was absent while I suffered, caring for our newborn son, unable to feel the same attachment to Harry as I had with Rosie. And he hadn't been there for me. And he refused to acknowledge that. And I lugged my shame around like a screaming toddler, clinging to my shins. Shame over needing Greg to rescue me, shame over drinking. The lawyer in court proclaimed, *These were the circumstances that led to the infant's death.*

But what came first: the chicken or the egg? The neglectful husband or the neglectful mother? And what came next? Journalists frothing over the news, lawyers trying to keep them well away, investigations into whether I murdered my son, police interviews with my four-year-old daughter, questions from my brother gently probing, *Did you do this deliberately, Pen?*

Suddenly, my life was no longer perfect, sunny, pink, golden, *House & Garden* magazine. The house was sold, Rosie and I moved into my parents' guest bedroom, and I needed someone to blame.

I couldn't face blaming myself. You only do that if you have no ego. But I had an ego. I was Perfect Penny. Penelope Perfect. If you blame yourself, you'll never be able to stand in front of the mirror and do your hair. You'll never be able to meet another man later down the track. If you blame yourself, there's no living with yourself.

Greg was no longer around to point fingers at. My mother and father were being much too compassionate for someone like me, who probably deserved jail. Friends told me they had no idea I was silently suffering, therefore I couldn't blame them. So, who did I blame?

I blamed Rosie.

MONDAY

Eloise, 12.33 a.m.

When Scott is out like a sagging drunk at a bar, when Levi snores from his bed, when Coco is bunched up beside her teddies on the bed, stinky blankies shoved under her nostrils, I know it's time to move. The handwritten note is left on the dining table with two crosses down the bottom. I want Scott to see that I care. I've taken one set of keys, my sneakers, my water bottle, the maps. Everything must look as though Rosie and I feel badly about not doing our bit to look for Edmund. I've got two torches the police lent us, along with Levi's waterproof backpack. And inside the pack, I have a pillowcase, along with my dry clothes stuffed inside a plastic bag, ready to put back on after we rescue Edmund from the boat. I'm not using the word *if*. I'm using the word *when*.

'Ready?' I ask Rosie when she meets me outside the villa. Lightning goes off like a strobe and her face is as pale and clammy as I imagined it'd be.

Rosie shrugs and I empathise. I'm not ready either. She's carrying a plastic bag of clothes and is dressed in her bathers. She knows nothing of my plan. I hook my arm around hers.

'We're prepared. We know which boat he's on.' I'm talking to convince myself as much as I need to convince Rosie. Thunder vibrates between the walls of the villas. We walk down the side of Brett and Sal's.

'Mum fell asleep in my bed, beside me,' Rosie tells me. Her voice is sad, not scared.

I squeeze my arm around hers. 'We're doing this for her. Remember that.'

She nods. 'But if we don't find him—'

'Shh.' I force a smile that she sees in the next flash of lightning. 'One of these days you're going to have to tell me what happened between the two of you.'

But Rosie shakes her head. She's never going to open up to me.

We hide our plastic bags and Rosie's phone in the long grass adjacent to the cliffs. The air is metallic and humid, the wind a hot sigh. I leave the backpack on.

She looks at me as she ties her hair in a ponytail. 'Why are you wearing that backpack?'

'There's a few bits and pieces we might need.' I turn away from her and head in the direction of the cliffs. I start running towards the caves, wanting everything to be quicker, hurried. The faster we do this, the faster my life goes back to normal. Freedom is just around the corner. And Barry's presence is felt and noted. Rescuing Edmund needs to be achieved before Barry discovers who I am.

'What have you got hidden?' Rosie keeps up with me, carefully stepping on the rocks.

'It's Levi's bodyboard. We'll need it to float Edmund back to shore.'

'Gosh, you've really thought about this, haven't you?'

It's stuck behind a gap in the rocks. I hand it to her. 'More than you realise.'

The map of the boats is in the backpack, so I take it out, unfold it and count back on the chequered plan. I point to *Black Swan*. Dark, no lights. Only a few boats are lit up. But that one remains obscure.

'We're going to sneak up and the only way to do that is by swimming out,' I tell Rosie. 'Edmund's either in there alone or with Nico.'

We start down to the shoreline. Water doesn't scare me. Levi and Scott often go surfing and at times, when Levi was much younger, I've gone out with them for company. But I've never swum at night. Rosie will be freaking out about this, and I can't have her feeling threatened. We have to stay silent. She follows me into the water, where she sucks in air. It's not cold, but the fear is making her think it is. Lightning cracks above the mainland, giving us a good picture of how far we have to swim. Not far. One hundred metres, one hundred and fifty max.

'I have a pillowcase that we will use to place over Edmund's head,' I say, dipping my body under to my shoulders. A chill washes over my skin. 'It's going to look strange and mean, but we have to do it so he doesn't recognise us.'

Her eyes are shiny and black. 'What? No. That's horrible to think of doing that to him. All he'd want is a cuddle and a familiar face—'

'Well, what other choice do we have?'

She's shivering, more from shock than cold. 'Nico said he's drugged him.'

'We can't rely on Nico.'

Dipping in, slimy seaweed circles around my feet as though tugging me back. I don't really want to talk, I just want to think. But Rosie's gasping, kicking behind me, using the bodyboard to float. She sounds panicked when she asks, 'If Nico's there, how are we going to get Edmund?'

It was only a matter of time until she'd ask this question. And if I tell her the truth, Rosie's likely to stop swimming and return to shore. But we're getting deeper now, unable to feel the sandy bottom.

'Just leave that bit to me, okay?'

Her toenails scratch my foot. I'm not a special forces operator, I'm not a spy or a cop or anyone who should know anything about sneaking up on a criminal to take back a kidnapped child. And the more I think about how ridiculously dangerous this all is, the more angry I become. Submerging my head under the water, I exhale a burst of angry bubbles, screaming. I pop up and wipe my eyes, ignoring Rosie's slippery, shiny face, and keep swimming, scooping away armfuls of water. I'm angry with Rosie and this anger propels me onwards. She dragged me into this fucking mess. I leave her a few metres behind and then come up beside a vacant mooring, which I hang on to, gathering my breath, waiting. Water sloshes into my face and I accidentally swallow a salty mouthful. I almost gag. I want to cry.

Rosie's looking down around her as though a shark will lunge up and grab her. She's freaking out. And it's hard to strategise when you're freaking. But I'm done with this now. She needs to help me for once.

'When we get Edmund, we don't talk, all right? At all. We stay silent. We put the pillowcase over his head, mean or not.' God. I close my eyes for a moment and squeeze them as despicable images of someone doing this to Levi or Coco flash like the lightning above my head.

'At least he'll be back with Mum and Kav in no time,' Rosie adds.

I nod. 'And that's always been the goal, hasn't it?'

We leave the rough rope of the mooring and keep swimming out, passing seven more boats – one with boisterous people on board listening to rock music. We make sure to swim around the light. Lightning flashes every now and then, creating a picture of choppy, pointed waves, each reminding me of sharks. Distant thunder. We're awaiting the storm because it's making itself known. We don't even think about the depth below, the seaweed, the creatures,

the black. There's too much to think about ahead of us. *Black Swan.*
From the water, it looms like a ghost ship. The hull is caked in barnacles, eating away at the hull like decay on teeth. The tiny crusted
particles tattoo the sides in ink.

'This is it,' I whisper to Rosie. 'From now on, no talking.'

She tugs my shoulder. 'Wait.'

'Rosie, we have to go on board.'

'I'm scared of Nico.'

I nod. 'I know you are. But don't be. Nico thought he could
push you around by intimidating you. He doesn't know how strong
you are. How much Edmund and your mum mean to you.'

I know how it feels to be controlled by a man, a thug, a criminal. *No more, Rosie.* She will escape this man the way I did.

We swim around the side of the boat, while water smacks
up against the hull. The lights are off inside the cabin and bedrooms below and by the time we reach the stern transom, it feels
somewhat comforting to lift ourselves out. No more dangling
legs pointed to the depths. At the same time, the idea of creeping in under the black canopy has me feeling nauseous. The salt
water has wrinkled my bottom lip. I point to the transom, wanting Rosie to leave the bodyboard there. She's shivering, holding
herself. In the flash of lightning, I spot goose bumps covering
her skin.

The black canopy is cut down the middle, displaying a short
doorway for easier access. I take the backpack from my back and
unzip it. Inside, I pull out a heavy Maglite torch the cops lent
us. I'm not using it for light, I'm using it as a weapon if we need
it. It's heavy enough to crack a skull, to send a man to the floor.
Plus, I have a knife. I don't want Rosie seeing it, but at some
stage, I'm going to need to take it out of the pack. If Nico's not
on board, then perfect. We can grab Edmund freely. But if he
is, then it may come in handy.

Rosie watches me for instructions. I step in first, waiting for my eyes to adjust to the darkness inside the canopy. Heavy diesel fumes clog the enclosed space, along with the smell of rotting fish, varnish and wet unwashed towels. I blink, looking around. Rosie ducks her head and follows me in, still holding herself like a child. And she is. That personal responsibility swirls in my sickly stomach.

Thunder rattles louder. I edge around the plastic table and chairs until I'm inside the cabin where old fabric loungers, a dining table and shabby curtains display a squalid lived-in quality.

I stop, holding up a hand. An old-fashioned news voice down towards the bedrooms. It's a radio. I turn to Rosie, holding up my finger, and step down the three stairs until I'm right outside the door of the main cabin. AM radio. I hear a man clear his throat and I flick Rosie a look. Nico. He's in there. But where's Edmund? In the other cabin? In the engine room? Stuck in the tiny bathroom? I poke my head around the door ever so slightly and then gasp when a man in his eighties, lying naked and exposed, dim book light over his newspaper, spots me in the doorway. I bump back against Rosie, knocking my skull into her nose.

'Who the bloody hell are you?' he thunders.

'Quick,' I say to Rosie, pushing her back up the stairs.

The old man steps out of his room, towel wrapped around his waist, and I turn and hold my hands up to my forehead. 'Oh my gosh, I am so, so sorry. This is not Paul and Linda's boat.'

'Wha—?' he says.

'We've come to the wrong boat, I'm so sorry. Friends of ours said they were out the back of the bay and we've got the wrong boat.'

'Get off here.' He flings his arm towards the stern. 'I don't care who you think this is.'

He doesn't make sense and he's clearly frazzled. I feel badly for the old man.

'I'm sorry,' I say again and run up the steps, back through the galley and out past the canopy to the transom. Rosie jumps into the water, sliding the bodyboard towards her, and I drop the torch into the backpack, zip it up and slip in next to her.

'Fuck,' I say, heart hammering. 'I did not expect that.'

We swim away from *Black Swan* before he can locate us in the water and grab on to the nearest mooring to catch our breath. We're behind another boat, so he won't see us.

'Now what?' Rosie says, flinging an arm up. 'I can't believe we just did that.'

'It's been unattended all day.'

'It hasn't. That old creepy dude has just been quiet in there.'

'But you can understand how I thought it was the one.'

'You said you had a vibe.'

'And I did.'

She rolls her eyes. 'What if he calls the police?'

I shake my head and listen in. I can't hear yelling or calling out like I expected. 'He won't. He probably just thought we were both drunk and foolish. It's okay.'

'No, it's not okay.' She adjusts the board directly under her. 'We've now got less than an hour until Nico does something to Edmund and—' She doesn't complete her sentence, because I know what this means.

I drift on my back for a moment, wetting the back of my hair. There are no stars, only dirty clouds, coloured by the lights of the mainland. There are no more boats. I cannot believe I got it wrong. But then again, of course I can. Did I really expect to find Edmund, to get away with taking drugs with a minor, to fool my husband into loving me again? For a short moment, a blink in time, I was able to live the life I wanted. And I screwed it up by screwing the

303

tradesman. I'm sick of lying. I'm sick of trying. Lifting my head, I stare across the water towards the villas where Penny and Kav and Scott and my kids rest. It would be easier to let Rosie win. Tell your mum, tell Kav, tell them what I did. I'm never getting away with my mistakes. But then Rosie's smartwatch flashes and it's a message from Nico.

15 min left. Say bye bye to your bro.

Penny, 1.43 a.m.

Thunder shatters my dream, rousing me from the deepest sleep, but melatonin drags me back. Her absent body can be felt, even through unconsciousness. Rosie's not with me. The sheets have slipped off the bed and I'm cold, remembering. *Edmund's gone. Edmund's gone.* And now Rosie.

My limbs are lifeless, unable to work, yearning for sleep. My eyelids remain stuck and I finger around the cold mattress for my daughter. Empty. Eventually, my brain signals to my eyes to open and they do, fluttering away the last vestiges of sleep.

The blurry phone reads 1.43 a.m. It's Rosie's phone. Where is she? It takes a few seconds for me to swing my legs off the mattress and stand. I've only felt exhaustion like this once, when Harry died, when my life evaporated in the space of seconds. Still, I need to know she's okay.

Out in the kitchen, the fridge moans and creaks. Outside, the wind knocks the windows together. Kav's snoring in our bedroom, oblivious to the storm. It's dark. No light. No Rosie. She's not on the balcony either. With my hands on my hips, I rotate, as though the couch, the sink, the dining table will present her to me. Instead, on the table there's a note stuck under a glass, flicking in the breeze. I lift the glass and take the note, reading it under the light of my own phone that's charging near the sink.

Mumma, I couldn't sleep. The guilt I feel about Edmund missing is keeping me awake. I haven't even hardly looked for him, either. I messaged Eloise and asked her to take me while you sleep and rest. She was happy to. I'll be back in the morning.

Your Rose X

Sighing, I fold the note and leave it on the bench. I don't know how I feel about this. Rosie asking Eloise to look for Edmund, Eloise taking Rosie. It's the middle of the night, for one thing. And I understand Rosie's guilt and *need* to look, but Eloise should know better. She should've told Rosie to wait until the morning. It's not as though they'll be able to see much during the night anyway, and with the rain coming. Still, I understand the desire to keep searching, because I *too* don't want to stop. It's our minds and bodies that need rest. I cup my stomach. Especially this body.

Rosie's guilt is a leftover symptom of how I've always made her feel. The blame, the distance, the withholding of love. She wants to do her part to show that she cares, but she doesn't need to prove anything to me anymore. I love her. She's more than enough. And tonight, our long-overdue conversation and affection has spurred Rosie's determination. She wants to attest her care for me, her brother and this family. So, for that, I'm not angry. I'm just wondering why she always leans towards Eloise?

I take a clean glass and fill it with water, groggy and sore in all parts of my body. I drink it down, imagining the liquid swimming through my arteries, swelling them with life.

Eloise is young at heart, I suppose, with her high-end fashion, teeny bikinis, blonde extensions. She's the Barbie doll teenage girls strive to be. Anyway, I'm certain this is just Eloise's way of sucking up to me. For what? I'm the one who did the yelling last night. I should be making amends with her. But what does she want from me? To form some kind of friendship?

My head eddies with fatigue. I shouldn't have screamed at her. I need to apologise to her for that. I head back into the bedroom, readjusting the pillows and sheets. I guess it's nice of her to take Rosie. Then again, the difference between nice and nasty is a messy distortion right now. How can I be the judge and jury on such things after my own past? How can I consider anything in my exhausted state of mind?

Climbing back under the covers, my body seems to heave, settling itself into a comfortable position. I can't deliberate anymore. I'm too, too tired. There's no thinking of Edmund, nor where he's gone. Eloise's face is blank to me, a stolen canvas. Rosie isn't anyone anymore. Kav's snores blend with the crashing waves. The baby in my stomach is now only breath and air. The room is black space. I am nothing. Only sleeping.

◆　◆　◆

We met on an autumn night when the chill licked my cheek and the cold bit my nose. We met on a street crammed with cafés and wine bars. Orange, red, brown, yellow, lime-green leaves curled around tree trunks, glistening with fairy lights. People in scarfs, long black coats and beanies exhaled mist from their mouths, stepping inside cosy cafés, filled with warmth, open fires, couches and romance. The bar belonged to a street that belonged to a town that belonged on a movie set. Friendly faces where friendly people dined, where expensive black SUVs rolled, where mansions with large gates opened to people with large wallets. He lived up the street. In one of the mansions. I lived ten kilometres away, with my parents and Rosie, in a bed with a trundle attached.

It was my friend's idea to go to this area, to snag a rich guy, to act rich, to drink expensive wine and to pretend we belonged here. You see, I didn't deserve it. Not the rich guy, the niceties of the venue, the time alone to be a single woman, looking for a man. An undeserving sense followed me through life like a stale perfume I could never wash off. I felt self-conscious the moment I followed the trench-coat-clad couple inside the café and bar. They knew how to do it, to unravel their scarfs, hand them to the manager, to point to a table and get given it, and to order French wines, pronouncing them correctly. I sat behind them, waiting for my friend, stifling hot in my coat and scarf, feeling too insecure to ask the manager to store it. I didn't know how to pronounce the name of the wine under the white wine section, so I ordered a sparkling water instead. My father would have known. If I was him, I would have felt like I belonged here.

I sat in the bar, people-watching, jealous of the carefree way they spoke to one another, with laughter and smiles coming naturally. I wanted to be like them again. The way I was before Harry came along.

I sipped my bitter sparkling water, sucked on the lemon and watched the door, the clientele exiting and entering. The chair opposite me remained empty. My friend was fifteen minutes late and I was getting hotter. I shrugged the coat off and then felt two hands take it from me from behind. It was Kav. A man who smiled and then motioned for the waiter to come and take my coat. A man who I remembered from high school. His face was instantly recognisable. The dimples, the sharp nose, those eyes. At school he was new, only coming during the last year of high school. I never got to speak to him properly. He was cool, yet kept to himself a lot of the time, never came to parties, always with a book under his arm. Now I know why. He was studying to get first-class grades for med school.

'You look hot.'

'Roasting, actually.'

He clicked his fingers. 'Penny, right?'

I smiled, sipping my water. 'How do you remember my name?'

He shrugged and didn't respond to that. 'Well, what's mine?'

'Kav. But yours is unusual.'

'I'm glad you remember.' He pulled up a chair and ran a hand through his blond-grey hair. I eyed up his hands, eyed up his empty ring finger. 'I hope you don't mind. I'm waiting for someone, and they haven't shown.'

I rolled my eyes. 'Same.'

'Well, then let's get a drink.'

He ordered us the French rosé and pronounced it correctly. He ordered us frites and mayonnaise and beef cheeks and cauliflower purée. He ordered us more wine, this time red, and I already knew I could love him. Because I told him right then and there about Rosie, about Greg, about trauma. I didn't tell him about Harry. But being a doctor, he listened, understood, empathised and nodded. And I knew if I went home with him that night, I'd have to resume the role of Perfect Penny, only this time I'd do it right. I'd fuck him when he needed it. I'd fill his fridge with meals. I'd get his clothes dry-cleaned and I'd watch every movie he wanted. He'd never leave me. He'd never neglect me. He'd do as I asked, because I'd be perfect. And everyone would know about us, and everyone would want to be us. We'd have our own babies and this time I'd love them all equally. Kav, the baby, Rosie. We'd live happily ever after.

Only it seemed we couldn't have babies. And so, we could only adopt.

And everything was working. Until Edmund went missing.

Eloise, 1.44 a.m.

He needs to give us more time, thirty minutes, fifteen – anything; we need more time. Rosie's shiny face looks to me for instruction, and as we cling on to a mooring, our legs dangling below us into the deep, it's the first time I have nothing to give. I shake my head. And she shakes hers back. 'Tell me what to do,' she shrieks, unfazed if anyone hears. I clap her mouth but she pushes my hand away, scratching my finger with her sharp nails.

'My brother is about to be killed.' She gasps, swallowing a mouthful of salty water, which she gags on, coughing. I'm aware of that. So aware of it I can't think. She coughs and cries, screams under water.

'We need more time,' I say, also dipping my face under the water. I open my eyes to deliberately sting them. It's black down there. So black. Rosie lifts my chin.

'How will I ask him for more?' Her voice is shrill, panicked, like I'm letting her down. And I feel like now I am. But I'm also frozen with fear.

'Is he really capable of killing?' I ask.

She gives me a foul look of disgust. 'You want to wait to find out?'

'No, I just mean, is this all a big threat, how do we know—'

'His own life is on the fucking line, Eloise.' Her face is wild. 'He will never stop, not on Edmund, on me, until he gets the money he owes.'

'But is he capable—'

'Yes he's fucking capable.' Her voice wobbles. 'I know he's capable because he's kidnapped my brother, drugged him and this isn't the first time he's done something like this. I've heard the fucking rumours, okay?' She starts swimming away from me, back to shore, as though utterly repulsed by me and my questioning. But her answers terrify me to the point of blankness. I can't move, I can't think, I can't speak. And for the first time, I wait for Rosie to tell me what to do.

After a few metres, she stops and swims around to look at me. 'Eloise, seriously, hurry the fuck up.' Her voice is deep and it breaks me out of my frozen fear. So I follow, releasing the mooring and kicking my legs to catch up to her. My body is absolutely freezing cold, my chin shivering uncontrollably. I try to silence my teeth chattering by clamping my jaw.

'We need to ask for more time,' I repeat to her back. She's like a bobbing seal. 'And we can only do that if we give him something.'

She stops and paddles around to me. We're beside a dark yacht, its mast swinging and chinking in the wind. 'But you have no money. You said.'

'What can we give him?' I'm feeling breathless and my shivering doesn't help. We need to get to the sand and solid ground so I can think logically about this. 'We need to give him something that will waylay him a bit so we know where he is.'

'You still think he's on a boat?' Rosie keeps swimming beside me this time. 'We checked them all.'

What if I was wrong and he's not on a boat? What if he's tucked in a villa somewhere? I ask Rosie for the time. She checks her watch. We have ten minutes to come up with a plan to buy us more time.

When our feet finally stroke the sand, my body loosens a little. We're on land, no longer free-dangling in the dark. I sit in front of an overturned dinghy and cuddle my knees, gazing out to the boats, all facing north. Rosie joins me, tapping at her watch.

'We need more time, please, Nico.'

'Wait, we need to offer him something first, or else he might go ballistic.'

Something scurries beside us and Rosie yelps. It's a water rat. Our movements scare it. It sprints back into the spinifex grass and rustles its way to safety. And then it hits me like a wave to the face. I lean back against the upturned dinghy and laugh out loud to the cloudy night sky. And Rosie looks at me, waiting. Why didn't I think of this all along? Nico is a fucking rat. And we just need to coax him out like we would a rat. With cheese, with treats, with something irresistible.

Eloise, 2.29 a.m.

He's agreed. The rat has said yes, just like I knew he would. This is an added extra, a bonus for being a good boy and letting us have more time. But he doesn't realise, because he's too greedy, that when he scurries out of his hidey-hole, we'll be watching.

My fifty-thousand-dollar Cartier diamond watch will be hidden for him at the cliffs on the edge of the bay. I'm certain the rat has matched our picture of the watch with photos online and I'm certain he'll peek from his hidey-hole, squinting his beady eyes to make sure we're planting the watch there. That's why he's agreed to give us until 6 a.m. Not that we'll need it. I'm so pumped, so ready to rescue Edmund from his predicament, that we only need one thing: to wait for the rat to exit his hole.

After sneaking past a sleeping Scott and grabbing my watch from my jewellery case, we messaged Nico from up on the street near our villa, where we hid the backpack and bodyboard. Once we'd snapped a shot of the watch, we made sure we came down from the street together, to nestle the watch among the rocks. We made sure to wrap it with one of our T-shirts to prevent scratches and damage. And now we've headed away from the cliffs and back up the steps alongside Brett and Sal's, dripping wet and cold, to wait and wonder how long and from where the rat will emerge.

We're quiet, so quiet we've not spoken since we hid the watch. It's the calm before the storm and we both feel it. This is a much better plan, and hopefully soon we'll discover where Nico has been hiding Edmund.

I have my pack on my back with a knife inside a long sock of Levi's. Should we need it, I will use it. I'm done with this crim.

I told Rosie we may have to wait a while. Because Nico has a rat's cunning, aware of roving police and holidaymakers who are all on alert for suspicious activity. Plus, he'll have to ensure Edmund is kept secure from accidental discovery. He also may have an accomplice, so we need to be aware of that.

I'm scanning the darkened villas, the steps and walkways leading down to the beach. I'm scanning the sand for movement. I'm listening in to chinking bike chains, the whirl of wheels. I'm aware of the wind picking up, the soft pelts of sporadic rain. And then finally, fifteen minutes after waiting against the shadow of Brett and Sal's villa, shivering and holding Rosie's icy cold hand, we hear it. A dinghy starting up somewhere out on the bay near the ferry jetty. Rosie squeezes my hand, but I whisper, 'Just wait. It may be someone else.' But I'm aware of the time, the pub being closed, nothing else open, everyone sleeping, the exhausted island resting. So, it could be Nico. 'Just wait.'

But I'm staring towards the sound.

'There.' Rosie releases my hand and points towards a cluster of boats near the jetty and a dinghy riding off between them in the direction of the cliffs. There's one man steering the dinghy. It came from a large, family-sized cruiser adjacent to the ferry jetty. It's him. We're certain it's him.

We can't risk being seen, yet we have to move fast. If Nico spots us, that's it. So, I direct Rosie along the street to the furthest walkway down to the beach and tell her to run. He can't see us behind villas and it's much easier to run on concrete than over sand. My backpack jostles against my wet back, my bare feet sting on the road, but we rush as fast as we can to the walkway leading down to the pavilions. We are at the other end of the bay, furthest away from Nico and the cliffs. And his dinghy drones in the distance. Great. He won't hear us. Once on the sand, we sprint to the water and dive in, kicking and splashing and swinging our arms through the ocean towards the cruiser. Towards Edmund.

Eloise, 3.09 a.m.

Maybe *Black Swan* was the practice run, a stepping stone into the real deal. What did I learn from it? Never judge a book by its cover, I suppose. Now, I feel we need to be more prepared, skilled, quiet, thinking smartly about where Edmund would be kept. Still, we have to be so quick and so quiet.

Amazing the way the adrenaline diminishes the fear of the water. I could be in a swimming pool the way I'm moving through the ocean, not focusing on what lurks beneath. For some strange reason, my arms feel stronger, tighter, as we swim towards the boat. And I'm ready to use the Maglite torch on anyone's head, should it come to it. I'm ready to bundle Edmund up, plonk him on the bodyboard and take him back to the shore. It doesn't fill me with twirling nausea like it did before. I'm ready for this arsehole to get his comeuppance so we can live a normal life.

Rosie kicks her legs like a frog, rather than splashing and drawing attention. However, a few fat drops of rain have started pelting my head. The thunder's travelling further away, but the clouds smell heavy and humid, ready to empty. This could be a good thing. Block the sound of us.

When we get to the slippery transom, this time Rosie doesn't have to be instructed to leave the bodyboard there. She gently lowers it while the rain sprays down harder on the white leather seats on the deck. Everything about this boat reeks of wealth and slime. White, stark white. Shiny. The boards are smooth on my feet, polished to perfection. How did the police not search this boat? We walk quietly along them, Rosie behind me, holding herself again. The dinghy has stopped droning, which means Nico is pulling it up to shore. Quick, we have to be quick.

This time, I have the torch in my firm grip, ready to smash it down on whoever Nico may be with. We don't need light because our eyes are well adjusted to the night. The back door is closed, so I twist the handle, slowly, slowly, to prevent squeaking. Luckily, the rain dumps down and a clap of thunder follows, masking noise. I quickly turn the knob and step on to a lush white carpet. Releasing the door handle slowly, I allow Rosie to step in after me, before closing the door again. Even though I'd prefer to keep it open, if someone's down in the cabin they'd wonder why the sound of rain, the breezy air comes through. I'm thanking the carpet for muffling our footsteps.

My hair drips down my back, on to the rug. Good, ruin the carpet. I wish I could light a match to this boat. Who is the owner? One of Nico's mates? One of the long-standing islanders who the police trust? I don't get why it hasn't been searched.

Rosie stays quiet behind me as we move through the kitchen and dining area, its leathery, wood polish scent richer than *Black Swan*'s rotting fish.

On the kitchen bench, a glass of half-drunk milk, a plate with crusts and something else Rosie points to steers our attention. She whacks my arm with wide eyes. Edmund's helmet is concealed under the oven. We're on the right boat.

This makes my legs tingle, while my grip on the Maglite stays constant. I swallow, quickly absorbing the other items around me – in the kitchen, on the dining-room table, the lounge chair. There's a pair of flashy sunglasses, Nico's. A car magazine. A few beer bottles and a half-drunk bottle of whisky on the dining table. A packet of cheesy crisps is open and, in the kitchen, an empty cigarette carton, an ashtray and a lighter sit beside the milk.

Up on the bench above the sink, a pack of needles. A bag of white powder. A bent spoon. I nod. Definitely the right boat.

There's something else, too. Two medicinal packets: OxyContin and sleeping tablets – his sedative for Edmund.

I stop, biting my bottom lip, conjuring up a plan. If Nico's mate is down there asleep, what would be the best way to get rid of him? Smash him over the head with a Maglite torch, highlighting a crime to police and whoever finds him? I don't think so. Rosie taps me and shrugs, wondering why I've stopped. I have a plan, that's why. But first we need to see whether someone else is on board.

Gesturing with my head for Rosie to follow, we then take the small set of stairs down to the cabins. The boat is set out the same as *Black Swan*. A master bedroom on the left, a larger family-sized bedroom in front with bunks, and a bathroom to the right. Before looking inside the master bedroom, I brace myself, taking in a slow, deep breath. Rain drums the top of the boat, and again, I'm thankful for its noise-cancelling quality. This is it.

I carefully lean my head around the door frame, only using one eye to scan the bed. And it's empty. The sheets are rumpled, the bed unmade, and pillows are plumped to hold his disgusting head. But it's empty. And I want to kiss Rosie with relief.

'Empty,' I whisper. 'No one is here. Nico is doing it alone.'

In front, the bunk beds are also empty, with their beds untouched and neatly made up. Only a canvas bag of luggage sits at the bottom end of it, against the wall. Nico's, I'm assuming. So, Edmund isn't in here.

I highly doubt Edmund would be kept in a squishy boat bathroom, but we can't discount it either. The door's closed. Again, I inhale deeply before gently twisting the doorknob. I feel so close to Edmund, the whole ordeal being over, my future with Scott and the kids. This is it. This is it. I grip the Maglite torch just in case.

The bathroom's empty. A shower drips with cologne-filled air. A razor, shaving cream, a shitty thick silver bracelet curls like a snake around a packet of painkillers. Rosie recognises the bracelet and shakes her head. It's a look of shame. As though she herself cannot believe she was ever attached to a guy like Nico. I'm guessing the spicy scent reminds her of their time together. But she looks pale and sick, as if the memory of him disgusts her. I squeeze her hand.

She exhales. 'Where's my brother?'

'Perhaps the engine room. There's always space down there.'

'How do we find that, though?'

'There should be a hatch somewhere, either up on the outside deck or under a piece of carpet. You look down here and I'll try the deck.'

I push past Rosie and stop at the kitchen to read the labels on the prescription packets. OxyContin. I don't know what that is, but judging by the red warning sticker, the cautionary instructions all over the packet, this medicine is potent and dangerous if taken incorrectly. The other packet is a sleeping tablet I recognise from the times Scott's needed them. Is Nico using these on Edmund to keep him quiet? Is this how they do it? Fill the poor kids with drugs? Edmund could be in a lot more danger than we realise.

'Eloise,' Rosie yells out from the bunk-bed cabin.

Leaving the medicines, I bolt down the stairs. She's pointing to a hatch under one of the bunks. 'I didn't see it at first, but I lifted the canvas bag to look through Nico's luggage and saw the hatch behind it.'

I remind her to shush. Although, if Nico *has* drugged Edmund to keep him quiet, Edmund wouldn't hear us anyway.

'It looks like the bag was used to hide the hatch,' I whisper. 'From police maybe?'

I slip my finger between the round silver piece of metal and pull. The hatch opens. It's a locker, used for storing ropes, fishing gear, linen. And I don't even have to look hard to know Edmund will be in there. Rosie starts crying and I tell her to shush. He cannot know it's us. I have the pillowcase stuffed in my pack, ready to place over Edmund's head, but I want to feel him first, and we need to hurry. I imagine Nico over by the cliffs now, ready to search.

Bending, I go to reach in, but my fingers clutch a bed sheet, an empty pillow. My hands knock an empty glass. I feel all of this, but not Edmund. My fingers extend, my arm moves left to right, but it's empty space.

Because Edmund's not here.

Edmund's not here.

Eloise, 3.31 a.m.

'He's gone.' I peer inside the space where Edmund once was. Rosie crouches to inspect for herself, mimicking my movements, yanking out the sheets, the pillow in a violent, panicked rage so the crumpled bedding lands at our feet.

'Where has he taken him?' Rosie speaks to the bed sheets, wet hair hanging in front of her.

But I'm not listening to her. About fifty metres away, a dinghy drones, rising and falling over the waves. 'Quickly, he's coming back.'

'But Edmund—'

'Get the bodyboard and go and hide on the other side of the boat.'

'What about you?' she asks.

'I'm staying here.' I cannot tell her why.

Rosie runs up the steps, almost slipping. She dashes out to the deck and I quickly collect the bed sheets and pillow and stuff them back into the hatch, closing it up. I dry our wet footprints in the kitchen with a tea towel, hoping that if his feet are wet, he won't notice the wet carpet, won't notice me in here.

Outside, the rain's flattening the sea into submission. Droplets bounce back up into the air and the bodyboard drums with rain. Rosie hides against the hull and I make sure she stays there, blinking, waiting, listening. She then lowers her head on to the board as though we're doomed and waiting for our death. She scrunches her eyes tight, and I leave her there and head back inside. We're not doomed. Not yet.

The dinghy motor rattles off and rubber squishes against the transom. Two feet step off. Down in the shadow of the bunk bed, I'm curled up behind one of Nico's oversized canvas duffel bags. He won't see me here, but from here I can see him. The door closes and, along with it, the sound of rain diminishes. And then finally, Nico appears before me, dumping a pair of sandy Converse shoes on the dining table. I can only half see him, but it's enough to observe as he opens the folded T-shirt and lifts the watch from inside. The smile on his face means he's thrilled. Thrilled to bits. But where the fuck has he taken Edmund?

Nico, all bald and beefy, tattooed up to his skull, gently places the watch back down on the shirt and I hear something crinkle. A flick of a lighter and the earthiness of nicotine follows. He's celebrating his win with a smoke. A few other noises I'm trying to decipher come from the kitchen. A drawer opening, utensils chinking, a gas stove bursting to life, the twisting pop of a beer bottle. And then Nico returns to the living area and sits behind the dining table, and it's now I get to see him in full as he sucks his smoke, leans back and places a needle and spoon on the table. He readies himself for a celebratory high. Belt buckle flicked open, tied around his arm, smoke dangling from the corner of his lip, eyes squinting. Nico goes about shooting up, with bliss quickly following. The belt slackens around his arm, falling, and he pulls the needle from his skin, head dropping back. It must be heroin. And I couldn't have asked for anything more flawless than this moment. This pure, relaxed moment of a crim settling down like an anaesthetised dog. The knife in my gripping hand loosens and I watch for a few minutes more. Until Nico is rested. So rested the cigarette falls from his lips and rolls down his chest, down his thigh and over on to the carpet, singeing it.

There were plans. I was going to hold the knife to Nico's throat from behind and ask him where Edmund was. There were plans to smash him over the head with my heavy torch. But I know what I am, and I know how much I value my family, my marriage, my freedom. I know how much I want Edmund back with his parents, how much I want Rosie to live a good life, to fix herself, make herself better the way I did. I know I don't want to get caught. Yet I also want this torture to end and end quickly. We'll find Edmund eventually, because he can't be far, not if Nico planned to drop him off on the beach. Getting rid of Nico now means I'll be unchained to him, Rosie, and the chaos they've pulled me into. It's now or never and I have to risk it.

There's no need to kill him in a messy, violent way. No, I can go one better.

Climbing out from the bunk, I tuck the knife back into the pack and zip it up, pulling it over my shoulder. Rain pelts down on the boat, shrouding noise, shrouding footsteps.

Nico's almost snoring, he's so chilled.

I'm going to crush and melt his powder, his sleeping tablets, his OxyContin into a liquid. Using one of the syringes, I will suck as much of it up as I can. Some sleeping tablets, some OxyContin, some of whatever he's injected himself with.

The syringe only needs to be jabbed in his neck. Just one swift movement.

I swallow a saltiness and hear Nico gurgling with sleep, or bliss, or near death.

He's so stupid he doesn't realise that someone got in. And *that* someone is creeping behind him right now, tiptoeing up the stairs, to the kitchen. Grabbing the lighter, the spare needle, the spoon and packets of drugs, I tiptoe back down the stairs.

The packet says to take one, with food, once a day. I'm guessing this'll have a lethal impact. It's what I'm aiming for, anyway. The label on the side of the medicine. *Caution: Do not mix with alcohol.* I bet he's been at the pub.

From the shadow of the bedroom, I crush up a lethal concoction on the bedside table, grinding the tablets with the back of the spoon and bottom of the lighter. I then use the lighter to melt the tablets on the spoon, until they're liquified and ready to suck. My hands tremble and it takes a while to melt and bubble. The spoon is heating up, burning my fingers, so I use the tea towel to shield the end. Eventually, though, it works.

Holding my breath, I make my way back up the stairs with my arm out, ready to stab the needle into his thick, tattooed neck. He needs to stay rested and zonked.

Up close, he's all bones and knuckles, with semi-closed eyes. It's now or never. I can't lose any time. I'm as quick as a flick, leaning down to him with the needle pinching the right side of his jaw. He gets one chance and that's all I'm offering.

Nico awakens with wide eyes staring at me, before realising what's happening.

So I speak low while threatening him. 'If you move, I'll jab this into your neck and you'll die. Where is Edmund?'

Nico goes to whack me away, to fight me off, leaving me no choice but to jab the needle in hard, pushing the contents into his bloodstream. Yanking the needle out, he twists on the couch and tries to smack my head with an open hand. How long until the drug affects him? How long? Minutes? Hours? He twists and recoils on the couch, pulling strange faces. And I don't know what I'm doing. I don't know what I'm doing. But I back away, waiting and watching. 'Where is Edmund?' I ask again.

Nico goes to stand, but then pauses, falls back down on the couch. He's lost his voice and body and any control over it. He's swaying, groaning, holding his head like it's crawling with bugs. It's working. The drug is taking its hold on him, but we don't know where Edmund is.

Nico slumps down sideways on to the couch, losing consciousness. And I'm up against the kitchen bench, breathing heavily, eyes fuzzy. And he doesn't stand back up. Nico's eyes are closed, mouth open, twitching. And I'm watching, shaking, blinking in disbelief at what I've just done.

I thought it'd take longer. But I know there are some major veins and arteries below the ear, so perhaps I hit a big one. Yuck, the thought makes me want to vomit. My stomach convulses watching him die.

Staring at the needle, which has been whacked to the floor, I realise my prints are all over it. When the police come, they'll check. I rub the needle and spoon and lighter and packets all over my wet bathers, cleaning them, and then dry them off with the wet tea towel I'd used for our footprints. Using the tea towel to grip them, I then place them all into Nico's hand, pressing his fingerprints against the needle and instruments. Using the back of my fingers, I check his pulse. Nothing. Gone. Nico died of an overdose.

The cops only have to see his drugs, delve into his lifestyle, his group of friends, to believe it. Everything has to look like it did before we came on here. I have to take his phone, which sits on the kitchen bench. I have to take out the SIM card, smash it and bury or hide it somewhere on the island. The medicine needs to go back on the shelf with the spoon, the lighter. No fingerprints. Edmund's prison needs to be closed up, used as a normal cupboard for storing ropes or snorkelling gear or extra linen.

When the cops come on board, it needs to appear like a drug overdose. And knowing Nico and his affiliates, the cops won't bat an eyelid. Just another crim dead. The world's a better place for it.

I quickly place Edmund's bed sheets and pillow back on the bed and I collect my Cartier watch, slipping it back on my wrist. I shove the T-shirt and tea towel into my backpack and all the while I'm shivering, shivering with anxiety. Taking Edmund's helmet from under the oven, when I think I've done all I can to leave this place clean and clear of Rosie and me, I leave Nico's body and stagger out to Rosie.

It's still raining heavily. And Rosie is lying with both arms over the bodyboard. 'Rosie.'

With teeth chattering and with dark lips, she looks up at me. 'Is he . . .' She doesn't finish her sentence, but I nod, throwing Edmund's helmet into the ocean. It floats, but that's okay. Eventually it'll wash up to shore and be found like a hundred other helmets and bikes left on the island every day with tourists too lazy to return them.

But now when Edmund is found, wherever he is, it has nothing to do with me.

Eloise, 3.52 a.m.

The long swim back is a grim struggle. Sudden pelting rain burns our eyes, stings our scalps, and the shore has vanished. Are we even heading in the right direction? I feel as though I'm one breath away from drowning. I'm swallowing waves. A queasy flip of my gut makes me gag, exhausting me to the point of slipping under. My coughing brings Rosie close until she makes me float on my back. Her firm hand clasps under my chin as she tows me along and I scrunch my eyes tight, allowing her to support me back to shore. My mind turns to Edmund's whereabouts. What did Nico do with him? I hardly notice the easing rain. I'm so mentally overwhelmed by this weekend and witnessing Nico spasming to his death. I was truly wishing he'd say something, point me in the right direction to Edmund.

'What if we don't find him?' Rosie says.

My throat is scratched with salt as I speak. 'We will.' I'm sure of it. 'He'll be somewhere on this island.'

Nico is gone. That's the main thing. Meaning, Edmund can no longer be hurt by him. That's what I keep telling myself anyway. Neither can Penny. Or Rosie. And most importantly, neither can I. But I'm too tired and waterlogged to let relief sink in.

As we draw close to shore, I ask, 'Did Edmund know Nico was your boyfriend?' My words are slurred and slow, my mouth dry with brine and cold. And Rosie's hot breath touches my ear as she drags me through the water. We need to make sure there's nothing linking us to him.

'I never told him. But Nico might have. And Edmund never saw us together.'

'Good,' I say, licking salty lips. 'Very good.' That's why we need to get rid of his phone and text messages to Rosie. I'm still thinking, planning, plotting, when all I want is peace. And I still need her to delete that photo.

The storm washes over us. I'm so sick with what these past few days have done to me, I almost don't believe I'm here right now, floating on my back with Rosie dragging me through cold black water.

When Rosie releases me, my legs kick against the sand beneath me. Thank God. We wade through waist-deep water.

'You have to delete that photo.' My voice sounds harsh from swallowing seawater. 'From the cloud, from your files, from wherever you stored it. I want to see you do it.'

'But what about Edmund?'

We stagger out of the ocean, breathless and weak. 'We'll find him, but you made a promise to me.'

Rosie wrings her hair out so it drips on to the beach, deliberately not answering me. Rain thuds the sand and waves lap the shore and I have a sick thought. What if she doesn't delete the photo?

'Rosie?' Something has caught her attention as she faces the sky and tells me to shush. 'Delete the photo, okay?' Her phone's back up in the bushes near the cliffs where we left it in a plastic bag.

She cocks her head. 'You hear that?'

Gentle sobbing, very faint. And then rain, and lapping waves and gusts chinking the yachts on the bay. We stare at each other. Where is that coming from? The sobbing drifts with the wind and

I face the direction of the cries, which I think are coming from the ferry jetty. So faint, so small, so tired. I see someone.

'You hear it too?' Rosie says.

Stumbling off without replying, my throat is tight. Not far ahead, a small body struggles to haul itself on to the beach. It's him. It has to be. I run with wobbled legs, with all my might, tears streaming in my wake.

Penny, 4.13 a.m.

Before the police start, before the search continues, before we live another day through this nightmare, I take my coffee mug up to the lighthouse, dressed in slippers, my pyjamas, my eyes swollen, my hair tied in a messy knot that'll take scissors to untangle. I don't want Kav. I don't want Georgia. I don't want encouraging words, silly questions, relentless media attention, hugs, pats on the shoulder. I want the lighthouse view, the vast ocean, the stormy sunrise, the orange nugget sun, sickly sweet in its pastel pinks, breaking through the slate clouds. I want the air, rough and wild, to beat my face. I want the salt mist of waves.

I take sips of coffee, its bitterness too sweet. Everything is too sweet and lovely and not matching my mood. I came up here for the shipwreck sign. This lighthouse was created to prevent any more from occurring. This is what I needed myself. A lighthouse.

I tip the dark liquid out on to a coarse bush, set the mug down and grip the splintered railing. I close my eyes. And then I open them.

Because below the lighthouse, a road weaves from the north of the island to the south, and I watch like a bird in a nest. And there are voices. Recognisable ones.

Rosie. Laughter.

I leave the fence, accidentally kicking the mug over so it rolls and rattles over the gravel, and stare down to the road. There's no one there. It's still too early for people to be out riding, running, especially with all the rain we've had. Perhaps this is what occurs after trauma. You go crazy, start hearing and seeing things you wish to hear and see.

It happened after Harry, too. Crying babies sounded just like him. I remember checking in a woman's trolley once, just to make sure it wasn't Harry. I pulled the blanket back to inspect the face. The mum whacked my hand, gave me a weird look and quickly pushed the baby away, reporting me to the store manager. My face burned with shame as I rushed out. From then on, I disregarded every baby wail. It could never be Harry, as much as I wanted to bring him back.

I head back to the mug, bend and pick it up. But I hear it again, laughter. So, I rush back to the railing and stare down. Walking out from underneath the gumtrees, I spot three people.

Two females. One boy.

I drop the mug and it shatters, splintering over the gravel. I jump the fence, landing on sharp spinifex, squashing it into hundreds of shards. And I run down the wet hill between spiky bushes and limestone rocks that cut into the soles of my flimsy slippers. My slippers come off and I don't care. I run barefoot over sodden sticks and pebbles.

'Edmund!' My voice is shrill, urgent, stuck. I can't breathe.

I jump over a boulder and weave between two bushes, pushing myself through them, scratching my skin. Finally, I'm at the bottom of the lighthouse hill, under gumtrees and a brewing sky. And in front of me, standing in the middle of the road, in between Eloise and my beautiful teenage daughter, is Edmund.

Blinking out two tears, I grin, running towards him. And in a second, I have my son back. I clutch his small body and he wails

331

like a baby. A newborn baby. A newborn who greatly needs his mother's comfort. I crouch, holding him, gripping him, kissing him. His shoulder, his clammy neck, his cheek, his small face. His eyelids, his smelly hair, the left ear, the right.

'I thought you'd gone. I thought you'd drowned,' I'm saying into his T-shirt. He's wet. All wet. 'I thought you'd drowned.'

'We found him on the shore, down by the ferry jetty,' Eloise says. 'He was totally out of it.'

'You were lost?' I speak up to his face. I'm lower than him. I'm lower because I want to see every part of him. He looks the same when he nods down at me. Only he looks horribly weak, tired, dehydrated. Like a child who's been through a war. He's not even talking.

'He needs water.' I pat down his body like I'm searching for him. Like he's not really here at all. A ghost, apparition. I don't deserve this, do I? A second chance? 'He needs water and a nice bit of food and a good bath. A bath at the hotel with bubbles. He needs a good sleep.' I'm checking things off my list. All the things he'll need and want. I'll give him everything. Anything.

'We gave him water,' Eloise tells me.

Edmund holds me tight around my neck and I burst into tears again, this time motioning for Rosie to join us. She's crying, hands up to her mouth, and so is Eloise. Her face is wet and worn out. I want to hug her too. My hero. They are both my heroes.

Rosie joins us on the road and I sit and cradle them both. 'Thank you,' I say to Rosie, kissing her wet hair and then Edmund's and then hers again. 'My special girl. You found him. You clever girl.' Rosie laughs once through her tears and wraps her arms around me and Edmund.

And then I look up at Eloise and stare at her, nodding with sincerity. 'Thank you.'

Eloise, 10.42 a.m.

The joyful scene in Penny and Kav's villa can only be described as denial or mental fatigue. I get that she's relieved to have her baby back, but this is not the reaction I would imagine only five hours after mother and son are reunited.

A banquet of takeaway coffees, fresh muffins, array of dough-nuts, rainbow fruit platters and juice are sprawled over Penny and Kav's dining table like we're back at their wedding. It's a party. Café music, guests everywhere. Relief. That's the word on everyone's lips. Relief.

The party guests have congregated back at the villa where it all started and Penny has instructed us all that we're to end this ordeal, this weekend, this nightmare event with smiles, laughter and good food. It's kind of bizarre the way Penny sweeps away the weekend. We're traumatised, exhausted, jittery and rough around the edges. And she's filling glasses with champagne and swanning around in a bright kaftan like we're all in one setting and she's in another.

'When we step on that ferry this afternoon,' she proclaims to the guests indoors, outdoors, filling the balcony, 'I want to step on it with relief.'

Someone pops open a third bottle of champagne and hands me a glass of golden bubbles. It's Penny, smiling, kissing the side of my face like I'm one of her children. She won't stop doing it either.

Squeezing my hand, touching my arm, leaning her forehead against mine and whispering the two words I've heard twenty times this morning. *Thank you. Thank you for finding him.*

And I thought I'd be bubbling like my champagne. I thought I'd feel the relief they're all experiencing. I thought I'd be laughing joyously with Penny, knowing Rosie and I achieved what we set out to do. Nico is dead. And no one will ever link his overdose with Edmund's disappearance. That boat moored in the bay will sit there for days, perhaps even weeks, before someone realises his body is on board. No one knows Nico and Rosie were together. Not her family, not her friends. Not now that I plan to smash and bury his phone.

Yet I don't feel relief. I don't even feel happy. Even with Coco on my lap, Levi pouring himself a juice, Edmund on the couch watching a movie, almost falling asleep after stuffing himself with muffins and cakes, I sit here numb and vacant. I should be somewhere else. A dark room in a bed with a cold pack on my head. Or jail. Or being interrogated thoroughly.

Edmund's been bathed in the hotel with bubbles, just like Penny promised. He's been questioned by police. Rosie and I have been questioned too, and our alibi checks out. We found him on the beach, wet and alone, and we recovered him from the water.

The clever little guy had swum away from Nico's boat. But when we found him there, on all fours on the beach, Edmund's account was hazy and disorientated, like he was sleepwalking. It proves the dangerous amount Nico must've given him to stay anaesthetised. He'd told us he'd fallen into the water. When we asked him where from, he couldn't remember. That he'd just woken somewhere dark, seen the lights on the island and kept swimming. So, everyone assumes it's from the cliffs. No one really knows but us.

Now, Rosie's sitting at the end of the couch, Edmund's feet on her lap, staring blankly at her phone. She's as worn out as I feel. But at least she's deleted the photos from her phone. While Edmund slowly sipped water in my lap, shivering with cold and shock, I watched as Rosie ran to the cliffs to retrieve her phone, erasing the foolish snapshot from her saved notes, her photo collection and her files. She then went on to erase Nico. She even hugged me straight after, and bawled, apologising for all she'd put me through. It doesn't matter now.

Now, Georgia circles around the group, pouring champagne while William talks with Brett out on the balcony. In the kitchen, Kav and Penny embrace, quietly discussing something that makes them both smile. She's shaking her head and grinning. The sight of it fizzes a lightness in my belly. But I guess I'm searching for more. Confirmation that this was all worth it. I look away from them and sip my champagne. It pinches my tastebuds.

And then Scott stands behind me and places a hot hand on my shoulder. I look up and he sips his champagne before looking down at me, winking. It's an unexpected gesture, a knowingness. And it's then I feel it.

Relief. *This* is what I've been seeking. This is what I've been searching for. The rest of the party are celebrating togetherness and right there in that wink, that touch, I'm joined to something solid again. *I did this all for you, for us, for our future.* I smile at Scott, leaning against his hairy arm while Coco wriggles off my lap.

'You must be exhausted,' he says. It warms me to hear someone recognise that.

I close my eyes. 'You have no idea.'

'I was worried when I woke up this morning and didn't see you,' he admits, sipping his drink again.

'You were?' If only you knew. I want to touch his hand and hold it. I want to tell him just how awful last night was for me.

To do what I needed to do to protect myself from losing him. The swim, the needle. Eventually, I'm going to have to find a way to forget it.

'And then I saw your note and realised how good you are.'

I look up at him again. 'Good?'

'Helping Pen and Kav like that.'

'Penny would have done the same for me,' I say, sipping my champagne. I don't need it. I've already got a massive headache. I've swallowed two painkillers but the ache is still there, a dull thrum that won't leave. I need rest and a big sleep. Scott shrugs, like he doesn't agree with me.

'You found him,' he says. 'That's the main thing. You're her hero now.'

William interrupts Scott, pointing to a large yacht out in the bay. And I'm still wondering how Nico got away with hiding Edmund on the boat. William tells Scott what it'd take to pull up the mast. And I'm happy to be left alone for a moment. Coco joins Edmund on the couch, so I readjust my legs and sit back in my chair, champagne between my thighs, cooling them, closing my eyes once more to the sound of waves and distant laughter.

Until I hear Barry's voice at the door. And I'm no longer relaxed.

◆ ◆ ◆

The police questioned Rosie and me after Edmund was found, but we'd prepped ourselves well on the story. The story was the main part of the plan. If the story didn't check out, they'd delve deeper, so it had to be tight, no mistakes, no crossed wires.

We told the police we'd found Edmund wet on the shore.

We found him there, cold, shaking, sleepy.

We sat for fifteen minutes with Edmund in the rain, giving him water, practising our story, waiting for Edmund to slip out of his drugged haze and back to reality. Would he mention Nico, Rosie's boyfriend? No. He didn't. Would he mention how she'd given him money for ice cream? Nope. He couldn't tell us where he'd been.

When he finally came to, he recognised us, reaching out to cuddle his big sister, who wept with relief. We told him how happy we were that we'd finally found him. We gave him water, he cried in Rosie's arms. We fed him the stories we wanted him to recount back to the police, to Penny, to everyone. How he'd ridden off too far because he wanted to go for a night ride. But then he got lost. Edmund stared at us, blinking through the darkness, weak and tired. The rain continued, wetting his hair, soaking his clothes. He said he couldn't remember anything. Only this. Only now.

'You rode too far away,' I told him.

'I didn't mean to,' he cried. And I cuddled him and told him he wasn't in trouble, that everyone would understand. He rode too far. He got lost. He got frightened and didn't know where he was. And he was so dehydrated, so hungry and so feeble, he eventually nodded and agreed. I'm not sure what drugs he'd been fed, but I think we could have lost Edmund had we not found him when we did.

'We'll take you back to Mum and Dad now, okay?' Rosie said, carrying him on her back. 'And you can just tell them the truth about this. You wandered and got lost.'

'Okay,' Edmund said, resting his little chin on her shoulder. He sucked on one of my mints. We had also given him more water, which I told him to sip slowly.

And then he saw his mum. And the police believed us. The police believed Edmund. After all, he was found well, unscathed, and that was the main thing. And they couldn't run the medical tests on him like they would back in the city. Being on an island meant they didn't have the resources. They checked his mouth, his eyes, his blood pressure, his body. Dehydrated and severely tired, they concluded. But no scratches or bruises, which the nurse deliberated on. He must have gone cross-country.

Whatever, Penny didn't want any more checks. She only wanted her son back, in the hotel, in warm lemon bubbles and fluffy towels. She wanted him fed with hot chips, a milkshake and whatever else he fancied. So, the police started to pack up, the ferry finally disembarked, the bay emptied, the visitors on the island left. And I went back to our own villa, to Scott, to rescue our marriage, while pretending to be the hero who saved Edmund.

Penny, 10.50 a.m.

Barry looks different in the daytime, now my son is back. His shirt isn't as stained as I once thought, but then again, perhaps he's changed? Possibly even brushed his thinning hair? He's clutching a bunch of yellow daisies, already wilting. Things only get delivered to the island once a day. Fruit, veg, fresh produce and flowers come at a hefty price. But when he noticed the bunch, he thought of me. And I guess this is his way of . . . apologising for being so abrupt when we met? It's cute and I'm looking at him like I would William, or my father, or a cheery old grandpa.

Taking the flowers off him, I lean in and kiss his clammy, red-veined cheek. It's soapy and proves he's bathed since yesterday. Barry blinks a few times as though he can't recall the last time someone kissed him. And then he touches his face. 'I'm glad he's been found safe.'

Kav hands him a glass of champagne as Georgia takes the daisies off me and fishes around in the cupboards above the fridge for a vase.

'Thanks for everything,' I say. 'I know you thought I was a useless mother—'

'Now, now.' He wags a finger. 'I've just seen irresponsible parenting in the past, that's all.' Barry sets his glass down on the sink. He hasn't even sipped it. 'Listen, Wallis just called me because he couldn't get a hold of you two. But there's something you may want to hear.'

'We've been busy celebrating.' Searching for my phone under bags of bread rolls and behind coffee cups, I can't find it. 'I haven't even looked at my phone.'

'What is it?' Kav says.

Nodding out the back, Barry opens the flyscreen for us both. 'You may want to talk outside, away from the little one.'

We follow him out beneath the clothesline where Edmund and Rosie's wet clothes drip in the warm breeze. It's already heating up, but the storm clouds produce a density in the air. It's harder to breathe out here.

'It's about Edmund's biological parents,' Barry says, folding his thick arms. Red and white hairs sprout from his pink, freckled skin. I'm staring at them and nodding slowly. What he's about to tell me, I knew all along. Even when we found Edmund, it still didn't feel right, *sit* right with me. How could he get himself so lost? Pearl is involved somehow.

'Edmund missing *does* have something to do with them, doesn't it?'

'Nah.' He shakes his head and smiles slightly, and I release my shoulders. 'Your little fella got too cocky for his own good. Lesson learnt for the little chap.'

'Okay, then what about his parents?' Kav asks, frowning.

'Apparently they had one of their mates come here this weekend to track your little guy.'

Oh my God. This news sickens me. I hold my arms and Kav strokes my back. 'Tracked? You mean stalked?'

'A few people reported him around town, acting suspiciously, stealing from the general store, scaring a few of the kids. Snatched a bike off a kid and pedalled away.'

Looking to Kav who's scowling intensely, I say, 'That man I was telling you about, the one who was staring at me. I wonder if it was him?'

Barry nods. 'Tall, lean, all in black—'

'That's the one.' I click my fingers at Kav. 'He was really weird. Looked out of place. They sent him here, to do what?'

Barry blows out a deep breath. 'We're not too sure, to be honest. He says Edmund's mother wanted pictures of your son. Said it's all harmless stuff, but police are questioning him and the parents back in the city as we speak.'

'But how do we know he didn't take Edmund and do something with him?' Kav asks Barry.

'Edmund never mentioned him.' I speak for Barry. 'And police asked him everything. I think he would've said if he was with someone.'

'True, and he was pulled in for questioning after a family caught him taking their daughter's bike yesterday morning,' Barry says. 'Before that, he stole from the store and he was acting drunk and disorderly at the pub last night. Then he was told to get off the island. He was present and everywhere around the town, not hiding out with your son.'

I shake my head. The person texting me from the city phone box. Pearl knew we were here and I wondered how, and this makes so much sense. I feel so disturbed by the news, but also grateful the police are aware of him and Pearl and her obsession with our family. Barry mentions restraining orders, and Pearl's experience in jail being enough of a threat to keep her away in future. The police are on it, he says, assuring me with a squeeze of my shoulder.

'If anything, Edmund going missing made the guy stand out like dog's balls,' he says. 'The island community were on to any strange behaviour.'

Eloise is at the kitchen, pouring herself another glass of champagne. 'Pen, do you want a top-up?' she asks through the flyscreen.

'No, I'm all good, thanks.' I turn back to Barry. 'How did he get here? Boat or ferry?'

'Ferry. All the boats on the island were searched, remember? Apart from Sam, Richie and the Deacon family boats,' he mutters to himself and scratches a flake of dry skin above his eyebrows.

'Why weren't those boats searched?' I ask as we head back inside and Barry collects his champagne. He downs it in one gulp, surprising me. I didn't think he'd take to expensive bubbles. Swiping his lips with the back of his arm, he looks at Eloise, squinting.

'Sam, Richie and the Deacons are our regular boaties, been around for donkey's years,' he says, with attention back on me. 'Practically live here on the island with their families. Sam's grandfather was on the bloody island board. No need to check their boats. They're as honest as they come.' He looks at me and winks. 'Although I probably wouldn't be telling you this if the little one was still missing.'

God, I'm seriously glad he didn't say this to me while Edmund was missing. I probably would have punched him for being so slack and not searching *all* the boats. This revelation is unsettling – Pearl was having us stalked by a friend. But Barry seems to think it's all going to be fine, and so does Kav, who assures me the police are aware now. She's never going to get away with coming near us. The first thing we'll do when we get back to the city is apply for a restraining order.

Barry keeps his eyes on Eloise as she walks away and calls out, 'Oi, Eloise, isn't it?'

Eloise turns and smiles. Blinks a few times as though there's dust in her eyes. 'Yes.'

'I know why I recognise you.' Barry clicks his fingers, then points them like a gun at her. 'My ex's daughter. Spitting image. Haven't seen her in about ten years, but God you look alike.'

He then turns and asks Georgia for another champers and Eloise just looks at him, expressionless, before heading back out to Scott. She leans her head against her husband's shoulder and Scott holds her, wrapping his arms around her waist. It's a lovely sight, a connection I'm sure she's been wanting.

The police are on to Pearl and this weirdo. All is well. I touch my stomach and breathe calmly. Around the villa, people are having normal conversations, and it feels right and comforting because it is what people strive for. Balance, normalcy, domestic bliss. We don't seek drama, conflict, pain. All we want is equal peace. Conversations about the weather, a warm home, a glass of Shiraz in front of the fire with the person you love.

People you love. I look at an exhausted Edmund and smile. And then I look at my beautiful Rosie and smile even wider. I've got both.

ONE YEAR LATER

Penny

We're here to do it right this time. Two picnic blankets, body-boards, a speaker and a cool-box of chilled drink are set out for both of our families.

If this was an ad for the tourist campaign, you'd want to come to the island. Eloise sits in between Scott's thighs, long blonde hair matching the sand and sun. She laughs at Scott, eyes twinkling with a new-found love that belongs to teenagers, or newlyweds or honeymooners. He kisses her head and she rests back while Kav passes me a wine. It's about time I can enjoy one without thinking of breast-feeding. Georgia and William mind baby Jack back at the hotel. We're going to meet them there later for a seafood dinner. There will be crisp wine and thick white napkins and glowing lights and suntans. We'll enjoy each other's company, together.

Brightly coloured striped towels are lined up beside us and the kids dig in the sand while Rosie and Levi balance out on a paddle-board between boats moored in the shallows.

This time, Eloise and Scott's villa is beside ours. We're here for seven nights and we plan to erase the past with beautiful dinners, rides around the island, sleep-ins, sunbathing, surfing trips out to the reef and spa massages back at the hotel. So far, it's working. Three days in and we're settling into the island groove. It has a way of relaxing the joints, softening the skin, converting frowns into smiles. Everything feels back to normal now.

Nothing bad ever happens on the island. But we heard the disgusting story about the druggie who rented Barry's pal's boat. The Deacons? Or maybe Sam. I can't recall the family name, but they were island royalty, practically owned the pub, restaurants and beaches and let a crim hire their boat for two weeks during and after Edmund's wandering. He died of an overdose, but police think the family have ties to bikie gangs. Whatever, it's just weird that in all the years of visiting this pristine place, two incidents occurred so close together.

After cutting up the cheese and feeding Kav, I pass the bowl of olives over to Eloise. She pops one in her mouth and stands, dusting off her sandy bum. She leaves our group and the radio music. Scott watches his wife's long figure sashaying down to the shoreline. I smile. I'm happy for them. I'm happy they're happy. She collects Coco in her arms and kisses her chubby legs. She's three and still as cute as ever.

My daughter paddles over to Eloise when she spots her standing on the shore. Rosie has always had a quiet connection to Eloise, ever since they found Edmund. It's as though that moment bound them together. It's not that I'm envious. My relationship with Rosie is wonderful, close, intimate and mended. We go shopping together. We have movie nights. We go out for dinner. She helps me cook and clean. We explore universities. We go to the theatre. No, I'm not jealous.

I suck on the olive stone and squint under my hat, watching Eloise take the paddle off Rosie. She helps Rosie back on to the shore and then, instead of taking her own turn on the paddleboard, Eloise and Rosie decide to sit at the shoreline, allowing the water to rush past their bottoms. I can't hear what they're saying. Their backs are to us. Rosie draws something in the sand with a finger. I'm not jealous. Not at all.

But there's something that makes me hold my breath a little, tense my stomach muscles slightly. Seeing them together is like running into an old enemy and smiling like you're happy to see them. It doesn't feel right or natural. I'm not jealous. I'm really not.

No, it's more than that, a deeper alarm that triggers. I've tried to switch it off, smile over it, distract myself. But it flicks on again and I'm there, tight, taut and holding my breath.

I'm not jealous.

I'm suspicious.

Edmund has been mentioning things since we've returned. Perhaps they're memories. Perhaps they're triggers. Perhaps he's smelling the sand, the pines, the salt, causing his brain to sift through his subconscious, making memories more distinct. Last night, in bed, he muttered something as he was falling asleep. *Rosie's boyfriend took me.* And this morning, he said he *swam from the boat.* But what boat? What boat could he mean? When I prompted him, he said it was *scary and cold* but he thinks he's dreamt it.

So I'm not jealous. I'm suspicious. I'm wondering.

Did they, *did they*? Did they have something to do with Edmund's disappearance?

'Mum, look.' Edmund points to a sandcastle and I smile, all my attention now on him.

'Good one, buddy,' I say. Never neglecting. Always present.

And the heat toasts my skin, and the shiny sand stings my eyes – a white, glaring brightness making my eyes water. A single tear drips down my cheek as I glance at Eloise and Rosie. Then the water, crystal clear, hiding nothing. Then the boats, facing north. Then the blue blanket sky. A seagull claims its territory, squawking, and the waves collide with the cliffs. Perfect. Everything so perfect. The way it needs to *be.*

But I stand anyway. Brush the sand off my bottom. Tell Edmund I'll be right back. And Scott speaks to Kav. And I walk down the beach towards Eloise and Rosie. It's hot and burns my soles. But I walk down there and they hear me coming because I clear my throat.

And then I stand directly between them, the water pooling around my toes. And they both look up, the sun blinding their eyes, wondering why I'm here.

ACKNOWLEDGEMENTS

Well, here we are again, and writing this is just as emotional as it was the first time. I want to start by thanking my readers who either loved *The Shallows* enough to want to read *The Rip*, or who are new to my books and chose to invest their time reading this. It means the world to me to have real readers enjoying my stories. Rottnest Island, Wadjemup, off Perth, Western Australia, is a dear place to me, and I hope you'll one day visit its white shores.

I recently met my agent, Jade Kavanagh, and editor, Victoria Haslam, in London and Harrogate and it was a truly memorable weekend. We had lunch, spoke about books, films, storytelling, and the industry. After that meeting, I felt lucky, connected and close to these two intelligent, lovely and supportive women, who both love my ideas and my writing. Thank you both so much for believing in me and my writing and for making me feel so welcome!

To the rest of the Darley Anderson team, especially Camilla Bolton, Georgia Fuller, Mary Darby, Rebecca Finch, I absolutely loved meeting you all at the office and feel extremely grateful to be so well looked after. And to the incredibly friendly and welcoming team at Amazon Publishing, Eoin Purcell, Sammia Hamer and Kasim Mohammed, thank you for your ongoing support.

I've met so many amazing authors since *The Shallows* was published, particularly the uplifting John Marrs, Mark Edwards, Lisa

Gray, Tina Payne, Andy Maslen, Susi Holliday, Sara Bragg, Emma Steele, Mercedes Mercier, Ali Lowe, Allie Reynolds, Matthew Spencer, Jo Leevers, Cat Steadman, Barry Divola, Kerry Mayne.

And to the lovely writing community who helped launch *The Shallows*: Josh Hortinela, Karina May, Shelley Gardner, Monique Mulligan, Louise Allan, Polly Phillips and my lovely members of The Write Club who are just as excited as I am: Deb, Fiona, Kristy, Carmelina, Skye, Sam, Kel, Camille, Sallyanne, Georgia, Ike, Ione, Sarah, Luci – there are forty of you Writeclubbers all up, some new and some old. I appreciate you all and I love our community!

Thanks again to my family for your interest, love and support, especially Darryl, who constantly reads my work and lets me excitedly rant and gush about the whole process! And to my closest friends for letting me 'have a break from discussing books and writing'.

And to Tiff for once again passionately promoting my work and encouraging me along. So lucky to have a sister who is an avid reader of thrillers (especially when they pick out how random it is for my character to be drinking tequila!).

To Kurt, for taking me to London so I could see my future 'in the flesh', for your unwavering, unconditional dedication to me and my dreams, for always putting me first, for plotting, for editing, for reading, for being the best partner a person could ever dream up. Thank you, thank you, thank you. And that still will never be enough.

And lastly and most importantly, Milly and Emme. Bright, intelligent, creative, passionate girls. I love Rottnest with you. I love holidays with you. I love it when you're home with me. I simply love you.

ABOUT THE AUTHOR

Holly Craig lives on the Western Australian coast. She spent her childhood on boats and on Rottnest Island, inspiring her novel *The Rip*, and her first #1 bestselling novel, *The Shallows*. The beach and river were her playground and have shaped the settings in her novels. Holly is an English teacher and now teaches adults how to write their novels, preparing their manuscripts for publication. She also co-hosts a podcast, *Off The Page*, which focuses on the highs and lows of author life.

You can follow Holly on her website: www.hollycraig.com, Instagram: @hollycraigauthor, and Twitter: @HolCraigAuthor.

Follow the Author on Amazon

If you enjoyed this book, follow Holly Craig on Amazon to be notified when the author releases a new book!
To do this, please follow these instructions:

Desktop:

1) Search for the author's name on Amazon or in the Amazon App.
2) Click on the author's name to arrive on their Amazon page.
3) Click the 'Follow' button.

Mobile and Tablet:

1) Search for the author's name on Amazon or in the Amazon App.
2) Click on one of the author's books.
3) Click on the author's name to arrive on their Amazon page.
4) Click the 'Follow' button.

Kindle eReader and Kindle App:

If you enjoyed this book on a Kindle eReader or in the Kindle App, you will find the author 'Follow' button after the last page.